ICE COLD
SPY

USA TODAY BESTSELLING AUTHORS

DAVID ARCHER
BLAKE BANNER

ICE COLD
SPY

AN ALEX
MASON
THRILLER

R

RIGHT HOUSE

ALEX MASON SERIES

Odin
Ice Cold Spy
Mason's Law
Assets and Liabilities

PROLOGUE

B ob Magnusson's great love was ice. The more the better. He had known since childhood that his spiritual home was Greenland, where the ice sheet —the size of Alaska, six times the size of Arizona and up to two miles thick—stretched for six hundred and sixty thousand square miles: white, pure and largely untouched by human madness. Others saw its infinite, frozen expanse and saw death. He saw the frozen vastness and saw home, safety, hope.

He had flown from Nuuk, the capital on the west coast, where he had his home and his office, nine hundred miles across the great frozen expanse to Ittoqqortoormiit, the gateway to the Northeast National Park. From there he had taken a King Air 360 four hundred miles north and slightly west into the interior, to the UCLA base camp, where he had most of his equipment set up. And from there, after greeting his team, he had taken a snowmobile fifty miles north to his sensor array, just three hundred and fifty miles south of the northernmost tip of Greenland. The sensor array and its data was something only he attended to.

He sped along under the pristine sky, ice-blue with not a cloud in sight. He slowed at the top of a hill and stopped, and, made cumbersome by his heavy, thermal clothes, climbed clumsily off the vehicle. It was probably only 49°F, but the chill factor of all that ice made it seem a lot colder. He stamped around a bit, clapping his hands, and stared at the broad, shallow valley ahead of him. He knew it well, and he knew that just at the far side, twenty minutes away, was the broad array of sensors. And just beyond the unmanned station where they were located were the moulins, vast, vertical ice-caves spreading and unpredictable, plunging a mile deep, sometimes up to thirty feet across at the mouth, but huge and cavernous beneath. He knew the area intimately, and he felt it posed no threat to him, but an inexperienced person might die within a few hours of a careless mistake.

He looked back the way he had come, and a different kind of cold twisted his belly. He felt his heart jolt and dread drained the blood from his face. On the horizon, barely visible in the glare of the ice, was a speck, moving fast toward him.

He clambered on his snowmobile again and accelerated away, down into the shallow valley, praying that its downward gradient would obscure him from view and render him invisible.

A sudden urgency told him he should call Silvia on the VHF radio-phone, but he dared not stop. In his mind he could see her in their apartment, lying on the sofa, reading the *National Geographic*. Her short, dark hair, her slim legs in Levi's, the big Aran sweater she had stolen from him. The image turned into an ache of desire and fear.

He rode on until soon he could see the blue hut, raised on stilts, where the sensor monitors were housed. He knew that once he stopped there the snowmobile would be visible, and it would be clear that he was there too. He would then have no escape.

With trembling hands and unsteady legs he came to a halt, parked at the bottom of the steps, and ran with a laborious lack of speed up the stairs to the door. He rattled the handle, pushed in and moved quickly to the monitors.

The data he saw there momentarily made him forget his fear. What he had suspected was true. The nightmare he had dreaded was now a reality.

In a flash some part of his mind took him back to California, to Professor Ruud van Dreiver's office. Rudy was the head of the climatology department and had called Bob to meet Daniel "Danny" Bludd, CEO of the Green Tomorrows Corporation. Ruud had stressed to Bob that this meeting was important, and could be worth a lot of money to the department.

They had sat around Ruud's mango wood coffee table in beige calico armchairs and drunk black, Fairtrade coffee from brightly colored African Attitude cups, even though Ruud always had it with cream and white sugar. Danny Bludd had sipped his coffee once and set it down on the mango table, then leaned back in his chair.

"Let me lay it out for you as plainly as possible. We are, as you are, as we all are, worried about the impact of human activity on the climate and this planet's natural resources."

Ruud had nodded somewhat more than was absolutely necessary, and Bob had thought to himself that, if that was as plain as possible, he might need to lace his coffee with something stronger to get through the meeting. Bludd was talking again.

"According to my research, the Greenland ice cap is pretty important in the whole...," he waved his hand in a circular motion, "climate change issue."

Ruud nodded some more. "Your research is accurate."

"And there is a chance, a good chance, that under Greenland, because of the weight of all that ice—I mean we are talking trillions upon trillions of tons of ice, right? All pressing down, crushing all that organic matter into..."

He paused, realizing perhaps that he was sounding too enthusiastic, and Ruud came to his rescue.

"Aside from oil," he smiled, "natural gas."

Bludd pointed at him. "Exactly, natural gas. We believe, our research shows, that there are vast reserves. And the Greenland government assures us that there *are* in fact such reserves, of gas and oil...," he shrugged and made a face of skepticism, "but then they want us to invest there, so they would say that, right?

"Now, Greenland is not rich. Exploration alone, simple drilling, could bring industry, work and money to Greenland. So they are keen for that to happen. On the other hand, Denmark, who pretty much run the show as far as foreign policy is concerned, is playing cute. 'Maybe there is, maybe there isn't, we want to talk to a lot of people, we might develop it ourselves...' Because they want to get every penny they can out of those natural resources. So what we need is an independent assessment of whether there is oil and natural gas under all that ice. And we also need to know how hard it's going to be to get at it—I mean," he laughed, "we're talking about getting through over a mile of ice before we even start drilling! So how hard is that going to be?"

Bob had interrupted at that point, struggling not to be distracted by the blue sky and the sun gleaming on the leaves outside Ruud's office.

"So basically you want a survey of the ground beneath the ice, and a feasibility study on whether you can drill." He scratched his head. "Most of northeastern Greenland is a national park, so drilling there is going to be difficult and controversial on two counts: first it's a national park, and second, we are supposed to be moving away from fossil fuels. Greenland is melting *because* of fossil fuels."

Ruud cut in laughing, "But nothing that can't be overcome, I'm sure."

Bob ignored him and spread his hands. "That's something you'd have to lobby for in Greenland and Denmark, I imagine. But I have to tell you, I don't know how likely they are to go along with it. I mean, the Greenland ice cap is a kind of linchpin that holds the world's weather to certain patterns. It's also a cooling system. If you start digging oil wells, extracting oil and gas, it's difficult to know how that's going to affect the ice. It could have a major impact at a global level."

There was something unmistakably hostile in Bludd's eyes. Bob tried to ignore it and went on, "So it might be wise, while we're doing the feasibility study, if we did some projections of climate impact too."

"Yeah." Bludd had nodded. "Yeah, do that too." He had stared at the coffee on the mango table for a while, then spread his hands like he was trying to channel energy. "Look, I am being as clear as I know how. We need to secure contracts with Greenland and Denmark for the exploitation of that natural gas. And we need you to make it happen. Make it happen and there is *a lot* of money in it for you."

Bob had been about to protest, but Ruud had cut

him short. "You can count on us. We're putting our best man on the job. Bob here has an impeccable reputation for integrity, so that is going to look good for the media, and it will reassure those people who may be concerned about the impact on climate that we are taking that seriously."

Looking through the window of the hut now, Bob saw the blurred spec of a figure entering the valley, speeding toward the station. He fumbled for the radio-phone beside the panel of monitors and called Silvia. It rang twice.

"Hello!"

"Honey, it's me, Bob."

"Hey, I miss you, baby."

"Me too, sugar. Look, I need you to listen very carefully, Silvie, I haven't much time."

"What's going on, baby?"

"I'm at the station, the sensor array monitor hut."

"OK, what's up?"

"There is a man approaching and I think he is going to try to kill me."

"*What?*" Her voice was shrill. "Honey, is this a joke? That is not funny!"

"Listen to me. I need you to get all my papers, clean out my account, and get the hell out of Greenland. Call Ittoqqortoormiit and see if they can send a rescue team. But you get out of here. Get out *now!*"

"*Baby!*"

He hung up. Through the window he could see the figure taking shape as it drew closer. He sat at the computer console which was connected to the sensors and started typing furiously, sending the data to Thor Olafson, his assistant, with the strict instructions, "Do not let

Monet anywhere near this material. Submit it immediately to Dr. van Dreiver at UCLA." Thor would know what to do.

He heard the boots tramping up the steps and then the door opened. Cold, bright air swept in behind the giant who stood in the doorway. He pulled back his hood, removed his goggles and the mask that covered the lower part of his face.

Bob frowned. "What the hell are you doing here?"

The deep, baritone voice spoke quietly. "I can't let you do it. You know what the GT Corporation wants. It was made clear to you. You know what the university wants. There is no third way. I'm sorry."

"No!" Bob rushed forward, reaching out to grab the huge shoulders. "You don't understand. The consequences..."

The blade was long and thick, and razor sharp. It had to be to cut through the heavy clothes and penetrate into his liver. At first there was shock, then a strange sense of normality, like there should be a sensible, simple fix for the relatively small cut. Then, as the blade withdrew, a sudden and growing sense of weakness as the blood drained out, and time drained away with it.

He watched the big man turn and walk out of the door, without looking back. He heard the thud of heavy boots descending the stairs. He took a couple of unsteady steps to the chair by the monitor and picked up the telephone. It was answered instantly.

"*Bobby?*"

"Silvie, honey, I've been stabbed."

She was weeping. "*Oh, Bobby!*"

"It's in the liver, baby, so it's pretty bad." He could

hear his voice beginning to slur. "You wanna hang up now and call Ittoqqortoormiit, and tell them it's urgent. And you, baby, you need to get out of Greenland, fast."

But she had already hung up. She was a good girl. She had your back. She was calling, and they'd send out the King Air 360 to get him. But he knew he wasn't going to make it that long.

He stood and hobbled to the door. Very carefully he descended the steps, feeling the warm blood trickling down his right leg. He walked away from the building a few feet, then sat down, looking north into the crystal-white ice, and the ice-blue sky. He remembered for a few moments the last modification the Green Tomorrows Corporation had made to his brief. He had had a sinking knowledge then that he was getting drawn into something he would not be able to get out of.

He had told Ruud it could not be. Even Ruud had been worried, and had promised he would talk to Bludd, but it had made no difference. Silvie and Thor had both agreed with Bob, but the relentless pressure of the corporation and the university had driven them on, with promises and assurance which, like the horizon, were always just out of reach.

He made a small pillow out of snow and lay down. He smiled as he felt the cool ice creeping in, chilling him, bringing him peace. He had been sitting with Ruud in his office, telling him, "The Green Tomorrows Corporation is owned by the NATOil Corporation, Rudy. It's a global giant, a giant that is anything but green. We are going to destroy our reputation and our credentials!"

Ruud had done what Ruud always did. He had flapped a hand at him and said, "Aah, relax, will ya? You worry too much! I already asked Danny about that. He said the Green Tomorrows Corporation was NATOil's first step toward establishing its green credentials. They *want* to change! They are going to start phasing out oil and non-renewable resources, replacing them with renewable ones. They, and we, are going to be spearheading that move. And you, Bob, will be the tip of that spear. This could make you, pal. The man who made the world a greener place. Just stay cool, will you? We have to go *through* the crap to get out of it, right?"

He lay smiling, allowing the cold and the ice to soothe him. California and UCLA seemed so far away. The battle to save the world belonged to others now. He was at peace, embraced in the bosom of that vast world of cool, cool ice and white, white snow. He closed his eyes, breathed softly, and went to sleep.

CHAPTER ONE

The phone rang in the dark.

I fumbled for it and uttered a noise something like, "Whaumngh?"

"Mason? You are unintelligible! You must enunciate clearly!"

I held the phone away from my face and squinted. It was dead center of the long dark night of the soul, three AM. It was also the Chief, the nefarious Nero. I put the phone back to my ear.

"It's the long dark night of the soul, sir…"

"Don't quote Fitzgerald at me at three in the morning. I will be there to collect you in twenty minutes. We will breakfast at the White House."

I skipped the hot part of the shower and stood under a stream of very cold water, gasping and grunting and repeating to myself, "Breakfast at the White House…"

Manny Pacquiao, my cat, was on the foot of the bed observing me with disgust as I toweled myself dry and got dressed. He had never forgiven me for having him castrated. I had never forgiven myself, for that matter, and he knew it and gloated.

"I don't often breakfast at the White House, Manny," I said, tightening my tie. I glanced at my watch and saw that I had five minutes in which to make coffee. "In fact, as far as I can recall, I have never actually had breakfast at the White House. This is a first."

He yawned and closed his eyes.

I took the stairs at a reckless three at a time, forwent coffee, grabbed my coat from the closet and stepped out onto predawn Adams Street. It was cold. The birds were still in bed and the light from the streetlamps cast inky shadows and evoked saxophones and dames with long legs and husky voices; and that made me want to go back to bed.

Two headlamps glowed at the corner of North Capitol and a black Caddy pulled up in front of my gate, with the Chief's huge head glowing like a moon in the back window. I pulled open the door and he shifted to make room for me. I climbed in and we took off as I closed the door. A smoked-glass partition segregated us from the driver. The Chief, whom some called Nero because he was allegedly a pyromaniac, scowled at me through the folds of his face.

"Did you have time for coffee?"

"No."

He grunted and looked away. "We'll have breakfast at the White House."

"You said that. Now is when you tell me *why* we will have breakfast at the White House."

"We are going to have a meeting with Stephen Adamopolous, Presidential Advisor on Sustainable Energy, regarding the van Dreiver Report requested by the Presidential Commission on Sustainable Energy."

"At four in the morning."

"I should have thought that was obvious." He remained silent, staring out at the empty streets, with his ghostly reflection staring in at him. The steady flow of amber lamps washed him with light and shadow. Suddenly he expostulated furiously, "I mean, Alex, if we were going to have breakfast at nine, like any civilized person, *we would not be driving to the White House at half-past three!*"

I smiled. Nero was so mad he was ready to set fire to the District of Columbia. He detested breaking his routine, and if he ever had to, you could count on his being as cheerful as a hornet with a hornet up its ass at least until dinnertime.

"I take it this is not a social call, and that Adamopolous has some reason for dragging us out of bed at this time of the morning to discuss the van Dreiver Report."

He grunted and sulked like a kid offered a lollipop instead of a double chocolate waffle cone.

"They have lost a scientist in Greenland. They should have three but they have only two."

"What's that got to do with us? He probably fell into one of those holes..."

"A moulin."

"Uh-huh, or a crevasse."

We entered Logan Circle and began the long curve to exit on Vermont, headed south.

"I have no doubt Mr. Adamopolous will enlighten us. Clearly he is not satisfied that he fell into a moulin or a crevasse. It seems there may be foul play involved. His girlfriend appears to have decamped, taking all his money and all his papers."

"Papers relating to the Presidential Committee on Sustainable Energy."

"Evidently. And the van Dreiver Report."

I groaned. "Climate change at four AM, before breakfast."

"Precisely."

We turned out of H Street onto Jackson Place and crossed Pennsylvania Avenue, where the gates to West Executive Avenue were opened to give us access. We pulled up outside the West Wing, where a long, white awning extended over the sidewalk. Two men in dark blue suits ran to the car and opened the doors for us, then led the way inside.

Everything in the White House is shiny. The parquet floors, the marble floors, the antique furniture that sits on those floors, the walls, the eighteenth-century lamps and clocks, the brass on the doors, everything, every bit of it shines, as though polished by the constant, daily brush with temporal power.

We were led along parquet corridors, over crimson carpets, past paintings and busts of men, and the occasional woman, who had wielded great temporal power in earlier times, and from there down a short, oddly arched passage to a heavy, white door with a brass handle. One of our two guides departed and the other knocked on the door, then pushed it open and allowed us in.

The room was roughly twenty foot square, painted cream and lined with books. The furniture all looked eighteenth century, with spindly legs and latticed sides, and floral cushions. There was a small, mahogany desk with a green leather blotter, and a couple of settees at either end of the room. In the middle of the floor a folding, mahogany table had been placed and set for four with white linen napkins and just about anything you might want for breakfast.

There was a fire in the grate, and a short man who seemed to be wearing his older brother's bargain basement suit was standing in front of it, watching us with his hands behind his back. When the door had closed behind us he stepped forward, holding out one of those hands.

"Mr...."

The Chief took his hand and cut him short. "No names, please! Well," he added as an afterthought, "You two may exchange names," he waved his two hands at us dismissively and hurried over to the table, removing his coat. "I am averse to the excessive use of my name. You know who I am. That is enough."

Adamopolous and I shook. I offered him a smile and said, "He's an eccentric genius."

"Right, Well, it's good of you to come. And my apologies for the hour. It is a matter of some urgency. Please, sit, I had the kitchen rustle up some breakfast."

The Chief was already sitting, pouring himself coffee. I sat opposite him and Adamopolous sat between us. I helped myself to bacon and eggs while he spoke.

"So here's the thing, we're running late because we only got to hear about this a few hours ago. This comes to us from Nuuk, in Greenland, via UCLA and the Danish police, and in a pretty garbled state."

The Chief was spooning jam onto a slice of toast and chewing at the same time. He said, "Perhaps you had better start from the beginning, Mr. Adamopolous."

Adamopolous nodded. "Yeah, it's been a long day. So, about a year ago, at the end of last August, the president established a Commission to look into the reserves of oil and natural gas under Greenland. Professor Ruud van Dreiver, head of the Climatology Department at the

University of California, was appointed head of the Commission. He in turn appointed Dr. Bob Magnusson to head up the team of scientists in Greenland to carry out the necessary research and tests."

The Chief interrupted. "Obviously you secured all the necessary permissions from Greenland and Denmark."

Adamopolous nodded. "Obviously. Greenland was very receptive, but Copenhagen was more cagy. It's a tricky relationship. Greenland is an autonomous nation within the Kingdom of Denmark. Greenland is a very poor nation sitting on vast mineral wealth, and the ownership of that mineral wealth is a moot point: Greenland? Denmark? Both jointly? Greenland has home rule, but does not conduct independent foreign policy, and that would include ceding mining rights."

The Chief said, "Greenland is keen to have someone tell them exactly what they are sitting on, while Denmark is cautious about America muscling in on a potential source of vast wealth."

"Right, so anyhow, we got the green light and Bob and his team shipped out there. Now, here is where it started to get a little complicated. The Green Tomorrows Corporation..."

"Daniel Bludd, CEO," the Chief interjected, and drained his coffee cup, then sat back and sighed, "an effective captain of dubious green credentials."

"Indeed, Daniel Bludd is the CEO of Green Tomorrows. He is an old friend of the head of the Commission, and of the president's, and he wished to donate funding for the research that would eventually lead to the report. That is irregular..."

"It reeks of corruption."

"Well, it certainly invites scrutiny from those who do not love us; however, the head of the Commission—"

"Ruud van Dreiver—"

"Indeed, Ruud van Dreiver, approved the donation by the Green Tomorrows, just so long as it was clearly a donation and nothing more. So the donation was made and Green Tomorrows became what we might call an interested party in the report. After which, and this is strictly between us three, Bludd began to exert influence so that the report should expand to include issues of interest to Green Tomorrows."

"Such as?"

"Such as particular details about oil deposits as well as gas, such as various different feasibility studies on gaining access to oil and gas through the ice, such as—and this was *very* controversial—creating artificial moulins so that drilling equipment could be inserted. We are talking about a mile of ice or more before you get to the soil, and then that soil might be frozen. Bludd was clearly trying to use the report in order to prepare a proposal for the Greenland and Danish governments, to exploit those minerals."

The Chief said, "Whereas the original purpose of the Commission was…?"

"Simply to know what lay under Greenland, but without the feasibility report. I think the president was more interested in keeping an eye on it, in case any predators like China or Russia came along seeking to mine it. Don't forget, Russia is just a thousand miles away, across the Arctic. And these days China seems to be just about everywhere."

I spoke for the first time.

"So what you're saying is that Bludd was trying to

turn it from a situation report into a feasibility report preparatory to a plan of action."

"Yes, that's it. Now, this was embarrassing because, from a strictly ethical point of view, Bludd and Green Tomorrows should not have been a part of the study at all, but it seems van Dreiver was unwilling to act, and he simply looked the other way. Honestly I suspect his thinking was, better Green Tomorrows makes the bid than Beijing or Moscow. At least he could control Green Tomorrows, right?"

"OK, so what happened?"

"Bob, the lead scientist, was a man of great integrity. That was one of the reasons van Dreiver chose him for the study. So he began to protest, rather vociferously, at the influence Bludd was beginning to exert over the direction of the study, and its ultimate purpose. He complained to the university, he complained to van Dreiver in person and he complained to the Presidential Commission officially as a body. It was causing a lot of embarrassment and the fear was that some of his memos and emails might be leaked."

"But they weren't."

"No, it was worse than that. He was murdered."

The Chief had his cup halfway to his mouth. He stopped, sighed and put it down again.

"Details."

"Sketchy so far."

Adamopolous hadn't touched his coffee until now. Now he picked up the cup, sipped it, made a face and put it down again. He thought for a moment, then started to speak.

"Wednesday morning, very early, Bob flew out

DAVID ARCHER

from Nuuk, across Greenland to Ittoqqortoormiit. Ittoqqortoormiit is a small town on the eastern side of the island, which serves as a last base before tourists and scientists make excursions into the national park. Here, apparently, he picked up a King Air 360 that flew him to the UCLA base camp, and from there it seems he took a snowmobile to what he referred to as the sensor array. It was a set of instruments he had set up about eighty miles north of the base camp. He had not shared the purpose of these instruments with anyone on the team, or the data he was receiving from them. He claimed it was confidential."

He paused and sighed. The Chief had become immobile, watching him. Adamopolous spread his hands and shrugged. "We have to assume that he arrived at this location at about four PM. The weather was good, visibility was good and there were no high winds. At shortly after four we know he made a call to his girlfriend. It was brief, less than a minute. And we know that about fifteen minutes after that he called her again. Obviously we have no information as to what they spoke about.

"However, we do know that very shortly after the second call, an anonymous woman telephoned the police at Ittoqqortoormiit and told them Dr. Robert Magnusson was in mortal danger, and gave them the correct coordinates to go and find him. It took them over an hour to get there, and by the time they did they found him lying in the snow outside a wooden shack kind of affair, raised on stilts, where he had all his equipment set up. He had been stabbed in the liver with a large hunting knife."

I asked, "What about his girlfriend?"

"So far it seems she's vanished without a trace, and she seems to have taken all his research with her: com-

18

puter records, files, hard drives—everything—it has just gone."

The Chief spoke suddenly. "So what precisely do you want from ODIN?"

"We want his research, above all. We want to get hold of his research before anybody else does." He gave a dry laugh. "If they don't have it already."

"Are you saying you think Daniel Bludd may have killed Bob Magnusson because he wasn't cooperating, and is now after his papers?"

Adamopolous licked his lips. "I am not saying that, no. But I am saying that any investigator would have to consider that as one of many possibilities."

"Understood."

"We also want to know who killed Bob. Aside from the fact that he was a good man who did not deserve to die like that, we can't have people running around killing agents of the president. And he *was* acting as an agent of the president, so he was entitled to the president's protection. We should have seen the risk, and we didn't. I feel bad about that."

I said: "So you want Bob's research recovered and you want his killer brought to justice."

"Yes. That's pretty much what we want."

"You realize," said the Chief carefully, "that this investigation could cause a great deal of embarrassment to friends of the government, and of the president."

"Yeah." He nodded. "I'm going to be advising him to distance himself from those friends."

"So be it."

He stood. I stood too.

"Thanks for breakfast."

I helped the Chief on with his coat. He said, absently, "We'll be in touch. I assume the car is waiting."

We made our way out again along the shiny, parquet and marble corridors and out to the waiting Caddy. There, dawn was thinking about breaking and the birds were going crazy about the idea. To the driver he said, "Adams Street."

To me he said, "You go home and make whatever arrangements you need for your cat. I'll have documents and instructions sent to you before lunch."

I sighed and figured I'd have a nap on the plane.

CHAPTER TWO

The flight was a little short of six hours. There are no flights direct from DC to Nuuk, so I had to fly first to Reykjavik in Iceland, then change to an Air Greenland airbus and fly back across the Atlantic to Nuuk.

Nuuk Airport is small and made of corrugated steel. It is strangely reminiscent of a dilapidated New England church crossed with the kind of space station you might have seen in a sci-fi movie from the '60s. The terminal was a short walk across the tarmac, the line for passport control was short and everybody seemed to know each other, and baggage reclaim took about four minutes. So twenty minutes after landing I was carrying my bag to a Ford Ranger parked out front.

Nuuk is the biggest city in Greenland, but it's actually a small town. It has about fifteen thousand in-habitants and covers an area two miles long by one and a half miles across. I guess it's smaller than most ranches in Wyoming, and the area it covers is sparsely populated. That suits me. In my book, being big and densely popu-lated is nothing to brag about.

It took me about seven minutes to cover the four miles from the airport to my hotel, on the other side of town. It could have taken a lot longer if I had stopped and got out to look at the views every time I wanted to. I have seen a lot of unusual places on Earth, but few were as stunning or as downright odd as the average view you see at every street corner in Nuuk. Most of the houses are clapboard and painted striking colors. And each one is unique. You get the feeling real humans live there, and the hive-mind has not taken root yet.

My hotel was the Sømandshjemmet, which translates as the Seaman's Home, located on a street that gloried in the name Aqqusinersuaq. Why anyone would feel the need to put three Qs in a single name, and two of those together, beats me, but that's the way they roll in Greenland. I checked in at the desk and was helped to my room by probably the friendliest staff on the planet. They were two women, one a six-foot-three blonde and the other a five-foot brunette. Neither of them stopped smiling, or talking to me in Danish, until they left the room, laughing, making cautioning sounds in Norse and wagging their fingers at me.

I had brought only hand baggage—I didn't plan to be there all that long. I unpacked, found my file and sat reading it for a while by the window, in the strange, burnished silver light that hangs over the Arctic from March till October.

Bob's closest associates, aside from his girlfriend, Silvia, had been Dr. Thor Olafson and Dr. Bernard Monet. Both were his assistants, though according to Stephen Adamopolous, Bob never really warmed to Monet. Both Monet and Olafsen were based in Nuuk, and both were nearby. I decided to go talk to them.

I had a shower, changed my clothes, flipped a coin and decided to talk to Dr. Bernard Monet first.

It was a five-minute drive among randomly scattered, colorfully painted clapboard houses with gabled roofs that looked like Viking halls and gave you the impression things hadn't changed much since Erik the Red settled here.

I came to Jesus Christ Square, which was really a circle, turned left into Aqqusinersuaq and after half a mile took a left into Noorlemut.

Number 3954 was an apartment block with four upper stories plus a ground floor. It had lots of blue, yellow and orange squares, oblongs and circles on it that made it look like a bad Cubist painting by an architect who wished he was Picasso but worked for IKEA instead. I parked out front and climbed out of the cab into a breeze that had turned suddenly icy after the sun had dipped toward the horizon.

Dr. Bernard Monet had his apartment on the fifth floor. I stepped out of the cramped elevator, crossed the small, dark landing and leaned on his bell. The man who opened the door was of above average height and build, with short dark hair and large brown eyes. He had a dark gray sweater on and managed to be completely unremarkable. I made a pleasant face.

"Dr. Bernard Monet?"

"Sure..." The accent was hybrid and might have been French Canadian.

"My name is Alex Mason, I work for the United States Office of the Director of Intelligence." Actually I work for ODIN, the Office of the Democratic Intelligence Network, but I like to mix it up a bit. I showed him my badge. He glanced at it and gave me an ironic smile.

"Must be a tough job. How can I help you?"

"I was hoping we could talk about Dr. Bob Magnusson."

He frowned at me a moment, then stepped back to let me in.

"Sure, come in, we'll go in the living room. My wife is cooking dinner in the kitchen." I looked at my watch and saw it was seven PM. He gave a small laugh. "Don't worry. This eternal light takes some getting used to. Then in the winter it is always dark."

The living room was bright and sparsely furnished. He gestured me to a cream sofa and sat in a cream-leather-and-pine chair a Swede would have thought was cool. Through the window I could see chunks of ice the size of city blocks sitting in the bay. He waited.

I said: "From my window I just see houses."

He didn't smile. He blinked in a way that suggested he was wise and said, "Every window has a different view. It is the emptiness inside that makes the window useful. What would you like to know about Bob?"

"That's a good question, Dr. Monet. I don't honestly know. He was murdered. What is your take on that?"

He had his feet on a very white sheepskin rug. He stared at it for a moment with his elbows on his knees, and sighed.

"My take? I am not sure I have a take, Mr. Mason. You may be surprised to learn that Greenland has a very high murder rate. Everybody loves the Danes, because they are so civilized and polite!" He laughed, but only for a moment and without humor. "But the Inuit do not see them like that. They seem them as an occupying, privileged force. There is a lot of racial tension between Danes and Inuit, and people get killed."

I studied his face for a moment. He held my eye.

"Dr. Bob Magnusson was not a Dane. He was an American."

"Of Danish extraction. If your name is Magnusson, the Inuit don't care where you were born. You are a Dane."

"He was murdered in Northeast Greenland National Park, five hundred miles from the nearest town, in the middle of a frozen wasteland."

"But only eighty miles from the UCLA base camp."

"OK, so how many people were at the base camp?"

"Four at any one time."

"And were there any Inuit researchers there who might have hated Dr. Magnusson for being a Dane?"

"I don't know who was on the roster for that day." He shrugged reluctantly. "But none of them was Inuit."

I frowned again. "You don't know who was on? I thought you were his assistant."

"I was. Me and Thor. But I had a couple of days off and I do not know who was on duty at the camp." He suddenly sat back and spread his hands in a helpless gesture. "I am sorry! I have no theory for why or how Bob was killed."

I nodded like I understood.

"What happened to all his research? He must have had files, papers, removable drives, a computer…"

He shrugged again. "As far as I know all of that was kept at his house. He shared with us what he wanted us to know, which was not so much. In fact it was increasingly little."

"He was secretive?"

"A bit."

What happened to his girlfriend?"

He gave a short, humorless laugh. "Silvia? I am

waiting for you to tell me. She disappeared." He made a very French gesture with his fingers, opening them like a small explosion, and said, "*Puff!*"

"How was your relationship with Dr. Magnusson?"

"Good." He made a Gallic face, shrugging and pulling down the corners of his mouth. "We worked well together. Of course his friend was Thor, you know how it is with Scandinavians, they stick together. So him and Thor were close friends, but we were good. OK. No problem."

"What was your opinion of the research?"

His face creased into an ironic smile and his gaze shifted to the icebergs in the bay.

"You know? When you move from graduate student to postgraduate, and you are working for your PhD, you move also from naïve idealist to pragmatist. Is industry causing global warming? No climate change, *global warming!* The answer is very simple. It is another question: Who is paying for the research? The research is funded by the United Nations with money from Third World countries who want to level the playing field? Then industry causes global warming. The research is funded by Shell or BP? Then we call it climate change and we say it is part of a natural process."

I shook my head. "You seem to be about ten years behind the times, Dr. Monet. The last IPCC report was more than unequivocal."

He snorted. "Nothing has changed but the language and the masks. Climate change is happening, of course! Global warming is happening, *of course!* So the vested interests put on their green suits and talk about renewable energy, *but there is no renewable energy! Because renewable energy must be made using non-renewable fossil fuels!*"

I went to speak but he interrupted me. "How do you make a solar cell? Do you know? All so-called *green* technologies are depending on fossil fuels. Every single step of the production of solar photovoltaic power systems—solar energy—requires the use of fossil fuels," he counted them off on his fingers, "for carbon reductants, for smelting silicon from ore, for providing heat and power for the manufacturing process, for the transport of materials across nations and continents, for construction and installation. The *only* truly renewable materials consumed in solar photovoltaic power systems production, you know what they are?" He waited. I shook my head. "Trees, torn down and obtained from the burning of vast areas of tropical rainforest, mainly in the Amazon, for creating charcoal—carbon—which is needed for extracting silicon. Now add to this the mineral resources and fossil fuels necessary for constructing factories, processing equipment and maintenance of the solar energy infrastructure! And at the end of this process, you know how long a solar panel last? Maybe twenty years. You know how long a solar battery lasts? Five, maybe ten years maximum. You think in five, ten, fifteen year this cell and this battery have balanced out all the CO_2 that was generated to manufacture them?"

"Probably not."

"Let me tell you, Mr. Mason, a silicon smelter, a polysilicon refinery, a crystal grower, all require nonstop energy input twenty-four hour a day, three hundred and sixty-five days of the year. And this power, where is it coming from? It is coming from coal, oil or gas. Solar energy, wind energy, cannot replace fossil fuels for *eight billion people!* The world, the global, consumer society, is totally *dependent* on fossil fuels!"

"OK, I get it, but my question was: What was your opinion of the research you were conducting?"

"You know who funds it?"

"Sure, the Commission on Sustainable..."

He flapped his hand at me like he was batting away a ball. "Pah!" he said. "The Commission puts in some little money from the taxpayer, the university puts in some money from its funds, but seventy or eighty percent of the money is coming from Green Tomorrows."

I was surprised but hid it by shrugging. "Who have an interest in developing green energy."

He laughed. "And so they are looking for oil and gas? They are looking for oil and gas because they have an interest in green, renewable energy? I want a banana so I go to my fridge looking for a burger?" He laughed. "And they want to know can they make artificial moulins to get drilling equipment down through the ice to get at the oil and the gas. This is legitimate research for a company dedicated to green, renewable energy?"

"So you did not approve of this research?"

He looked at me like he'd just found me stuck to the sole of his shoe.

"No, I did not approve of this research."

"How about Bob and Thor?"

He spread his hands and shrugged, like he was rendered helpless by my stupidity. "I do not understand what is your question. What is my opinion of Bob and Thor? Or what was their opinion of the research?"

"How about both?" I smiled pleasantly at him while I imagined throwing him out of the window. "Let's start with their opinion of the research."

"We all agreed that Green Tomorrows, and their

parent company NATOil, had an agenda with this report. They were seeking to make a deal with the Greenland government, and maybe also with Denmark if Denmark was willing. But if Denmark was not willing, I think they would be happy to foment separatist feelings and fund the independence movement, if that will help them secure the sole rights to Greenland gas and oil. But we all were resigned. If we want to keep our jobs, pay the rent and eat, then we must accept the job and do the research."

"Green Tomorrows' parent company, the NATOil Corporation."

"One of the so-called Big Eight."

I was quiet a moment, thinking. "Bob knew this, obviously."

"Obviously. It was Thor who discovered the fact. Bob confronted Rudy, Ruud van Dreiver, who commissioned Bob to make the report. They had a meeting with Daniel Bludd, the CEO of Green Tomorrows. Bludd was all, 'Oh we are fighting to make the transition, we want to give you so much money so you can help us to break free of fossil fuels...,' but is all bullshit. If you want to break free, why you are looking for ways to drill through the fucking ice, man?" He waved his hands in the air, saying, "Transition, transition... But there is no transition! Who are you fucking kidding, man? You want to make cars, and TVs and cell phones and fashion sneakers and houses and planes and airports and food and so on and so on for *eight thousand millions of peoples*—with windmills? With solar panels? Come on!"

"OK." I nodded. "Then, I have to ask you the obvious question. Had Bob decided to challenge van Dreiver and Bludd? Was he threatening to go public, expose them...?"

He was laughing and shaking his head before I had finished. "Bob? No, man. That was not Bob's style. Bob was all about the compromise. We can all work together and find an answer. Bob was the one who used to say, 'The cure for climate change would cause more harm, suffering and hunger than a managed transition to sustainable energy.' And that was his goal."

"Was he wrong?"

He gave a small, exasperated snort. "It depends what you expect to do with sustainable energy. Yeah, you can run Greenland, *maybe* Iceland, on sustainable energy, when you are keeping population in the thousands or hundreds of thousands. But keep the world like it is today, with eight billions of people? You gotta be kidding me."

"So let me be clear about this, Dr. Monet. Bob was not in conflict with the university or the corporation?"

"No, no way, not Bob. Bob was never in conflict with nobody. He was a diplomat, even an appeaser."

I watched him a moment and he watched me back. In the end I said, "So if I understand you correctly, you are telling me his relationship with his employers was good and they had no reason to eliminate him."

"I don't know if that is what I am telling you. I am just telling you that as far as I know, they were happy with him, and he was trying to make everybody happy."

"He didn't manage to make you happy, clearly."

He shrugged and pulled down the corners of his mouth.

"He didn't make me happy or unhappy. I am an existentialist, Mr. Mason." He gave a small laugh. "Let me ask you: Do you realize that in the next hundred years more than eight thousand millions of people will die?"

I frowned. "Why is that?"

He raised his eyebrows, shrugged and spread his hands in that Gallic expression that says, *It's obvious!* "It is obvious! Because nobody lives for one 'undred years! So in one 'undred years, all of us who are alive today, will be dead! *Voila!* So, when you adopt this perspective, you do not get so upset. *Carpe diem!*"

I grunted. "So you can't offer me any guidance on who might have wanted to kill Dr. Magnusson."

"No," he shook his head, "and I do not believe anybody *wanted* to kill Bob. Greenlanders, like Icelanders, they are crazy people. Bob had a very attractive girlfriend, maybe somebody was jealous. The ice, the cold, no day in winter, no night in summer, it makes people crazy." He gave another Gallic shrug. "What is important is that the research goes on. The research must continue."

I looked out at the massive icebergs sitting in the bay, at the strange silver light, and wondered if Dr. Bob Magnusson had been killed in a moment of crazy hot blood, or ice-cold pragmatism.

CHAPTER THREE

Wednesday dawn Silvia felt movement in the bed, but she didn't want to open her eyes. Heavy, warm blankets lay on her eyelids and drew her back into sleep. She heard Bob groan and rub his face, then stomp sleepily to the bathroom.

She complained, stretched and sat up. Outside the window the air over the water was gunmetal gray touched with silver. She looked at her phone. Four AM. At first guilt made her stand and make for the kitchen downstairs. He worked so hard, he was so devoted and loyal, and good. She had to be with him when he left. But as she started making breakfast, thinking about him brought a smile to her face. It was not just guilt.

After ten minutes he came down dragging his rucksack with one hand and drying his hair with the other. She parted his straggly moustache and kissed him.

"Coffee and pancakes. I'll have mine later. How long you going to be, baby?"

"You're the best, baby." He put his foot on the chair to pull on his heavy boots. "I should be back tomorrow, Friday the latest. I just need to check some readings."

He sat and she watched him drink the milky, sweet coffee and eat the pancakes, thick with butter and maple syrup.

"You're pretty sure of what you're going to find, aren't you?"

He nodded with his mouth full, then licked his fingers. She threw his napkin at him. "Don't do that!" Then, "You think they're gonna listen to you? I'm not so sure, baby."

He drained his cup and she refilled it as he buttered another pancake.

"They have to," he said simply. "It's like the Cold War. We were never at risk because nobody was ever going to fire the first shot."

"How is this the same as that?"

"Because nobody was going to choose extinction. When they see the consequences they will back up, stop and think. People, especially these people, will push as far as they can to make a profit. But as soon as they realize they're going to die if they push any further, they stop. When I explain to them the repercussions, and I prove it to them with hard data, they'll understand."

She sighed. "I thought you and your colleagues had been doing that for the past twenty years. I thought the IPCC did that last month."

"Nobody listens to the IPCC, you know that. Anyway, they'll listen. I'll make them listen, I promise."

He had finished dressing, pulled on his rucksack and she had walked him to the door. There she had kissed him until he became impatient.

"Honey, I have to go."

They had both laughed, kissed again, and he had gone to the Defender he had parked in the drive. He climbed in, slammed the door and took off up Niels Hammekenip Aqqutaa, toward the airport. She watched the car till it was out of sight, standing in her pajamas. The air was cold, touched with the promise of the snow and ice that was to come. She shuddered and closed the door.

She peered in at the kitchen, regarded the dirty plate and the cups, then, giggling to herself, she tiptoed up the stairs as though someone might see or hear her, and fell back into the bed. Where she almost immediately fell asleep.

She awoke again at twelve and stayed in bed till one, then she rose feeling a mixture of guilt and smugness. She went down to the kitchen again, put the plates beside the sink, made herself a stack of pancakes and a pot of coffee which she took to the living room to eat while she gazed at the milky sea and, by turns, read the *National Geographic*. It was a lazy Wednesday, and good to do nothing for a while.

She dozed on the sofa for a while and then at a little before four her phone rang. She fumbled for it and answered.

"Hello?"

"Honey, it's me, Bob."

She smiled and stretched. "Hey, I miss you, baby."

"Me too, sugar. Look, I need you to listen very carefully, Silvie, I haven't much time."

She frowned and sat up. "What's going on, baby?"

"I'm at the station, the sensor array monitor hut."

She nodded, like he could see her. "OK, what's up?"

"There is a man approaching and I think he is going to try to kill me."

The blood drained from her head. The room rocked and her belly twisted. "*What?*" She heard her own voice shrill as she got to her feet. "Honey, is this a joke?"

"Listen to me. I need you to get all my papers, clean out my account, and get the hell out of Greenland. Call Ittoqqortoormiit and see if they can send a rescue team. But you get out of here. Get out *now!*"

She was on her feet, panicking. *"Baby!"*

But he had hung up. She fumbled with the phone. Her fingers would not work. She found the emergency number for the police and called. It rang once and was answered immediately. She half screamed into the phone.

"Please, for god's sake, you have to act fast!"

"What is your emergency?"

"My boyfriend, Dr. Bob Magnusson! He is at...wait!" She ran to the kitchen and looked on the corkboard for the coordinates. "At his field lab, coordinates, latitude, 77°26'1.08"N, longitude, 32°33'51.33"W. He just called me, he said there is a man trying to kill him. Please go to him! Please, for god's sake."

"OK, caller, I am informing the emergency services. Please hang up in case he calls again. Somebody will be in touch."

She walked in circles around the room, with her hand over her mouth and tears flooding her cheeks. All she could think was, *It can't be true!*

But Bob did not panic, Bob did not imagine things, Bob was anything but dramatic.

She found herself in the kitchen, staring at the plate and cup he had used that morning, the knife he had held in his hand, the butter on the knife. It couldn't be real. The phone rang and made her jump and scream. She answered it with fumbling fingers.

"Bobby?"

"Silvie, honey, I've been stabbed."

She sank into the chair, hollow inside. *"Oh, Bobby..."*

"It's in the liver, baby, so it's pretty bad. You wanna hang up now and call Ittoqqortoormiit, and tell them it's urgent. And you, baby, you need to get out of Greenland, fast."

She hung up and frantically dialed 112 again.

"What is your..."

She cut across the woman's voice, trying not to scream, trying to control her hysteria.

"My boyfriend, Bob, Dr. Robert Magnusson..."

"Yes, caller, we are dispatching a plane..."

"He's been stabbed in the liver, please hurry! He has been stabbed! He's dying!"

"There is a team on its way. What is your name, caller? Do you need help?"

She hung up and dropped the phone to the floor. Slowly realization dawned, that if Bob was telling her to get out of Greenland, with his papers, he feared that the killer might next come for her.

The killer, or his accomplice, who might be in Nuuk right now. She scrambled to her feet and ran to the front door, which she locked. Her car was in the garage. Which was locked and had access from the kitchen. She returned to the kitchen, took the large knife from the block and opened the door to the garage. It was dark. She turned on the light and started, then whimpered. But it was locked and there was nobody there.

She turned off the light, closed the door and ran up the stairs to the bedroom. There she packed a change of clothes and spent half an hour gathering up Bob's papers, pen drives and removable hard drives.

Twice she had to run to the bathroom to vomit.

At half past four she sat in front of the computer and transferred everything from Bob's account and their joint account to her personal account. Then she went to book a ticket and realized she had no idea where to go or what to do. So, wiping the tears from her eyes and struggling to control her bottom lip, she called the only person she could think of.

"Rudy?"

"Who is this, please?"

"It's Silvia. Bob's..."

"Oh, *Silvia!* How are you? How's Bob? You OK? You sound odd."

"No, I am not OK. Rudy—" Her control over her voice began to slip. "I think Bob has been murdered."

"*What?* What are you talking about, Silvia?"

"He called me. He was at the station, where he has the sensors. In the national park. He said he thought somebody was coming to kill him. Then a little later he called again and said somebody had stabbed him in the liver." She started sobbing again. "It doesn't make any *sense!* I am terrified, Rudy. I don't know what to do."

He was quiet for a moment, like he was thinking. Then he said, "Well, have you called 911?"

"Yes, 112, they are on their way."

"To you or to him?"

"To *him!*"

"Then all you can do is wait. Listen, I'll book a flight, Mary will come with me..."

"No! He told me they might come for me. He told me to take all his papers and get out of Greenland."

"That they might come after *you?* Why on *Earth*...?"

She had started to shiver and knew she was going into shock. Outside a cold wind had whipped up. "Rudy, I don't know what to do."

"You said you have his papers?"

"Everything that was at the house, yes."

"Did he tell you who he thought these people were?"

"No. He'd been talking for a few weeks about how there might be people who wanted to hurt him, but he said he had it all under *control*..." She started to cry again.

"OK, Silvia, take it easy. Now if Bob told you to get out of Greenland with his papers, then that is exactly what you must do. I'll get in touch with the Greenland police, but meantime let's get you to a safe place. I want you to book yourself on the next flight to London, you hear? Have you got money?"

"Yes. But why London?"

"Because it is closer and faster, and I have friends there. Now, as soon as you get your ticket you let me know the flight number and the arrival time, and I'll have someone meet you. OK?"

"Yes, all right. Thanks, Rudy. I don't know what I would have done."

"That's OK, Silvia. You go and get your ticket and I'll get on to the Icelandic police and see if they can tell me anything. I can't help feeling this is some crazy mix-up."

She thanked him again and hung up. Half an hour later she had made the reservation, checked in and printed her boarding pass. She called Rudy, gave him the details and, at a quarter past five, she ran down the stairs, unlocked the kitchen door to the garage, threw two bags on the back seat and pressed the remote control to open the door. It rose slowly with a loud rattle as she climbed behind the wheel, locked the doors and started the engine. Light began to flood the garage. She screamed involuntarily, expecting at any second to see a figure standing outside. But there was no one there and she drove out onto the street and headed for the airport.

Ten minutes later she arrived at the airport parking lot and parked beside Bob's Land Rover. For the next fifteen minutes she was unable to get out of the car, or do anything. She cried convulsively and had to cover her mouth with her sleeve to stop herself from shouting out loud with pain and grief. She pleaded to God that there would be a miracle and that Bob would be all right. But she knew, in her gut, that there would be no miracles.

The next hours were interminable. She spent the night at the airport. Her flight was scheduled to depart at seven thirty AM. Boarding would commence at six thirty. The seats, like all seats at airports, were hard and uncomfortable. She tried to doze, but as soon as she closed her eyes nightmarish images crowded in of the frozen wasteland, and Bob's dying thoughts and feelings. And then she would start to cry silently, until by four in the morning her grief had drained itself into a state of numbness. And it seemed no sooner had she slipped, exhausted, into darkness than her alarm jangled her into wakefulness, and it was time to board.

The flight, or flights, lasted twenty-six hours. Nuuk to Kangerlussuaq, just a hundred and eighty miles north. Then a four-and-a-half-hour wait before changing planes and departing for Copenhagen at twenty minutes before one PM, to arrive at nine o'clock that night. There another wait for over ten hours before flying on again, at seven fifteen the next morning, east instead of southwest, to Kaunas in Lithuania. There, in Lithuania, another wait for almost two hours and finally, at twenty minutes past eleven, she boarded her last plane bound for London, Luton, where she touched down at just after noon on Friday.

She emerged from arrivals, haggard on the outside and on the inside, drained of emotion and numb. She crossed through the barrier, not sure for a moment if she was supposed to connect with another flight or find a bench to curl up and sleep.

A hand touched her shoulder. She stared at it for a moment, before tracing the arm to a face that was both frowning and smiling.

"Silvia Gordon?"

It was a woman, small, maybe five foot two, with a face like a pixie: very blonde hair, very blue, slightly slanted eyes. Before Silvia could say anything the woman said, "I am Joanna Jeffries, a friend of Rudy's. He telephoned me and asked me to meet you."

Silvia didn't answer straight away and the woman's frown deepened. "You poor child," she said, "you must be exhausted. Come along, you'll stay with me for a day or two until you're rested."

She put her arm around her and guided her toward the parking lot. Silvia let herself be led. The woman spoke some more. She was saying something about a frightful journey.

"Where are we going?" she asked. She was aware that everything was very different to Nuuk. But the last day had been a succession of different places and pictures, and streams of people leading her down long passages.

She tried to get a grip on her mind. Somewhere she was aware that there was danger. Bob had been murdered. Somebody wanted to kill her. "You're Ruud van Dreiver's friend?"

"Yes," said the woman, smiling at her. "He asked me to meet you and take care of you." They had arrived at a green Range Rover in the parking lot. The woman opened the passenger side and Silvia climbed in. Then the driver's door opened and the woman got in behind the wheel. She placed her hand on Silvia's knee and peered into her face. "Are you OK?"

"I think so."

"Everything is going to be all right. I'm going to take you home and pack you into bed with a couple of sleeping tablets. You sleep and rest and recover. Then, when you're feeling stronger, Rudy will call and tell you what to do. OK?"

Silvia nodded and spoke very quietly. "Thank you."

Then she closed her eyes and sleep enveloped her.

CHAPTER FOUR

D
r. Thor Olafson lived about five hundred yards away from Dr. Bernard Monet, if you followed the roads. As the crow flies it was more like a bow-shot.

A few clouds had appeared in the sky and when they obscured the sun the air turned very cold, and I found myself shuddering as I climbed into the truck. A single thought kept going around in my head and I couldn't shake it. It was a stupid thing, but I wished I'd asked him: If his philosophy was so bleak, existential and French, why the hell was it so important for the show—or the research—to go on? And also, if the research was just another way of shafting the sheep so they could extract and burn more fossil fuels, why was it so important that the research go on?

At first I thought he'd got on my nerves because he was some jerk playing at being Albert Camus or Jean-Paul Sartre. But then, as I climbed in the truck and fired up the engine, I realized that wasn't it. What was wrong was that he'd been putting on the act to hide something.

I pulled away and headed up Noorlemut to the intersection with Aqquirsinersuaq, where I turned right, thinking to myself that what Monet had been hiding was precisely what he had let slip at the end. Throughout our whole interview he had been acting like he didn't give a damn about anything. Everyone was corrupted, the universities were corrupted, the professors were corrupted, the governments were corrupted, so nothing mattered and he didn't give a damn. But right there, at the end, he had slipped. He did care, he did give a damn: "The research must go on."

I remembered a quote from Sartre, from *The Flies*, "Human life begins on the far side of despair."

I drove down Aqquirsinersuaq making "Hmmm..." sounds to myself and frowning until I turned into Dronning Ingridsvej, wondering who Ingrid was and what she'd done to earn such a name.

Number 385 was an eight-story apartment block with the ground floor clad in peeling white clapboard, and the rest of the building in dark chocolate brown with large balconies overlooking Queen Ingrid's Hospital and the bay beyond. I left the Ford in the parking lot and entered the lobby. It was dark and functional and occupied mainly by bicycles. Thor's apartment was letter A on the sixth floor. I rang the bell and waited.

The man who opened the door after a couple of minutes seemed to block out more light than the door itself. He must have been six foot six, and you'd have to make a stopover to get from his left shoulder to the right. He had thick, wiry blond hair that hung below his shoulders and the lower part of his face was lost somewhere in the undergrowth of his beard and his moustache. He regarded me with no particular expression. He held the door in his right hand, and a large jug of beer in his left.

"Yuh," he said.

It seemed a redundant question, but I asked it anyway.

"Dr. Thor Olafson?"

"Yuh."

"My name is Alex Mason. I am here on behalf of the Presidential Commission on Sustainable Energy. We are looking into Dr. Robert Magnusson's death. Can you spare me a few minutes?"

He took a few moments, gave the ghost of a nod and said, "Yuh." Then he stood back to let me through. He used his jug to point toward his living room, closed the door and followed me in.

The walls were lined with books. There was a desk in the corner with books stacked in towers around the computer. There were also books on the floor, beside stacks of papers, bound reports, magazines and newspapers. Two armchairs and a sofa sat around a coffee table in the center of the floor. All four pieces of furniture were partially covered in snowdrifts of papers and books. He used the jug to point at a chair and rumbled, "You can make space on the chair. You want a beer?"

I was going to say no, but something about the giant made you want to drink beer, heroically, and perhaps pillage and plunder a bit. So I said, "Yeah, thanks."

He brought me a dark brown pint bottle from the kitchen with a chilled mug. I poured as he sat and watched me. The beer was a dark, nutty red-brown with very little froth. I took a pull and got a mouthful of spices, malt and toffee. I savored it and nodded.

"That's beer," I said.

"Nanoq. Danish."

I cleared a space on the table and set the jug down where I found a ring from a previous jug.

"Dr. Olafson—"

"Thor. My name is Thor. Before I go to college I was Thor. Then I was go to college and I wrote my thesis and publish it. But I am still the same man. So my name is still Thor. I don't need a new name."

I wondered if everyone in Greenland was hooked on deep thinking and philosophizing. Maybe it was the six months of darkness that did it.

"OK, Thor, my first and obvious question, have you any thoughts or feelings about who killed Dr. Magnusson?"

He gave one slow blink.

"Yuh."

"Who?"

"You."

It was probably only a couple of seconds, but we sat and stared at each other for what felt like a long time, and I was acutely aware that his size, his strength and his temperament all made this man potentially very dangerous.

"Let me see if I understand you. You think I killed Dr. Magnusson? What possible grounds do you have for that belief? I only arrived in Greenland today. I have neither motive nor opportunity."

"For you names are so important. You introduce yourself, 'I am here on behalf of the Presidential Commission on Sustainable Energy.' So you are the agent of the Presidential Commission on Sustainable Energy. So you *are* the Presidential Commission on Sustainable Energy. I believe the Presidential Commission on Sustainable Energy killed Bob. His name is Bob. He is my friend."

I sighed. "OK, Thor, I am Alex Mason. You can call

me Alex or Mason, I don't care. The Commission employed me to come and find out who killed Bob. What makes you think the Commission killed their own researcher?"

He drained his jug and wiped the foam from his moustache with the back of his hand.

"The Commission, and the corporations who bought the Commission, employed Bob and me to find some information. We can divide this information into three parts." He held up a fist like a sledgehammer and raised an index finger the size of a small arm. "One, how much oil is under Greenland?" He raised his middle finger. "Two, how much gas?" He raised his ring finger. "How difficult is it to access this oil and this gas? These three things they wanted to know."

"But?"

"But this was not the information Bob was going to give them. We answered these questions, for sure. But we gave them more information also, about the consequences of mining gas and oil."

He was quiet so long I began to think that was the extent of his answer. Finally he made a grunting noise I realized was a sigh.

"The issue of climate change is complicated. It is very hard to understand, and making predictions is harder. Understanding climate change and making forecasts in Greenland is much more difficult than that again." He paused and I waited. "Because we have so much ice here. Ice has complicated dynamics. It is not behaving like you think it is going to behave. You don't know nothing about ice. So I cannot explain it to you. But I tell you what Bob was telling Ruud van Dreiver, Daniel Bludd and Tony Gorr. If you once are starting to drill in the ice,

you can destabilize the ice cap with catastrophic consequences."

"Wait, Tony Gorr?"

"Yuh, CEO of NATOil Corporation, which is owning
Green Tomorrows."

"What kind of catastrophic consequences?"

"The partial collapse of the ice sheet, melting and
calving on a catastrophic scale, glaciers moving like rivers
of ice and mud, catastrophic flooding, tsunamis across
North Atlantic, earthquakes ten and eleven on the Richter
scale, maybe even crust displacement."

I scratched my head. "Thor, forgive me, but it is
hard to believe that drilling through the ice could trigger
such extreme results."

"Yuh."

I waited, but apparently that was it. So I pressed
him. "How?"

"I told you. Is hard to explain to somebody like
you."

"Try me."

Again the groaning sigh. "OK, see we have one or
two mile of ice, and you are imagining that at the bottom, the ice is stuck, bonded to the rock by freezing.
But you are wrong. That two mile of ice is sitting, all
over Greenland continent, on maybe three feet of mud.
You have more than six hundred thousand square miles
of ice, one or two miles deep, floating..." He moved his
hands one slowly above the other to illustrate. "...float-
ing on an ocean of mud. If above temperatures are minus
twenty, thirty, forty centigrade," he shrugged, "OK. Ice is
holding good. But if temperatures above are minus one,
or one, two, three degree above freezing, then ice begins

to make moulins, big holes in the ice, three hundred feet across, with melt water pouring all the way, two miles down to the mud. And the ice sheet begins to look like a Gruyère cheese. So if you understand a little about physics, imagine you have enough ice to make an area of the Earth's crust so big it reaches from the southernmost tip of Texas, the Mexican border, on the gulf, across the Canadian border into Saskatchewan, and from Utah right the way across to Missouri, you got an idea of the size, right?"

"I got it."

"So this ice is so heavy, we are talking about hundreds of quadrillions of tons, so heavy it has made that land sink below the level of the sea. All of that weight pushing down, pushing the land under the sea. Imagine the size and the weight: from Mexico to Canada, from Utah to Missouri, two miles deep of ice. Now imagine all that weight pushing down on a block of ice that is looking like a Gruyère cheese, like a colander, with holes going in through it, thousands, maybe millions of holes, all the way down to that ocean of mud. You know what that weight wants to do when it reaches the mud?" I shook my head. "It can't go down, so it wants to go out." He pointed right and left with his fingers and repeated, "It wants to go out to the sides, so the ice begins to crack and pull apart."

I sat in silence, staring out at the silent blue sky over the bay, imagining that much ice pushing down with an unimaginable pressure of quadrillions of tons, and starting to tear apart under its own weight. I felt a cold chill of something truly unimaginable about to happen.

His voice broke in on my thoughts. "Now all I need to do to trigger the biggest catastrophe in sixty-five million years, is to start industrial-scale drilling through that ice, and increase the geothermal energy in the bedrock, releasing hot gas and oil."

"It's hard to visualize."

He made a noise like "Hm," then added, "So he told the Commission something they did not want to hear, and they send a man like you to kill him."

"A man like me?"

He shrugged. "An agent. An instrument."

"So your theory is that they killed him to silence him, and now they'll find somebody more sympathetic..."

"Or easier to bribe."

"...or easier to bribe, to finish his research with more favorable findings."

"Yuh."

I scratched my head. "Thor, if you are right, your telling me this would put your life at risk too."

He nodded. "I hope they try. I would like to pay the Commission for Bob's death. He was a good man and a good friend."

"I'm sorry." I meant it.

"Did you kill him?"

"No, Thor. I'm trying to find the person who killed him. Things are not as simple and black and white as you think."

"Maybe."

"Where is his research?"

"I don't know."

"You were his closest colleague."

"Yuh."

"He must have had files, notebooks, computers, data storage..."

"Yuh."

"You must have some idea where it is."

He shrugged his massive shoulders again. "I don't know."

I sighed. "What can you tell me about Silvia, his girlfriend?"

"I can tell you she was his girlfriend, they were living together, now she is gone."

"You know where?"

"No, maybe she is dead also."

I sighed again and scratched my head again. Thor was not easy to talk to. "I am not the enemy, Thor. Maybe you're right and people from the Commission arranged Bob's death. If that's true I will find out and bring them to justice. If you help me, that will be easier to do."

"Maybe. But right now my heart hurts for losing my friend. I do not trust the Commission and I do not trust you because you are their man. Do you have more questions?"

"Yeah, just one. Do you have Bob's research?"

I watched his eyes carefully. They were about as telling as an igloo.

"No."

"Do you know where it is?"

"No. You are asking the same questions again. That means you have asked all your questions."

"I have one last one, Thor, and then I'll leave you in peace. The question is this: if you have told me the substance of what you and Bob had found, about the drilling, what is the point in hiding his research notes and the report from me?"

If I had hoped for a telling reaction, I didn't get it.

He remained completely impassive.

"You say I am hiding it. I did not say I was hiding it."

"OK." I sighed and stood. "Thanks for the beer."

"If you come back, bring Bob's killer with you."

I held his eye for a long moment. "Help me catch him, and you might have yourself a deal."

He didn't answer, but something in his eyes said he was thinking about it. It was about as expressive as I had seen him, so maybe I had got to him somehow. I nodded.

"I'll be seeing you."

I opened my door and went out into the bright, cold wind. I climbed in behind the wheel and sat looking out at that strange town with its strange Arctic architecture, its steep, gabled roofs and brightly colored houses in red, green, blue and yellow; and the roads which were really just the broad spaces between houses. I had one more thing I had to do that day before my pre-dinner martini. I needed to contact the local police liaison officer and have him tell me about Silvia and the house she shared with Bob. The cop-shop was on Lundsteensvej, half a mile northwest of where I was, along the blessedly pronounceable Imaneq. I started the engine and rolled up Dronning Ingridsvej, which would forever be for me Droning Ingrid's Way, and turned left onto Aqqusinersuaq, with all its Qs.

CHAPTER FIVE

The cop-shop was a long, two-storey brown clapboard structure with a big blue and white sign on a post outside that said POLITI, and another sign over the door that read, surprisingly, POLITIGARDEN. I figured it meant police station, climbed out of the truck and pushed inside.

It wasn't like a New York police station. Everything was open, blond wood and there were lots of windows. There was a sergeant sitting at a desk who smiled at me as I walked in. He looked more Danish than Inuit. All Danes speak English so I smiled back and said, "My name is Alex Mason, I'm here from the United States to inquire into the death of Dr. Robert Magnusson. I believe you have a liaison officer for me to talk to..."

I trailed off because he was still smiling at me. When I had finished he nodded once, picked up his phone and spoke into it in Danish.

"*Amerikaneren er her. Skal jeg sende ham op?*"

Yeah, I know, when you see it written it's easy. But it doesn't sound how it looks. He nodded a couple of times, said "OK, OK," and hung up. Then he offered me his nice smile again and said, "You can go right on up. Take the stairs," he pointed at the blond wood, blue-carpeted stairs, "and the office is the first on your right."

I gave him the thumbs-up and said, "Thanks."

He winked and gave his head a little tilt. "Y'all have a nice day now."

As I climbed the stairs he was looking at his computer screen like he was pleased with himself. I came to a landing with more blond wood, blue carpets and lots of glass, crossed to a corridor on my right and stopped at the first door I came to. I knocked and went in.

The office was relatively small and functional, with a steel desk, a steel filing cabinet, IKEA bookcase and lots of papers and files stashed everywhere. Behind the desk was a very pretty blonde with dark blue eyes that made her uniform look sexy. She gave me a very friendly smile and pointed at the chair opposite.

"Mr. Mason? Please sit down. I am Detective Sergeant Elise Knudson. When did you get in? I hope the journey was not too exhausting? Greenland is not easy to get to! How can I help you? Will you have some coffee?"

I said, "Um," while I tried to decide which question to answer first. I couldn't make up my mind so I said, "Hi, Elise, it's good of you to see me. Thanks."

She got up, which didn't raise her very far from where she'd been—I figured her at five-two or five-three, with a small waist and nice hips—and made us two cups of instant coffee that would have had the Chief frothing at the mouth and playing with matches.

"Milk? Sugar?" she asked over her shoulder.

"Black will be fine. Um..."

"What do you know?" she said, sitting down. "You want to see his team? The house? Where do you want to start?"

"I think," I said, "I would like to see the house. I understand all his papers, computer, notes..."

"Gone," she said, raising the paper cup to her lips and sipping. "All gone."

"You've been to the house?"

"I was the first to go to the house." She sat back in her chair with her hands folded over her small, flat belly and her legs stretched out under the desk. "There was so much telephoning that day. And we have to use the radio-telephones here, and all day back and forth, everybody's running around asking, 'What the hell is going on?' And the guys at Ittoqqortoormiit are like, 'We got a call somebody is trying to kill Bob. Is it a joke?' And we are like, 'Who is going to want to kill Bob?' Right? And the plane has just landed—it has just taken him out to the UCLA camp—and they are making it turn around again to go back and get him, with a couple of cops now, because the caller says Bob is out at his station and somebody is trying to kill him. Crazy. Everybody liked Bob. He was a nice guy. And then they found him..." She trailed off, frowned, winced and shook her head. "And it was true, somebody had killed him. Stabbed him once in the liver. He was lying in the snow."

"Once."

She gave three slow nods. "Just once, deep, big knife, very sharp. Much intention, but no rage."

"A hunter?"

"Maybe. Knife, yuh, location, yuh, but then what about his papers? A hunter did not take his papers."

"Opportunism?"

She raised an eyebrow and laughed. "Opportunism? How?"

"He called his girlfriend, right? He tells her what has happened or what is happening. She calls the emergency services and after that one of two things happens: She lets either Thor or Monet know what has gone down, and one or both of them steal his work because they know it will be worth big bucks to Green Tomorrows; or, she takes it herself for the same reason and with the same purpose."

She ran both hands through her hair, staring at the wall behind me. She shook her head.

"I don't believe it. We can explore that possibility, but I don't believe it."

"Why?"

She stuck up her thumb as number one. "Silvia and Bob were like the dream couple. Always so close and in love. She would not steal from him." She stuck up her index. "Two, Bob and Thor were like brothers. Such close friends. And Thor I have known all my life. He is a good man and would never do nothing that was bad. He would not steal from his friend. Monet..." Her hand dropped into her lap.

"What about Monet?"

"Look, this is what I know from speaking to them in the pub and chatting and talking..."

"You were friends?"

"Of course. So, Monet never really was fitting in. Nobody ever really got to like him or trust him. So he would never have had access to anything that valuable. Monet was excluded. He did his work but he was not given serious responsibilities."

I frowned. "Sounds like you knew them quite well."

"Like I said, Thor I have known all my life. We were

at school together." She laughed. "There are fifteen thousand people in this town. First divide out the Danes from the Inuit, we don't mix. It's a shame but it's a fact. Now, how many do you think are in their early thirties? How many do you think are interested in doing something that is not fishing, merchant navy or building? So you go for a drink, there is Thor with Bob and Silvia. We join them and we talk."

She spread her hands. It was self-explanatory. I nodded.

"OK, so how about we go and look at the house, and then I buy us some real coffee?"

"Good."

She got to her feet and strode down the corridor before I could stand. As I exited the office she was leaning in through a door and shouting, *"Jeg tager amerikaneren med til Bobs hus!"*

She pulled on her jacket as we went down the stairs. "We go in my car. I bring you back after and you get your car."

I smiled. "Do I get a choice?"

"No." She pushed through the glass door and I followed her out into the street. Chill had turned to cold and there were darker clouds accumulating in the sky. She made a backward and forward motion with her hand. "We can talk by radio, you in your car, me in mine, but that would be stupid."

"Right, good point."

She had a twenty-year-old Land Rover Defender. She hauled open the door and clambered in. The doors slammed and we were reversing and turning as she spun the wheel and kept talking.

"What you are going to find at Bob's house? I can tell you. Nothing. I was the police officer who went to the house when we got the message from Ittoqqortoormiit. You are going to find same thing I found."

"Nothing."

"Nothing."

"Well, I have to look, anyway."

"You got to look anyway. I would look. You probably asking, 'Who is this Danish sergeant who knows everything?' But you will see."

We did a little bit of a fishtail left into Kuusuaqq and, a hundred yards on, another little fishtail right into Imaneq. Then she put the siren on and it was a long diagonal race across Nuuk. She waved and smiled at people five times during the dash.

At Niels Hammekenip Aqqutaa she did another little fishtail right and we rolled sedately to the end of the road, a hundred yards from the ocean. There she killed the engine outside a large, brown and white clapboard house with a gabled roof, which you might have found in any coastal town in Maine.

She jumped down from the cab and I followed her to the front door as she fished the keys from her pocket.

"Officially we are looking for Silvia, but we have no idea where she is by now."

"By now?"

"Thursday she flew to London. Three long stops on the way to London. We are waiting for the British police to tell us if she arrived. All is time."

I pulled my cell from my pocket as she stepped inside the shadows of the house. After a second Lovelock's husky voice answered.

"Listen, Bob Magnusson's girlfriend boarded a flight for London Thursday. She has either just arrived or is about to arrive. We need to know if she got to London..." Elise reemerged through the door with her hands in her pockets and said, "Luton—"

"London Luton airport. Otherwise she might have left the flight at..." I glanced at Elise.

"Copenhagen or Kaunas, in Latvia."

"Copenhagen or Kaunas, in Latvia. Get somebody on that. I need to know by yesterday at the latest."

I hung up, shutting out the acid reply. Elise sighed and shook her head. "Greenland Politi ask and maybe we get an answer next month. Big American demands and he gets his reply yesterday."

"Quit griping and enjoy it while it lasts. Show me inside."

The ground floor was mainly an open-plan space roughly divided into a living area with a fore on the right and a dining area on the left. The back wall was mainly sliding-glass doors that gave onto a long veranda with views of the sea. The only other rooms on the ground floor were a modern kitchen and a bathroom. There were a lot of books. The sofa and the armchairs were cream and I noticed a *National Geographic* lying open and crumpled on the floor beside the sofa. On the table, within reach, was a pot of coffee and a cup.

I pointed at the magazine. "So he goes to check his station and leaves her here. She's having a lazy day reading the *National Geographic* when he calls. She drops the magazine to call the cops at..." I looked at her and screwed up my brow.

"112," she said.

"OK, 112."

She shrugged. "Yuh, sounds obvious."

"Yeah, it also suggests that she was not expecting the news. And if that is correct, we will probably hear shortly that she made it to London instead of jumping ship in Copenhagen or Latvia."

She frowned at me. "Why?"

"You ever lie on the sofa reading a magazine or a book?"

"Yeah."

"What do you do if the phone rings?" She shrugged. I said, "You lay the book or the magazine carefully on your belly, right? Pick up the phone and answer it. Correct?"

She gave another, smaller shrug. "Yeah, maybe, probably, yeah."

"Now you get news you were expecting and you have to do something quickly and efficiently. You sit up, close the book or magazine, set it down on the table and go about your business."

"OK."

"But now you receive totally unexpected news that puts you into a panic. You jump up, sending the magazine flying, and go into a flap." I pointed to the stack of *National Geographics* on the bookcase beside the sofa. They were all neat and well kept. "People collect them and bind them. You won't find another one with a creased page. Guaranteed."

"Huh…"

I moved to the kitchen and peered in. "So the natural inference is the conversation she had with Bob scared her. She called the cops…"

"Emergency 112—"

"Yup, threw a load of stuff in a couple of cases and ran, leaving the dishes unwashed, the coffee on the table, chances are the bed is unmade." She nodded. "She was having a lazy day, and she was not prepared for the call. So it's unlikely she planned it, therefore it is likely she booked her flight for where she wanted to go." I turned to face her. "London. So the question becomes..."

"Why London? Why not California, where they are from?"

"What, or who, is in London?"

She followed me up the stairs, talking as she went. "The other question is, what did Bob tell her on the phone? 'I have been attacked, I am dying, call the police.' OK. But this is not a reason to escape from the country. Especially, they have a friend who is a police. So what did he tell her?"

"Good. Correct. And the answer is, in so many words, 'Get the hell out of here because they'll be coming for you.'"

She frowned a moment, then her face began to clear and she nodded. "Yuh, that is what he told her. It is the only logical thing."

I stepped into the bedroom. The bed was rumpled and unmade. In the bathroom I pointed at the sink, then at the bath.

"Look, she didn't even take her toothbrush. Everything, she left everything—except his papers."

I turned and sat on the bath while she leaned on the doorjamb with her arms crossed.

"This all tells us one more important thing. He was not killed because an Inuit hated him and wanted his girl

—the murder was not racially motivated. His murder was directly related to his work. She dropped everything and ran in a panic. She didn't even pick up her toothbrush. Two things she prioritized and did do: she called the cops at emergency 112." She nodded. I went on, "And she took all of his work. So we can infer that he called her and said, 'Get the hell out of Greenland. They will come for you now, and take my work. They must not get my work.'"

"That makes sense."

"When I asked Thor Olafson who he thought had killed Bob, he said he thought American agents of the Presidential Commission on Sustainable Energy had done it, because he and Bob were reaching conclusions the Commission did not like."

"Yuh, Bob used to say he was upsetting his employers."

"So, it's pretty urgent we find out who's in London. It could be a safe haven for her, or…"

She grunted. "Or it could not. It could be a trap."

"Yeah. Did he have a den or a study or something here?"

"Down here."

She led the way down the landing to a small bedroom which had been converted into an office. There was nothing in there but some bookcases and a desk.

"We took the desktop computer for forensic analysis. Apart from that there was nothing here related to his work."

"So either somebody got here and took her and her stuff…"

She shook her head. "No, neighbors saw her leave in her own car."

"So she's definitely running from Bob's killer."

CHAPTER SIX

I t was raining. No Indian summer this year, unless it rained all summer in India.

The trees in Holland Park bowed and tossed gently against the uniform gunmetal gray of the sky. The gray sidewalks gleamed slightly, reflecting the amber headlamps of the cars, already glowing at four PM. The blacktop hissed wetly as a car slid past, leaving snaking ripples of light in the water.

Captain Aila Gallin glanced at her companion in the car. He was holding a Canon EOS 2000D in his lap while he stared at the tall, cream house that stood detached from the rest of the terrace on Holland Park. Holland Park was the name of the road that skirted the park of the same name.

"Lavi, you like poetry?" she asked him.

He looked at her like she'd made an unwelcome proposal and shrugged.

"What kind of poetry?"

"There's a poem I like," she said, looking out through the drops of rain on the windshield. "The rain it raineth on the just, and also on the unjust fella, but mainly on the just because, the unjust has the just's umbrella."

Her companion groaned softly and returned his attention to the house. "Are you always like this when you are bored?"

"Who says I'm bored?"

"I am going to request to head office they don't post me with you again. You call attention to us, you make noise, and you can't keep your attention on the job. You are crazy, Aila. I am going to file the request today."

"Too late."

She said it as she frowned down the road at an approaching Bentley. He scowled at her. "Eh?"

"I already filed that request, Lavi. Here they come. See, you don't pay attention. You missed four shots already."

He raised the camera and started shooting. The car cut across the sidewalk and descended a short drive where a garage door opened automatically and admitted the vehicle. Gallin pulled an attaché case from behind the passenger seat, flipped the catches and opened it. The inside of the case was comprised largely of a built-in computer with a lift-up screen, and a couple of pockets that contained pieces of hardware. From one of these she withdrew a small tripod with what looked like a long, slim flashlight attached. This she connected by means of a USB cable to the laptop, and settled it on the dash, aimed at the ground-floor window. She flipped a switch, a light came on and the computer made a small "ping" sound. There was silence for about a minute. Then there was the sound of a door opening and voices. The door closed and a man was speaking. He sounded smug.

"Good of you to come out in this weather."

The reply came from a girl, London, maybe Caribbean. "Well, I'm not going to say no to *you*, am I? Especially if you send a Bentley for me."

A little giggle and an embarrassing growl from him. "I should hope not! The bloody money I spend on you!" He pronounced "bloody" and "money" with a long "u" sound, like "woody," placing his accent around Lancashire, right where Gallin needed it to be.

A gasp of mock shock from the girl. "Well, I should think I'm worth it, ain't I?"

"Every penny! Come on, drink up and we'll go upstairs."

A hint of mischief in her voice as she asked, "So where's your wife today, Toby?"

"I packed 'er off to bloody Preston with her mother for the weekend."

"Naughty Toby!"

More giggling, then some disturbing grunting, a couple of squeals and the door opened and closed.

Lavi said, "Which one is the bedroom?"

"There are five bedrooms," she said as she repositioned the laser mic. "Do your homework."

The invisible beam hit the glass of the master bedroom and picked up the vibrations from the room, translating them into sound through the computer. They sat through a painfully embarrassing half hour in which the Shadow Foreign Minister said nothing of any use to his favorite call girl, and the girl did little but giggle and shriek.

Gallin said, "We'll have to take her. Pay her, blackmail her, threaten her. Whatever. I cannot sit through another session of King Kong and the Tart. We have to take her and turn her."

Lavi shrugged.

"The British are our allies, remember? We cannot

honey trap members of the British government, even the opposition."

"Are you sure they are our allies? They seem much more interested in appeasing Arab oil princes than in supporting their Israeli friends. Besides," she looked up at the bedroom window again, "you're saying we can't set a honey trap, but we can sit outside his house spying on him?"

"One leaves no fingerprints and no witnesses, Gallin. We listen and we go away. The other leaves witnesses, bruises, fingerprints... It's too risky."

She slapped both hands on the steering wheel. "But all they talk about is sex! Sex, sex, sex! Bums, legs..."

"OK, stop."

"Wait, what's this?"

A cell phone was playing a ringtone. Toby Grimes grunted and swore. The tart's voice could be heard: "Ow, leave it, Toby!"

"It's me bloody private number, you silly bitch! It could be anyone!" Then after a second, in a businesslike voice, "Hul-lo! Toby Grimes, speaking."

Gallin barked a harsh laugh. "Ha! I'd pay money to see him right now, stark naked but for his socks!"

"Shut up, Aila!"

"Oh! Your Highness! What an unexpected pleasure! Oh, *Abdul*," a nervous laugh, "I see, well, I am honored, Abdul." A few seconds of silence, then, "Now? Why I would be delighted! You are always welcome at my humble abode, your...um...Abdul! I'll see you in a few minutes, then!" He hung up and then his voice rasped. "*Get dressed! Get out of here! Hurry, you silly bitch! I've got a bloody Arab prince turning up any minute!*"

"What about me money?"

"Here! *Here!*"

"Don't throw it on the bloody floor!"

"Pick it up! Pick it up and get out! Quick!"

Five minutes later a pretty girl in a rain mac came trotting out from the rear of the house and started walking toward Holland Park Avenue. Two minutes after that an Aston Martin pulled in from the same direction and did a U-turn to pull up in front of the house. The driver's door opened and an elegant man in his early thirties climbed out. He was dressed in an exquisite suit and trotted up the stairs to the front door and pressed the bell. The door opened almost instantly and the man was admitted.

Gallin said, "Did you get him?"

Lavi put down the camera. "Three-quarters profile. This is a crap position."

"It's the only position we have."

"Did you recognize him?"

"Prince Abdulazziz-bin-Nayef."

He covered his face with his hand. "*Elohim Adirim!* Are you kidding me?"

"Believe me, if I was going to joke with somebody, it would not be you."

"What the hell is he doing visiting the Shadow Foreign Minister?"

"If you shut up maybe we can find out."

The noise of the door opening and closing sounded again on the computer. Toby Grimes's voice asking, "Champagne? A cocktail?"

"If you have a single malt that will do fine."

Gallin snorted. "He probably had bacon for breakfast!"

"Two Macallans coming right up! No ice, I take it?"

"Indeed, no ice. So, Toby, a very interesting evening last Saturday. It is the first time I have ever seen a Shadow Cabinet Minister dancing the Watusi with a girl in a wet T-shirt. I hope nobody posted it on Facebook!" He laughed and while Grimes made noises of distress in the background, the prince went on smoothly, "The Watusi! I thought that had died out in the '60s. with Steve McQueen and Johnson's daughter."

"Well, I didn't know what it was, really. Sixties-themed party, weren't it."

"It was indeed, and you acquitted yourself admirably. I hope you were...," he paused and you could hear the smile in his voice, "up to the later challenge in the bedroom!"

"Oh, no, I mean, we didn't..."

"Come, Mr. Grimes! We Muslims are not judgmental in these matters. We believe a real man needs many women. We invented the harem, remember. Besides, I am very well informed, I can afford to be, and I would take it as a grave insult if my good friend were to lie to me."

There was a leaden silence for twenty long seconds. Then the idiot Grimes, swallowing and unsteady: "Well, I mean, we were a bit playful, but, but, but nothing serious. I mean, I'm a married man..."

"Toby, Toby, don't fret so. I am your friend. I'll tell you the truth, there was a defect in one of the security cameras, and it caught you in the act, so to speak. Your bottom shining like a great moon rising over the blue, satin sheets of the ocean, and the creamy white skin of your wet T-shirt friend. Sharon? Tracy?"

Toby couldn't talk. All he could say was, "On, on,

on..."

"On film, yes, Toby. Very good quality, too. Only the best for Abdul. But please don't be afraid. I will get you the original and place it in your hand. No strings attached. One friend helping another in need."

"Yes." A shrill, nervous laugh. "Yes, friends helping each other out, that's right."

"And speaking of which, Toby, I have a dear friend who is in need of help. He is an extremely wealthy man and I know if you are able to help him out with a small problem he will be able to make it worth your while. Not a bribe! Heavens no! A mere matter of mutual and legitimate back scratching. But, I'll tell you what. Let's take a little drive, I have a table booked at a nice restaurant where we can chat without fear of eavesdroppers. It belongs to my uncle, and he has it scanned for bugs every day, twice!"

They both laughed and after a moment the door opened and closed again, and two minutes later they emerged from the house and climbed into the Prince's Aston Martin.

Gallin watched them pull away and roar past. She sat in silence for fifteen seconds then pounded the wheel of the rental Mercedes with her fist.

"Ben-zonna! Zoobie! Zoobie! Zoobie! Zoobie! Zoobie!"

Each *"Zoobie!"* was accompanied by a thump of her fist on the wheel. She snatched her phone from her pocket, pressed a number and after a moment spoke.

"Abdulazziz-bin-Nayef showed up... Yes! That's what I said. The prince, yes. He is blackmailing him. Grimes has a weakness for women. Nayef claims he has footage of Grimes with a woman in bed. Now he has taken him to a restaurant that belongs to his uncle and which is swept twice a day for bugs… No, of course I am not following them! They have seen us parked outside Grimes's house. I have no idea where the restaurant is, but he is taking him there to discuss how he can help a very rich friend. He is blackmailing him and sweetening it with bribery."

She listened a moment longer and then recited the license plate of the Aston Martin. Then she fired up the engine and headed south and then west along Holland Park and south again into Abbotsbury Road.

After a while Lavi asked, "Where are we going?"

"You are going home. I am going to a meeting with David."

"Why?"

"That's none of your damn business."

"It is my business if you're cutting me out."

"He's not cutting you out. It's a separate matter. Didn't you want to be shot of me? Well now you will be."

She dropped him on the corner of Melbury Road and High Street Ken, and watched him for a second as he walked away into the rain and the growing gloom, with the wet, colored lights glowing all about him. When she could go she took an illegal right onto the High Street and followed it west as far as Russell Road. There she turned in and parked outside a four-storey, yellow-brick house with a basement and a big, bow window. Eight steps led up to a small porch and a big, dark blue door with a brass knob. There was light filtering through the net drapes on the ground floor. She climbed out of the Mercedes, hunched into her shoulders and ran across the road. Behind her the car lights flashed and bleeped.

She buzzed on the bell and a moment later a muscular guy in a T-shirt opened the door. He had a can of

Coke in one hand and a burger in the other. In the background she could hear the TV.

"What did you do, open the door with your teeth?"

She stepped in out of the rain. He didn't smile. He shoved the door closed with his foot. "Boss is upstairs. He wants to see you."

She scowled and started up the stairs, muttering, "I guess you used your prehensile toes."

A door slammed, cutting off the TV. She climbed the eight flights of stairs and came at last to a door on the top floor. She knocked and the door buzzed open. The room was large and had two tall sash windows overlooking Russell Road. On the far left there was a coal fire burning in the grate, a couple of chairs were arranged around it, and directly in front of her there was a desk at right angles to the window, affording a clear view of the entrance to Russell Road from Kensington High Street.

Sitting in front of the fire was a man in a charcoal gray suit. He was heavy set, with dark pouches under his eyes, and his dark hair was turning gray at the temples. He looked fifty, but she knew he was sixty-two. She knew that because he was her father.

When he spoke his English was exquisite, the product of Eton and Oxford, and forty generations of financing and bankrolling the British aristocracy. She crossed the room and kissed him.

"Papa, how are you?"

"I'm still alive, Aila, so I can't complain. It's not allowed." He waved a finger in the direction of a recess beside the fire. "Pour yourself a whisky. Get the damp out of your joints."

As she poured she spoke. "Abdulaziz showed up..."

"Never mind him now. What about Lavi? Is he any good?"

She sat opposite her father. Outside thunder rolled in the distance and water tapped on the windowsill like an accelerated clock.

"He's an errand boy. He is career-minded in that he wants to make the right connections and get promoted, but he has no initiative, no drive. He will not take risks and he has no imagination."

He sighed heavily. "So hard to find good people these days. Everybody is looking for security, and the quick, easy fix."

"Papa, why is Prince Abdulaziz-bin-Nayef talking to the Shadow Foreign Secretary?"

"I don't know. The Left in this country have always been friends of Palestine, and close with Saudi. I am surprised the prince feels the need to blackmail where normally all they have to do is ask."

"Did you manage to pick them up?"

"Of course, Aila. I had a car watching you, and they followed them to the Lubyanka."

She sipped and frowned. "The *Lubyanka?*"

"An exquisite French restaurant in Mayfair. Six month waiting list. It does not belong to Nayef's uncle. It belongs to a Russian billionaire, Gabriel Yushbaev, one of a thousand small businesses which he uses to launder his wealth. The name is obviously a private joke. It is known to be a safe place to discuss business."

"So we have no idea what they are talking about."

"Not at this stage, no. We have alerted MI6, of course, but at the moment all we know is that they are cornering him for something. They want to use him, obviously."

"What do you want me to do?"

He took a pull on his whisky and savored it for a long while, gazing into the flames.

"I don't know," he said at last, very quietly. "I don't know."

CHAPTER SEVEN

Meanwhile, six thousand three hundred miles away, in the foothills of the Suleiman Mountains, just fifty miles southeast of Kandahar city and perched above the Kandahar desert in sand-colored tents, the six men of the Al-Qaeda cell known as Alfajr Aliaslamiu settled down to eat their supper of rice, chicken and vegetables, and to read the word of God in quiet contemplation.

After a day of violent training in the mountains and in the desert, it was good to be at peace and feel God's love for those who subjugate themselves to His will.

Islam.

Jamil closed his eyes and repeated the word: "Islam."

Subjugation.

And it was as though God flowed into his body and his mind and took loving possession of him. Fear evaporated and was replaced by the infinite strength and courage of Allah. All was peace. All was certainty.

The flap of his tent pulled back. He opened his eyes and saw a young man in baggy linen trousers and a waistcoat lean in.

"Jamil, Mustafa wants to see you."

He closed his Quran and rose to his feet. Outside his tent the sky was turning to dark turquoise above the sand. The moon was rising in the east, casting a translucent halo over the horizon. The air was cold and made him shudder. He followed in the soldier's footsteps across the small camp of low bivouacs nestled among the sheer walls of the mountain canyon. Eventually they came to a larger, khaki tent which had been placed hard against the rock face so that it was invisible from the air. Here the soldier stepped in, muttered something and told Jamil to enter.

"*Allahu akbar.*"

There was a bedroll on the floor to the right of the flap. Directly ahead there were cushions and mats. Mustafa, tall, lean, in his late thirties, wearing desert fatigues, was seated there and placed his hand over his heart in acknowledgment of Jamil's praise of God.

"*Allahu akbar*," he replied, then gestured to some cushions opposite him. "Please, sit, Jamil." Jamil sat and Mustafa smiled at him.

"You have done well in training."

"I try to train for God. I train with Him in my heart and He gives me strength."

"That is the way we must live. We must have faith and allow God to guide us in all things." He paused a moment, watching Jamil, then added, "In everything we do we serve God, if we subjugate ourselves to Him. This is the path of Islam."

"*Allahu akbar.*"

"*Allahu akbar.*"

"I want you to get ready, Jamil. I want you to go to God's glory."

A stab of adrenaline made Jamil's heart thud once, then his gut was twisted with fear, anxiety and elation. He rocked forward, repeating his praise for God.

Mustafa smiled and placed his hand on Jamil's head.

"Be at peace, Jamil, I will pray for your safe return. But know that if you fall, great glory and bountiful gifts await you in paradise. However, in this particular mission, it is very important for us that you are successful. This is one mission that must not fail. We do not need another martyr. We need a victory. The future of the world, Jamil, depends on you. God is great; have faith in His guiding hand and you will succeed."

"I have faith, *Sayyid*..."

"Mustafa. You may call me Mustafa now—we are brothers."

Jamil began to weep, covering his face with his hands. He got on his knees and prostrated himself before the older man, repeating over and over the words that had become his life's mantra: "*Allahu akbar, Allahu akbar*..."

Mustafa put his hand on the young man's head. "Come now, there is work to do. I want you to collect your items. A car is coming for you. You have many hours of travel ahead of you."

"Where am I going, *Say*...Mustafa?"

"First, you are going to Islamabad, to see some friends. You can tell nobody, and you must talk to nobody until the car comes for you. Pray, and if you need anything, come to me. You talk to nobody else. Do you understand?"

"I understand."

"Go and prepare. The car will be here in half an hour."

Jamil hastened back to his tent, weeping as much with fear as with joy, and began to pack his few possessions into his small rucksack. God was great. God had chosen him. So he must prostrate himself in body, soul and mind, and serve God. That way, success became inevitable.

* * *

Silvia opened her eyes. She saw a tall, sash window on her left. Through it she could see gray sky, the backs of brick houses, trees. There were raindrops on the glass, but they were stationary. The window was open a few inches and for the first time she was aware of the cool air touching her skin.

Across the room there was a freestanding wardrobe. Her mind began to work, slowly, cautiously. She was in a bedroom, in England. At first she didn't know why. There was a chunk missing from her reality. What was she doing here? Why was she not at home in Nuuk?

And then the bleak, ugly, irreversible truth oozed in, infecting everything with despair. She cried for half an hour, until she had exhausted herself, but afraid of sleep she climbed out of the bed and crossed the small room to the door. She was wearing a nightdress she did not remember putting on, and on the back of the door there was a soft pink dressing gown which she climbed into.

She found herself on a landing. The floor was carpeted wall to wall in gray. The walls were white and the doors were cream. At the far end of the landing a door stood half open onto a bathroom, and immediately in front of her, stairs descended to the ground floor. There she could see a patch of dull light lying crooked on the floor, and within it a newspaper.

A woman appeared in the angle of the stairs and the landing. She had her back to Silvia as she crouched to pick up the paper. She had short, blonde hair, a trim waist, jeans and a neat, silk blouse. More memories crept in. This woman had met her at the airport. She was a friend of Rudy's.

A wave of grief came and passed. Silvia took a deep breath and started down the stairs, wiping her damp face with her hands and running her fingers through her matted hair.

She found a short passage running to the back of the house, with two doors on the left-hand side, and a third facing her, which stood open. It gave onto a small breakfast room that opened out into a large kitchen. The small, blonde woman was sitting at a heavy pine table. She had the table set for breakfast for two. The newspaper was open in front of her, but she was looking up at Silvia, waiting. When Silvia did and said nothing the woman smiled.

"Good morning, Silvia. You've been asleep for a little over twelve hours." The smile deepened. "Almost sixteen, in fact. How do you feel? Could you manage some tea, or coffee?"

Silvia nodded and moved to the chair, where she sat. She nodded yes to milk and sugar and sat staring at a plate of bacon and eggs, wondering if she could eat.

"I'm Jo," said the woman, pouring coffee into a china cup. "I don't know if you remember much. I imagine you are quite disorientated."

"You met me at the airport. Ruud asked you to

meet me. Is he going to come?"

"I'm not sure yet, Silvia. I thought we'd let you come round and find your feet before we discussed any plans. Can you manage a piece of bacon and some toast?"

"I'll try." Jo helped her to a small slice of bacon and a piece of toast. Silvia picked up the bacon in her fingers and frowned at it. "I had a couple of bags..."

"In your wardrobe. Untouched. I thought you'd rather unpack yourself once you were rested."

She reached across the table and gave Silvia's hand a little clasp. "You sit there and have your breakfast. I'm going to give Rudy a call and tell him you're up and about."

She stood and went through the kitchen out to the backyard. Through the kitchen window Silvia watched her pace up and down with her cell to her ear, the wind moving her fine, platinum hair as she spoke. She stopped, with the nail of her left baby finger gently clasped between her teeth, listening. Then she nodded a few times, slowly, said something and hung up. Silvia put the bacon in her mouth and tried to chew it.

The kitchen door opened and Jo entered, bringing damp, patchy sunlight with her.

"He's going to book a ticket and he hopes to be here in the next couple of days. Meantime he wants you to talk to a friend of his here, whenever you feel ready. He's a very close friend of Rudy's, and a friend of mine as it happens."

Silvia frowned. "Why does he want me to talk to this man? Who is he?"

"Well, as you know, Bob was involved in some very important research. Rudy is not very confident about how well the Greenland police are going to manage the investigation. So we want to do everything we can..."

"We?"

Jo stopped a moment and smiled. Then she sat again and reached out for Silvia's hand.

"Silvia, poor child, who do you think I am?"

"You said you're a friend of Ruud's."

"And I am. But how do you think we met? Who do you think I am?"

A hot twist in her stomach made her withdraw her hand and put down the bacon.

"I don't know what you mean."

"There is no need to be alarmed, Silvia. I work for the British government. Have you ever heard of MI6?"

"Like James Bond?"

"Well, without all the toys and without the 007 license to kill, but yes, more or less. We often cooperate with the Americans, and this business affects us both. So we would like to know what happened, and we are co-operating. Does that make sense?"

"I guess."

"But I don't want you to be worried. We're going to take care of you and make sure you are safe. And when you feel up to it you just tell me, and we'll arrange it."

She looked around the room, as though searching for some kind of point of reference, something familiar she could hold on to. She blurted suddenly, "I really need my family. I don't know why Ruud told me to come here."

"Quite simply because it was the quickest way to get you safe. Please don't worry. We'll have you back home with your family in no time flat. But first let's make sure you're safe, and that we don't attract unwanted attention to your family."

Silvia nodded. "Yes. OK, let's do it. Tell Ruud's

friend whenever he wants. It's never going to be easy. We may as well get it over and done with."

"That's the spirit. Good girl."

So Silvia finished her slice of bacon while Jo cleared the table, and while Jo made a call, Silvia went up and showered and dressed, and checked Bob's papers. Everything she had grabbed was there, and as far as she could tell, it had not been touched.

At shortly after three that afternoon a car drew up outside. Silvia was lying down, reliving what she could remember of the last two days since Bob had kissed her and driven away. She heard the car arrive, she heard the doorbell chime and she heard the door open and close, then quiet voices: Jo's and a man's, after that feet on the stairs, a tap at the door.

"Silvia?"

She sat up, wiping her face on her sleeve. "It's open."

Jo slipped in and closed the door behind her. "He's here. Are you sure you feel up to this? I can make him go away if you want." She sat beside Silvia on the bed and put her arm around her. "It would be nonsense to say I know what you're going through. But I've lost people, and I know what that's like. I am so sorry. It must be hell, and for what it's worth, I think you're being very brave."

They sat like that for a while, with Silvia clinging on to Jo and Jo stroking her hair. Finally, after ten minutes or a little more, Jo gave her a handkerchief. She blew her nose and dried her eyes and said, "OK, let's do this."

Toby Grimes stood as they came into the living room. His suit was Savile Row, though even that couldn't make him look elegant. He was big, shabby and rotund, like a character from Dickens. He hurried across the carpet on small, eager feet, unsure what to do with his hands, until he clasped them together like a priest and said, "Silvia, call me Toby," and then, like a man who had seen on TV that this was what Americans said when somebody died, "I am sorry for your loss."

"Thank you."

"Please," he gestured with both hands at the sofa, "won't you sit down? I know this must be very distressing for you."

She sat. He returned to his armchair and Jo sat too, offering Silvia a secret roll of her eyes.

"How can I help you, Toby? I'm not sure why Ruud sent me here. What I would really like to do is to get back to my family. I don't mean to be rude, but I'm not sure what the death of an American scientist in Greenland has to do with the British government."

He coughed, glanced at Jo and fumbled. "No, well, it's a good question. Of course, as you know, we and the Americans have what we call a special relationship. At least, we had until Mr. Biden decided to pull out of Afghanistan!" He gave a short laugh and plowed on. "No, I jest! So we do a lot of intelligence sharing and we often help each other out when we can…"

Jo interrupted. "Rudy saw that a flight to Los Angeles would take a lot longer than the flight to London. He was worried about you and wanted to get you somewhere safe as soon as possible. So he asked me and Toby to take care of you."

Grimes nodded. "Rudy and I go back a long way. So really, it's not a case of what you can do for me, but what I can do for you. I'm here, unofficially, to take care of you and make sure you get home all right. The one who's going to want to ask you questions is this one." He jerked his thumb at Jo.

She looked at Silvia and smiled a little sadly.

Jo said, "Our first priority is your safety and well-being, Silvia. Before I asked you any serious questions I wanted you to have somebody here looking out for you. Think of Toby as Rudy's representative."

Silvia studied the floor a moment. She asked, without looking up, "So which one of you is Ruud's friend, and which one is the spy?"

Jo was very serious when she answered.

"We are both old friends of Rudy's. Toby has known him considerably longer than I have. You may not realize it, Silvia, but Toby is an important member of the opposition. He is a politician and he has a lot of influence. He and Ruud van Dreiver met twenty years ago at a Democratic convention in Washington, where Toby was a guest speaker. They have been close friends ever since."

Grimes added, "My being here is totally unofficial, and if it weren't for the fact that Rudy is such a close friend, I could not possibly be associated with this. Presumably the Greenland police are looking for you. I don't mind telling you," he scowled at Jo, "this could cost me my career!"

"Don't stay on my account," said Silvia quickly, with a little asperity. "I'll manage."

Grimes shook his big head. "I'm not. I'm doing this for Rudy. And I am happy to help you. I just want you to understand that I have no vested interest here. I can't speak for Jo, though."

Jo cut in. "All right. I won't beat about the bush. Rudy *did* ask me to get you, bring you home with me and call Toby. We want to help you, but we also want very badly to know what happened to Dr. Magnusson, who did this to him and why. We *are* on the same side, Silvia."

Silvia rubbed her face with her hands, suddenly panicking inside. Jo saw the panic and spoke softly, "Rudy will be here very soon." She gave a small laugh. "I don't know what time it is there, but we can call him if you like, if that will reassure you."

Silvia shook her head. "No, I'm sorry. I just feel all at sea. I don't know what to think, or do, or *feel*. What do you want to know?"

Silvia sat forward, with her elbows on her knees.

"Silvia, were you aware of the nature of Robert's work?"

She thought for a long moment, transported back to the bar in Nuuk, where she and Bob used to meet with Thor and Elise, and talk sedition and revolution. She could hear the noise of the crowded voices, the loud music; she could feel the bustle, the hustling bodies, their heat. She could taste the cold beer.

"No," she lied at last, "not really. In very general terms. I wasn't all that interested in what he was doing, and he was pretty secretive. So that suited us both."

"What about documents, draughts for his report, notes, computer drives? You said he asked you to take all that."

She nodded once. "Everything I could. But he only kept very basic, rough notes at home."

Jo nodded and smiled. "Of course. So where did he keep the serious stuff?"

Silvia looked her square in the eye. "I don't know. I think Bernard was charged with compiling everything into the final report. So he probably has the bulk of the important stuff."

"Bernard?"

"Bernard Monet. Bob's assistant."

CHAPTER EIGHT

Silvia had gone up to her room to lie down. Jo was standing by the French windows looking out at her garden in the drizzle. Toby had moved to the sofa where he could watch her. His face was flushed and his eyes were bright with anger.

"I am the bloody *Shadow Foreign Secretary!* Have you *any bloody idea* what this could do to me if the press gets a hold of it? I could be Foreign Secretary in a couple of years! The future bloody Foreign Secretary conspiring to hide and conceal an American woman sought in connection with the murder of an American scientist!"

"It means the same thing," she said absently to the gray glass.

"*What?*"

"Hide and conceal. They mean the same thing, Toby. It's a redundancy."

"*I* am talking about my bloody future as..."

"Foreign bloody Secretary,"

"*Foreign bloody Secretary*, and you're talking about grammar!"

She turned and stared at him with open dislike. "Toby, let's face it. The chances of your ever being Foreign-bloody-Secretary are about as slim as my ever voting for you or your gang of proletarian thugs. How you ever got appointed to the Shadow Cabinet is a mystery known only to you, the party leader and presumably the party treasurer. But having got that far, if you had learned to keep your winkle in its shell, you would not be in this trouble now, would you?"

He sulked and for a moment had the appearance of a very large baby. "But still…!" he said, "I should not be here!"

"But you are, and you are going to help us get her back to the States *the long way* and on that long way, you are going to help us get his report."

"How am I supposed to do that? I'm not a *spy!* I'm a politician, for Christ's sake!"

"By being nice, not making a pass at her and leaving everything else up to me. We'll take her back to the States via Canada or some other roundabout route. And along the way I will befriend her and make her see how important that research is. If that doesn't work, we'll have to resort to more drastic measures."

He half got to his feet. "Don't you bloody involve me in a bloody murder!"

She closed her eyes and sighed. "Do try not to be so obtuse, Toby. Just organize a family holiday or something, out of the country and close to the States."

He stared at her, helpless, with his fat face sagging at the jaw. "And how am I going to explain that to Keir? I can't just…"

"I don't really care what you tell that minor grammar school yob, Toby. As far as I can see you are in a mess and fighting to save your career. So you had better start by ensuring you keep the few friends you still have, and help us get Silvia to a safe location near the States."

He glowered at her sullenly. "I can't just snap me fingers and make things happen, you know!"

She laughed. "I am well aware of that, Toby. But we also both know that if you take a trip to Canada through the VIP channels, nobody is going to check on your personal secretary or your other traveling companions."

"I already have a personal secretary. I can't go changing my secretary without causing a ruckus and drawing attention to meself."

"Just work something out, Toby. Get Silvia somewhere reasonably safe and remote where I can talk to her. Get it right and who knows, maybe your career might get back on track again."

He stared at her for a long moment. "Are you serious?"

"Stop shagging every tart you come across, get serious and get this right, and there are people who are willing to help you. But clean up your act, Toby, or neither you nor your socialist buddies will ever see office again." He grunted. She added, "If there is nothing else, I'll expect to hear from you tomorrow morning."

"All right. I know when I'm not wanted." He stood and made his way to the door. There he hesitated. "We, government, Parliament, I mean, left and right, we like the Arabs, don't we?"

Jo frowned hard. "*What?*"

"That is, we need the oil. I mean, the Americans are the friends of the Jews, but us…"

"Your anti-Semitic credentials are well known, Toby. And believe me, they are not approved of on the other side of the Atlantic *or* here!"

"No, I don't mean that. I mean…," he dithered,

shuffling his feet. "I mean if a prince—"

"Toby, are you losing your mind?"

"No, I mean a Saudi prince, asked you to do something, I mean, we want to be on good terms, right...?"

"What have you done, Toby?"

"No, nothing, I was just wondering. Forget it. It's nothing."

She followed him to the front door and watched him climb into his car and drive away into the night. Once indoors again she dialed a number and sat in the drawing room watching her reflection in the French windows. It rang twice and was answered.

"Yes?"

"He's done something stupid. He's talking about Arab princes asking favors of him."

"He's a dick."

"We have to move fast. He's a liability and I am pretty sure they'll sack him from the Shadow Cabinet soon. Without that he's about as much use as an ejector seat in a helicopter."

A soft grunt. "He appeals to the working man. That carries weight with socialists, even today."

"Let's play this safe and get it sorted tomorrow. Who's this Arab prince?"

"The Mossad shared with us yesterday. Prince Abdulaziz-bin-Nayef visited him. They think it means something."

"We don't?"

"They know each other socially."

She felt anger arising in her gut. "There is hardly an Arab billionaire in London that Toby Grimes doesn't know socially. After what he has just said to me, considering Nayef's connections with al-Qaeda, I would say this warrants a closer look. Wouldn't you? I mean, remind me, when was the last time the Mossad gave us dud intel?"

"We'll look into it."

Her voice was like a shard of ice. "I would recommend you do."

She hung up and sat a while on the sofa, still staring at her reflection, toying with the idea of advising the Circus to call off the operation. She had not liked it from the start. It was too elaborate, too convoluted, and she could not see the real purpose of it. But apparently it had come from the top, so unless she could find some serious flaw with it, she would have to go with it.

Fifty yards down the road, on the corner of York Close, the young agent watched the red rear lights of Grimes's car turn right toward Westley Road. He knew it would be picked up pretty soon. Grimes had driven himself, and while he had been inside he had slipped a tracking device under the trunk.

He pulled his phone from his pocket and made the call.

Gallin answered on the second ring. "Paul, what?"

"I followed him to Bury St. Edmunds. You'll be surprised who he went to see. Jo Jeffries."

"Jo Jeffries, Jo Jeffries…"

He heard a man's voice in the background and nodded as though they could see him.

"Yeah, that's right. Senior intelligence officer in the SIS."

"Did you manage to listen?"

"No, they were at the back of the house and there was no way to get at the windows. But she has somebody staying with her, a young woman. I caught snatches of conversation. I…"

He hesitated. She said, "What?"

"I got the impression he came to see the girl."

"Why? What gave you that impression?"

"He arrived and the girl came down. The girl went up and shortly afterwards he left."

"We need to know who that girl is. Stay on the house."

* * *

Three thousand, seven hundred miles away, as the crow flies, Jamil entered Islamabad along the N80, sitting in the passenger seat of a Ford Ranger pickup. It was nine o'clock at night, but the traffic was still heavy and as they moved along the Kashmir Highway into the city, among the bright streetlamps and traffic lights, he was momentarily overwhelmed after the weeks of seclusion and meditation in the pristine desert. But that feeling was soon replaced by a rush of adrenaline, a sense of coming home to a metropolis devoted to God, to the holy mission of jihad.

"*Allahu akbar*," he said softly.

His driver, a big, taciturn man who had spoken little during the long drive, nodded once. "*Allahu akbar*."

They turned into Rohtas Road and moved north for a couple of blocks along the tree-lined avenue. At Street 32 they turned again. The road was practically empty, but for the parked cars reflecting the dead light of the streetlamps. The truck pulled up outside the guest house and the big man pulled an envelope from his robe. He handed it to Jamil and jerked his head at the door.

"Go, they have a bed for you. *Yuajihuk Allah!*"

God would guide him. He turned and looked at the

hostel. Dull light spilled from its open door. He crossed the sidewalk into a small lobby. The reception desk was on the left. A man in a dull gray robe and a dark gray waistcoat, with a kufi on his head, looked up.

"Yes?"

"You have a room for me?"

The man's eyes fell on the envelope in Jamil's fingers. "I think that is for me."

Jamil stared at him for a moment, then read the scrawl on the envelope. Ahmed Patel. A cast name, probably a Pakistani convert.

"Are you Ahmed Patel?"

The man reached out his hand. "I am Ahmed Patel. Give me the envelope."

Jamil handed it over. The man opened it, smiled at the contents, opened a drawer and removed a key. "One B." He pointed at the stairs. "First floor."

The room was small and narrow, with barely enough room for the bed and the wardrobe. He dumped his rucksack on the floor and opened the window, to let in the muggy air and the silence of the night street. Then he stretched out on the bed and closed his eyes, letting his exhaustion drain from his muscles. The darkness closed in. He must try not to sleep. He must wait for instructions. A messenger would come. He was the warrior of God.

Distant traffic. A distant beep. The frozen stars above Kandahar.

And then a loud rap on the door. He sat up, panic pounding in his chest.

"Who is it?"

"*Allahu akbar, sadiq.*"

A friend. He rose and moved to the door, flattening himself against the wall.

Jamil felt the heavy knife in his hand. As instructed, he asked his visitor who had sent him: *"Man 'arsal laky a, sadiqi?"*

His answer would decide whether he lived or died.

"Allah yuqarir kula al'aqdar."

God decides all destinies. This was his contact. He opened the door. A tall man with a straggly beard and traditional dress, with a kufi perched on his head. In his hand he had a suitcase. He said no word but handed the case to Jamil, then turned and left, hurrying down the stairs.

Jamil closed the door and laid the case on the bed. He flipped the catches and threw back the top. A strange sensation of sickness, revulsion and excitement. The clothes were Western clothes: three suits, two in charcoal gray and one blue. Seven shirts, three ties, underwear, two pairs of shoes, one black, one brown, a Rolex watch, a sports jacket and a pair of beige chinos. A toilet bag with deodorant and aftershave. There was a large manila envelope. Inside it was a British passport in the name of Sammy Patel, a driving license, a Visa and a debit card for HSBC Bank. There was an airline ticket and a boarding pass, Virgin Atlantic, nine hours and forty minutes direct to London Heathrow. He would arrive at eight forty in the morning. There was a note too attached. It read:

Shave. You are a Western playboy. Somebody will meet you at Heathrow. Your flight departs three AM tonight.

He sat a while in deep thought. Then made his way to the bathroom, shaved very carefully into a plastic bag.

After that he washed, sprayed himself with deodorant and splashed aftershave on his cheeks. It felt wrong, sinful, but he knew it was necessary for the jihad. Even so, he begged Allah for forgiveness.

He changed into the chinos and the sports jacket, with a light blue shirt, and made his way downstairs to look for a taxi. At the reception desk he paused. The receptionist raised his eyebrows and smiled. "My goodness!" he said. "You look the proper gentleman now! Very nice jacket! How can I help you, sir?"

"Don't talk," Jamil said, quietly.

"Oh, no, I do not talk," he laughed, shaking his head.

The movement was extremely fast and very violent: faster almost than the eye could follow he slammed the middle knuckles of his bent fingers into the windpipe of the receptionist. The man clawed at his throat, unable to suck in air. The veins bulged in his head and his neck as he turned first red, and then very quickly blue. Jamil walked quickly around to the flap. He opened it and moved in behind the counter. The receptionist had his back to him and was making a ghastly croaking noise. Jamil smashed his elbow into the back of the man's head, and when he fell facedown on the floor he stamped with his heel into the back of his neck. He felt the vertebrae crunch.

He found the thousand US dollars in the envelope, took them for himself, and left quickly to find a cab. The man had noticed too much. He was too smug, too clever, and besides, he had kept the filthy name Patel. He was not a true convert. Mohamed had said that a man who converts to Islam for convenience is as hateful to God as any other infidel. If he cannot be converted or enslaved, then he should be killed.

At the airport he had something to eat and tried to doze on a seat for a couple of hours. When he could not sleep he recited the Quran to himself, prostrating himself before God in his mind, subjugating his body, his mind and his soul, giving himself to the Almighty. Soon, he told himself over and over, he would strike down the great Shaytān and allow the glory of God's Kingdom to reign supreme forever on Earth, *Allahu akbar*.

He awoke in a panic. His heart pounding in his chest, he went to the board and saw the gate had been announced for his flight. His stomach twisted and he had to fight back the vomit. And then he was walking, walking fast down the long, anonymous tiled passages, plunging deeper and deeper, mixing with the stream of humanity, all flowing, flowing toward the Virgin Atlantic plane that would carry him to his destiny.

CHAPTER NINE

Heavy clouds had closed in and desultory flakes of baby snow had started to drift down like they were in no great hurry to reach the ground. Elise had suggested coffee at the Kristinemuy Mutten, on yet another street that started with an A and had three Qs in it, which was, she said, preferable to the overpriced restaurant next door, which gloried in the name, Restaurant Charoen Porn.

I sipped as she submerged her face in a large cream bun and emerged chewing.

"I need to go and see his site north of the UCLA camp."

She nodded and chewed, said, "I come with you," and buried her face in the bun again. Watching her was making me hungry. I kept sipping coffee.

"How long will it take to get there?"

"Few hours. Depends on the weather. If this passes we can go soon, be back tonight. But if this becomes a storm, then we have to wait. We don't get a lot of storm in September, but weather is crazy now. Hard to predict."

I shook my head. "I have to go today, storm or no storm. A snowstorm could completely destroy what I am looking for."

"What are you looking for?"

"I don't know. But I'll know it when I see it."

"Fantastic."

She said it with no expression, so it was hard to know if she was being sarcastic, but I figured she was.

"OK," she said, stuffing more bun than you'd think possible into her mouth, "so finish and we go talk to the airport. You know how to fly a plane?"

"Of course."

"Your government is paying."

"Again, of course."

I drained my coffee and we made our way to her truck. She headed north along Imaneq toward the airport, and on the way she made a call on the radio. A man answered in Danish. She waited till he'd finished, then said, "Yuh, OK, Boss. We are talking English because I am here with Alex Mason."

"Ah, OK, hello, Alex."

I stared at her a moment. She smiled encouragement and nodded.

I said, "Hi..." She mouthed at me "*Chief.*" I said, "Chief, hi, Chief."

"All is good?"

Elise cut in. "We need a plane to go to Ittoqqortoormiit, then the chopper to go to the UCLA camp."

"Oh, yuh, well, we expected this. But the weather is not so good."

"Alex Mason is paying. And he can fly."

"Oh, that's good." He laughed. "Very good."

"You call the airport, Boss, tell them we are coming."

"Yuh, yuh, so..."

DAVID ARCHER

The connection went dead. She took a deep breath. "So, eight hundred and seventy miles to Ittoqqortoormiit, maybe four hours. Five hundred miles to Bob's camp, another two hours. So seven hours total, because you always waste time somehow." She looked at her watch. "It's ten thirty, we gonna get there at five thirty. Not a good time. You have half an hour for looking for something you don't know what it is. Then we go back to Ittoqqortoormiit. We gonna get there eight o'clock earliest. So we will have to stay the night. There is one hotel, which is really bad, and there is a tavern with a couple of rooms upstairs. We will stay there."

We pulled into the airport and parked.

"Half an hour?"

"What?" She opened the door and sat staring at me with the door open.

"Half an hour is all the time I get to inspect the site?"

Her face lit up. "Inspect the site?" She burst out laughing and jumped down from the cab. She was still laughing as she walked ahead of me toward the airport. I decided that, despite making me want to put her across my knee and spank her butt, it was a very pretty laugh.

She led me to the small police office in the airport where she and the desk sergeant sorted some papers, after which she spoke to him in Danish and I caught what sounded like, "*Han siger, at han vil inspicere stedet!*"

At which they both laughed loudly and avoided looking at me.

She led me out onto the now very cold, blustery tarmac, where small flakes of snow were falling with a greater sense, if not of urgency, of intent. They stung when they hit your face, snuck down your collar.

"They say the weather is not going to get worse yet. There are jackets in the chopper, in Ittoqqortoormiit," she added, "so if you don't stay out too long, you might live."

"That's nice. That's good."

She smiled up at me with very red cheeks and eyes half closed against the wind. "You think I'm joking?"

The plane was a Gulfstream G280 which had seen a lot of service and better days. We clambered aboard and after ten minutes we were hurtling down the runway under a heavy lead sky you could practically reach out and touch.

There was little of any interest about the flight, except that seeing nothing but white ice for eight hundred and seventy miles really made me start to understand the vastness of the ice sheet beneath me. It was like flying from Manhattan to Miami and seeing nothing but ice in all directions, as far as the eye could reach.

After four hours and ten minutes I made a terrifying landing on what was basically a heliport adapted for small planes to land, and there, in increasingly cold, blustery conditions, we transferred to a police chopper and, within five minutes, we were rising and swinging away again over the mind-boggling expanse of snow and ice.

She leaned into me, stabbing her thumb back south and shouting over the noise of the rotors.

"What we crossed there is the thin bit, now, out here in the national park, this is the wide bit. If you get lost in the Sahara, you will die in maybe two or three days. If you get lost out here you will die in maybe two or three hours. Really, even though Bob was stabbed in the liver, and without urgent medical attention he would probably have died anyway, what killed him was the cold."

"OK, I get it, inspecting the site has to be quick."

She snorted and smiled, but kept her eyes out on the snow. The cloud cover was not as heavy here as it had been further south, but there was still no blue, just relentless gunmetal gray above, pure white below, with the odd melt-water lake, and speckles of sleet in between.

After a couple of hours she pointed ahead and said, "There, see the shack. The small dark blue speck…"

I squinted through the sleet and after a moment spotted the building. It was on stilts, about fifteen feet above the ice, with a wooden staircase climbing up the outside. The building itself looked like a small cottage, with blue clapboard walls and a gabled roof. I approached to within thirty feet and brought the chopper down on the ice and gathering snow. For a moment all there was, was a vast storm of white mist thrown up by the rotors, but as they slowed, the wind gathered up the cloud and carried it south. Gradually the building emerged, tall, eerie and blue against the claustrophobic gray of the sky.

Elise reached back and stuffed a huge, quilted jacket onto my lap.

"Did you wear your long underwear?"

"Did you wear your frilly pink knickers?"

"Yuh, I put them over my long johns."

"I might freeze to death, but at least I'll take that image to the grave with me."

I zipped up and swung down from the chopper. It was colder than you could imagine and I instantly wished I had brought heavier boots.

I joined Elise on the far side of the cockpit and she pointed to a spot about fifteen feet away, about eight paces from the first rung of the steps that led to the house on stilts.

"That was where they found him." She wiped the sleet from her face. "There is nothing to see now, but he had made a pillow for himself from the snow."

I pointed at the structure. "So he came down from up there?"

"Yuh."

"Was there blood on the steps?"

"Yes, and upstairs."

"He came down, knowing he was dying, we know that because he called Silvia, lay down in the snow, and went to sleep."

"That's right."

I looked up at the large windows that overlooked the white desert. "What's up there?"

She had started stamping her feet and slapping her arms.

"It is a multi-function station where you can put monitors which are attached to sensors out here. It is equipped with computer terminals and it has a supply of wind-generated energy. There is no shortage of wind up here. Bob had an array of sensors a little farther on."

The wind was gusting stronger and I had to raise my voice. I had also started stamping unconsciously. "Where are the sensors?"

"We left them here, upstairs, for you to see them. They are sealed in plastic and labeled. So now we can go upstairs."

We stomped our way up twenty steps and Elise unlocked the door. We pushed in and she closed the door behind us. The first thing that struck me was the awe-inspiring view through the large windows. The heavy cloud cover had blocked out the sun and the light was a dull gray, but the snow and the ice were a kind of luminous blue.

Just beneath those windows there was a long bench, and ranged along the bench were an array of electronic instruments of various types which I did not immediately recognize. All of them seemed to be connected, one way or another, to a large computer terminal on a second bench which was at a right angle to the first. I sat at the computer and started checking its recent activity. Elise stood behind my left shoulder, watching.

I looked up at her as I scrolled through the actions.

"This is the day he died."

"Yes."

"He deleted everything. All the data from the instruments has been deleted."

"He knew he was being followed. He knew they were coming to kill him and he wanted to protect the data."

"But he must have sent it to somebody first. He would not have simply deleted it."

She leaned in next to me and rattled at the keyboard.

"Yeah, look here, he did not have time to delete everything. Here is where he sent the data he recovered from the instruments. Thor Olafsen. There are many, many files sent."

"We need to get this drive to a forensic IT expert to see what he can get out of it." I frowned. "I'm seeing data here from a seismograph. What the hell would he be doing with a seismograph out here?"

She didn't say anything, but crossed to the far side of the room where there was a table. On it I saw a number of plastic bags of varying sizes. She said:

"This was the sensor array. We disconnected them and brought them in here because we assumed you would want to inspect them as they were when he died. When you have seen them we can send them to forensics."

"That's good thinking."

I went and had a superficial look at them. They didn't mean a whole lot to me. They seemed mainly to be related to air temperature, CO^2, methane and the temperature of the ice at the surface and at various depths below the surface. But what struck me most was the triaxial broadband seismometer.

"This would make sense in Iceland. It doesn't make a lot of sense here."

She stared at it a moment, then looked up at me. "Thor told me, there is a volcano below the ice, in this location. It is dormant. It has been dormant for many thousands of years. Geologists said the cold and the weight of the ice made it completely not active."

She took my arm and pointed to the windows. It was suddenly dark outside. "OK, we have to go."

"We need to take these instruments."

"No, we need to go, now, or we will die. If this wind rises to hurricane, we will not make it to Ittoqqortoormiit."

I grabbed an armful of instruments, Elise grabbed the hard drive, and we bolted for the chopper. As we clambered in she shouted above the wind. "The irony of Greenland is that it preserves forensic evidence perfectly, but if you try to get to the evidence, it kills you."

We clambered in and I powered up the rotors. The wind was strong but I had flown in worse at sea.

"It kills you?" I asked, without really thinking about what I was asking.

"Greenland," she said. "Greenland kills you."

And that got me thinking, really hard. Because the whole thing was wrong and didn't make any sense. Outside the late afternoon had turned almost black, and an ever denser snowstorm was bringing visibility down to practically zero.

"I thought the weather was meant to remain stable!"

"Yuh," she said, and shrugged, "but the weather is never predictable up here, and especially now. It can change in minutes."

We flew on in silence for a while, with the nerve-wracking sensation that we were not moving, when we were probably doing close to two hundred and fifty miles an hour.

"OK," I said, "help me think this through. Thor was not only Bob's colleague, but his closest friend, correct?"

"Yuh."

"So it makes perfect sense that, when faced with the threat to his life, he would send all his findings and the data from the sensors to him. But, when I asked Thor where the report was, he told me he had no idea. Which means either he was being super cautious..."

"Or he identified you with the killer." I nodded. She went on, "Which is basically what he told you."

"Yes, it is."

"Bob told Silvia to take what there was of his papers at home and run, and Thor either knew already because they had discussed it, or when Bob sent the data he included a message telling Thor what to do."

So far the wind had been behind us and I had been able to outrun it, but as we started angling east toward Ittoqqortoormiit, the gale started buffeting the port side of the chopper, making it hard to control, lifting it violently several hundred feet one moment, and dropping it dangerously the next. I spoke as I struggled to keep it on course.

"So how far does this take us? It means that Bob and Thor were agreed that they suspected the Presidential Commission, but of what? They were producing the report that the Commission had asked for."

The helicopter lurched sideways and tipped. I corrected and it plummeted under the pressure of the wind coming in from the portside. I pulled her up and wondered silently if we were going to make it.

"Or not," I said after a moment.

She nodded, apparently unfazed by our death ride. "Yuh, or not. And this we already knew. The question is, what instructions has Bob given to Thor. What did they intend to do with this data they were finding?"

Ahead, an ethereal, otherworldly glow emerged among the blizzard and told me we were approaching the ocean, and shortly after that the sparse speckling of lights from Ittoqqortoormiit began to pepper the darkness with a faint promise of warmth.

A final gust battered us as we began to sink toward the town, and the landing lights of the heliport appeared ahead and to our right. I felt the tension in my back and my shoulders begin to relax and heard Elise blow a heavy sigh beside me.

I smiled at her and gave a small laugh.

"You thought we'd be spending the next century in a block of ice out in the wilderness?"

She didn't answer for a moment, then said, "Now you owe me a big dish of mussels, a musk ox steak, and lots and lots of beer."

"Is that all?"

"That is for starters, then we'll see."

CHAPTER TEN

We made it back to Nuuk the next day just after noon and had Bob's instruments and the hard drive sent to Copenhagen, where they would be pored over by forensic scientists from the Danish police with an observer from ODIN.

Elise dropped me beside my truck outside the cop-shop and we sat for a moment in silence, with me staring at my car and her staring at me.

"You gonna go back to USA now?"

"Soon."

"You think I am married?"

I was surprised by the question. "I have no idea."

"Last night you were like, the perfect gentleman. But I am not married."

"Oh..."

"You wanna have dinner tonight before you go?"

"Yeah, that would be good."

I climbed into my truck, watched her push through the door into the station house and made my way slowly, thinking, down Imaneq and onto the unpronounceable Aqqusinersuaq. I slowed at the intersection with Dronning Ingridsvej and, on an impulse, turned in and parked outside Thor's apartment.

He opened the door almost immediately and stood, taking up the whole doorway, as he had before. He didn't say anything, just watched me.

"You got a minute?"

"For what?"

"I'd like to tell you about where I've been, and where I just got back from."

"Why is this interesting for me?"

"You won't know unless you let me in and I tell you."

He stood back and I went inside. The room was as I had seen it the last time, only perhaps a little more chaotic. I looked around. The space I had cleared on the chair last time I'd been there had been refilled with what looked like files and reports. He was standing in the living-room doorway, blocking it completely. I smiled.

"Looks like I was sitting right next to what I was looking for all along, huh, Thor?"

"What do you want?"

"I want the report Bob was preparing, and I also want all the data he sent you the day he died."

"I told you. I haven't got it."

"I've just got back from the sensor array in the national park. All the sensors, including the seismograph, have gone to Copenhagen to be analyzed, along with the hard drive." He didn't react, so I went on. "But before sending it off, I had a good look at the computer you had out there. It showed that he sent all the data he had collected to you, and he then wiped the computer clean."

He took a couple of steps toward me. The menace was palpable.

I gave my head a single shake. "Don't do it, Thor. I

ICE COLD SPY

won't kill you, I'll maim you, and then you'll have to go to prison for attempted murder. Be smart. I'm here to help you."

"You are here to help Green Tomorrows and the NATOil Corporation."

I jerked my head at his chair. "Sit down, Thor." I made a space on the chair behind me and sat. He blended a sigh and a grunt into an earth tremor and perched on the edge of his chair with his elbows on his knees.

"Thor, I don't work for either Green Tomorrows, the NATOil Corporation, or the Presidential Commission on Sustainable Energy for that matter. I work for the Office of the Democratic Intelligence Network."

He raised an eyebrow. "ODIN?"

"Old One-Eye."

"United States?"

"Yes. Bob was preparing a report that was commissioned by the White House, by the president. Now Bob has been murdered and the president wants to know why. I don't know what Green Tomorrows' interest in the report is, or the NATOil Corporation's, but I can guess."

He shook his head. "You don't know."

"I'll grant you that there may be private interests involved, but they are not my concern. My interest is to uncover the truth."

"You talk good, but when my back is turned, you will stick a knife between my ribs."

I lopsided my smile onto my left cheek, where it looks benignly ironic.

"We on a bit of an ego-trip, Thor?"

He scowled. "What?"

"The only honorable, decent man in the world is

you?"

He shook his head. "I am not an honorable, decent man. I have done bad things. But if Green Tomorrows and the NATOil Corporation are not stopped, there will be no tomorrows. They do not understand. They will destroy Greenland. They will kill us all."

"Does Bob's report say that?"

"Bob was a scientist. He talks in percentages, in probability margins, in margins of error. If you are a scientist you understand that he is talking about a catastrophic event that can kill many thousands of people, possibly much more. But if you are a money man at the head of a corporation in Texas or San Francisco, you see only access to natural gas and oil which you can exploit while you wait for the United Nations to take its finger out of its ass and make steps to ban oil and natural gas."

He stood and walked to the window. "But this is never going to happen. Because we are trapped in a vicious circle. All these bullshit renewable energies depend on coal, oil and gas to be manufactured, and to be backed up, because only coal, oil and gas can produce enough energy for eight billion people, and counting." He nodded. "Yes, solar energy is free, wind is free, waves are free. But the machines that exploit them must be manufactured and replaced and fixed and maintained, and that requires coal, oil and gas. So they have become one more industry making rich bastards richer, and destroying our world. But Bob's report does not say this. Bob's report talks about conservative margins of error, and conservative projections to the future."

"Governments have scientific advisors, Thor."

"I don't trust government scientific advisors." He turned from the window to look at me. "You know when the IPCC was founded?"

"No."

"Thirty-three years ago. Thirty-three years of making conservative estimates that were *always too* conservative. Thirty-three years of being careful not to overstate a problem that could not be overstated. Only this year have they used language that non-scientists can understand; this year, when it is already too late. I don't trust government advisors."

"I can't say I blame you, but it's all we have. That report belongs to the Presidential Commission—you can't simply take possession of it and suppress it because you don't trust what they are going to do with it."

"I can't?" He stared at me for a long moment. "Who is going to stop me?"

"I have to report back to my superiors..."

"That is a shame, Mason. It is a shame that you have superiors. No man should have superiors."

I sighed. "My government will report to your government and sooner or later..."

"Sooner or later they will come to destroy Greenland, and the Inuit government will be complicit in the crime, and that day, when that day is come, let me die like a man, not like a sheep."

"Cut the dramatics, Thor. Where is the report? If it is that serious, let's air it in the press, let's debate it on TV, maybe it will help to change things..."

"The report is dead. It died with Bob in the snow."

"He sent you the data."

"I did not receive it. Send your forensic scientists to inspect my computers, to steal my papers, to interrogate me. They will find nothing."

I took a long shot. I knew it was the wrong moment, but it was the only shot I had left.

"Did he find there was an active volcano down there?" He stared at me but said nothing. The tension in the air was palpable. "That's it, isn't it? And that is what is going to melt the ice. Tell me. If that is the problem, then the government needs to know. The world needs to know."

He still said nothing, did nothing, just stared at me.

"You're making a big mistake, Thor."

He gave his huge head a single shake. "The mistake is yours, if you stay here another minute trying to sell me your bullshit. You are fighting for the parasites who will melt the ice and bring famine to the world. Go. Get out of my house. Get out of my sight."

I could have pulled a gun on him. I could have shot him and worked my way through the hundreds of reports and thousands of pages he had in his apartment. I was pretty sure he had the data, and possibly the report, right there. I thought about it, but I could not bring myself to do it.

I nodded and stood. "I'm sorry. They will come, you know that, and I can't stop them."

"Can't?"

"It's not in my hands."

"Sheep have hooves, not hands, Alex Mason. Only men have hands."

I left and made my way down to my truck, feeling a bit like a rag that has been left too long in dirty water and bleach. I drove back to the hotel, stood under a piping hot shower for ten minutes, then switched it to cold not realizing just how cold cold water can be in Greenland. The shock was invigorating enough to make me resort to extreme blasphemy before toweling myself dry and dressing for the afternoon. Then I poured myself a strong martini and called the office. Lovelock put me through to the Chief and he spoke to me with his mouth full.

"Mason, I am eating small…" He trailed off and then came back, "…small pieces of smoked Norwegian salmon on homemade rye bread with caraway seeds. My neighbor bakes it. She finds it a comfort since her husband died. It is exceedingly delicious. I was forced to open a bottle of *Blanc Pescador* from Catalonia. What do you want?"

"Hello."

"Get to the point, Mason."

"I think there is a volcano under the Greenland ice cap, in the northeast of the island. I think the rapid loss of ice and water over the last decades has caused a spring-back mechanism, forcing the crust of the earth to bounce back as the enormous weight of the ice cap is relieved. That has caused geothermal activity and pressure which has activated the volcano which has been dormant for…" I shook my head and shrugged. "God knows how long. And I think Bob was going to tell the Presidential Commission and Green Tomorrows that drilling in that area, relieving the pressure of the gas trapped under the crust, could trigger an eruption which could cause a catastrophic collapse and melt of the ice cap."

"Have you gone mad, Mason? Has the cold frozen your neurons? What in the name of Beelzebub are you wittering about?"

He didn't say it maliciously. There was actually a smile in his voice. The salmon and the caraway seeds.

"I visited the site where Dr. Magnusson was killed yesterday. He had an array of sensors out there that nobody was aware of but him—" I was about to add, *and Dr. Thor Olafson*, but bit back the words, unsure exactly why. "One of those sensors was a seismograph. Greenland has no history of earthquakes, so it makes no sense that he would have a seismograph there unless he was looking for some specific geological activity. I think it was a volcano."

"Where are those sensors now?"

"In the hands of the Danish police's forensic scientists, with an observer from ODIN."

"You should have sought my authorization."

"You were busy dreaming of Norwegian salmon."

"Very well. Now, presumably these sensors were connected to some form of computer that processed the data received from them."

"It had been partially wiped. It is also being analyzed by the same forensic team."

"So if your absurd notion is correct they will find the relevant data."

"Yes."

"Then we must assume that an assassin was dispatched by somebody directly or indirectly working for the NATOil-cum-Green Tomorrows Corporation, trying to salvage their mining venture."

"That's how I see it right now. And I think I might know who that is, sir."

"Well..." I could see him, a frosted glass of white wine in his left hand, looking around the room as though he had all his thoughts displayed there. "I mean, Mason, logic dictates that it must be your Dr. Bernard Monet, doesn't it. Planted there by the corporation to keep an eye on things, and thus unpopular with the rest of the team, called to action at the last minute in the face of this unwelcome news."

"I think I'll retire, sir, and save the taxpayer some money. You're so good you don't need me."

"Go and talk to Monet, Mason. Get some proof for this absurd notion of yours."

So I did that. I went down, got back in my truck and drove the short distance to the road that was called Noorlemut at the north end, and Noorlernut at the south end. I was fairly convinced by then that road-naming in Greenland was in the hands of some kind of evil, dyslexic genius. I parked in the lot in front of his strange Cubist block in salmon pink, yellow and green against a functional white background and rode the elevator to the fifth floor, where I rang the bell. Nothing happened for a while and I rang again. Nothing happened again and I listened at the door to see if I could hear anything happening inside. Nothing was happening in there too.

I stood a moment and listened to the block. Nothing much seemed to be happening anywhere, so I did a handy trick with my Swiss Army knife and opened the door, slipped inside and closed it behind me. There was a lot of silence in the apartment. Monet and Thor were on extended leave pending the outcome of the investigation, so I figured Monet and his wife had probably gone out. Absently I noted they had forgotten to take out the garbage. I knew the living room was on the left, so I moved down a corridor to what I assumed were the bedrooms and his office.

The first door I found was a bathroom. It was empty and I moved on. The next door was not an office.

It was the master bedroom. I inched the door open and saw a woman lying on the bed, staring at me. I figured she must be Monet's wife. She was wearing a nightgown and a horrible rigid grin. By now I knew they hadn't forgotten to take out the garbage. What I was smelling was the nauseating smell of death.

The nails of her right hand had torn through the duvet and were held as a rigid claw. The bed on the left side of her body was saturated with blood, which had oozed from a deep cut in the side of her neck which had severed the carotid artery and the aorta. I approached carefully, wondering why she had not clawed the duvet with her left hand. The answer was simple. Under the nails of her left hand was quite a lot of her killer's arm.

I left the room and went to the living room. Monet was sitting in an armchair in front of the TV. The TV was switched off, but he didn't seem to mind. He seemed happy just to stare at the blank screen. I peered at the back of his neck. The wound was easy to miss unless you knew what you were looking for: a razor-sharp stiletto blade that slips in, between the vertebrae at the base of the skull, and severs all communication between the brain and the organs it depends on for continued living. Death, one assumes, is instantaneous.

I spent a quiet half hour in his study, and then called Elise.

"You miss me so much already?"

"Can't live without you, babe. And speaking of not being able to live, there are two people here who seem to be having some difficulty in that department, too."

"Again, in English."

"Dr. Bernard Monet and his wife have been murdered in their apartment."

"*For Satan! Lort!*" And then again with more emphasis, "*Lort!*"

"Lort?"

"Shit."

"Oh, right, I agree. But it gets better. This was done by a professional."

"OK, don't move, I am there in a minute."

CHAPTER ELEVEN

W hile I waited for her I called the Chief.

"Mason, report."

"I came to visit Monet."

"And?"

"He and his wife have been murdered."

"Do we know by whom?"

"Not yet, and two gets you twenty whoever it was is by now catching a flight from Copenhagen to anywhere in the world."

"More than likely. Are the Nuuk police competent?"

"I'd say so."

"Then leave the investigation to them. The forensics will go to Copenhagen and they will keep us up to date. In any case they will serve only to confirm what we know. This is a hit. But we have a paradox…"

He waited. I said, "If Monet was working for the NATOil Corporation and Green Tomorrows, why did they kill him? He may have been a loose end, but now they have just swapped one loose end for another."

"Precisely."

"I think Greenland has given me about all it has to offer. I want to go and talk to Silvia Gordon."

"Reason?"

"She ran. Logic dictates she should either have tried to disappear, or run back to her parents. Instead she ran to London. Why London? Have we any update on that?"

He grunted. "Perhaps. The Mossad have eyes on her, as have the Defence Security Service."

"MI5."

"But they are both being very coy."

"Will they tell us where she is?"

"If we tell them what our interest is. I am not sure whether we are ready to do that."

"No? Well, however well Bob and Thor were keeping their data close to their chests, Monet was getting it too—some of it at least. Whether he was visiting the sensor array without Bob knowing it, or whether he was getting it some other way, he knew about the volcano and his data about its activity was pretty up-to-date. It goes back just over a week."

"Don't share that with the Danish police."

"I don't plan to. I need to talk to the British DSS and Mossad. You need to get me a liaison. I'm going to fly out tomorrow."

"Why not this afternoon? You are wasting time."

"There are a couple of loose ends I need to tie up this evening."

"What loose ends?"

"Nothing you would want to waste your vast intellect on, sir. The cops are here, I'd better go. I'll call you from London."

I opened the door and Elise was there with the ME and a bunch of crime scene officers in space suits. She didn't look happy.

"Come to the kitchen," she said.

I followed her to the kitchen. She stood close to the sink and turned on the tap.

"What are you doing?"

"I read it in a book. If the place is bugged, the water makes it difficult for the microphones to pick up your sound vibrations."

"That's true."

"You didn't kill Monet and his wife."

"Is that a question?"

"Yuh, kind of."

"Of course I didn't. Why on earth would I want to kill Bernard Monet and his wife?"

"Don't answer my questions with another question. So they were dead when you arrived. Yes or no?"

"Yes, of course."

"So if they were dead, how the hell did you get in?"

I winced. "If I say I broke in, will we still have dinner tonight?"

She sighed, rubbed her face and ran her fingers through her hair. "The door was open and you came in because you were worried?"

"No."

"You heard something, or you had some other reason to believe they were in danger?"

"No."

"Mason, you cannot just go around breaking into people's apartments, especially in foreign countries!"

"You're right."

"Give me something to work with!"

"Um…"

"The smell! You rang on the bell and became aware of the odor. You have a lot of experience in this field and you realized it was the smell of a body. So you broke in and found the bodies, whereupon you immediately telephoned the police."

"Nnn...yup! That was exactly the way it happened."

"OK, that is the official story. An official story is not a lie."

"What is it?"

"The official story. Now tell me what really happened."

"I came to talk to Monet—"

"Why?"

"Because I suspect that he killed Bob Magnusson."

"You think he was a spy planted by the NATOil Corporation?"

"It's a possibility."

"It makes sense. He killed Bob so that he could take over the investigation and deliver the required results in the report."

I nodded. "He did insist a lot that the research must go on."

"Yuh, but if it makes sense up to that point, then we have to ask, so who killed *him* and his wife, and why? You said this looks like a professional job."

"It doesn't look like a professional hit. It *is* a professional hit. I figure they had to eliminate Monet because he had information that compromised NATOil and Green Tomorrows executives, and maybe even people in the Presidential Commission. Monet would have been in a position to do them a lot of damage. Once the investigation started, they had to get rid of him."

She nodded and grunted softly. "Maybe."

"You have some other idea?"

She stared hard into my eyes. "Maybe Thor."

The unlikelihood of it made me frown. "Thor? Revenge?"

"It is possible. Thor is very passionate, very intense."

I wasn't going to inquire into how she knew that, so instead I said, "I believe you, but he was convinced I was the killer, or if not me some agent of the NATOil Corporation, or the Presidential Commission."

"He is a very intelligent man. How long do you think it took him to conclude Monet was that agent?"

"Not long... Are you going to bring him in?"

"I have not decided."

"The report Bob Magnusson was working on, I think it may be among the million and one papers Thor has in his apartment. There may also be data on his computer."

"The stuff Bob sent to him before he died, I know. I will get a court order to examine all his stuff, but I think we won't find it. He has either hidden it out in the snow where nobody will find it. Or he has destroyed it."

"Yeah," I nodded, "but we'd better look anyway."

"OK, anything else?"

"Not right now."

"Good, are you married?"

I frowned. "*What?* No. Why?"

"I don't sleep with married men. OK." She turned off the tap. "You can go now. I call for you at your hotel, seven thirty sharp. Keep yourself available."

She went to leave. I reached for her arm.

"Hey, you'll keep me in the loop, right?"

Her very blue eyes looked amused. "The loop? I can bring my handcuffs, but a loop I haven't got."

She left the kitchen and headed for the bedroom, where the medical examiner was inspecting Mrs. Monet, and I returned to my Ford Ranger downstairs trying not to think about loops and handcuffs.

I returned to my hotel and started to pack my stuff. The explanation seemed simple enough. Dr. Robert Magnusson had not wanted to play ball with the big corporations. He knew, or suspected, that the volcano was there and feared that if they started drilling for gas and oil, coupled with the accelerating loss of weight from melting ice, it could trigger violent seismic activity resulting in the reactivation of the dormant volcano. The consequences for the ice cap, and the North Atlantic as a whole, could be devastating.

Corporations who live above the common mass of humanity are notorious for not giving a damn about the people they have to climb over to get a profit, and politicians bent on accruing power and achieving—or withholding—independence are notorious for being pretty shortsighted. So maybe Bob was justified in fearing that if he delivered the report it would be suppressed, and Greenland and the NATOil Corporation, in the form of Green Tomorrows, would go right ahead and sign a deal.

But.

I dumped my packed cases on the bed and went to lean on the balcony, looking out across the cold, dark water.

What about Denmark? Denmark would have something to say about the deal. And perhaps that was part of the problem. If the Nuuk government saw the deal as a chance for independence from Denmark, but Denmark saw the possible seismic activity as an excuse to veto it...

But then that put the Greenland government in the frame for the killing. And that didn't feel right at all, not least because I had not been hindered at all in my investigation so far.

There was something wrong about the whole picture, and I couldn't pinpoint exactly what it was. To have a corporation the size of NATOil scrambling for natural gas and oil under the Greenland ice cap at this stage of the game seemed unnatural, even surreal. And the fact was that, however ruthless they may be, to push ahead with drilling in the face of triggering a volcanic eruption under the ice was improbable in the extreme. And all Bob had to do was to present the findings to the Presidential Commission. They were the true owners of the report, and they would stop any attempt to exploit the oil reserves, if the risk was that high.

Wouldn't they?

I was still turning it over like a half-cooked pancake at seven thirty when reception called me to say that Detective Sergeant Elise Knudson was here for me.

She was still in uniform when I got down, and she didn't look like she was in any mood to play with handcuffs or loops.

I smiled blandly. "You dressed especially. That was thoughtful."

"I just left the *politigården*. I bought a nice red dress..." Her hands hovered over her body, moving up and down. She sighed and shook her head. "Not possible. It's more complicated than we thought."

"You have to go back?"

"No."

"You feel like having a drink and a meal."

She nodded. "Yuh, yuh. Sure, we go." She turned and pushed through the door. I thought I'd be a gentleman and as I followed I added, "You look just as good to me in uniform as in a red dress."

She snorted a laugh. "You haven't seen the red dress."

We dined at a restaurant called A Hereford Beefstouw, which sounded promising in spite of the tortured vowels at the end, which was located on the fifth floor of the less promising Hotel Pissifik.

They had candles on the table, there were good, original paintings on the walls and the chefs were visible in tubular paper hats behind a semicircular bar. We took a table by the window with a pretty good view of the fjord and the Akia plain. We ordered two vodka martinis and the waitress brought them with a couple of menus.

We both had pickled salmon to start, I ordered a musk ox loin and she ordered a T-bone. We had a white Bourgogne with the salmon and Trus, *Ribera del Duero* with the meat.

When the waitress had left us we toasted and sipped, and fell silent as we put down our glasses.

"You want to talk shop until they bring the salmon?"

She offered me a smile that was rueful and nodded.

"They had been tortured."

I felt a sick hollow in my belly. "I didn't see that."

"It was not anything you would see unless you were looking for it. The medical examiner found it. It changes everything. It shoots our theory to hell."

I thought about it, looking out at the gathering dusk above the still, silver water of the fjord. "It means Bernard Monet had information his killer wanted very badly, and Monet didn't want to give it to him—"

She shook her head. "Monet was no hero—"

"Or..."

"Or his killer thought he had it, but he didn't. This is more likely."

"So why the hell..." I trailed off, trying to encompass the whole thing with my mind. Elise took over, leaning back in her chair with her eyes closed.

"So, why, if he is working for them, to keep an eye on Bob and Thor... No, wait." She sat forward. "We have three groups of people here, the Presidential Commission, Green Tomorrows, and the NATOil Corporation. Now, we are talking and thinking like *all* of these people have employed Monet. But this is not so. Some people from the top of Green Tomorrows and the NATOil Corporation have employed Bernard to watch Bob and Thor because they had too much conscience. Good?"

"Good."

"But the job was, find oil, find gas, find how we can mine it. Right?"

"Correct. But then Bob goes and finds a volcano."

"This is new. Nobody was expecting this."

"So Bob and Thor are going to go ahead and publish the data—"

She snapped her finger and pointed at me. "They are going to submit the report, but the data about the volcano is extra, it does not come inside the brief which the Presidential Commission has given him, so they are going to publish this separately! This will trigger a huge debate and make it impossible for the drilling to go ahead."

"Because the drilling, coupled with the ice loss, could trigger the seismic activity and the volcano. Good."

She sat back again and held both hands up. "OK, up to there good. But now somebody in…" She spread her hands and shrugged.

I said, "The NATOil Corporation."

"OK." She nodded.

"Somebody in the NATOil Corporation decides that Bob is about to become a pain in the ass, so they instruct Bernard to eliminate him, and they will then arrange for him to take over the report."

She raised a hand. "Question."

"Why didn't he eliminate Thor at the same time?"

"Exactly."

I nodded. "If we were talking about a professional hit man, I'd agree. But if our killer is Monet, he wouldn't stand a chance. So maybe he was planning a more subtle hit at a later stage, if Thor gave him trouble. The real problem was Bob."

"Yuh, OK, that is possible."

"So now, Bob, knowing or at least suspecting he is about to get hit, desperately sends all the data to Thor and instructs him not to let Monet anywhere near it. Monet kills him, tries to recover the data but finds he can't. When he tries to explain this to his employer, they think he is trying to double-cross them or blackmail them, so they send someone to get the report."

She nodded again. "That makes sense."

The waitress came with the salmon and the bottle of wine in an ice bucket. She poured, smiled and left. I leaned forward.

"You need to put a twenty-four-hour guard on Thor. If they have found that Monet hasn't got the report and the data, they will go after Thor."

"I have warned him, and I have a car outside his house."

We ate in silence for a while. Then she sighed and sat back.

"So, my job is almost done. I close the airport, I close the ports, I use Thor as bait and wait for this killer to move. He is already in prison. But you, you still must find this report, and the data. Thor has it, but you are leaving. I don't understand."

I drained my glass and refilled.

"Maybe Thor has it. I am not so convinced. Maybe he had it once, but he is pretty crazy and I wouldn't be surprised if he has destroyed it. That's what he told me he had done."

She frowned. "Yuh? What for?"

I thought back. "I asked him where the report was. I told him if it was that serious we could leak it to the press, debate it on TV... You know the kind of thing. But he told me the report was destroyed. His exact words were, 'The report is dead. It died with Bob in the snow.'"

"But Bob sent him the data."

"That's what I told him. He said he didn't receive it, and challenged me to send forensic scientists and cops to look for it. He said they would find nothing. I think he has destroyed it."

She was frowning hard. "But that doesn't make sense. It's crazy."

"Well, Thor is a bit crazy."

"But if the data shows the presence of a volcano that might become active, he should *want* that fact publicized." She stared at me a while. "Maybe he is afraid you, as an agent of the Presidential Commission, will suppress the data, and he plans to make it public himself."

"That's possible. The other possibility is that Silvia has it. She ran, remember, and Bob told her to take all his papers with her."

"Ah, so you are going to look for Silvia."

"Yeah, but I am going to do that tomorrow."

CHAPTER TWELVE

A few hours later, at two o'clock the next morning, there was frost in the air. Sergeant Mogens Andersen and his partner, Officer Lars Christensen, were sitting in the unmarked Cherokee, steadily drinking hot coffee from a couple of flasks. They were outside Thor's apartment block on Dronning Ingridsvej, with just one streetlamp thirty feet to their left, and another thirty yards ahead. The combined light of the two on that freezing night was enough to induce chronic depression.

The lights in the apartment block were all out, except for one, solitary lamp in the entrance porch.

Lars studied the porch sullenly and wondered how it was that the light of that bulb could induce hopelessness and despair, where the much dimmer light of the stars could inspire hope and magical possibilities. He was about to put this thought to Mogens, when he saw a man in his late twenties or early thirties, approaching the intersection ahead of him at a brisk walk, with puffs of condensation billowing from his mouth.

"What kind of fool is out on a night like this, at this time of the morning?"

The man turned into the street and walked toward them, keeping his head down.

Mogens grunted. "Maybe all the crazies are out today. There is another fool coming down the hill behind us. We don't get involved unless we have to. Our mission is to watch Thor. Understood?"

"Understood."

The guy drew level, stopped and leaned down to the window. Lars scowled, thinking he would have to open the window and let in the cold air. But the thought froze in his mind when he saw the man pull a suppressed semiautomatic from his jacket. He saw the cannon loom large against the glass. His heart beat wildly. He heard a pop and a splintering of glass beside him, and Mogens utter something like, "*Yoh!*" An instant later he saw the flash of fire, and that was the last thing he was conscious of in this life.

About seventy feet above them, Thor rose from the chair he had placed beside the window, where he had been looking out at the frosted stars over the fjord, and made his way to the bedroom. There he yawned and stretched and pulled back the covers.

Seventy feet below the two men made their way in silence to the dull porch where Lars had seen no hope. One stood with his hands in his jacket pocket, looking out at the dull, cold night while the other hunched over the lock. A moment later the door opened and the two men slipped inside.

They didn't ride the elevator. They needed silence. Silence to get into the apartment. Silence to take Thor by surprise, to cripple him before they gagged and incapacitated him. Then he would talk, but he would talk quietly.

They arrived at the sixth floor. Garry was the smaller of the two. He was married and had two children he barely knew. They lived in Glasgow, but after this job he was going to buy a villa on the Costa del Sol, in Spain. He knelt and picked the lock while Jimmy looked and listened. There was nothing to see but darkness, and nothing to hear, not even the soft scratch of Garry's tools. Jimmy knew Garry was a pro. One of the best.

When this job was done, Jimmy was going to go to Las Vegas and blow the whole damn lot on coke, booze and whores. Jimmy was with the Zen masters. There was no future. There was no past. There was only now.

The door moved softly open. They both remained motionless. There was not a breath to be heard. Garry nodded to Jimmy and they stepped softly inside.

There was a small entrance hall. The living room was to the left, and to the right a corridor ran down to the kitchen, the bathroom and the bedrooms. Jimmy led the way as far as the first door. Now they could hear the slow, heavy breathing of deep sleep. Jimmy gave the door a quick push to avoid squeaky hinges, and saw the bed in the dull glow from the window, and the huge, massive bulk in the bed, turned away from him.

Garry came up beside him. He knew what he had to do. Jimmy would plug him in the knee, precisely as Garry smothered his face with a heavy, woolen scarf. After that they would gag him and begin the slow process of interrogation.

Jimmy was the first to hear the movement. He turned to his right just as the thirty-inch, razor-sharp blade buried itself into the angle of his neck and his shoulder with a nauseating thud. Garry hadn't noticed the noise but now looked up at the thud and the shifting shadows just as Thor's massive boot smashed into his balls.

With a single, fluid movement Thor pulled the sword from the deep gash and a fountain of dark blood shot up toward the ceiling. He swung the blade again and brought it down again into the angle of the other shoulder, carving out a deep V from which Jimmy's head dropped to the floor. The decapitated body, drenched in its own blood, folded and sank beside it.

Next to the headless body, Garry was on his knees, clutching his genitals and whimpering. With a single swing of his right hand Thor brought the blade of his battle-ready, ninth-century replica slicing in a wide arc down through the back of Garry's neck, severing the vertebrae and slicing through the thin muscles. His head dropped and rolled, and came to rest beside Jimmy's.

Thor had the plastic bag and the box ready. He placed the two heads in the bag, sealed it and put the bag in the box. He then taped it up with packing tape. He washed his sword with bleach, dried and oiled the blade and hung it where he kept it always, on the wall in the living room. Finally he went down, climbed in his truck and drove to his favorite whorehouse in Quingorput, three miles away, by Lake Nuuk. There he would have a dozen witnesses who would swear he was there all night.

Meanwhile, just half a mile away, a mere ten-minute walk, in the very last house on Saqqarliit, overlooking the icy water of the fjord, while Thor finished his grim task, Elisa slept with her head upon Mason's chest, with the windows to her terrace thrown wide open, and the cold, starlit air wafting the curtains. Mason was not asleep. He watched the molten silver light on the ocean and told himself for the millionth time that something was wrong with his perfect theory.

Something was wrong that wasn't right.

CHAPTER THIRTEEN

Somebody else who felt something was wrong that wasn't right was Jamil. In his heart, or that part of his imagining which he held dear as his heart, he could see the translucent skies of the desert, peppered with shards of crystal ice, whispering of peace and God's eternal love and mercy. But all about him, as he was herded down tiled passage after tiled passage, among swarming humanity of every race under the sun, he saw madness, chaos and confusion—and filth. He saw godless people: Chinese, Hindu, Mediterranean, hulking blond northerners, and to him it seemed they were the legions of the lost, scrabbling like rats in their daily fight for money and profit, willfully lost and ignorant of the Word of God.

Willfully lost! That was the most disgusting aspect of these godless beings, who were lower even than rats in God's eye. For had they not been offered God's Word and God's mercy? And had they not knowingly rejected it?

And when he thought that he felt a great, sacred rage well up inside him. For these were the people who were loathsome to God: those who had heard the Word, those who had been called, but chose to ignore God's almighty will. These would surely burn in Hell, where daemons would force them to drink boiling water while the angels watched and laughed.

Evoking again in his mind the clean sands and the turquoise night skies of his home, he recited silently, fervently under his breath, *"Surah Al-Wāqi`ah, verse fifty-six, They will dwell amid scorching wind and scalding water in the shadow of black smoke, neither cool nor refreshing. Surah Al-Hajj, verse nineteen, Garments of fire will be tailored for those who disbelieve; scalding water will be poured over their heads, melting their insides as well as their skin; there will be iron crooks to restrain them; whenever, in their anguish, they try to escape, they will be pushed back in and told, 'Taste the suffering of the fire.'"*

He passed through passport control as though he were invisible, and he thanked Allah and his guardian angels for their protective mantels. He waited for his case in baggage reclaim with a sickness of anxiety in his belly and his eyes fixed on the floor. He had never seen such a place as this and a wild claustrophobia threatened to overwhelm him. His heart cried out for the bright, clear open spaces, his family, his home and his brothers. He repeated fervently under his breath, *"Allah humma'h fathny min bayne yaday wa min khalfi, wa'an yameeny wa 'an shimaly, wa min fawqi, wa a'uthu bi 'athamatika an ughtala min tahty!*

"O Allah, protect me from my front, behind me, from my right and my left, and from above me, and I seek refuge in Your Magnificence from being taken unaware from beneath me!"

With a jolt of joy he saw his case spill out onto the conveyor. He snatched it and hurried toward the arrivals exit, remembering Mustafa's instructions to him to appear at all times calm and relaxed. "For every step you take on jihad, Jamil, Allah takes that step at your side, and we, your brothers, all walk with you. So walk with God in your heart."

He emerged from one of the seemingly endless tunnels into a large room with people swarming and teeming all around him. The ceiling towered three floors above him, and at each level he could see shops, bars, people moving. All about him was a barrier, where people cried out to each other and embraced. There were bareheaded women everywhere. He saw one now openly kissing a man on the mouth. He tore his eyes away, invoking God to guide him through this antechamber of hell, and scanned the crowd beyond the barrier. He had been told that somebody would meet him there. But he saw no one.

He pushed on, through the opening in the barrier, and headed toward the coffee shop, where he had been told to wait. As he joined the line to buy a drink, he felt the pressure of a hand on his shoulder. He jumped and looked, and saw the smiling, elegant face of an Arab. He was not what Jamil thought of as a true Arab, a man of God. He was Westernized, touched by the Shaitan. He had beautifully cut black hair, brushed back from his face. He had an exquisitely well-cut suit, a white shirt and a tie, and his near-black eyes were amused.

"Sammy?"

He shook his head and his voice caught in his throat. "No, you have made a mistake."

The dark eyes were doubly amused now.

"Truly? You are not Sammy Patel? What is wrong, Sammy, you do not recognize your own cousin?"

Terror and confusion gripped Jamil's heart. He had no sooner stepped off the plane than he had made his first bungling mistake.

He stammered, "I am sorry!"

The man laughed and slapped him on the shoulder. "Don't tell me you are hungover again! Was the stewardess feeding you whisky?"

Jamil's scandalized denial was smothered as the man put his arm around his neck and pulled him into a brotherly embrace, ruffling his hair in the process.

"Come on, I have the car outside, Mama is dying to see you. We have so much to talk about, and I have so much to show you." Jamil drew breath but his new friend raised a cautionary finger. "Remember what I used to tell you when we were children? Sammy, never say anything unless you have thought about it at least three times!"

Jamil bit back his words while his mind cast about wildly for a point of reference, something familiar and solid he could hold on to. In his mind he kept repeating, "Allah, help me, Allah!"

They stepped into a VIP elevator that took them down to the VIP parking lot. His so-called cousin kept talking nonstop.

"I know what you are feeling right now, Sammy. This is like nothing you have ever experienced before. I know. Everything you have been taught, everything that has been drilled into you for so long, suddenly it does not apply. But you have to adapt, my brother. Adapt or die! So, until we are safely in my car, keep your mouth shut!"

The elevator came to a halt and the doors hissed open. They walked ten paces to a Bentley Continental GT V8. Jamil stopped dead.

"This is your car?"

"Get in."

He opened the trunk, threw in Jamil's case and opened the passenger door for him. Jamil climbed in. The door clunked and a moment later his new cousin climbed in behind the wheel. When the door was closed the man turned to face Jamil.

"This is the first and last time I will talk to you as Jamil. You are new to this, you are fresh out of training and you are confused, so I am being patient. But you need to start reacting. Now."

Jamil shook his head. "This car, your clothes…"

"This is the sacrifice we make for the jihad. This is how we get close to them. They see us and they think, 'Oh, he not like an Arab, he is so elegant and civilized, he went to Oxford and Harvard, he speaks English like an Englishman, I can trust him. They let us get close to their hearts, and then we drive in the knife. Do you know who I am?"

"No."

"I am Prince Abdulazziz-bin-Nayef, do you trust my commitment to jihad?"

Jamil's mouth had sagged. "Yes, of course, your highness."

The prince raised a long index finger. "Jamil, listen to me very carefully if you want to live until tomorrow. From now on you will refer to me as Abdul and treat me like your own brother. You will drink with me, you will whore with me, and you will behave like an arrogant aristocrat, because that is what you are from now on. This behavior is granted by Allah to those who fight for His greater glory. Give me your papers."

Jamil handed over Sammy Patel's cards and documents, and bin-Nayef handed him a new set. Jamil looked at them. He was now Jamil-bin-Nayef.

"You are now truly my brother. We fight together, we walk together with God by our side. Whatever you do in the next few days, Jamil, remember, you do it for God's greater glory. Enjoy it, for it will not last, and the time will come to take up your sword and fight like a lion. Do you understand?"

Jamil was weeping. "Yes, your..." He squeezed his eyes shut. "Yes my brother, Abdul."

"Good man! So now, let's go!"

"Where are we going?"

The prince laughed. "To practice! I must introduce you to some very important people, so I must teach you how to behave like a very important person." The huge V8 growled and they moved toward the exit. "You know how very important people behave in the West, Jamil?"

"No, how? Like the Great Shaitan?"

"Let that be the last time you talk about Islam. We *never* talk about Islam to these people."

The big beast of a car roared out onto the blacktop under a clear blue September sky among the rolling green hills and the golden trees.

"Very important Westerners do whatever they like. They drink too much, they take cocaine at parties, they have sex with each other's wives and husbands, they gamble at casinos..." He shook his head and glanced at Jamil. "They do whatever they want whenever they want. So for the next few days we must do as they do, with one important difference."

"What difference?"

"In our hearts we know we do it for Allah. They do it for themselves. So when the time comes to get up and fight, we will have God in our hearts, but they will have only decadence and greed."

Prince Abdulazziz-bin-Nayef settled back in his seat and felt the five hundred and forty horses surge under him. He smiled. "I think we will start by dressing you appropriately," he said. "Then we will go to a good restaurant and I will teach you the right things to say about wine, and then a nightclub. Tomorrow I will introduce you to..." He paused. "To the Right Honorable Toby Grimes."

Jamil's brow furrowed with anxiety. This was not his idea of jihad. "I don't understand," he said. "*Allahu akbar*, Mustafa said we would be making war on Shaitan. But this, the car, the clothes, the alcohol, the women..."

"You will understand, little brother. You will understand. You must walk among them, invisible as a ghost. Keep the fire burning in your heart, but walk among them so that they cannot see you, so that in their blindness they see only another like themselves. God will keep you strong. I will explain everything to you."

They drove to Mayfair, where Prince Abdulazziz took Jamil shopping for everything a billionaire in London needed: from shirts and evening suits, to socks and cuff links, ties and handkerchiefs. Slowly Jamil's sense of panic faded and became merely a background anxiety. He longed to talk to Mustafa, who was always so clear and unambiguous, who always explained everything in clear terms of black and white, Allah and His prophet and the word of God. Jamil knew that the prince was a great hero of the jihad, but his words and his actions confused him.

They returned to the prince's mansion on Charles Street, where Jamil was shown to his room by a young maid. There he showered and changed and the prince came to him personally to see that he was suitably dressed for the evening. He made a few alterations, settled his handkerchief, changed his cuff links and gave him advice.

"Smile always, but not like an idiot. Smile as though everything amuses you. Smile as though you consider all humanity beneath you, but you regard them with kindly affection. Smile, my brother, as though you have many billions of dollars in the bank, and nothing worries you. Show me that smile now."

Jamil frowned. The prince stood back and spread his hands wide. "Look at you! Your entire village could live for a year on what your suit cost! Your shirt is the finest shirt money can buy. How does it feel to be dressed like that?"

"I feel guilty."

The prince scowled. "You feel guilty for doing God's will?"

"No!" He took a deep breath and closed his eyes. "The clothes feel good, your high... My brother Abdul."

"The creams, the aftershave, the perfumes... They feel good?"

"Of course."

"So now, for God, for the jihad, show me the smile of a man who is amused that nobody on the planet is as rich as he is." Jamil hesitated. The prince's face became like wood. "If you cannot do it, Jamil, we will have to kill you. By tomorrow morning you must be a rich, Arab playboy, or die."

There was a moment of ice-cold stillness. Then the prince burst out laughing. A second passed and Jamil began to laugh. The two men embraced and the prince stepped over to a sideboard where three vintage, crystal decanters stood on a silver tray. He poured two generous measures of single malt and gave one to Jamil.

"Sip," he said, "carefully. By tomorrow this must be your favorite drink."

They dined at Le Gavroche and the prince quietly guided Jamil through which knives and forks to use, and, as Jamil began to relax, he explained to him what exactly was going to happen over the next few days, and exactly what Jamil's mission was.

Jamil, who had had by then a large whisky, a dry martini and a glass of wine, frowned at his new brother and said, "That is all? That is all I have to do?"

The prince smiled, leaned back and swirled his wine before inhaling the bouquet.

"For now, Jamil, that is all you need to know. This is your first time, your first job, we will take it one step at a time. For now you are learning the skills of camouflage. Show me you have dedication and talent, Jamil, and I promise you, you will not be disappointed."

After dinner they went to a nightclub where everybody knew the prince and showed him great reverence and respect. He was shown to his own table and six girls came to sit with them. They drank champagne that the prince told him cost five thousand pounds sterling the bottle. When Jamil looked scandalized and was about to protest that this was immoral, and that there were people who worked all their lives in his village who never saw that much money, the prince raised a finger, then raised his glass and said, "We make this sacrifice for Allah. *Allahu akbar!*"

Perhaps because he was drunk, perhaps because after so many months of grueling abstinence and training he was enjoying the girls' caresses too much to argue, he laughed at the prince's toast and drained his glass.

Shortly after that another girl came to the table with a silver box and a mirror, and Jamil was introduced for the first time to cocaine. He did not remember much after that. He remembered feeling that he had finally come to understand the mystery of God, he remembered standing in an elegant Georgian square looking up at a crescent moon and knowing that God had chosen him for a great destiny, and he remembered being in bed with three girls, knowing that this was the rightful due of God's warrior.

But he remembered nothing after that.

CHAPTER FOURTEEN

Tedium made the flight seem longer than it was. I touched down at London Heathrow at four thirty in the afternoon, feeling it should be at least midnight. I had only hand luggage, so I was able to skip baggage reclaim, but passport control was slow and heavy going, and added to the feeling that Britain was in the slow but relentless process of turning itself into a fortress. "Built by Nature for herself," I muttered to myself as we shuffled toward the booths, "against infection and the hand of war."

"Business or pleasure, sir?"

"Pleasure."

He glanced at my passport and my Five Eyes card, stamped the visa and told me to enjoy my stay.

I strolled through arrivals, collected an F-Type Jag that ODIN's London office had left for me in the VIP car park and headed in to the Dorchester where Lovelock had booked me in. As I cruised down the Great West Road I was smiling to myself, thinking I was going to enjoy a few days of civilization, Dorchester hospitality and city life. Greenland had been fascinating, but a little intense.

I rolled down Knightsbridge, past Hyde Park and the Albert Hall, then turned north into Park Lane. There

I gave my keys to the valet and strolled in to the understated elegance of the Dorchester lobby. The concierge saw me come in and smiled.

"Mr. Mason, welcome back. Have you reserved?"

"Yup, my usual."

"Ah, yes, the deluxe king."

I took the key and told him I didn't need a bellhop. I dropped my bag in my room, had a shower and a shave, dressed for the evening and made my way down to the bar. There I sat myself on a stool and ordered a vodka martini.

A body in a violet silk dress with a slash all the way up one exquisite leg slid onto the stool beside me. I didn't look and tried not to smile. A voice that made your toes curl said, "Is this seat taken?"

I still didn't look. I spoke to the polished surface of the bar.

"It is now, and whoever had it before can go to hell."

"That's so nice."

Now I looked at her and smiled. "What are you doing here, Gallin?"

"Looking for you, what else. I knew I'd find you either in the bar or in the restaurant."

"You could have tried my room. You would have found me there a little earlier."

"A little earlier I wasn't dressed."

"Neither was I."

She turned to the barman. "Give me a Manhattan, rye not bourbon."

"So," I said, turning to face her, "why are you looking for me?"

"You didn't call."

"You told me not to."

"Well, that shouldn't stop a man like you."

I arched an eyebrow. "Whatever it is, it's obviously not urgent."

The barman gave her her Manhattan and a bowl of peanuts. She put one in her mouth and watched me a moment.

"I am your liaison officer."

"Again? Now you work for the British DSS?"

"Don't be silly, Mason. Your Big Boss called my Big Boss and asked that we work together."

She swung around in her chair so her bare knee was touching mine. I said, "On what? I'm here on holiday."

She sipped her drink. "You're here looking for Silvia Gordon, Dr. Robert Magnusson's ex-girlfriend."

"I'm afraid you have me confused with somebody else. However, would you like to dine with me?"

"Do I have to call Nero again?"

"Just for the sake of the argument, what possible interest can the Mossad have in Dr. Robert Magnusson's girlfriend?"

She shook her head gently, gazing at her glass on the bar. "None."

"So?"

"So, not that it's any of your business, if you're only here on holiday, we *are* interested in Prince Abdulazziz-bin-Nayef."

I picked up my drink and frowned at it. After a sip I was still frowning.

"The Mossad are interested in Prince Abdulazziz-bin-Nayef. That's like saying 'Bakers make bread,' or 'My tailor makes my suits.' What has Prince Abdulazziz-bin-Nayef got to do with Silvia Gordon and Dr. Robert Magnusson?"

"Ah!" She shrugged and raised her eyebrows. "You're on holiday. Nero must have made a mistake when he said you were flying in from Nuuk to look for Silvia. I suppose you won't be interested to know where she's staying either."

My cell rang. I pulled it from my pocket. It was the office. Lovelock's husky growl asked me, "Are you there yet?"

"Yes."

"You just don't bother to follow protocol and let me know."

"I was busy having a martini."

"Cute. Mossad's katsa, Aila Gallin will be contacting you. We are not liaising with MI6 on this one. We want to cooperate with Mossad. They have an interesting angle.. She'll brief you."

"Thanks for letting me know."

"Yeah? Follow protocol, handsome. It makes life easier for all of us."

She hung up. Gallin blinked at me. I said, "It seems I'm not on holiday after all."

"Shucks. Bummer."

We ordered two more drinks and moved to a table in the corner. As we sat I said, "Before you tell me where Silvia is, or better still, before you take me to her, explain to me what bin-Nayef has to do with this. What kind of connection are you making here?"

"That's the thing. We don't know, and I was actually hoping you could tell me."

"Give me the background."

"OK." She sat back and thought for a moment, organizing her thoughts. "As I am sure you know, there are certain countries in Europe that are a kind of home away from home for Islamic jihadists. In the European Union you have France and Germany, who make things pretty easy for them, and then you have the United Kingdom. It's surprising, you'd think that being the jihadists' number two preferred target, and with the longstanding relationship the Bank of England and the Royal Family have with Jewish bankers—Goldsmith, Schuster, Warburg, Rothschild, to name but a few—you'd think the UK might be a little tougher on Islamic terrorists, but the fact is they make it surprisingly easy for them. I guess oil talks."

"Is this a soapbox?"

"Partly. So we make a point of watching not just known terrorists, but also their friends in high places. Prince Abdulazziz-bin-Nayef is known to finance terrorism and to be very sympathetic to al-Qaeda and to the Taliban. He spends about half the year here in London. So, while he is here, we watch him and we keep tabs on his friends too."

"I have a feeling you are about to tell me about one of his friends."

"The British Labour Party, that's the socialists, are notoriously anti-Semitic, and extremely pro-Palestinian. Not surprisingly, Nayef has close friends among the Labour Party elite. Mostly they just hang out in expensive clubs and drink champagne at two thousand dollars a bottle, like good socialists should, but sometimes the relationship goes a little deeper, and recently our prince in shining oil has started to get cozy with the Right Honorable Toby Grimes, the Shadow Foreign Minister."

"So you have been spying on leading members of the British government's Shadow Cabinet. Does MI6 know about this?"

She smiled. "They let us know indirectly that they could not possibly, ever, find out about it. And as long as they didn't know about it, we could do whatever the hell we liked. The Right Honorable Toby Grimes is not a popular man, except with Prince Abdulazziz-bin-Nayef, who courts his company, takes him out to dinner, invites him to private parties—you name it."

I made a face that said I was unimpressed. "So far that's just the usual money and oil for interest exchange that goes on from Berlin, Paris and London to Washington DC. What has this to do with Silvia?"

"OK, so it was a rainy night in September—"

"I'm already hooked."

"I am watching Grimes's house while he is playing house with a hooker, when Nayef shows up in his Aston Martin. The hooker leaves by the back door and Nayef enters the house and the living room. They drink whisky. In the conversation it emerges that Nayef has Grimes on video making the beast with two backs with a girl at a party the previous Saturday. Nayef tells him the film was made by accident and he will bring him the original, no strings attached."

"Son of a bitch."

"Yeah, smooth as a snake. Friends, he tells him, are there to help each other. And goes on to tell him he has a very rich friend who needs a favor. He will tell Grimes all about it at the Lubyanka."

"That restaurant is bug-proof. The Russian mafia

set it up, and anyone who has a secret they need to discuss, goes there. You want to know who are the leading spies in London today, drop by the Lubyanka."

"Exactly, so we were not able to record the conversation. However, dinner was brief and when Grimes left he collected his own car and drove to Bury St. Edmunds, just north of London. There he went, alone, to a private house where he was admitted by an attractive woman in her thirties. I was not able to listen in because they moved to a room at the back of the house for their conversation. But we did hear how she went upstairs and brought down with her one Silvia Gordon, whom she had collected from the airport off a flight from Copenhagen."

We sat in silence for a long moment. Eventually I said, "My brain hurts."

"Don't sweat it, I have had a little longer to put the pieces together, and my brain also hurts. Try as we might, we cannot find a connection between Silvia Gordon and Toby Grimes, but there is absolutely no doubt in my mind that he went there for the express purpose of meeting her. And now get this, the woman who collected her from Heathrow Airport is Joanna Jeffries, senior intelligence office at MI6."

"Have you..."

She interrupted me. "We have made discreet inquiries at the Circus, but they are not talking. Either they don't know what she's up to, or they're not telling." She took a pull on her drink and jerked her chin at me. "Your turn."

I told her about Bob Magnusson's murder, and that we suspected he may have been assassinated by the NATOil Corporation, or its subsidiary Green Tomorrows, because his findings, if made public, could jeopardize their plan to drill in Greenland.

"Before he died he called Silvia and probably told her to take his report and run."

"So she ran to London and was picked up at Heathrow by a senior MI6 intelligence officer who took her home and immediately called a senior opposition cabinet minister, the Shadow Foreign Secretary, and introduced them."

I took a long pull on my drink and drained it.

"It is very, very unlikely, but it may be that there is no connection. That Toby Grimes just happens to be connected to Prince Abdulazziz-bin-Nayef, and to Silvia Gordon."

"Nah…"

"OK, listen, the UK, like every other major Western economy, is interested in the Presidential Commission's report. We are running out of oil and we have nothing to put in its place. So we all want to know what is under Greenland. Now, when MI6 get word that Bob is dead, they move in and somehow contact Silvia and tell her to come to London. Jo Jeffries goes to collect her at the airport and Grimes, off his own bat, goes to get a preview. Weirder things happen in politics."

Her face said she was unimpressed. I went on.

"Meanwhile, Prince Abdulazziz-bin-Nayef is sucking up to the man who will probably be the UK's next Foreign Minister, and blackmailing him while he's at it."

She shook her head. "Nah. Maybe you don't follow British politics, but aside from anything else, it is very unlikely Grimes will ever be Foreign Minister. One thing, and one thing only, connects Bob Magnusson, Silvia Gordon, Toby Grimes, MI6 and Nayef."

"Oil."

She nodded. "Oil." She signaled the waiter for two more drinks and went on. "Like you said, everybody was curious about the outcome of the Presidential Commission's report. When Bob Magnusson was killed and his girlfriend ran, I guess everybody jumped to the same conclusion. 'She's got the data he collected.' British intelligence stepped in quick and smooth, like they do, and got hold of her. Meanwhile Prince Abdulazziz-bin-Nayef, who as well as financing terrorism is an oil billionaire, deployed Grimes to get access to the girl."

"That's one reading of it, but it doesn't ring true. You don't recruit a high-ranking, high-profile opposition politician for a job like that. No, they are using Toby Grimes *because* he is high profile and high ranking. But what for?"

"Beats me. The prize is obviously Silvia Gordon. And right now the Brits have her. You want to get Joe to call Boris and ask for her back."

"Yeah, something tells me Boris might tell Joe to go to hell. They're not the best of friends since Afghanistan and the shelved trade deal."

She gave a soft grunt. "So what then?"

"I think maybe I should go and introduce myself to Jo Jeffries in Bury St. Edmunds."

"And cut me out of the loop? Think again, pal."

"No way, Tonto, you'll have my back, sitting outside in the car. I'll tell you what I really want to know, Gallin. How the hell did these people know she had run? The Commission knew because the Danish police called them. I was notified at four AM the next morning and flew direct to Greenland, and as of then ODIN knew, the Commission knew and the Danish Police knew. So how the hell did MI6 and Prince Nayef find out so fast?"

The waiter delivered our drinks and Gallin took a deep breath. "I am speaking off the top of my head here, and I am not really sure why, but this makes sense to me. They knew, because they were told by the only other person who knew she'd run."

I frowned. "Who?"

"The killer."

"That's deep. It would mean a leak."

"Somehow that makes sense."

"OK, so we go and ask. Meantime..."

I pulled out my cell and called ODIN. I was put through to the Chief who immediately asked, "Where are you?"

"The Dorchester."

"They have a new chef. He is superb. Will you dine at the Grill?"

"Yes, but I didn't call you to talk about food, sir."

"No. What then?"

"Silvia Gordon is staying with a senior MI6 intelligence officer,"

"You mean SIS."

"Yes. Now, what I am wondering is whether her employers know she has her."

"Why? Because there was no time for them to find out she had run and probably had her boyfriend's data?"

For a moment I sat and hated him. When I was done I said, "Yes, sir."

"Who informed her, then? Either she has a random, and entirely unlikely contact within the Danish police, or she is in touch with the elements within NATOil and Green Tomorrows who ordered Dr. Robert Magnusson's death. I find the latter far more likely. You have arrived at the same conclusion and now you would like me to make discreet inquiries and find out whether the British SIS realize that one of their operatives is holding Silvia Gordon."

"Yes, sir."

"Well, why didn't you say so, man? I'll be in touch."

He hung up and Gallin said, "So?"

"He'll make discreet inquires as to whether the SIS realize that one of their operatives is holding Silvia Gordon." I paused. "If they don't, it means she is freelancing for NATOil."

"Good. So I suggest we have a late dinner in your room and right now we go and talk to Joanna Jeffries."

CHAPTER FIFTEEN

The package arrived at the head offices of the Green Tomorrows Corporation in Newark, California, by FedEx. It was addressed to Mr. Daniel Bludd and Anthony Gorr.

When it was deposited on his desk, in Danny Bludd's office, he sat slumped in his huge leather chair, with his double-breasted suit bunched up around his head, and stared at it for a long while without opening it. The postage was from Nuuk, in Greenland. He could not think of anyone who might send him anything from Greenland, or anyone from whom he would want to receive anything from Greenland. Greenland was a place that right now he wanted no connection with.

And it made him very unhappy that alongside his name on the address there was Anthony Gorr's. He and Tony should not be connected in people's minds. After a long, careful inner debate he reached out his short arm, picked up the telephone and called Tony.

"Yeah, Danny, I'm kind of busy. What can I get my secretary to do for you?"

They both laughed. Danny's laughter was a little strained. When they were done he said, "Listen, I just received a parcel."

"Is it your birthday? You're getting old, you son of a bitch."

"Tony, listen, the parcel is from Greenland, from Nuuk, and it's addressed to both of us."

The laughter died and was replaced by a prolonged silence. Then, suddenly, "OK, right, out. Everybody out. Danny, don't say anything. Get out, everyone. Yeah, yeah, I'll call."

Danny heard the shuffling of bodies over the phone, then the clunk of the door. Then, "Is it the report, or the data?"

"I don't see how."

"Well, open it."

"Let me ask you something, buddy. Would you be so keen if you were sitting here next to me?"

"Well, is it ticking? What are you going to do, drop it in water before you open it? Come on, Danny. You can't call the cops. You don't know what's in there. Just open the damn thing."

He took a deep breath. "OK." He stood, took his letter opener and slipped it through the thick, brown tape. The flaps of the box sprung back and he pushed them fully open. Inside there were Styrofoam chips surrounding a thick, black plastic, garden refuse sack. He could hear Tony's voice demanding, "Well, what is it?"

He switched the call to video and trained the camera on the bag. He could hear Tony asking, "Is there a note? Open the bag. See what's inside!"

Keeping the lens focused on the bag, Danny folded back the shiny, black edges. The smell that wafted up to him made him retch, but he bit back the reflex and peered inside. That was when he saw the two goggling heads, white as wax, staring up at him with bulging eyes. His cell phone clattered to the floor, he shied away clasping his hand over his mouth and vomited over his desk. He grabbed the handkerchief from his pocket, trembling violently and repeating over and over, "Oh, God! Oh, dear God! Oh Jesus!" before vomiting again on the floor.

His secretary burst through the door, her eyes wide. "Mr. Bludd! What is it?"

"*Get out!*" he screamed at her. "*Get out! Close the damned door! Get out!*"

Wiping his fingers he dropped to all fours, scrabbling for his cell under the desk. He could hear Tony, tiny as Tom Thumb, shouting from the phone.

"*Danny! What the hell! Answer me! What the hell is going on? Danny!*"

He clamped the phone to his ear.

"It's two heads."

"*What?*"

"It's two damned heads!"

"You're not making any sense, Danny. What's in the damned box? Who's it from?"

"Listen to me." He spoke with elaborate precision. "Inside the box there-are-two-damned-heads! Two human heads. The heads that used to belong to *two living human beings!*"

"...Jesus. Do you know them?"

"Well, surprisingly, Tony, I did not stop to take a close look. I was too busy retching."

"Where are you now?"

"Sitting under my desk."

"What? *Why?* Danny, get a grip!"

"I dropped the cell and—ah, forget it!" Laboriously

he clambered out from under the desk, still holding the cell to his ear. "I think..." He hesitated. "The parcel came from Greenland. I think these may be the guys who were sent to take care of Monet and Olafson."

"Sweet Jesus."

"Yeah, well, something tells me he ain't going to help us much."

"Who did you delegate that to? We shouldn't be talking about this on the phone."

"Don't even think about hanging up on me! I gave it to Harragan, my head of security."

"Call him now, get him to clean it up. Let's meet. We'll have lunch at Bird Dog."

"You expect me to *eat?* You expect me to eat *Japanese food* after what I have just seen?"

"Come on! Don't be a pussy! Cowboy up, Danny. Have a couple of Scotch..."

"Ok, OK, but we eat Italian, not friggin' Japanese. All I need now is raw fish! We'll go to the Terún."

He hung up and called Harragan on the internal phone.

"Y'Boss!"

"Get up here. I want you in my office fifteen minutes ago."

"M'onmaway!"

He crossed his office, avoiding the splatter on the floor, and poured himself a stiff whisky which he downed in two gulps and shuddered. He dipped his handkerchief in the decanter of water and wiped his hands and his mouth, then poured himself another stiff Scotch.

There was a knock at the door and Harragan stepped in. He was big, with a barrel chest and a hard, broad Irish face. He stood a good six-two and had hands like slabs of concrete. His suit was expensive, but would always look out of place on him.

He glanced around the room, taking in the details. He closed the door behind him and said, "What's in the box?"

Danny Bludd jerked his chin at it, indicating Harragan should have a look for himself. He crossed the room, stepping over the patches of vomit on the floor, and looked inside the box without touching it. He didn't react, except to say, "Garry and Jimmy. That's a shame. They were mates."

"I don't want to know their names," Danny said through his teeth. "I want to know what it means, and what you are going to do about it."

Harragan regarded Danny with distaste.

"It's a pretty clear message that whoever did this does not intend to give in, and is happy to deliver this kind of treatment to whomsoever we send after him. That's what it means. You didn't ask who did it, but I'll tell you fer nothing. You told me to go after two targets, the French scientist, and the Icelandic scientist. Well no French scientist ever did *this*. Besides I know fer a fact, because they told me, that they went and asked him a few questions. They didn't like his answers so they killed him and his wife."

"Jesus Christ!"

"I'm sorry, was that not what you wanted? I must have misunderstood when you said, 'Get rid of the bastard.'"

"Don't be impertinent. I have just had a shock."

"Yeah, right. So they said they was going to go and have a chat with the Icelandic fellah, Thor Olafson. Looks like he had a chat with them first. He knows how to use a blade. I reckon he used a sword or an axe." He pointed into the box. "He took Garry's head clean off with a single stroke, but Jimmy's was done very nicely." He made diagonal stroke motions with the blade of his hand. "Right, then left. That's the right way to do it."

Danny was regarding his head of security with baleful eyes. "Are you done?"

"What am I going to do about it? Whatever you tell me to do. You're the boss. But I think it's going to get expensive and messy if you keep sending guys after this boy. I'd recommend trying to negotiate with him. He's a dangerous bastard and no mistake."

Danny pointed at the box. "Get rid of that. And get the cleaners in to get rid of that smell," he waved his finger at the carpet, "and all this. I'm going out for a bit."

Harragan closed the box and sealed it with Scotch tape. He picked it up in his arms and maneuvered his way out the door. As he passed Bludd's secretary he said, "Get a team to clean the office, will you? It stinks in there."

Danny's driver dropped him on California Avenue beside the blue parasols outside the Terún and was instructed to find some place to park and await his call. Then Danny Bludd strutted on short legs across the blacktop and found Tony Gorr, tall, slim and elegant with one long leg crossed over the other, seated outside, under a parasol, with a tall gin and tonic in front of him.

"Danny, you look stressed. Sit down and have something soothing." He laughed with good-humored malice. "Shall I ask them to warm some milk for you?"

"Take a hike, Tony," he said as he sat, "I am not in the mood."

The other chuckled. "What have you done?"

"Harragan identified them. They're the boys he sent to deal with Bernard and Thor."

"That's very unfortunate."

"OK, you got your degree in understatement. Moving on, they dealt with Bernard, but it looks like Thor lived up to his name."

"Never trust a Norwegian with an axe."

"Icelander."

"You mean there's a difference? What'll you have?" The waiter had arrived.

He told him, "Glenfiddich, no ice." The waiter went away. To Tony Gorr he said: "We are looking at a situation that could blow up in our faces and land us both behind bars, or worse."

"Relax, we'll contain it. The danger is if you start getting hysterical."

"I am not hysterical!" he spat back savagely. "I just opened a carton with two human heads in it!"

"So it happened. Get over it. And sooner rather than later, Danny. I need you cool and focused. What's your man going to do about it?"

"For starters I told him to get rid of the heads."

"OK, what else."

"Nothing else. He recommends negotiating with Thor Olafsen. He figures sending somebody else after him will aggravate the problem."

Tony Gorr grunted. "He may be right. It reads to me like he was warning us off, not threatening us. What we need to be focusing on right now is getting our hands on that girl. We need that report, Danny. We need that data and we need to control its contents and who reads it."

"Obviously," Danny snarled sullenly, "but the Icelander is a loose end and we'd be crazy to leave him at large. This has got badly out of hand and we need him and the girl silenced."

"See? There you go panicking and getting hysterical again, making things worse instead of better. There are many ways to silence somebody, Danny. You don't have to shoot them or cut off their heads."

"OK, genius, like what?"

"Well, Danny, we start by making Bob Magnusson our friend and *our* hero. The three of us were out there trying to make the world a better place. His brains, our dream and our money. And then we highlight what an amazing guy he was looking after his girlfriend the way he did, after her history of mental instability and drug abuse."

Danny sat forward, his face suddenly alight. "What? She's a junkie?"

Tony smiled. "Not yet, but she will be once I get through talking to the director of the clinic where my ex-wife is in permanent residence."

"Son of a gun! You can't make that stick!"

Tony laughed. "Are you kidding? If she has to choose between being labeled a junkie and accepting a six-figure bribe, what do you think she'll choose? She'll hand over the stuff without a moment's hesitation. I guarantee it."

Danny sagged back in his chair. "That would work, if we could get our hands on her."

"Of course it'll work. Her brand-new medical records are being delivered to the Hope Clinic as we speak."

"And how do you intend to make this offer to her?"

"She's in London right now, staying with..." He

hesitated for just a second. "...a friend of a friend."

"Who?"

"You can't know. But she'll be flying somewhere closer to home pretty soon, maybe Canada, maybe the Caribbean. Then we'll go and see her, and make her the offer. She'll accept."

"You're a dangerous, devious bastard, Tony."

"Never forget it, Danny."

"And what about Thor Olafson?"

"He is the least of our worries. We simply need to make him understand that we can and will put him in the frame for Bob's murder."

"Why?" Danny shook his head. "Why would he kill Dr. Magnusson?"

"The oldest reason on Earth. So he could steal his girl, with whom he was insanely in love—and for the groundbreaking research." He spread his hands and shrugged. "We muddy the waters, we manufacture evidence, we point fingers and, if the courts don't convict, the press and the people will. Either way he goes down."

The waiter reappeared.

"Are you ready to order, gentlemen?"

Danny looked squeamish. "I want a pepperoni pizza, and a cold beer."

Tony smiled at his partner and there was ill-concealed malice in his eyes. "I'll have a sirloin steak, rare, and a glass of Barolo."

The waiter left and Danny asked, "So are you going to have her brought to San Francisco?"

"No, I told you, she'll be stopping off somewhere quiet and perhaps remote. It's not clear where yet. I am just waiting for news. Wherever it is, we'll go and see her.

After we've made the deal we can send her back to Los Angeles. From what I hear she's so broken it will take only a little fatherly pressure from me to bring her round."

Danny thought about it. "She'll be wondering why van Dreiver hasn't come for her."

He shook his head. "Van Dreiver's position is much too delicate. He cannot be seen to be involved with this. But it's easy enough. Van Dreiver's been a friend of mine for years, so has the president, for that matter. When Rudy told me what had happened, and how the Commission had been thrown into chaos with this thing, I immediately volunteered to go and get the poor girl. She will feel grateful, and that much more inclined to give me what I want."

Danny sighed and rubbed his face. He had to admit that Tony was right. He usually was. "OK," he said at last, "but when she gets back to LA, the pain of losing her boyfriend has to become too much for her. She has to cut her wrists or something, take an overdose, whatever. I don't want that bitch out there haunting my dreams at night with her slack mouth."

Tony pulled down the corners of his mouth and shrugged. "You take care of it. I want full deniability. And you make damn sure it does not kick back on the company."

"And Thor Olafson? That bastard sent me two severed heads. I want him to pay!"

"Sure, but give it a year. He will not be a threat for us. Just relax and take it easy, Danny. Everything is going to be OK." His smile returned. "You'll get your revenge."

* * *

Three thousand three hundred and sixty-eight miles away, Elise stood beside Dr. Thor Olafson on the shore of Qinngorput Bay, looking out at the boats resting on the milk-smooth water. The fall was closing in and you could feel the promise of snow in the air as the sun slid day by day down toward the southern horizon, which would soon swallow it up and bring on the long night.

Elise had her hands thrust deep into her pockets and she spoke to the tiny, transparent waves that lapped at her boots.

"Are you going to lie to me, Thor?"

"No." He narrowed his eyes at the distant mountains across the fjord. "Are you going to put me in prison, in Denmark?"

"No."

"I will tell you. But if you tell anyone else, I will say you are lying. I have a dozen witnesses who will swear I was here all night."

"Whores."

"So what? They are people. I have met as many honest prostitutes as I have met lying policemen."

"Why do you go with whores?"

"You know why. There is no woman for me." They were silent for a while. Elise's nose and cheeks were turning pink in the icy air. Thor said, "They came to kill me. I knew they would. They killed Bernard, and they tortured him for Bob's data. They did not get it. So they came to me. I saw them arrive. I was waiting for them." For a moment there was a grim smile in his eyes. "I introduced them to Sigrún, and she drank deep. Then I came here."

"Where are their heads, Thor?"

"I sent them to their owners." She frowned at him,

not understanding. "Those men were not free men, Elise. They were slaves. They did not own their own heads. Their heads, their hearts and their souls belonged to another. So I sent their heads to their true owners."

She took a deep breath and shook her head. "This is why there is no woman for you, Thor. You are a very attractive man. You are strong, and intelligent, and noble, a woman could love you, but you are crazy. You are completely crazy."

"You are also a bit crazy, Elise. Could you ever love me, and be my woman?"

"Could you ever be less crazy?"

He thought about it, then shook his head. "No."

They stood like that for a while longer, staring at the ice-cold water, and then turned and walked away from the shore in the dying light.

CHAPTER SIXTEEN

The Right Honorable Toby Grimes grunted, groaned and rolled himself out of bed. He sat a moment staring down at his feet on his bedside rug. He grunted again and staggered to the bathroom where he showered and shaved before going downstairs in his dressing gown to the kitchen, where Olga was making breakfast.

Olga was from Colombia and had learned early on that it was best not to talk to the Right Honorable before eleven AM, unless it was to answer one of his curt questions. She placed his five newspapers beside his plate and ignored him. His plate contained eggs, bacon, sausages, fried tomatoes and two slices of fried bread. Beside his plate also there was a teacup, a fat, blue teapot, a jug of milk and a silver sugar bowl.

He sat and she poured his tea while he scanned the front page of the *Telegraph*, seeing what the enemy was up to. As he folded it and set it down, and picked up his knife and fork, the doorbell rang. He ignored it, but glanced at Olga's shapely posterior as she ran up the steps to answer the door.

He read about the alliance between the UK, Australia and the US to provide Australia with nuclear submarines to check China's power in the South Pacific. He smiled smugly. He had been part of the consultation process on that one. Voices were raised above. Olga sounded distressed. He glowered at the stairs and heard a reassuring male voice, then shoes on the stairs and Prince Abdulazziz-bin-Nayef came into view.

Grimes's scowl turned to an expression of dismay, which deepened when he saw a well-dressed young man behind the prince, and Olga looking distressed saying, "I am sorry, Mr. Grimes, I told them you were..."

She trailed off because bin-Nayef was talking over her, as though she was not there.

"Forgive me, forgive me, Toby, I know you are breakfasting, and I know that breakfast is sacred to you —" His face lit up and he stopped dead on the stairs. "Bacon and eggs? Do my eyes deceive me? A *full English breakfast*? I adore the full English breakfast!" He turned to his young companion. "Jamil, have you ever had a full English? It is the food of gods! May we join you? Would that be an impossible impertinence and an imposition?"

Grimes was getting to his feet, wiping his mouth with his napkin, confused and floundering.

"No! Yes! I mean, please do! Join me, you are most welcome. If I'd known you were coming I would have... Olga, please, can you rustle up some more eggs and bacon for our guests? And you'd better make another pot of tea."

She put her hands to her head, muttered, "*Oh Dios!*" and set about preparing two more breakfasts, while bin-Nayef introduced Grimes to Jamil.

"My cousin, who is here for a brief visit, and as soon as he arrived I thought, 'I must take him to meet my good friend Toby. I am sure you are going to be great friends.'"

Toby gave his new friend a nervous smile and shook his hand. They all sat and bin-Nayef gestured with both hands at Toby's plate. "Please, my friend, continue. Do not let us interrupt you. You eat and I will talk. How's that?"

He laughed, Toby nodded and smiled and Jamil regarded him with no expression at all. As Toby picked up his knife and fork again, bin-Nayef wasted no time in coming to the point.

"It is my cousin's intention to settle in the UK and start a business here, importing and exporting, and I thought to myself, what better experience could he get than working with the Right Honorable Toby Grimes, Shadow Foreign Secretary? I thought perhaps you could employ him as a personal secretary and mentor him for a year or two. What do you say?"

Grimes had frozen with a forkful of food halfway to his mouth. His mouth, already open, stayed open and a piece of egg slowly slid from the fork and splatted on the plate.

"My, mymymy..." he said. "But I already *have* a personal secretary. I can't sack her without a good reason. There will be questions asked. It would draw a lot of unwelcome attention."

Bin-Nayef laughed again and waved a dismissive hand. "My dear friend, I do not mean anything official, or that the party need know about. Just an excuse for him to hang out with you, carry your briefcase, meet useful people, get your tea. You know the sort of thing."

"Well, I mean..."

"And, to show you my gratitude, I have arranged a very special gift for you. It comes in two parts. The first is on this pen drive." He reached in his pocket and pulled out a manila envelope which he tossed across the table with a wink. "A souvenir from a rather special party where we watched the moon rise."

Grimes went pale and picked up the envelope. He stared at bin-Nayef, who was apparently oblivious to Grimes's distress. He went on.

"The other is a week's holiday in the Bahamas for you, your immediate staff," he gestured absently at Olga, "any family members you care to invite, and of course your new personal secretary."

Grimes swallowed hard and stared at Jamil. "I'll have to clear it with party headquarters."

"Nonsense. I have already cleared it with them. We will call it a session of trade negotiations. You will stay at my villa outside Adelaide Village, on New Providence Island. You will have full use of my yacht, and you are just ten miles from the center of Nassau. It will do wonders for you. You will feel like a new man when you get back." He winked at Grimes and pointed at the manila envelope. "Come on, old chap, one good turn deserves another. What do you say?"

The threat, overlaid with elegance and charm as it was, was nevertheless palpable. Grimes nodded, licked his lips and forced a smile.

"Well, would you look at me, ungrateful and graceless! What a kind gesture, and naturally I would be delighted to accept your very generous offer. The Bahamas, ay? Well, that is unexpected. Something to look forward to next summer."

Bin-Nayef threw back his head and laughed. "Next summer? My dear friend, next summer I will regale you with gifts for next summer. This gift is for now! *Carpe diem!* Who knows where we will be next summer? We might be with O'Leary in the grave! No, my friend, no. 'But little time had they to pray, for whom the hangman's rope was spun, And what, God help us, could they save?' Seize the day! You depart tomorrow at noon from the City Airport in a private, chartered jet. My car will meet you at Nassau airport, and take you to the villa."

"I'm overwhelmed, your highness. But I really should talk to Keir..."

The prince's smile faded. He looked at Grimes steadily. The kitchen became very quiet.

"What in the world for, Toby?" he asked, softly. "I have told you. I have cleared it with your head office and with Keir. We had dinner last night at my house. Now, you really should start packing and getting ready to go. Jamil will come with me to get a few last-minute things, but we'll leave his passport with you."

Jamil reached in his pocket and pulled out a British passport which he dropped in front of Grimes. "That way you can take care of all the arrangements and transit through the airport."

They stood and made for the stairs. Grimes stood too. The prince waved a hand at him. "Please, don't get up. If you need anything at all, I have left a car out front with a couple of my most trusted friends in it. They will take care of you."

They climbed the stairs and left a dreadful silence behind them. Dimly he heard the front door slam. Olga said, "What should I do with the eggs and bacon?"

His face clenched like a spiteful fist. "*Oh, shut up will you, you silly bitch!*"

He pulled his cell from his dressing gown pocket and dialed.

"Toby, what is it."

"Look, this is embarrassing, I've just had Prince Abdulazziz-bin-Nayef here. He's sort of latched on to me a bit, become quite friendly..."

"He wants you to go to his villa in the Bahamas, Toby. We discussed it last night. He has some very interesting propositions to put to us. Could be quite a coup."

"There won't be a comeback because I stayed at his private villa?"

"Don't worry about it. The deals we get from this will be good for Britain and good for the working man. I was about to call you, as a matter of fact. Has he gone?"

"Yes."

"Try playing hardball with him once you're there. A good deal could put us in the running. Highlight us as the ones with the profitable international relationships, know what I mean?"

"Yeah, yeah, I get it. All right then. It's all a bit last minute, that's all. I'll be in touch."

"Good man."

He hung up and sat staring at the table for a bit, then he called Jo Jeffries in Bury St. Edmunds. He forced a fatuous grin onto his face and into his voice. "Fancy a holiday in the Bahamas?"

"What are you talking about?"

"I think I may have solved our little problem."

"Oh?"

"I have an unexpected trip to the Bahamas tomorrow."

"That was quick."

"Came out of left field. I'll be there a week. Private jet. Private villa on the beach. All the trimmings. I'll be taking a private secretary and my cook, so I suppose there would be room for your friend."

"You come and collect her. I shouldn't be seen at your place."

"Agreed, I'll come and get her. Meantime book yourself a room in Adelaide Village and we'll bump into each other out there."

"I'll stay at the Hilton, thanks very much."

"Suit yourself. See you in a bit."

He hung up and rubbed his face with his hands. After a moment he became aware of Olga leaning with her backside against the sink, watching him.

"You takin' your cook..." she said, with an arched eyebrow.

He sighed. "Of course I am. Don't be mad at me. You don't know what it's like, all this stress, making decisions that could affect all of history! All this power comes with responsibility, you know? The destiny of entire countries...*the planet!*"

"Poor papito. So you takin' me, so I hel' relieve all that stress?"

"Course I'm takin' you! You don't think I'd spend a whole week in the Bahamas without you, do you?"

"So who is this you gonna collect now?"

"Oh, it's complicated. You wouldn't understand."

"Is she pretty?"

"Not like you!"

"Come on, papito. I give you a nice massage and a shower, an' you can tell me all about it. Then I go shopping for some nice bikinis while you go collect this girl."

He grinned, then growled. "Oh, come here you temptress, you!"

* * *

Jo Jeffries set down the phone carefully on the pine table, as though a careless move might upset more than simply her plate and her cup of tea. Silvia watched her do it and waited. She had a slice of untouched toast on her plate and a cup of coffee held in both her hands.

Jo finished buttering her toast and took a deep breath. "That was Toby. He is flying to the Bahamas tomorrow and he has offered to take you with him. It will be very safe." She raised her eyebrows and gave a small laugh. "You'll be going in style, in a private jet to stay at a private villa on the beach. If we're careful, no one will know you've left the country. You'll go VIP with tight security as part of his retinue." She paused. "Once you're there it's less than two hundred miles to Miami or Fort Lauderdale, and you're back home in the USA."

Silvia sat very still. She could feel the beginning of panic in her belly. She asked, "Will you be coming?"

Jo frowned. "Would you like me to?"

"I know it's a lot to ask. You have your work and your life to get back to. I guess I'm being stupid."

"Not at all, Silvie. You poor child. I can't go with Toby, but I'll catch a flight out to Nassau and I'll be there shortly after you arrive."

"But the cost..."

"I'll talk to Rudy about it. Don't you worry about that. The important thing is that we get you safely home and find out what has happened here."

Silvia rose and came around the big pine table, where she got on her knees and flung her arms around Jo, and sobbed into her lap. Jo stroked her hair and made soothing noises, and looked unhappily at the poor child's wet cheek and her eye screwed shut.

* * *

At ten to four o'clock that afternoon Lavi was sitting in an anonymous Toyota outside Jo Jeffries' house, watching the drizzle. He saw a dark blue Audi pull up in front of Jo Jeffries' house. He took photographs and waited. He saw a man get out whom he did not recognize. He wore a bulky coat and a hat and walked to the front door where he knocked and rang the bell. He was admitted, but they must have gone to a back room because the laser picked up no sound from the windows at the front.

Five minutes later the front door opened and the man emerged again with Jo Jeffries. The man was talking and she was looking up at him as he spoke. They made their way toward the Audi and Lavi called in. Gallin answered.

"What?"

"Unidentified male has arrived in an Audi RS6." He recited the license plate. "He was admitted to the house and is now returning to his car with Jeffries. Do I stay and watch the house or do I follow Jeffries?"

Gallin didn't hesitate. "Follow Jeffries."

He gave them a few seconds' head start and once they were moving he tailed them along Newmarket Road and out onto the A14. He then followed them to Cambridge and eventually to London, where they finally pulled up outside the very house he had been watching a couple of days earlier with Gallin: the Holland Park home of the Shadow Foreign Secretary, Toby Grimes. There he watched them climb out into the growing dusk and hurry to the house through the drizzle.

He called it in and Gallin told him: "Stay on the house. Tell me if she leaves."

At six PM, in the growing dark, he watched a Bentley roll up and saw Grimes, a young, well-dressed Arab, a very attractive dark-haired young woman and a young blonde in a business suit, carrying Grimes's attaché case, all spill out of the house. The young Arab and the chauffer carried an abundance of cases to the car while Grimes and the two girls climbed in the back.

He called it in again.

"Was Jeffries with them?"

"No, just his retinue: secretary, PA, chauffer. Jeffries is not there."

"Stay on the house until she emerges."

"Will do."

He hung up and sat and waited.

CHAPTER SEVENTEEN

Gallin hung up and sighed.

"That kid."

I glanced at her but kept my eyes on the road. The traffic was heavy and the drizzle was turning to rain.

"He makes me nervous. I can't put my finger on this or that and say, 'He's no good because!' No. He just..."

She trailed off. I flicked my eyes at the GPS. It said we were ten minutes away.

"He's got no imagination. You need imagination in this job. He's always looking for somebody to tell him what to do. Sometimes you have to have initiative and imagination. One of these days he's going to screw up. I know it. And the other me is going to say, 'I told you so.'"

"There's another you?"

"According to my shrink there are fifteen of me, and each one is worse than the other, whichever way you count them. Heavy, huh?"

"Sounds like your shrink needs a shrink. We're here."

I came off the A14 at exit forty-two onto a big circus, or what the Brits call a roundabout. I followed it around to Newmarket Road and came off. After a little over a mile I turned onto York Road and Gallin pointed to a cute, redbrick suburban house surrounded by trees, hedges and rosebushes.

"There," she said.

I pulled up and we climbed out.

Gallin said, "She's not going to open the door. It's the first thing Jeffries will have told her. 'Do not open the door to anybody unless I am here.'"

I nodded and rang on the bell, then stood back to look at the windows. There was no movement in the drapes, but after thirty seconds or so the door opened and Jo Jeffries stood looking out at us. She gave a small frown when she saw Gallin, like she remembered her, then looked at me.

"Yes?"

I heard Gallin swear violently under her breath and storm back toward the car. I smiled pleasantly. "Are you Joanna Jeffries?"

"Yes."

"My name is Alex Mason, I work for the Office of the Director of Intelligence. I'm here on behalf of the Presidential Commission on Sustainable Energy." As I spoke I pulled out my badge and showed it to her. "That person stomping toward the car is my colleague, Captain Aila Gallin, of the Institute for Intelligence and Special Operations."

She handed back my badge. "You mean the Mossad. What do you want?"

"Ms. Jeffries, we know that you have, or have had until very recently, Silvia Gordon staying with you."

Gallin had climbed in the car and we could hear her muffled shouting. Jeffries shook her head. "Silvia Gordon is not with me. And in any case, what possible interest could you have in Silvia?"

"Do you mind if we come inside? Ms. Jeffries, I know you are an intelligence officer with the Secret Intelligence Service, and I am sure you must be aware that Silvia Gordon is a person of special interest at the moment. Not least," I added, "because the Danish police want to talk to her about her boyfriend's death."

I saw Jeffries' eyes travel past me and heard the car door slam. Gallin's boots approached along the path. "How do you do?" she said to Jeffries.

Jeffries sighed. "I suppose you had better come inside."

She closed the door behind us and went ahead to the kitchen. There, she pointed to her big pine table and leaned against the sink. "Do sit, I'm afraid I haven't time to offer you a drink."

I pulled out a chair and sat, with my elbows on the table. Gallin sat at the end, with her hands in her pockets.

I said, "Are you going somewhere, Ms. Jeffries?"

"I'm sure you didn't come here all the way from Wilshire Boulevard in Arlington to ask me if I am going anywhere nice. Now, we all know who we are. Please tell me what you are doing so far from your jurisdictions, knocking on my door."

"As I am sure you know, Ms. Jeffries, Silvia's boyfriend was Dr. Robert Magnusson, who was commissioned by Ruud van Dreiver, the head of the Presidential Commission on Sustainable Energy, to make a report on the oil and gas reserves under Greenland."

"Of course."

"Then I am sure you also know that Bob Magnusson was murdered a few days ago." She didn't answer. She just waited. "On the day that Bob was killed, Silvia fled Greenland with, we assume, all of Bob's research notes and the data he had accumulated. We need to talk to Silvia, and the Danish and Greenland police need to talk to her too. Where is she, Ms. Jeffries? If you make it necessary I can get my boss to talk to your boss, and then your boss will tell you to talk to me, but it was my impression that we were supposed to cooperate with each other."

She shook her head. "There is really not very much I can give you, and I have to say that I strongly object to the fact that you have not made this approach through official channels."

Gallin spoke up. "We would have, Jo, if we had known she was here. But as you didn't inform anyone that she was with you..."

Jeffries' eyes narrowed. "So how *did* you find out?"

"Pure chance," I said. "But as things stand I don't think I am at liberty to tell you."

She sighed. "It's quite simple. I am a close friend of Ruud van Dreiver. I have been for many years. Silvia phoned him from Nuuk airport in a panic, telling him that Bob had told her to leave Greenland immediately. But she was in a state emotionally, very frightened as you can imagine, and wanted guidance. So Rudy told her to come here, to London. Then he called me to go and collect her from the airport. That's really all there is to it."

Gallin asked, "Why didn't he tell her to go to LA and pick her up himself?"

"Quite simply because it would take much longer, there were more changes and she would have spent more time alone and uncared for."

I nodded. "OK, so where is she?"

She hesitated for a fraction of a second, then

seemed to make a decision. "She's on her way to the Bahamas. I am afraid you are much too late. They took off from the City Airport about an hour ago."

Gallin's voice was incredulous. "The *Bahamas?* Why the hell is she going to the Bahamas? You can't get a flight direct from London to LA?"

Jeffries regarded her a moment without expression. "She was terrified. It was why she came here in the first place. Her boyfriend had just been murdered, for no apparent reason, and while the killing was in process he called her—"

I cut in: "While it was in process?"

"Just before—minutes before—while the killer was approaching him, and immediately after he had been stabbed. And he told her in no uncertain terms to get out of Greenland. Obviously she was, and still is, terrified."

Gallin narrowed her eyes. "I still don't get why she's gone to the Bahamas. If I went to the Bahamas every time I got scared I'd have to buy a house there."

Jeffries sighed and closed her eyes. She pulled out a chair and sat. "Rudy has another close friend here in London."

Gallin said, "Don't tell me. Toby Grimes, the Shadow Foreign Secretary."

"Yes. You've been watching him?"

"Haven't you?"

Jeffries didn't answer the question. Instead she said, "Rudy called Toby as well as me. He was afraid that whoever had killed Bobby might go after her."

I asked, "Why? What made him think that?"

She shrugged. "Simply the fact that Bobby seemed to think so. He asked me to look after her, and he wanted

Toby to use his political influence to get her back to Los Angeles incognito and protected. It just so happened that Toby had a trip arranged to the Bahamas to meet a trade delegation or something. So he suggested Silvia go with him, and from there it's a quick flight to Florida, where Rudy could meet her and take care of her."

I scratched my head and did a lot of frowning. Finally I turned the frown on Jeffries and shook my head.

"We are colleagues, right?" She didn't answer. Her face was like a library window at four AM. Dark, with all the information on the inside. "I mean, our respective nations are allies, there's the old special relationship, the Five Eyes, AUKUS, so we, you and I, are colleagues. So here are the things I don't understand: first, if I am here, looking for Silvia, on behalf of the Presidential Commission on Sustainable Energy, and Professor Ruud van Dreiver, the head of the Climatology Department at the University of California, was appointed, by the president, as *head of that Commission*, why the hell did he call you and the British Shadow Secretary of Foreign Affairs, in England, instead of calling me? I wasn't even in Greenland at that time. At around the time he called you and Grimes, I was being briefed in DC. He could have called, or joined the damned meeting and told me, 'Hey, on your way to Greenland, stop off in London, get Silvia Gordon and get her safely back to LA.' All this time I have been looking for Silvia Gordon, *on behalf of the damned Presidential Commission*, and all the while the head of that Commission knew where she was! You want to explain that to me, colleague?"

"I have no idea, Mr. Mason, and I will thank you not to raise your voice at me. All I know is that Rudy called and asked me to pick Silvia up at the airport and look after her, which I did. Then he asked Toby to get her safely to the States, which he is doing. I know absolutely nothing about your Presidential Commission or why Rudy did things as he did."

I stood, signaling to her by doing so that the interview was over and, I hoped, allowing her to relax her guard. Then, dismissively, like it wasn't really important, I asked, "Who's the trade delegation Grimes is meeting?"

It worked. She was momentarily taken off guard. She hesitated.

"Um... I..."

"Prince Abdulazziz-bin-Nayef?"

For a fraction of a second she looked alarmed. "I don't know. I have no idea."

I smiled. "I'll tell you something, Joanna, for a senior intelligence officer, there is an awful lot of important, relevant stuff you don't know. And I'll tell you something else. For a senior SIS officer, you are remarkably lacking in curiosity."

"If you have questions you want answered, Mr. Mason, I suggest you get your boss to ask my boss. And by the way, in case you think we are stupid on this side of the Atlantic, there is no Office of the Director of Intelligence. You are either ODIN or ODNI, but you are not ODI."

I opened the kitchen door. "Thanks for your help."

She moved ahead of us and opened the front door. Outside it was still drizzling.

"Next time you call, do it through the proper channels."

We climbed in the car and Gallin beat the steering wheel with her fist. "When I get my hands on Lavi I am going to rip his head off and shove it so far up..."

"Yeah? I'll hold him while you do it."

"They dressed Silvia up as Jeffries, took her to Grimes's place in Holland Park, then hid her in plain view made up to look like his PA or his secretary. God damn it! By now they are halfway to Nassau!"

"You want to be quiet a minute?"

I was hearing the phone ring at ODIN. She started the engine and we pulled away, back toward London, hissing over the damp blacktop. Lovelock's dark chocolate voice oozed into my ear.

"Office of Data Processing and Information Networks. How may I direct your call?"

"It's Mason. I need to talk to the Chief. Make it snappy."

"Please hold."

She put my voice through recognition software and a few seconds later the Chief said, "What?"

"Joanna Jeffries, British SIS intelligence officer and the Shadow Foreign Secretary, Toby Grimes, acting on Ruud van Dreiver's request, have helped Silvia Gordon escape from the UK and she is now flying with Grimes to Nassau. Silvia called van Dreiver from Nuuk Airport and asked him for help. He told her to fly to London."

There was a soft grunt. That was his answer, so I went on.

"I want to know, if Silvia called van Dreiver from Nuuk Airport, why the hell were we not informed of that at our briefing at the White House? Why was I sent to Greenland instead of London?"

Another grunt.

"Is that it? Is that all you are going to say? Ungh?"

"Shut up, Alex. Go to Nassau."

"By the time we get to Nassau she'll be on her way to LA!"

"Shut up, Alex, is a phrasal verb in which the preposition 'up' modifies the verb 'shut' and changes its meaning to 'be silent.' Do you understand, Alex? Shut up."

He waited. I didn't answer because he had told me to shut up. So I did. Satisfied, he went on.

"I will have somebody watching Miami, Fort Lauderdale and Nassau airports. I am not satisfied that she will come directly from the Bahamas to the United States. I think she will stay there. Now you, kindly do as I say and get the first available flight to Nassau."

"Yes sir."

I hung up. Gallin was smirking. "Daddy told you off."

"I'm going to the Bahamas. Are you coming, or do you have to ask *your* daddy?"

She looked at me along her eyes without turning her head.

"ODIN's going to be watching the airports?"

"Mm-hmm."

"Meanwhile we find Grimes and Silvia."

"Yup. You guys have been keeping tabs on bin-Nayef, right?"

"Yeah. You're wondering if he has any property in the Bahamas. He has. The Bahamas are a tax haven. They are also a damned nice place. So he spends a good part of the year there. He has a beachfront villa in Adelaide Village."

"So two gets you twenty that's where Grimes is taking Silvia."

We moved onto the freeway, headed toward London. The traffic was heavy, the hiss of the tires was loud and the spray from the other cars made a dense mist on the road. Gallin licked her lips and asked, "Is this MI6 playing fast and loose? Those guys are subtle."

"That would mean that Ruud van Dreiver was in MI6's pocket, which I doubt. And anyway," I screwed up my brow, "why would van Dreiver conspire to get the report or the data from Silvia, when she's going to give it to him anyway? *She* called *him!*"

"It doesn't make any sense."

"It only makes sense if Grimes, Jeffries and van Dreiver are acting independently."

She stared at me. I said, "Eyes on the road."

She looked back at the wall of mist. "Explain."

"The report is worth a fortune. The world is running out of oil. Oil's days are numbered and the Western world is gearing up to phase oil out and make it illegal. Right?"

"Right. The problem is, so far nobody has a viable alternative to oil."

"But now Bob discovers oil under Greenland, and natural gas. Now, we all knew it was probably there, but Bob—and I am just guessing here—Bob discovers there is an enormous amount. So whoever controls that oil will rival Saudi in terms of wealth, power and influence, at least until an alternative source of energy is found, which could be a very long time. But just as things are looking up, Bob discovers a volcano and starts to create problems."

"Now, van Dreiver, having seen the preliminary reports, is aware of the potential and turns to two very unlikely friends who are, nonetheless in a position to help him bring home the bacon, so to speak. He eliminates Bob and Monet, tries to eliminate Thor, and when Silvia runs, he diverts her to London where Jeffries takes control of her..." She trailed off. "The only thing that's different, Mason, is that we are saying that the head of the Presidential Commission is complicit with NATOil and Green Tomorrows in this. It sounds far-fetched. But," she shook her head, "but I'll be damned if I can think of another explanation."

I nodded, gazing out at the speeding traffic and the broad freeway channeling us toward the vast metropolis, burning that vital fuel as we went; and all about us millions upon millions of humans were doing the same thing, burning fuel in their cars, in their homes, in their offices and in their factories. And for a moment it seemed to me that the entire planet had become a vast, ravenous machine, drinking and burning that fuel.

CHAPTER EIGHTEEN

We were able to get a nonstop, British Airways flight to Nassau's Lynden Pindling international airport, by the skin of our teeth. It was a nine-hour flight and got in at four thirty-five PM local time, about twelve hours behind Grimes and Silvia. We picked up our rental F-Type from Luxury Rentals and headed for the hotel, west along the Windsor Field Road. The hotel was just a couple of miles from the airport, but a good six miles by road from Adelaide.

The relentless blue skies and turquoise oceans were a treat after the relentless gray skies and rain of London. "But I confess I was looking forward to a few days at the Dorchester, a play, a show, some fine dining."

Gallin nodded. "It's a great town, but there are too many people, and the weather gets to you in the end."

Something in the way she said it, and that odd, transatlantic accent of hers made me realize: "You live there?"

She shrugged. "Well, you know, I move about a lot."

"But you live in London."

"Yeah, kind of. My dad lives in London."

"And your mother?"

"Cut it out. Stop. Respect the boundaries, Mason."

I smiled to myself and kept on driving through the lush, topical landscape of banana trees and palms. After a while, as I turned off the Western Road into Mahogany Hill, she said, "So how do you want to do this?"

I pulled in to the front of the hotel and killed the engine.

"Option one, we go up to the front door, ring the bell, tell Grimes who we are and take Silvia with us back to DC. We have the law on our side, we have very close ties with the Bahamas—"

"You do."

"The USA does. We are not overstepping our jurisdiction because we are not arresting anybody, we are here to help her, and if they kick up a fuss, we allege they are kidnapping her."

"It's nice." She nodded. "Clean, elegant."

"Option two, we watch them, note their movements and plan a snatch."

She shook her head. "Time is too short."

"Option three, we simply wait, watching and follow her back to the States when she leaves."

"No good because it gives Grimes and Jeffries all the time they need to do whatever it is they want to do. Option one is the only viable option."

I nodded. "OK, agreed."

"And it has the advantage that they won't be expecting it."

We entered the lobby and made for the reception desk. Lovelock had told me she had made the reservation for Brown. I conveyed this to the receptionist and he smiled. "Ah, yes, here we have it, Mr. and Mrs. Brown, the honeymoon suite, you have wonderful views of the marina, and we have left a complimentary bottle of champagne in the refrigerator."

"How very kind."

Gallin clung to my arm. "Darling, and I didn't even know we were married! Was it in Vegas, when I blacked out? Tell me the truth."

I ignored her and smiled at the receptionist as he handed me the key, trying to look like he hadn't heard it all before. "We have a couple of bags in the trunk. The Jaguar's out front."

"I'll have the bellhop take them up."

In the elevator I told her, "It's company policy. Two agents in separate rooms, especially when they are young and attractive, like us, it draws attention."

"I'm young. You're not young."

"So I *am* attractive?"

"You're a pain in the ass, is what you are. You get the couch."

We didn't bother to shower or change. When the boy had delivered the cases we went back down, climbed into the F-Type and rolled out under the eternal blue skies and headed west along the Western Road. Though Adelaide was in fact only about two miles away as the crow flies, a lot of western Providence is taken up with forests and parkland. So we had to drive west as far as Clifton Bay and then loop back east through the port of Adelaide, which was a mean, ugly-looking place, and finally entered Adelaide Village along the south coast, with palm trees and sparkling lime-green beaches on our right-hand side.

"I vote we come back after we have delivered Silvia and spend a few days eating lobster and lying on the beach."

She gave me a sly smile but said nothing.

We wound through the village, past the glistening marina populated by gleaming white yachts, wound through lush parkland and, at long last, came to a long, rambling road of beaten earth with green pasture and woodland on the left, and palatial houses on the right, with occasional glimpses of empty, white beaches between one house and another. After a little more than half an hour we came to a large, white wall, about eight to ten feet in height, with a solid steel gate in it. I glanced at my watch. It was closing on six PM. Beyond the gate all you could see were banana trees, and beyond those a couple of palms.

There was an intercom beside the gate. I climbed out and went and pressed the call button. Nothing happened so I pressed again. As Einstein would have predicted, nothing happened again. Gallin climbed out of the car and came and stood next to me. I said, "Now what? It's the one scenario we didn't think about."

"Maybe they're on the beach."

I nodded. "A little farther down there's a track that leads to the sand. Let's go have a look."

Two minutes later we parked the Jag beside the road and walked fifty yards to the vast expanse of white beach. The sea was dark blue about a half mile out, but where it lapped at the shore it was a pale transparent blue, with occasional patches of lime green. There were practically no people. A couple of girls sunbathing and a handful of guys playing ball.

For all the security bin-Nayef had at the back of his house, the front was just a low wall, a gate and a path through a tropical garden to a colonial verandah outside a large, Spanish-style colonial house.

We pushed through the gate, crossed the garden, climbed four steps to the porch and rang on the bell. Einstein would have shrugged and spread his hands and said, "See? I told you!"

I said, "So they are not here and they are not on the beach. Maybe they went into town for lunch, or they went to meet someone. What do we do? Wait for them? Have a swim? Ask a neighbor?"

We looked up and down the long strip of sand and the elegant houses set back among tropical gardens. They didn't look much like the kind of neighbors who spend their time peering through their drapes to see what the Joneses are up to.

"You don't happen to have a Mossad field office in Nassau, do you?"

She looked at me blankly for a moment. "No, we don't get a lot of trouble from the Bahamians. They haven't sworn to wipe us off the face of the Earth recently."

"No, I guess not. Go away and come back later doesn't seem much of a plan."

She looked past my right ear and said, "Is that a neighbor? She's coming this way and staring at us."

I turned and tried to smile the way George Clooney would. Everybody trusts George Clooney's reassuring smile. She was about fifteen paces away at the gate, peering at us. Her voice, when she spoke, said she was from Miami.

"Are you looking for the prince, Abdul?"

Gallin replied. "Actually, we were looking for his guests. He asked us to drop in on them and see how they were, but there is no reply when we ring on the bell."

The woman looked mildly affronted, like she'd been accused of lying. "Well, they're in there. An ugly fat man, two gorgeous dolls, one Caribbean and the other white, and a well-dressed young man. I think he's Mexican, or an A-rab. Arrived yesterday and have kept to themselves, 'cept the A-rab boy went out in Abdul's Bentley this morning. Ain't come back yet. Sometimes he lends his house to people. I ask him not to. Sometimes they're A-rabs, sometimes they're English. I don't mind the English so much, but the A-rabs, you never can tell what they're gonna do. You're not an A-rab, are you?"

"No, I'm not an A-rab."

"I don't like this fat man. I don't know what he's doin' with them two young girls."

I was already walking away. I heard Gallin thank the woman, who called out after her, "You tell him when you see him to stop sendin' them damn A-rabs!"

"I'll tell him!" Gallin called back.

"Too many callers!" said the woman. But it didn't register then, because my mind was on something else.

She caught up with me as I turned off the path to cross the sand toward the car.

"You want to tell me where you're going?"

"We gonna git us an A-rab boy—"

"The person we want is in the house."

"But they won't let us in. Call Nero, get the license plate of Nayef's Bentley, and get him to request a Bolo. They inform *us*, they do not act. A professional courtesy."

She stuck out her hand. "You call him. Gimme the keys. I wanna drive."

"Get your own car."

I climbed behind the wheel and we headed north

toward Adelaide Road, through more banana groves and palms, and then east toward Nassau. The sky was turning grainy and you could feel evening in the air. Gallin called ODIN and put it on speaker. When the Chief came on I told him, "I need a favor from the Nassau PD."

"What favor?"

"First I need to know the license plate of Prince Abdulazziz-bin-Nayef's Bentley, registered to him in Adelaide, Providence Island, Bahamas."

"Wait..."

I waited thirty seconds while he made the request. Then he said, "What else?"

"I need the PD in Nassau to put out a BOLO on that car, to inform us when it is located, and not to intervene."

"That is asking a lot. Too much."

"It's a professional courtesy, sir. We're not going to cause trouble. We will be very discreet. We just need to know where it is. Time is running out and we cannot get to Silvia without it."

He sighed using all four hundred and twenty pounds of him. "All right. I'll see to it."

* * *

They had arrived at the villa at just after four AM and everyone had retired to bed with desultory yawns and good nights. Grimes had stayed downstairs in the living room drinking a nightcap and reading the messages on his phone, while the girls went upstairs. Jamil had locked himself in his room telling himself he could allow himself six hours sleep. He knew that what lay ahead of him would be exhausting, and he needed to be fresh and wide awake when the time came. So he undressed, showered, said his prayers and lay down, feeling God's presence with him, enfolding him and soothing him. He slept deeply through the dawn and early morning, until eleven AM.

He rose as soon as his eyes opened. He checked his watch and was satisfied he had not overslept. He showered, shaved and dressed. Then he pulled the Samsonite case the prince had given him from the wardrobe, dumped his clothes on the bed, slid back the false bottom and extracted the Glock 17, the suppressor and the two magazines. He assembled these, took a towel from his en suite bathroom and draped it over his right arm so that it concealed the weapon.

He was pretty sure that Grimes and the girls would be having what Grimes had called a "lazy morning," and would still be in bed. He was not wrong. He trotted down the sweeping marble staircase to the checkerboard entrance hall and found the house empty. So he made his way to the kitchen at the back. Olga was their cook and he knew she would still be in bed. Again he was right. There in the kitchen he found only Joe, the chauffeur who had collected them from the airport last night. He was making coffee and had a bottle of bourbon on the table. He smiled at Jamil as he entered the kitchen.

"Good morning, Mr. bin-Nayef. You're up early." He glanced at the towel. "You plannin' on takin' a swim? Miss Olga ain't up yet, to make breakfast, but I can..."

He never got to what he could do because Jamil shot him through the head. It was a brief moment, a *phut!* and Joe sagged back in his chair with his eyebrows still raised in surprise. Jamil stepped behind him to the blood-spattered stove and turned off the ring where the coffee pot sat.

DAVID ARCHER

He felt no emotion. He had long ago become used to death and had learnt that if you killed for God, God took the dark emotions from you and gave you peace.

He sprinted back up the stairs, making no noise, and entered the master bedroom. Grimes was at the window looking out at the gently sparkling ocean. He had his cell to his ear. In the bed Olga lay with a pillow over her head. Both were naked and shameless.

Grimes was saying: "I don't bloody care *what* Mr. Biden thinks. Mr. Biden doesn't vote in the bloody UK elections! I want promises I can make to my constituents, and I'd like to be able to deliver on at least one of them. Hang on, I've got another call..."

Jamil killed Olga first, because her sinful flesh disgusted him. He knew she would go to Hell, where she would writhe for eternity among scorching fires, as an infidel whore. Grimes heard the small noise but did not turn immediately. He said into the phone: "Jo, where are you? Good, and I would thank you to come and take this girl off my hands as soon as... Hang on..."

He trailed off because he was staring in astonishment at Jamil. Jamil shot the servant of Shaitan, Grimes, right between his bulging eyes.

That was one future Foreign Secretary who would not order strikes against jihadist heroes.

He left the room and walked down the corridor to Silvia Gordon's door. He opened it and stood looking down at her. She too was asleep. She always looked tired, always looked sad. He felt in his heart that if he'd had time, perhaps he could have shown her a path to God. He allowed himself a moment to look at her golden hair, her very white skin. He thought that he would like to give her a humane, honorable death for a non-believer, and with a

196

sharp blade remove her head. It would be a compassionate thing to do.

He smiled. The great Western giant, so proud of its power and its strength, was always sleeping. He raised the Glock. In that moment perhaps she sensed something, for she opened her eyes and looked deep into his. A small frown twitched her brow. Then she seemed to relax and smile.

He did not understand the smile, and that made him hesitate for a moment. Then he shot her in the head, angered by her smile. She should have been in awe and fear of the horrors that lay ahead for her. He left the room.

From there he ran down to the kitchen again and opened the cellar door. He flipped the switch in the wall and a dull, yellow light came on, painting the white-washed walls with a hint of bronze. He descended the steps into a vast, cavernous area with great arched pillars which threw long, sinuous shadows across the terracotta floor. Against the walls there were shelves, hundreds of shelves, all filled with bottles of wine. Some of the bottles were worth thousands of dollars, the prince had told him, and had forbade him to destroy them.

Each section was labeled, and as he approached the end of the first rack of Bordeaux, he saw the label, Baron Rothschild. There he knelt, removed the bottom shelf and extracted a box. It was about eighteen inches square and twelve inches deep. It was very heavy. He didn't open it, but carried it up the stairs to his room. There he placed it in the false bottom of the Samsonite case, slid the false bottom closed and repacked the suitcase.

Now he took his case out to the garage. He went via the kitchen and collected the keys for the Bentley from the chauffeur's pocket. He placed the suitcase in the trunk and took the car out, down the driveway, flanked by banana trees and palms, out of the big steel gate and out onto the broad road of beaten earth, headed toward Nassau.

CHAPTER NINETEEN

J amil followed Carmichael Road through attractive,
quiet suburbs, under a gentle sun and blue skies. He
was oddly aware of his extremely expensive clothes.
He had the soft top down, the breeze was in his hair and
his shades had cost a man's salary for two months. He
asked God for forgiveness because he felt good. He felt like
smiling. He felt cool.

He wrenched his mind back and forced himself to
focus on the sacred job at hand. He turned the smooth
monster of a car onto Bailou Hill Road and accelerated
effortlessly for three miles until he came to the intersection with Marlborough Street. There he slowed and
turned in to park outside the British Colonial Hilton. The
name made his gut churn with heat and anger. But he dis-
guised it, as Prince Abdulazziz-bin-Nayef had taught him,
by placing on his face a smile: the smile of one who knows
that God walks with him, guiding his hand as he strikes
down each and every one of those who deny Allah.

"I am the sword of God," he told himself as he entered the magnificent marble lobby, with its huge potted
palms and neo-classical art. He approached the desk, as
the prince had shown him, with amiable arrogance and
condescension. "You have a suite for me, the name is bin-

Nayef."

"Ah yes, ocean view. You have luggage, Mr. Nayef? You wish valet parking?"

"Not now. Later. I just wish to see my room. Give me the key, I do not need the bellboy."

"Naturally, as you wish." He handed over the card. "Top floor, the elevators are just here, on the right."

Jamil rode the antique concertina elevator, all dark wood, brass and engraved mirrors, to the top floor, where he walked quickly to his suite. There he let himself in and went immediately to the wardrobe and opened it. There he found a Samsonite case identical to his own. He did not open it. He had been told expressly not to open it. He left the room immediately and returned to the lobby, where, for the sheer devilry of it, he returned to the desk. The concierge gave a small frown when he saw the suitcase. Jamil ignored him.

"I will be expecting some guests for dinner. There will be eleven of them, one of whom will be my cousin, Prince Abdulazziz-bin-Nayef. Please reserve me a table. We will have oysters..."

"Shall I get the *maître* for you, sir?"

"I have no time. Make a note. Oysters, I want them in dishes, three large bowls along the table so that we can help ourselves, champagne, the best you have, six bottles, then a small leg of spring lamb for each guest, with couscous..." He thought back to the wine he had had with the prince in London. "Château Margaux, 2016 was good. We'll need six bottles, I think, the *premier grand cru*, obviously."

"Of course, sir. At what time shall we be dining?"

"Cocktails from seven thirty for dinner at eight. Open the wine at seven so that it gets a good two hours before we drink it."

"Naturally."

Jamil smiled to himself as he trotted down the steps. He had taken all the attention away from the suitcase. All they would be thinking about now was securing the oysters and the spring lamb, and the six thousand dollars' worth of wine which they were going to be opening, and that would never get drunk.

He placed the case in the trunk of the Bentley, beside the other one, climbed in and made his way at a sedate pace toward Lynden Pindling International Airport. He arrived at shortly after one, parked the Bentley in the VIP parking lot and carried his cases to the private departure desk in the VIP lounge. There he showed his papers and was informed by the clerk that the jet had been made ready.

"You have submitted your flight plan...um...Quebec in Canada?" Jamil nodded. "Will you require a pilot, sir? I note you have not requested one."

"I'll be flying it myself."

"Very good, sir."

A sudden stab of panic twisted his gut, flooding it with adrenaline. Fear momentarily distorted his mind and he wanted to cry out and run, back away from the madness that was enfolding him, escape from the killing and the cruelty. But he called on Allah, "*Allahu akbar,*" whispering the sacred name to himself, and God brought him peace again.

He noticed the clerk watching him curiously. "Are you all right, sir?"

"Yes, I am fine."

"We can easily arrange a pilot for you if you don't

feel well."

"No." His voice was firm. "I will fly it myself. Please ensure that the cases are stowed on the plane, within the cabin. When will I be clear for takeoff?"

He checked his computer screen. "Oh, I think not more than three-quarters of an hour, Mr. Nayef."

"Good, I will have coffee."

He went and poured himself a cup of strong, black brew. He had not eaten since the night before and he was hungry. But he had decided to fast as a penance, as a sacrifice to Allah for the pleasure he had taken in the charade, in the alcohol, the women and the decadent Western luxury. He had allowed his pride and his greed to overcome him. Now he would fast as a token of his penance to the One True God, Allah.

He drank the coffee, went to the lavatory and splashed his face with cold water, and returned to the lounge where the clerk led him to a private gate, and a pretty, black stewardess led him across the tarmac to the prince's Gulfstream G650ER.

"Here you are, sir. Is there anything else I can do for you before your departure?"

He stared at her. Noted her eyes, huge and dark. *Nubian,* he thought. She should be in a burka, sacred and exclusive to her man. She could be saved.

"You are beautiful," he said. "You are a good girl, I can tell you have the light of God in your eyes. You should repent..." He gestured with his hands at her hair. "Cover your hair. Ask for God's forgiveness and serve Him."

The woman's face changed. She arched her eyebrow and smiled, ridiculing him. "Excuse me?" She turned to go. "You have a nice flight, sir."

This was the curse of humanity. This right here was the work of Shaitan: the hubris, the arrogance. Had he not given her the word of God? Had he not cast light on the path, for her to follow?

He found himself reaching for his pistol. He remembered he had not been able to bring it into the airport. It was in the Bentley. He thought about going to get it and shooting all the whores in the airport, *Allahu akbar!* But as he uttered the name peace came to him again, and God illumined his path. It was not for him to punish these people. Allah was great, He would punish each one for eternity, forcing them to drink boiling, scalding water, while the angels watched and laughed. His path was to fly, like an eagle, north to Quebec. To the land of ice and snow. He turned and climbed aboard the luxurious private jet.

* * *

Despite Grimes's demand that she come and take Silvia off his hands, Jo had preferred to be wise and take things easy. Aside from the rude way he had hung up on her, she had been unsettled by the ODIN agent, and particularly by the Mossad agent, whom she knew to be the daughter of the permanent field office chief in London. If she was involved, it meant the Mossad were very interested, and that was not good.

So she took the morning to try and get over her jet lag, and thought very carefully about every angle of the case. Three times she thought about calling Rudy, and three times she decided against it.

Finally, shortly before lunchtime, she climbed in her rental car and headed over to Adelaide. She reached the villa where Grimes and his small retinue were staying shortly before two. Spent ten minutes ringing the intercom at the big, steel gate, and then made her way round to the beach and spent a while on the verandah, ringing the bell and peering through the window. Grimes's phone brought her no joy either.

"They're in."

Jo turned and saw a woman at the dividing fence. She had been mature a good ten years earlier. Now she looked as though too much sunbathing had sapped all the goodness out of her. She was holding a folding chair and a paperback, and a colorful Hessian basket with a towel, sunblock and a bottle that might have been tequila.

"They appear not to be." Jo smiled.

"There's a fat man and two girls. And a young man in a suit."

"You don't know where they've gone, by any chance?"

"They ain't gone nowhere. I'm tellin' ya they're in there. The boy in the suit went out this mornin', but the fat man's in there with the two girls. You a friend of the A-rab prince, Abdulah?"

Jo lied without hesitation. "Yes, we went to school together."

"Well you tell him I don't like the people he sends here. That fat man shouldn't be in there with them girls, not openin' the door like that."

"Quite right."

"What they doin' up there?"

"Nothing Mummy would approve of," Jo answered absently, frowning up at the second-floor windows. The woman cackled and went on her way to the beach. Jo waited till she was out of sight and slipped a skeleton key in the latch. After a couple of seconds it clicked and the door swung open. She stood frozen for a second waiting for the alarm. It had been a risk, but as far as Miss Marple's horrid colonial cousin was concerned, only the secretary had left. The rest of them were inside, either sleeping off their jet lag, or last night's elbow-bending session. So it was unlikely the alarm would be armed.

It wasn't. She stepped inside, closed the door and listened.

The ground floor showed her nothing, except Grimes's cognac glass from the night before. So she made her way up the stairs. The door to the master bedroom was slightly ajar and, with her sleeve pulled over her fingers, she nudged it all the way. There was an exotic beauty lying dead in the bed, and over by the window, sitting obscenely on the floor in a toweling dressing gown, was Grimes, gaping at the floor with his cell on the floor beside him. She stooped and picked up his phone.

"Shadow Foreign Secretary found dead in Prince Abdulazziz-bin-Nayef's villa in the Bahamas," she muttered to herself. The government were going to be laughing all the way to the next elections after that headline. "What the hell was he doing here anyway?" she asked herself, but got no reply. Then she frowned and there was a shadow of grief on her face. "Oh, no..." she said quietly, and went down the passage to where another bedroom door also stood slightly open. "Oh, no..." she said again and pushed through the door.

She walked to the bed and sat beside Silvia. Her eyes were closed and she looked peaceful. The pillow under her head was sodden with recent blood, but the hole in her forehead was only small, like a caste mark. She stroked her hair and her cheek.

"Poor child."

She was innocent of anything more serious than loving a climate nerd. But she had paid for that with her life. Jo wasn't aware that she was crying until a tear touched the corner of her mouth. Then she wiped it away with her knuckle and stood. She made a rapid, efficient search of the room and found Silvia's two rucksacks stuffed with papers, drives and USB pens. She sighed, said, "Bingo," with not much enthusiasm and descended the stairs to the front door, taking care not to touch anything.

She wiped her prints from the lock and made her way quickly to the back of the house, where she slung the rucksacks in the trunk, got in her car and started back toward Nassau. On the way she called the Circus and was put through to her boss.

"We have an almighty cockup on our hands."

Her boss sounded peevish. "You're supposed to avoid problems, not create them. What's gone wrong?"

"Grimes is dead."

"Oh, shit! Did you kill him?"

"Don't be ridiculous, sir. I have just found the body. But it's worse than that."

"Worse? How can it be worse?"

"He's in Prince Abdulazziz-bin-Nayef's villa, in his bedroom with a naked woman in his bed. She is also dead."

"Oh, for Christ's sake! What is wrong with these people?"

"I hope you're sitting down, because there's more."

"*More?*"

"In the next bedroom down the hall, was Silvia

Gordon..."

"Oh, hell! Don't tell me she was dead too!"

"She is also dead. They were all executed. Single shot through the head."

"Well, what the hell was *she* doing there?"

She took a deep breath and carefully sidestepped her own involvement. "Grimes was a friend of Professor van Dreiver's. When he heard Grimes was going to the Bahamas he asked him to bring the girl with him and he would collect her at Miami or Fort Lauderdale."

"Jesus aitch Christ! Who has done this, Jeffries? And why, for goodness's sake?"

"It looks as though it might have been Grimes's private secretary. I warned you to look into Grimes's connection with Prince Abdulazziz-bin-Nayef. This new secretary was a young Arab he had just employed in the last few days. Remember I told you bin-Nayef had asked for a favor?"

"Oh, bloody hell, that's all we bloody need. More racial tension with the Muslims! What are you going to do?"

"Go home. I was never here."

"Good. Yes, that's good. All right."

"But sir, I think perhaps I should have a word with that American, and the Mossad operative."

"Aila Gallin..." He said the name as though he was savoring it and wasn't sure if he liked it. "She's Old Man Woolf's daughter."

"I know, sir. She seems to be cooperating with ODIN. You recall she came to see me..."

"I know, I know. Did you find Magnusson's notes or his report?"

She didn't hesitate for a moment. "No, sir. I haven't

found anything."

"God damn it!" and then, after a moment, "All right. Tell them we found the body and that it seems to have been the secretary, don't tell them anything else."

She hung up and as she turned onto Carmichael Road, she said aloud to her phone, sitting in the cradle on her dash, "Rudy!"

The phone answered, "Calling Ruud van Dreiver."

It rang twice and a deep voice said, "Jo, how's it going?"

"I have it. At least, I am pretty sure I have it."

"That's good. Good work."

"I'm going to examine it in my room at the hotel, and in the morning I'll take it back to London with me."

There was a long silence on the other end. Jo smiled to herself.

"That would be a mistake."

"Oh, Rudy, you have more trouble on your hands right now than you would know what to do with. You don't want to add the murder of a British intelligence officer to your troubles, believe me."

"What do you know that I don't?"

"Quite a lot, actually. But quite aside from the growing string of murders that seem to be attaching themselves to the van Dreiver Report, there is also the fact that I suddenly seem to have come over all patriotic, and I think this information could be of great interest to my new, independent, global Britain."

"I know a cure for that."

"I know several. What did you have in mind?"

"How about a six-figure transfer to a numbered account in the Bahamas?"

"The Bahamas is good, but the banks here do dance a little to the American tune. Make it Belize, make those six figures zeros and tack a couple of units on the front, then we'll be talking business."

"Patriotic, huh?"

"I have good friends in Moscow and Beijing if you're not interested."

"I'll get back to you in an hour."

CHAPTER TWENTY

When I got the call dusk was closing in and I was standing at the airport staring at a Bentley Continental GT V8, wishing I could afford one. Gallin was smiling at it like she wanted it to take her home.

"Jeremy Clarkson described it as Led Zeppelin at fifty-thousand watts with the volume turned to zero."

I answered the phone while saying, "Who's Jeremy Clarkson? Mason."

Jo Jeffries' agreeable voice said, "It's not the strangest greeting I've ever had, but it's in the top twenty percent."

"Joanna Jeffries. What can I do for you?"

"It's more a case of what I can do for you, Mr. Mason. Am I right in supposing you came to Nassau anyway?"

"I figure we were on the flight just ahead of yours."

"What makes you think I am in Nassau, Mr. Mason?"

"You said 'came'—'Am I right in supposing you *came* to Nassau anyway?' Jet lag will do that to you."

She gave a small laugh. "Fair enough. I wonder if we could talk?"

"Sure, where are you?"

"At the Hilton. We'll be there in…" I glanced over at Gallin, who was staring at me like she had nothing else in the world to do. She shrugged. "Twenty minutes, half an hour."

"Twenty minutes to half an hour. What's it about?"

"Grimes has been murdered."

I scowled at the Bentley. "What about…?"

"We'll talk when you get here. I have what you're looking for. I'll meet you in the bar."

The line went dead. Gallin was frowning. "What is it?"

My mind was racing, making impossible connections. There was a police sergeant approaching across the parking lot. I turned to look at him. He was holding some papers and didn't look happy.

"Mr. Mason, this situation is very irregular. I should not give you this information but my superiors have prevailed upon me…"

The look on my face made him stop. I growled, "Where did his flight manifest say he was going?"

"Quebec, but I must insist…"

I held up my phone and pointed to it. "I just got a tip-off. There are three people lying dead in Prince Abdulazziz-bin-Nayef's villa on Adelaide beach. And one of them is the British Shadow Foreign Minister. Now you'd better alert your superiors and get out of my face." I turned to Gallin. "Let's go."

He was still staring at me as I climbed in the Jag. I snarled, "Go!" and he ran back toward his office.

The tires complained bitterly as I pulled out of the parking lot and let the big V8 surge onto the John F. Kennedy Drive. We hurtled along the seafront, with the evening glistening on the transparent ocean on our left, and lapping at the pristine white beaches. Gallin was not looking at the beaches, though, or the towering palms that rose from them. She was staring, unseeing, at the road ahead as we growled along the fast lane, weaving among the slower traffic, as one by one the lights started to come on.

"The A-rab, well-dressed personal secretary killed all of them, took the Bentley and is flying to Quebec."

I nodded once but said nothing.

"It's ugly," she said. "I don't understand it and it is ugly."

"He's not going to Quebec," I said.

She turned quickly and frowned. "The flight manifest..."

"I know what the flight manifest said. But he's not going to Quebec."

"How do you know?"

I braked hard as we turned into Marlborough Street and pulled into the hotel forecourt. We climbed out of the Jag, pushed into the lobby and made our way quickly to the cocktail bar. Jeffries was sitting in the corner with a large palm on one side, a window overlooking the pool and the beach on the other and a gin and tonic in front of her. We crossed the room and sat. A waiter approached.

"Whiskey, straight up, and a vodka martini." When he'd gone I said to Jeffries, "You have what I want?"

She nodded. "I went to bin-Nayef's villa earlier today. Nobody answered the door, but their neighbor insisted they were all in there, except for Jamil, Grimes's new personal secretary. So I let myself in and had a look around. Grimes was dead in his room, along with Olga his cook, who saw to other general duties too. Silvia was also dead, in her room. They had all three been shot with a single round through the head at short range."

"You said you were friends with Grimes; what do you know about this new personal secretary?" I asked.

"Not a lot, except that bin-Nayef asked Grimes, as a favor, to take this boy on. It looks very much now as though he was planted to assassinate him. His name seems to be Jamil bin-Nayef."

Gallin shook her head. "That doesn't make sense. He was notoriously pro-Arab and anti-Semitic. Why would bin-Nayef want to kill him? He would be an ally for them in the British government."

Jeffries nodded. "I know, it doesn't make much sense, I agree."

I asked, "What about the girl, Silvia? Why was she here?"

She took a deep breath and sighed. "That's down to me. I asked Toby to bring her with him. I was to join them. I was in the process of gaining Silvia's confidence, to try and persuade her to hand over Bob's files and tell me where the report was."

I held up a hand to stop her. "Wait, questions, in the first place, what interest has MI6 got in Magnusson's report?"

"None, and we would have opposed any attempt to exploit the reserves under Greenland. But it fell in with another investigation we were carrying out."

"OK. We'll come back to that. Meantime, what the hell has Jamil bin-Nayef got to do with Magnusson's report?"

"Again, nothing as far as we are aware. He killed the three of them, left all of Silvia's notes where they were, didn't even search her room. It seems he simply took the Bentley and left."

We were silent for a moment. I sighed and shook my head.

"So he was using Grimes the same way you were."

Gallin muttered, "Jesus!" and slumped back in her seat. Jeffries frowned. "What are you talking about?"

"You used Grimes to get Silvia out of the UK without anyone noticing her, as one of his entourage. Prince Abdulazziz-bin-Nayef did exactly the same thing. He wanted to get Jamil to wherever he is going undetected. Getting him as far as the UK was comparatively easy. But getting him out of the UK might have proved harder. So they slipped him in among Grimes's entourage."

"Dear God..."

"And that tells us something else." Gallin knew what I was going to say. So did Jeffries.

"If they have taken that much trouble, to blackmail Grimes and set Jamil up as a private secretary, it means this was the final leg of his journey, and it was essential he make it. They were not taking any risks."

Gallin was watching me. Now she asked, "Where the hell is he going? What's in Quebec that would interest al-Qaeda?"

I didn't answer. I turned to Jeffries. "Why the change of heart? Why are you telling us all this?"

"Because I am about to arrange a meeting, and I think perhaps you should be there."

"What meeting?"

"A meeting with three men: Ruud van Dreiver,

Danny Bludd and Tony Gorr. Those three men have been riding the crest of a wave their whole lives. They were born to privilege, were raised among privilege, and their whole professional existence has been based on the exploitation of vulnerable and defenseless people, from the rainforests of South America to the poppy fields of Afghanistan and the sweatshops of India. I am not a goody two-shoes, but men and women like that make me sick. The FBI knows, the CIA knows, you in ODIN know and we know, these men have murdered, stolen, defrauded and extorted their way into Forbes One Hundred. They have subcontracted to companies that use slaves and children, they have poisoned villages with chemical waste—" She threw up her hands in despair at the sheer number of their crimes. "The list of their crimes goes on and on, but they are untouchable. They are above the law. They are too rich, too powerful and too clever. We have been monitoring them for a long time, but we have never had a clear shot."

Gallin asked, "Is that why you became van Dreiver's friend?"

"He was the brain, the lynchpin. Several years ago I used Grimes as a way to get close to him. We became friends and I made a point of being useful for him, facilitating things for him in exchange for money, so I could gain his trust. And just the other day we had our first big break. When Bob Magnusson was killed and Silvia called van Dreiver. I knew if I could get hold of that report, or the data or his files even, I would be able to lure the three of them into a trap. I have told van Dreiver I might sell the data to Moscow or Beijing if he won't play ball. So now I have to arrange a meeting, here, in Nassau. It would be good if you were there, present but not seen."

Gallin said, "What are you thinking?"

"The meeting is in my hotel room. I have time to install bugs and a video camera. You could be in the room next door, recording. I make them the offer and get them to incriminate themselves. When they take the bait, you make your entrance."

Again Gallin answered. "It's pretty slapdash."

Jeffries smiled. "Well, I'm making it up as I go along. The situation is fluid, to say the least, and changing from moment to moment. I think we have a real chance to nail these bustards, but I need your help."

Gallin shrugged, then nodded. "Yeah, I'll play."

I sighed and drained my glass. "I wish you luck, and I'd love to help, but I can't."

Gallin scowled at me. "What do you mean, you can't? Why not?"

"Because I have to go after Jamil."

"To Quebec? You don't even know if he's going to Quebec. He could be going anywhere!"

"I think I know where he's going."

"Where?"

I shook my head and smiled at Jeffries. "You're very believable and very convincing, Joanna, but I don't know what to make of you. For a woman who was not connected in any way with this case, in the end it turned out you were all over it like a rash. And I think you might be just about the best liar I ever met."

"Forgive me if I don't take that as a compliment."

I turned to Gallin. "Stay with her. Take down the Terrible Trio. Watch her. Maybe she's on the level, maybe she ain't."

Gallin arched an exquisite eyebrow at me. "Who

named you head honcho?"

"Just humor me this once. I am going to go get Jamil. Believe me, you'll be glad I did."

"*Where* are you going to get Jamil?"

I shrugged. "Quebec."

She frowned at me like I was crazy. "But…"

I interrupted her. "Think about it! The whole thing was geared up for this."

She blinked a couple of times, but other than that showed no expression. I stood. "I'll be in touch."

As I turned to go, Gallin said, "Mason?" I stopped and looked back. "You're an asshole."

I smiled. "I love you too, baby."

* * *

I took the Jag and sent Gallin a message to get a cab and collect the car at the airport. On the way I called the Chief and after the usual voice recognition palaver Lovelock put me through.

"What?"

"I can't explain so don't waste your time asking. Here's the thing. I need to charter a fast jet with a three-thousand-mile range."

"You will bankrupt us with your madness, Mason," he said, without much feeling.

"Sir, I saw on the Conspiracy dot Com website that we have a budget of one point seven trillion dollars. So don't give me that baloney."

"Don't be impertinent, Mason!"

"Fine. But can I have the jet?"

"What, in the name of all that is holy, do you need it for?" he asked with somewhat more feeling. "A jet, no less!"

"If I told you it was to ship Russian caviar to DC, would you say yes?"

There was a prolonged silence, then, quietly, "*Is* it?"

"No, but listen..."

And then I told him what it *was* for.

I got to the airport, went to the private, VIP charter office. A very pretty girl in a blue uniform told me there was nothing for me.

"Can you check again? I spoke to the party ten minutes ago. There definitely should be a plane for me."

She gave me a kindly smile and tilted her head on one side. "It'll take more than ten minutes, sir. Perhaps you'd like some coffee while you wait?"

She made it sound like she was offering me a back rub and a strong martini. It was hard to say no.

Another ten minutes passed, and each one of them seemed like a lifetime. The phone rang and the pretty girl answered it. She listened quietly, said, "OK," a couple of times and finally hung up.

"Mr. Mason?"

I was already on my feet. "Yup?"

"We have a Cessna Citation Longitude, it's a popular plane with a good range of about three thousand five hundred nautical miles..."

I cut her monologue short. "That'll do fine. Is it fueled up?"

"It certainly is..."

"The flight manifest..." I started to say, but she frowned and interrupted me.

"I understand it has already been submitted, Mr. Mason."

Nothing cuts through red tape like privilege. I smiled, showed her my documents, and ran across the dark tarmac, where dim amber lay in dull reflections under the translucent evening sky. I sprinted up the stairs and ten minutes later I was hurtling along the runway. The bird gave a small jump and then I was rising above the island, soaring above the starlit ocean, plunging into the darkness of the sky. He had a couple of hours head start, and I didn't know precisely where he was going.

After twenty minutes I got a call from ODIN.

"Mason?"

"Speaking."

"This is Lieutenant Peter Jones speaking. I was asked to talk to Canadian Air Traffic Control about the Gulfstream G280 piloted by Mr. Jamil bin-Nayef…"

I cut him short. "Sure, what have you got?"

"He filed a flight plan for Quebec, in Canada,"

"Yup. Did he land there?"

"No, sir. He came in slightly off course, over the sea just south of the Bay of Fundy. He radioed in to advise he was approaching land." He paused and gave a small, nerdish laugh. "Which is a little early really. You'd expect that at about a hundred miles."

"You would. So what happened next, Lieutenant?"

"Well, again, very odd, he then apparently dropped to below a thousand feet and disappeared from the radar."

The US is pretty much covered end to end by radar. You might be able to mask a small plane by brushing the treetops. Ocean waves, on the other hand, would offer good camouflage as RF reflection off of the waves can cause strong clutter returns. That would account for his approach over the ocean rather than over New York and

Vermont. But if he wanted to continue undetected, he was either going to have to risk flying over Nova Scotia and Newfoundland, or skirt around them flying low over the North Atlantic, adding about four hundred miles to his trajectory. They had been so careful up till now, my money was on the latter. Which meant I had the chance now to close the gap and shave off maybe an hour of the start he had over me.

"Roger that." I said. "Thanks for your help, Lieutenant."

After that I observed radio silence and set a course slightly north of northeast.

CHAPTER TWENTY-ONE

Jo Jeffries was not surprised to see that Rudy, Danny and Tony did not arrive alone. There were three other men in suits, each one the size and consistency of a concrete pile. Jo greeted Ruud with a kiss on the cheek, shook hands with Danny and Tony and ignored the three bodyguards, who took up positions by the door, the balcony and the window. Jeffries gestured her guests toward the sofa and the chairs which were set around a coffee table in the middle of the floor. As they sat she moved to the fridge in the small kitchen of her suite.

"Drinks?"

Rudy answered. "Yeah, we'll all have Scotch. You know what, Jo? We'd like to get down to business before we relax."

She hesitated a moment. "Sure, Rudy." She grabbed a bottle of single malt, a bowl of ice and four tumblers, and carried them to the table. As she sat, Rudy said, "Have you got the papers? We'd like to see them."

Jo laughed. "I am sure you would, Rudy, but it's not that simple, I am not that stupid, and what's more, you know it. Why don't we cut the fencing and get to the point where we actually make some progress. Let's start with the questions: how much are you offering, and for what, exactly?"

"What have you got, exactly?"

Jeffries was able to answer with some confidence, because ODIN had forwarded a preliminary forensics report from the Danish police, detailing what they had found on Bob's hard drive.

"I have the final draft of Dr. Magnusson's report, I have all of his notes, which Silvia Gordon took before fleeing Greenland, and I have all the data from his sensor array, which he gathered minutes before he was killed."

Van Dreiver remained impassive. Tony Gorr cleared his throat and crossed one leg over the other. Danny Bludd shifted his ass and his padded shoulders rose up near his ears. Jo Jeffries thought, *Gotcha!*

Van Dreiver asked, "What about the actual report?"

She shook her head. "No such thing, and you know it. The report was derailed because he had made other discoveries. The report was put on hold while he pursued this other research. And it is that other research that you are interested in. Keep fencing with me and this meeting is over."

Van Dreiver smiled. "Don't be silly, Joanna. You know you can't do that."

She threw back her head and laughed. "Dear Rudy. Do you know how many years I have been in intelligence? Fifteen years. And in that time I have had to deal with much more dangerous men than you three clowns. Don't think I haven't taken out insurance." She glanced at her watch. "This meeting ends in one hour at the latest. At that time you leave here with Magnusson's papers and I leave here a very rich woman. But if by then I have not made a call for those papers to be delivered, my partner will go directly to the Chinese Embassy. Now, do you still feel like playing hardball?"

"How much do you want?"

"For what, exactly?"

It was Danny who answered, leaning forward in his chair.

"Come on! You're the one who wanted to stop fencing! All of it! The rough draft, the data from the sensors...!"

Jeffries gave a small laugh and raised a hand. She deliberately uttered the words she knew would rile the little man. "Just stay calm, Danny. Let's be clear. Part of these papers are technically Rudy's. They belong to the Presidential Commission. You could sue me for them if you wanted to. But others are not strictly part of the report. You are not entitled to them. So, what is it you want?"

Tony Gorr growled, "What are you playing at, Jeffries? We want all of it. What's your price?"

"One hundred million, pounds sterling."

Danny expostulated. "You have got to be kidding!"

Jeffries smiled. "OK, thank you for coming, gentlemen. I'm sorry you wasted your time."

The man at the door stepped forward. Van Dreiver lifted his hand. "Wait! Shut up, Bludd. Don't talk. Understood?"

Bludd gaped at him. "*One hundred million pounds sterling?*"

"I said shut up." He studied Jeffries for a moment. "What about the volcano?"

"What about it? That's the information you're paying for. If I tell you, you don't need the report."

He sighed. "Is it worth it?" There was something

dangerous in Van Dreiver's eyes. "If I spend a hundred and forty million dollars on this and find it's junk..."

He let the words hang. Jeffries felt a twist of a thrill in her gut. She raised an eyebrow. "What, Rudy? You'll smack me on the wrist?"

There was a tense silence. Rudy repeated, "Is it worth it?"

"Yes, Rudy, I think it's worth it. But if you get your grubby hands on it and it doesn't say what you want it to say, don't come running to me."

Danny's face had been turning ever deeper shades of red. Now he burst. "Don't you try and screw us, sister!" He pointed a trembling finger at her. "You are playing with the big boys now. This is the big league. You *do not* want to mess with us!"

Her eyes were rich with ridicule and she threw back her head and laughed. "Rudy, where did you find this little man?"

Rudy tried to talk over her. "Just shut up, Danny. I told you not to talk!"

"Shut up yourself, Rudy! We need that damned report and this bitch is going to shaft us!"

Tony could see the chaos setting in, and he was studying Jeffries carefully. Too carefully, she thought. She addressed herself to Danny, and her voice was a scalpel that sliced cruelly through his balls.

"Look here, Danny, perhaps in small-town America you can get what you want by hurling around empty threats. To me you are just a very small man in an oversized, badly cut suit. Never make a threat you can't follow through on. I have seen bigger, more dangerous men than you brought to their knees because, like you, they couldn't follow through."

He got to his feet. Jeffries smirked. He flushed. "You think I can't follow through, you stupid bitch?"

Van Dreiver and Gorr both shouted at him to sit down, but it was too late.

"*You think I can't follow through?* You know who Bernard Monet was?"

Gorr's face turned suddenly puce. Van Dreiver looked away. Jeffries frowned. "Dr. Roberts' assistant? Of course I know who he is. Rudy? What is your little man talking about?"

Van Dreiver flared at her. "Just cut it out, Joanna!"

But Bludd was shouting over him, "*Call him! Call him and his wife in Nuuk! Ask how they are, you stupid bitch! You think I won't follow through! Just try me! Just try me!*"

The big bruiser by the door stepped forward, put his hand on Danny's shoulder and rumbled, "Sit down, Mr. Bludd."

Danny straightened his jacket and sat.

Joanna was looking both serious and very worried. "Are you telling me that you had Bernard Monet and his wife murdered? That was you?"

The implication for the three men was tantalizing. For once Bludd's lack of self-control might have paid off. Maybe, just maybe, he had scared her into compliance. It was Bludd, once again, who replied. "Yes! So you'd better watch your damn step!"

She cleared her throat and poured herself a shot of Scotch. She frowned with the glass halfway to her mouth, and paused.

"Did you kill Magnusson?"

It was Gorr who answered this time. "No. Why the hell would we kill him? We wanted his report." He turned and grinned at van Dreiver. "We might have killed him *after* he'd given us the report, but not before."

Ruud van Dreiver closed his eyes and sighed. When he opened them the threat of death was palpable. "There is more at stake here than you imagine, Joanna. I like you and I value your friendship, but don't overplay your hand. We need those papers. We need to know the status of that volcano, and it is imperative that the data does not get into the hands of the Russians or the Chinese. You want a hundred million sterling. Fine, you shall have it. But you have to stop playing hardball and you have to show us the data and the first draft."

She nodded, like a worried, chastened woman.

"OK," she said, "but I need you to clarify something for me."

He sighed. "Make it short and sweet, Joanna. I haven't got time to waste."

"I've looked at the papers, not in depth, I haven't had time, but enough to see that sustained drilling through the ice could cause the catastrophic collapse of the ice. The consequences for London, Brussels, New York would be beyond catastrophic, and the knock-on effect for the world economy would be unimaginable. How can you just go ahead and do this, knowing what the consequences will be?"

The three of them stared at her impassively. Eventually van Dreiver leaned forward, with his elbows on his knees, and stared down at his cupped hands.

"You're not entitled to this, Joanna, but in deference to our old friendship," he gave a small laugh, "and the fact that you will probably soon be one of the club, I'll tell you this much. There is Us and there is Them. It has always been Us and Them. Would this unimaginable catastrophic event be worse than the First World War? Twenty million people died in that conflict, and the entire infrastructure of Europe was torn down and destroyed."

He shrugged and shook his head. "What about the Second World War? Is it more unimaginable than that? The demented, obsessive drive to annihilate an entire race of people, the madness driving an entire nation to assert its racial superiority over the whole world, the Third Reich's flirtation with the dark arts, the seventy to eighty million deaths, about three percent of the world's population. Is it more unimaginable than that? But you know what, Joanna? After every one of these unimaginable events, the world grows, technology improves, quality of life improves, medicine improves, societies improve."

She stared into his face and saw that he was deadly serious.

She said, "You are talking about human beings, Rudy. About children, families, people."

He nodded. "Human suffering, I know. But we are all going to die, Joanna, each and every one of us. There is nothing remarkable about death. It is alarmingly banal. What is at stake here is not your life or mine, it is the survival of the planet's ecosystem. And if you don't know what is the biggest threat faced by our ecosystem today, then I am not going to tell you. The bottom line is, we will go after that gas and that oil, and if the Greenland ice sheet has a partial catastrophic collapse, then that will bring with it an abundance of opportunities, just like the Great Depression, the two World Wars, Covid and so many other challenges we have faced in the past as a species."

Bludd laughed suddenly. "There are about seven billion too many people anyhow!"

He laughed some more and Gorr laughed with him, but more quietly. Van Dreiver said, "OK, Joanna, my patience is all used up. Let me have the papers."

Jeffries shook her head. "I have one last question, and this relates to my own, personal security, so I need it answered. What has Prince Abdulazziz-bin-Nayef got to do with all this?"

They all stared at each other.

Van Dreiver shook his head and she could see he was getting mad. "Cut it out, Joanna. I'm beginning to think you haven't got the damned papers. Maybe you need a bit of persuading."

"Take it easy, Rudy."

"Take it easy? Seems to me the only time we got some sense out of you was when Danny let rip. Are you going to give us the papers or not?"

She scowled at him. "What are you saying, Rudy? Are you threatening an officer of the British Government?"

He stood. "You know what, boys? I think it's getting stuffy in here. I think we should step out on the balcony and get some air. What do you say, Joanna? You want to have a good look at the view of the Bahamas from your balcony?"

Joanna spoke quietly and carefully. "Rudy, get a grip. You would not seriously throw me off the balcony."

"I am going to count to three, and either I see those papers or I get my boys here to upend your pretty ass over the railing! I *am not kidding!*"

Jeffries picked up her phone and pressed a number. She said, "OK, you can bring it in."

A moment later there was a knock at the door. The

gorilla who had told Danny Bludd to sit down glanced at his boss. Van Dreiver nodded and the ape opened the door. Gallin had both hands held behind her back. She smiled up at his huge simian face and smashed her right instep into his balls. As he doubled up she shoved him stumbling back and brought the Sig Sauer P226 TacOps with laser targeting and suppressor up in front of her, held in both hands. She didn't flinch. She shot both bodyguards in the head and trained the laser sight on van Dreiver's forehead.

"Go ahead, punk," she said, "make my day."

Suddenly, horrifically, Danny Bludd screamed. He vaulted over his chair and launched himself at Gallin. He clung to her and the two of them stumbled back against the wall. There was a moment of hesitation, then Gorr charged at the two struggling bodies.

Gallin took a step back and to the side, putting Bludd between her and Gorr. Bludd had her left hand holding the Sig stretched up and pointing at the ceiling. Now Gorr collided with Bludd and both of them were grappling at her gun hand.

She lashed out hard and fast and kicked Bludd where she had kicked the bodyguard. Without pause, as he doubled up, her foot touched the floor for a fraction of a second, she twisted and smashed the heel of her right boot into his knee. He collapsed into the fetal position and she was face to face with Gorr, both his arms forming a frame for his face as he grappled with her left hand. She slammed the heel of her hand into the tip of his jaw, his eyes rolled up into his head and he collapsed on his back. She shot them both in the head and looked at van Dreiver. "You want to have a go, or you want to have a conversation?"

"I'll take the conversation," he said.

She nodded once. "I am going to ask you one more time. What has Prince Abdulazziz-bin-Nayef got to do with this?"

He shook his head and frowned at her and at Jeffries. "Nothing. I don't even know the man."

She swore quietly. "Monet was your man, right?"

Van Dreiver nodded. "He kept an eye on Bob and Thor and supplied us with information which they withheld."

She looked at Jeffries. Jeffries was already on the phone. "We need a laundry service, and we have Ruud van Dreiver in custody. We'd better not tell our American friends until we have him safely in London. It's a bit of an almighty mess, actually." She paused and nodded. "Bludd and Gorr?" She looked down at the two bodies on the floor. "They are just, well, Bludd and Gorr..."

CHAPTER TWENTY-TWO

My cell rang as I was crossing the Greenland coastline just south of Nuuk. It was Gallin.

"Are you where I think you are?"

"Probably."

"You put two and two together and made four, right? You're headed back to Greenland."

"Yeah."

"OK, let me give you what news I have. Ruud van Dreiver is in custody on his way back to the UK. Bludd and Gorr are dead."

"How?"

"I killed them. They attacked me so I shot them. Parasites we got enough in the world."

"OK, it sends a message. What else?"

"The Bahamian police reported to ODIN and Nero relayed it to me to share with you."

"What?"

"The bin-Nayef Villa in Adelaide. The cops broke in and found what Jeffries told us, plus the chauffeur dead in the kitchen. But they found something else. They searched the whole house and found in the cellar one of the wine shelves removed and behind it a cavity in the wall."

"Ah, that's why he had to come here."

"I had a hunch what you were thinking, so I asked if I could bring a Geiger counter along."

"And?"

"And you were right. The cavity and the area around it had high levels of radiation."

"Damn. I could have been wrong this time."

"That would have been good."

Her voice felt suddenly oddly comforting in the dark, flying over the slightly luminous world of ice below. She kept talking.

"I called Nuuk police and talked to your friend Elise."

"Yeah?"

"She said two men were found beheaded in Thor Olafson's apartment. But it wasn't him because he had spent the night at some cat house a few miles away."

"Nothing like a cat for an alibi."

"I asked her to review Bernard Monet's emails and phone records, also his bank accounts. Bob Magnusson was holding back information from van Dreiver and Danny Bludd, preparing a damning report on the corporation's plans, and Bernard Monet was feeding what information he could get to van Dreiver, Bludd and Gorr, but I have a hunch somebody else had approached him for information too."

I nodded, like she could see me. "That was what I thought. Bin-Nayef, moving in the circles he does, got word of the report and of the possibility of a volcano down there. He had somebody approach Monet and when he got confirmation of the volcano, he started making his plans. When you have that kind of money, a few pounds of plutonium is not that hard to get from Russia these days."

She was quiet for a while. Then, "Do you know where it is? Do you know where he's going?"

"I have a pretty good idea."

"Will you get there in time? I'm in the Bahamas right now. Have I got time to get to the Andes?"

"I don't know what to tell you, Gallin. I'm taking shortcuts. I'm going directly to the target. I've never tried a snow landing before. Should be fun."

I heard her puff air through her lips. "You want me to keep talking to you? Maybe you need to focus on what you're doing."

"I think you should probably get on a flight to San Francisco. It's nice talking to you. It helps. But I really don't know how this is going to play out."

A long silence. Then, "OK. Listen, uh, I could lie to you and say stupid stuff like even though you're an asshole, working with you I have, you've kind of, you know I really kind of got to have feelings for you. That mattered. But that would just be to kind of, give you courage and strength. But, I know you're going to pull through this, because you have to. So I am not going to say any of that stupid stuff. You understand what I am saying?"

"Yeah, I love you too, kiddo. I'll see you on the other side. Now get to high ground, will you!"

She didn't hang up, but we flew in silence, without talking, somehow connected.

Eventually my instruments told me I was approaching my target, though there was nothing below to tell me where I was, except flying over ice. The sky was clear above and I dropped to just a few hundred feet, closing in on the coordinates for Bob's sensor array, and the shack on stilts where he had kept them. I slowed, trying to pierce the vast, white wasteland with my eyes and suddenly, as though out of nowhere, the shack appeared, flashed past, and I raised the nose, banked to port and came around in a wide arc, slowing as I went and losing height. I left the undercarriage retracted, raised the nose slightly and smashed, belly-first into the ice. The jolt felt like it had loosened all my bones in my body. The head lashed back and I was thrown hard forward. The Cessna bounced, leapt into the air and smashed down again.

Then she was grinding along the ice. The noise was horrific, like steel being torn by frozen teeth. But the jet slowed, slid sideways and came to a halt. I sat for a few seconds wondering if I had broken my spine. I checked each limb, and everything seemed to be working, if in a state of shock.

My grandmother's voice spoke to me in my head and told me, "No time for shock now. Up you get!"

I undid my seat belt, got carefully to my feet and went to open the emergency hatch. The cold, when I did, was beyond what a person can imagine. I was in a light, cotton suit designed for the Caribbean, and the temperature outside must have been minus twenty-five Fahrenheit. I went to the storage area, found a couple of blankets and wrapped them around me like a cape, then clambered down into the ice and snow. The blankets didn't do much and pretty soon I was shivering uncontrollably and my teeth were chattering so hard I thought they were going to shake my brain loose.

There was no sign of Jamil and I wondered with

sudden despair if I had completely misread the situation, jumped to some crazy conclusion and gone hara-kiri for no good purpose. We all had to die, but this was a real stupid way of dying, especially if it left Jamil on the loose with some kind of radioactive device, who knew where in the northern hemisphere.

I was shivering too hard to swear, and I just kept trudging through the snow, with my feet growing steadily numb, toward where I knew the moulin was. It was just a hunch, and I had gambled so much on a hunch, but there was no other way of reading the clues. It had to be here.

That was when I saw the light up ahead. It was like the headlamps of a car, or more like a large motorbike. I wondered if the cold was making me hallucinate, screwing up the wiring of my brain, making connections between Hell's Angels, Valkyries and dying like a hero in the snow. A hero with frostbitten feet and two blankets wrapped around him. Some hero.

I trudged closer, with my feet turning from numb to painful. I knew I could lose my toes and my numbing brain wondered if Elise and Gallin would still find me attractive. I gave a short laugh. "Who are you kidding?" I asked myself, watching the light grow larger and brighter. "Elise would, because she is a good woman," I told myself. "You should marry a woman like Elise. She doesn't care about appearances or how many toes you got. But Manny Pacquiao would never accept her. It would be an impossible situation."

There was a noise, a rhythmic, persistent noise. But I was lost in the freezing cold, thinking about how I could reconcile my cat with Elise.

"Now, Gallin, that is a different proposition altogether," I told myself. "She would never accept anything less than perfect, and face it, chump, you do not stand a chance with that babe. She is waaaay out of your class."

I didn't know how long I had been walking, maybe ten or fifteen minutes, but the pain in my feet was spreading to my hands and I was finding it increasingly hard to walk. A terrible, compelling sleepiness was overwhelming me and all I wanted to do was lie down, as Bob had done, and think about Elise, Gallin and Manny Pacquiao, all living happily together in my warm, cozy house in DC.

But I couldn't because of the blinding light that was now glaring in my face, and the rhythmic rumble of what I now realized was a diesel engine. Then a huge shadow loomed in front of the glaring light. For a moment I thought it was an alien, with huge black eyes and a featureless face, but then I saw, on the ground behind it, two cases. One was an attaché case which stood open and contained two highly polished cylinders with the nuclear hazard symbol on them. The other was a large, Samsonite case which was also open, and contained a housing for the plutonium, to make a portable, tactical nuclear device.

Suddenly I remembered why I was there. From deep in my memory facts emerged. There were, at a guess, about twenty pounds of plutonium in the case. Two pounds of plutonium could give you a yield of about twenty kilotons, the same as the bomb we dropped on Nagasaki. This would be ten times bigger. Its blast wave would be enough to cause complete destruction in a radius of ten miles. And this man, with the mask and the goggles was going down, a mile under the ice, to place it in the sleeping volcano that lay beneath us.

I stood, hugging my shoulders and trembling, and

tried to shake my head and speak.

"Don't do it," I said, but I don't think he heard me over the sound of his snowmobile. He hesitated for a moment, then unzipped his jacket and reached inside. I knew what he was going to do and I shook my head again, and shouted, "*Don't do it! Don't do it!*"

He pulled out a semiautomatic and pointed it at me. I was acutely aware of my weakness, of my strength draining out of me, and a furious, impotent rage welled up inside me. I saw in my mind the inconceivable impact of that massive explosion, held down by the incalculable weight of the snow, driven down into the crust of the earth, rupturing the dormant volcano, aggravating the growing geothermal activity. I saw the huge eruption in my mind's eye, I saw the rivers of lava eating into the steaming ice, tearing the vast, continent-sized ice sheet apart.

The consequences were unimaginable.

And suddenly I was screaming, stumbling forward, grabbing the cannon of his Glock in my left hand. The gun exploded and heat seared through my freezing finger, but I could not let go. I hadn't the strength to kick or punch. All I could do was push and scream at him, "*No! No! You can't do it!*"

He lost his footing in the ice, slipped and fell, knocking the attaché case with his boot as he went down. The case slid and for the first time I noticed that the ice sloped away from where he had parked the snowmobile. I heard a scream and realized it was Jamil, the man in the goggles, scrabbling away from me over the snow, like he was trying to swim after the attaché case. I grabbed at his foot but he kicked free, and as I got to my feet I saw that we were at the edge of what looked like a crater, and at the center there was a vast, black hole, maybe thirty feet across. The sloping surface, where Jamil was now attempting unsteadily to get to his feet, was slick with meltwater that was draining steadily into the moulin.

He took a couple of careful steps toward the case, where it had come to a stop, near the edge of the moulin. Trembling violently, I picked up the blankets and wrapped them around me. Then I heard an inhuman howl as Jamil threw back his head and cried to the infinite, empty, freezing sky, "*Allahu akbar! Allah! Allah! Allahu akbar!*"

He took another step closer, bent to take a hold of the case and lost his footing. He slipped and fell, grabbed the case in both hands and I watched as they spun together and tumbled over the edge into the blackness, in total silence. I stood staring for a moment that might have been an eternity. Then I picked up the red, Samsonite casing, climbed onto the snowmobile and headed back to the shack on stilts, where I climbed, in increasing pain, up the steps to the shack, to the monitors.

There with numb fingers I managed to punch out the numbers on the radio-phone. It rang a few times, nobody answered, it seemed to switch then and started ringing again, like the call had been forwarded. Then a voice that was far too cheerful said, "God aften, Nuuk Politi."

Through chattering teeth, barely audible, I said, "This is Alex Mason, I need to talk to Elise, Detective Sergeant Elise..."

"Oh, hello, Mr. Mason. No, she is not here. Did you go to Dr. Magnusson array?"

Then I knew I was delirious, hypothermia was setting in and it was just a matter of time before I joined Bob in Valhalla. I laughed. "Yes," I said. "I guess we all end up here sooner or later, huh?"

"Yoh, is true. She will be there soon. Try stay warm, yoh?"

"Yoh," I said, slid down to the floor, wrapped the blankets around me and thought about making peace with my maker. Instead I thought about Manny Pacquiao, and hoped he would find a good human to serve him. Maybe Elise would be OK, I thought, but how would they get him out here? A voice from the back of my mind told me I was killing time. Better to close my eyes, allow the peace to envelop me, and find a path to the light.

I smiled. I could see the light coming to get me, glowing bright in the black glass of the windows. They were here, the Valkyrie, I had died like a hero after all. I just hoped they would find me, up here in the shack.

Then I heard the tramping boots on the steps and smiled again. They knew I was here. I chuckled. I couldn't speak because the shivering and the chattering of my teeth wouldn't let me, but I told myself in my head that from here on in it was going to be mead and ale for me, haunches of beef and singing and wenching around huge fires in the hall of the brave, the hall of the valiant, Valhalla.

Then the door burst open and cruel cold air blasted in. A huge man stood in the doorway looking down at me. I tried to shake my head and say, "No, the Valkyrie are women," but I couldn't make the words come out.

Then there was a woman. There was a woman dressed like an Eskimo. She pushed the man aside and rushed to my side. I smiled. She removed her hood and I saw Elise's face frowning at me.

"Now the Valkyrie have arrived," I said, "I can die

happy."

"You are crazy!" she said, and after that it was darkness.

EPILOGUE

I didn't die, and I didn't go to Valhalla. But two weeks later I did go back to the Bahamas, to the British Colonial Hilton, and I sat on their terrace at lunch overlooking the turquoise swimming pool, the white, white beach and the exquisite green and turquoise ocean beyond. Before me I had a dozen oysters, beside me I had a bucket of ice with a bottle of Mumm in it, and across from me I had Gallin, looking very desirable in a hint of bikini and a transparent robe, and pulling bits off a lobster. She was talking and I was only half listening.

"OK, so I get it. We were confused for a long time because we did not realize that Grimes was being used by two separate groups for a similar thing. Prince Abdulazziz-bin-Nayef wanted to get Jamil to the Bahamas to collect the components of the bomb, and then fly to Greenland. And Ruud van Dreiver wanted to use Grimes to get Silvia out of London and to a quiet place where Jo Jeffries could get Bob's papers and research and hand them over—not to the Presidential Commission, but to van Dreiver, Bludd and Gorr."

I nodded. "Because they realized, from the information Monet had given them, that he was planning to go public with his findings about the volcano, which would forever make drilling for oil and gas impossible."

She frowned. "I would have thought at this stage *nobody* would be prospecting for oil and gas!"

"You'd think so, but as Monet pointed out to me, there are eight billion people on this planet, and the number is growing exponentially. There is as yet no viable alternative to oil and gas. Until we find one, he who has the oil has the power."

She grunted. "So they wanted to suppress the data about the volcano and use the rest to strike a deal with Greenland to drill for oil."

"Pretty much."

I swallowed an oyster and followed up with champagne.

"Meanwhile Prince Abdulazziz-bin-Nayef had heard about the report on the grapevine and had bribed Monet into informing him, too. Oil was his trade and he wanted to know if there was viable oil under Greenland. But when Monet told him about the volcano becoming active because of the increased geothermal activity triggered by the melting ice, he had another idea. The jihadist blow to end all jihadist blows: take out London and New York in one devastating blow, a massive flooding to bring the two cities to their knees, and with the Western economies crippled, step in and make Greenland an offer they can't refuse, so that Saudi once again controls all the oil."

"That was it, two quite separate but interwoven plots."

"So here is what I don't understand. Why did van Dreiver, Bludd and Gorr have Bob killed *before* he had finished the report? They were running around like headless chickens trying to find it. If they had just timed it better, they would have had the report before he died. And, after all, it was Monet who killed him, so he would have known."

I shook my head. "It wasn't Monet who killed him."

She shook her head. "Who, then?"

I drained my glass, refilled hers and then mine.

"We may never be able to prove it. But my reading of the facts is that Bob was naïve. He believed that if people had all the facts, they would do the right thing. He believed, as a lot of people did, that van Dreiver was a reasonable, moderate."

"Huh! Was he ever not!"

"Thor was exactly the opposite. Thor is a cynic from the top of his head to the soles of his feet. He believed that once van Dreiver had the report, Bob and he—Thor—would be cut out, silenced, even murdered, and the report would be sanitized to show that drilling would be a benefit to the Greenland economy and, probably thanks to Green Tomorrows' technology, the natural gas and oil could be rendered almost clean. This, I imagine, was what was going through Thor's mind. I imagine they discussed it at length. In fact from what Elise told me, I know they did. But what Thor could not offer Bob was an alternative. Perhaps what he was advocating was to falsify the report and say the gas and the oil would be too expensive to get at. I don't know because he wouldn't talk to me. What I do know is that he was passionately opposed to handing that report over to van Dreiver and the NATOil Corporation."

She stared at me, with a hunk of lobster halfway to her mouth. "Are you telling me you think Thor Olafson killed his best friend?"

"To try and save Greenland, and much of the North Atlantic, I believe so. Look what he did to the boys Danny Bludd sent after him. He don't mess about."

"Holy crap."

"Have you told your Valkyrie friend?"

"My Valkyrie friend?"

"Yeah, you know, your little cop from Nuuk. Elise."

I nodded. "Mm-hmm."

"What did she say?"

"She said, 'Yoh, I know.'"

"Huh."

"So, Gallin, when I was in the plane, why didn't you hang up?"

"What? Hang up? I did hang up. I know because I took a call from an old boyfriend."

"You're lying."

"I'm not lying. I hung up, I swear to God. Why would I *not* hang up?"

"That's what I am asking you."

And so it went, for the two weeks that we happened to coincide in Nassau, in the British Colonial Hilton, in the Bahamas.

Read on for a sneak peak of Mason's Law (Alex Mason book 3), or buy your copy now:
davidarcherbooks.com/masons-law

Be the first to receive Alex Mason updates. Sign up here:
davidarcherbooks.com/alex-updates

EXCERPT OF
MASON'S LAW

To most people the threat of a nuclear holocaust was something that belonged to the years of the Cold War, something they associated with the United States and the Soviet Union, something that was laid to rest by Gorbachev and Reagan, back in the '80s, when the Berlin Wall came down.

So when Alia Gallin's murder was reported to ODIN agent Alex Mason, the last thing he thought of was that this could be part of the build up to a nuclear war. All Mason could think of was his rage, finding the killers and punishing them.

Only his boss, the man they called Nero, had ordered him not to touch it: It was the Mossad's investigation and the Mossad's jurisdiction, not ODIN's. But wherever he looked and whomever he turned to, all he could find were lies and betrayal.

That was when Mason decided he was going to do things his own way. Little did he realize that his way would take him to London, Tel Aviv, Tehran and the very brink of Nuclear Armageddon.

And perhaps beyond...

MASON'S LAW
PROLOGUE

Aila Gallin killed the engine and the lights and watched the desultory raindrops slowly gather as amber globules on the windshield. They didn't seem to be in any kind of hurry. She slipped the small Sig Sauer P365 behind her back into her left-handed pancake, butt facing down, contrary to recommended practice. She climbed out of the anonymous, cream-colored 2010 Honda Civic and slammed the door.

She was on Old Queen Street. The name made her chuckle. She knew she had the sense of humor of a twelve year-old schoolboy, but she didn't care. She lifted her collar against the drizzle, shoved her hands into the pockets of her black leather bomber jacket and turned into Storey's Gate. The Westminster Arms pub was just forty paces away, painted shiny black with gold letters: the haunt of politicians, journalists and crooks.

She pushed through the door and was immediately struck by the warmth, the noise of conversation and laughter and the agreeable smell of beer. She scanned the room and saw Ahmed sitting at a table in the corner, ignoring a gin and tonic and looking at his cell phone. She elbowed her way to the bar, asked for a pint of best bitter and carried it to the table. He looked up as she sat.

"You're late."

"So is the Apocalypse, what can I say? Shit happens. Cheers." She raised her glass and pulled off a quarter of the pint. He didn't respond but settled back in his chair.

"You don't talk much like a rocket engineer."

She sighed, rolled her eyes, spread her hands and shrugged. "No. You're right. You know what? You're right. And my mother would agree with you. You know why?" He sighed and looked at the wall. She went on. "She would agree with you because, you know what she wanted me to be? She wanted me to be a good, Jewish wife, have five sons and for all of them to be doctors, lawyers and engineers. But it seems to be a curse I have, Ahmed, never to be what other people expect me to be. If I was the kind of person you expect me to be, I wouldn't be here right now talking to you, would I? I'd be in a lab somewhere, engineering rockets."

"Fine! OK, I have to be careful..."

She paused with the pint halfway on its return journey to her mouth. "You want me to start talking about vectors, thrust, parabolic arcs?"

"I said OK!"

She pulled off another quarter pint, smacked her lips and put the glass back on the table. Ahmed said, "You're Jewish."

"Jesus! Give the man a peanut! I just told you that, fifteen seconds ago. You think I don't know I'm Jewish? My parents reminded me every day of my life for the last twenty-eight years!"

"Will you please shut up?"

DAVID ARCHER

"Will you please say something intelligent?"

"We are trying to keep a low profile!"

"So I'm Jewish. What's your point?"

He leaned forward and spoke in a harsh whisper. "You're applying for a job with the Iranian government, the people who fund Hezbollah. How can you betray your country and your people like that?"

She stared at him for a very long moment. Her arched eyebrows and her tight mouth said she had lost hope of any kind of intelligent discussion.

"*My* country? *My* people? That piece of land belongs to the United States of America in all but name. And they did not steal it from us. They stole it from the Palestinians. And the people who live there are not my people. They are Russian, German, American, Palestinian, British, French—they are from the whole world, united by an idea that should have died out two thousand years ago! Me? I am English and I am not proud of it. I am ashamed of it. I am the daughter of a nation that has pillaged and plundered and stolen its way through twelve centuries of history. The people *I* have are my grandmother's people. She was a good, Palestinian woman, married to a Jew."

Ahmed frowned. "So you are a Muslim?"

"No. I am not a Muslim, I am not a Jew, I am not a Christian. I am not even a Buddhist or an atheist. I don't give a rat's ass about religion. I am a realist. I live here and now. And you know what the most important thing is, right now?"

He scowled. "Allah."

She gave a short, mocking laugh. "Money. You give me the money, and I will give you one of the best minds ever to come out of Cambridge University and the Massachusetts Institute of Technology."

"Your attitude disgusts me."

"And your teeth disgust me, Ahmed. But what can we do? Grin and bear it. Or in your case, please, just smile and bear it."

"If you talked like that in my country..."

"Yeah, I know. Tell me something I don't know, like what the salary is and when I start. You have my resumé, you've had time to check it out. So what's the deal?"

He took a piece of paper from his pocket and wrote a number on it. He slid it across the table to her. At first she thought it was a telephone number. She raised an eyebrow at him. "American dollars or British pounds?"

"Dollars. Don't get greedy. That is your fee over three years. You will be given accommodation and food. Payment will be made when you have finished the job."

"What guarantee have I got that you will honor this?"

"That is very simple. If you are successful we will want to use you again. Also, you will be useful to us installed in an American university."

"What university and what position?"

"I cannot be certain yet. Maybe Colorado. It cannot be too high profile. Your position will depend on what is available, but it will be a senior position."

She shook her head. "That is tempting, but there is no deal unless I get fifty percent upfront in an offshore numbered account."

"I will have to consult."

"That's crap and you know it. No one is going to accept the deal you're offering, Ahmed. Least of all if they have the kind of intellect you're looking for. You knew I'd ask for half upfront and you are ready to agree to that."

"I still have to report back. I cannot make that decision."

"OK, when do I start?"

"First of the month."

"Where?"

"You'll be given the details at the next meeting. Someone will inform you of the address."

"What about my expenses tonight?"

"What? You are joking!"

"Joking? You brought me out here in the rain to waste my time on this bullshit? No way, pal. Let's see how generous the Ayatollah can be."

He sighed and pulled two twenties and a ten from his wallet and tossed them across the table to her. She folded them carefully and smiled. "That's more like it." She drained her glass. "Pleasure doing business with you, Ahmed. How about a restaurant next time, and the Ayatollah buys me dinner?"

"Do not mock the Ayatollah. It will be bad for you if you do. The next meeting will be in a private house."

"Yeah, sure. Hang loose, dude."

She stood and pushed out of the pub without looking back. She lifted her collar against the steady drizzle and walked quickly back along Storey's Gate toward Old Queen Street. The only light was the limpid yellow from the tall, iron lampposts, which reflected wet and oily on the blacktop.

She climbed into her car, slammed the door, locked it and took a deep breath. Scanning her mirrors and finding nothing untoward, she took a transparent plastic bag from her glove compartment, folded the money and the note with her salary scrawled on it, and dropped them in the bag. Then fired up the engine and backed up illegally the hundred and fifty yards to The Two Chairmen pub, saying, "You got all that?"

Aaron's voice came back to her in the nano-speaker in her right ear.

"Affirmative. Where are you now?"

She spun the wheel so the car wound up facing west.

"On my way home. I'll drop the car at Oxford Street. Have someone collect it and give it a thorough cleaning."

"OK. Do you want company on the way home? Do you think they are buying it?"

She drove another hundred and thirty yards down Dartmouth Street to Tothill, chewing her lip. As she made a left toward Parliament Square she said:

"No, I'll be OK. I am pretty sure they are buying it."

She said it with more confidence than she felt. Ahmed was about as easy to read as Chinese algebra. Frankly, a little company on the way home in the form of four six-foot *katsas* seasoned in Krav Maga would have been reassuring. But she was playing a game she had to play alone. So she kept her eyes on her mirrors and drove.

At the Westminster Station Subway she turned left onto Parliament Street and Whitehall as far as Trafalgar Square, and there went five times around the circus to see if anyone had followed her. They hadn't, at least not in a car.

She made her way to Oxford Street and left the car at the Oxford Street Multi-Story Parking Garage. She left the key in the glove compartment, made her way down to the crowded, wet street and walked round the corner to the Boots Chemist, where they sold just about everything from aspirin and saline solution to sandwiches and newspapers, by way of pens and wrapping paper. There she bought a large envelope which she addressed to a house in Washington DC, and stepped out onto the damp street again before dropping the transparent plastic bag containing the note with her proposed salary and the fifty pounds into the envelope.

From the Boots Chemist she hurried half a mile up Edgeware Road to the DHL office on the corner of Harrowby Street and pushed through the plate-glass doors. She handed over the envelope and told the Australian kid behind the counter:

"I need it there in twenty-four hours,"

He gave his head a twitch. "No worries. It'll be there."

"It had better be."

But she said that to herself, as she stepped out of the shop and into the rain, and scanned the street for a taxi. She saw the warm yellow light of a cab and raised her arm, emitting a piercing whistle at the same time. The cab swerved and pulled in, and she leaned in the window.

"Campden Hill Square, Holland Park."

They drove in silence. She watched the London streets move past, eternally wet, an ocean of bobbing umbrellas. It was a city she normally associated with safety and security, and homely common sense. But right then, riding through the dark among the millions of inhabitants that swarmed over its sidewalks and crammed into its roads, it seemed to her there was a madness that had infected the city; a craziness that somehow nobody else could sense. Because they all seemed to be possessed by it. All they could see was their wet feet pounding the wet sidewalks, the six feet in front of them as they pushed and elbowed and dodged through the crowds, tunnel-visioned into getting home to their TVs, where they would plug into the hive-mind, to be fed...

"What number, love?"

She snapped out of it and said, "Oh, right here is fine." She paid him, gave him a generous tip and pushed through the gate to the front yard of the elegant, four-story Georgian house. The path ran down the right side of the yard to the big, dark blue door with the big brass handle in the center. On the left were hedges and rosebushes. And dark shadows.

She fished her keys from her jeans' pocket as she walked. She slipped the key in the lock and paused. There was something, something she could not identify. She scanned the shadows, saw nothing, listened to the sounds behind the sound of the distant traffic. A rustle? A breath? But there was nothing. So why were the alarms going crazy in her head?

"I need a holiday," she told herself, and wondered about suggesting a couple of weeks in the Caribbean to Mason, as she pushed the door open and stepped into the hall. He might get the wrong idea. She smiled. That could be fun.

It was as she pulled the key out and closed the door with her foot that she realized what it had been—the noise. The key in the lock had sounded wrong.

She dropped, hunkered down and moved up against the wall. The house was absolutely silent. She pulled the P365 from behind her back and inched her way to the living-room door. It was open. She stood with her back pressed against the wall, listening for breathing. She heard nothing, moved in with the pistol held in front of her and smacked on the light. The room was empty.

She snapped off the light again and moved back into the hall, moving fast toward the kitchen. She made no effort to be silent. If there was anyone in the house they had already heard her switch on the living-room light. She kicked in the kitchen door, palmed the switch and nothing happened. Blackness. Her skin went cold and terror struck at her belly. She dropped to the ground and rolled and heard a heavy thud and a curse above her. Automatically she fired in the direction of the curse. There was a curse, "*Al'ama!*" a thud and a gurgle. Scuffling feet. The darkness seemed to shift. A boot stamped painfully on her leg. She bit back the scream of pain and swung savagely with the butt of her weapon, aimed blindly and fired again. A weeping, "*Allah!*" Then an arm like a vice around her neck. Hot, moist breath in her ear, "*Ya sharmoota!*" She couldn't breathe. She tried to twist the Sig behind her back, but a hand grabbed her wrist and levered the gun out of her fingers.

A savage voice in the dark: "*Kol khara!*"

Then a flash and an explosion, and darkness closed in.

Just a quarter of a mile away, in Ladbroke Square Garden, Aaron sat in the control car drumming his fingers on the wheel. For the fifteenth time he repeated, "Captain, come in please. Do you need assistance?"

Finally he took his secure cell and called the Chief at Russell Road.

"Yes."

"Sir, I have lost contact with the captain."

"What do you mean, lost contact?"

"She said she was going home. She left the car at Oxford Street. The car has been recovered according to plan. But I have been trying to contact the captain to confirm she has arrived home and there is no reply."

A sigh. "Perhaps she removed the earpiece."

"She would have notified me."

"Where are you?"

"Two minutes from her house."

"Come in. I'll send a car."

Aaron failed to suppress the note of anxiety in his voice. "Yes, sir," he said, and hung up.

MASON'S LAW
CHAPTER ONE

Maria Garcia leaned forward into the candlelight. Her long, silver earrings hung down beside her long neck. A single pearl set among diamonds rested smugly in her perfect cleavage.

"This *is* the cognac talking," she said.

"It is very good cognac," I replied. "I can't wait to hear what it has to say."

"You're a bad man, Alex Mason."

"Come! That's the cognac talking."

"Be serious. I have always felt very drawn to you. I have fought against it, but it's an itch that just won't seem to go away."

"You must scratch, Maria. It's the only thing to do."

"Take me home, to your place, and scratch me. Do very, very bad things to me, Alex."

Coming from a woman who would send most supermodels crying back to Mommy, it was an offer I could not refuse. Except at that very moment, my cell vibrated in my pocket. It had to be the office because only the office had that number. My other phone I had deliberately left at home, so as not to be disturbed.

I ignored the vibration and signaled the waiter for the bill. It vibrated again. I leaned forward and breathed in her ear, "I'll be right back." And made my way to the bathroom.

Checking my teeth in the mirror, I asked severely into the cell, "What?"

It was not Lovelock. It was the Chief. "Be in my office in ten minutes."

"Sir, I am not only well over half an hour from your office, I am dining with the most desirable, carnal woman on the planet. And she likes me!"

A snort of amusement. "She won't like you that much when you tell her you have to go to the office, will she?"

"That's funny, sir. I didn't know you had a sense of humor."

But he'd already hung up.

She sat in the far corner of the cab and stared out the window all the way to her apartment. Once there she closed the door with unnecessary force and didn't say goodnight.

"Seventeen-oh-one, Fort Myer Drive," I told the driver and settled back in the cab to consider the magnitude of my loss.

I was still considering the magnitude of my loss when I settled myself into the leather armchair opposite the Chief, in his office on the eighteenth floor of the Commonwealth Building on Wilson Boulevard, in Arlington, Virginia. We watched each other for a moment and finally he took a deep breath and sighed.

"Sex is not good for you," he announced, massively. "It dissipates one's fibers and uses up one's vital energy.

As a pleasure it is overrated. Caviar, Chateau Lafite-Rothschild, 2016—Left Bank, of course. An Armand de Brignac Gold, brut."

"Sir, I dearly hope you did not call me here to discuss food and wine."

He shook his vast head. "No. I was merely trying to console you. I am going to send you to Iran. You will be impersonating a rocketry engineer, specializing in delivery systems for nuclear warheads."

The facetious humor drained out of me, leaving my skin feeling cold and pasty.

"They have warheads?"

"That is something I need you to confirm. However, everything seems to be pointing in that direction. What we could get, before our informant was silenced, was that there is a camouflaged laboratory-cum-facility in the desert to the south of Tehran..."

"Nine-tenths of Iran is to the south of Tehran."

"...thank you—where they have been working around the clock on developing nuclear devices for deployment against Israel. It also seems the device, or devices, in question are nearing completion." He shrugged. "Or have been completed."

"And you want me to infiltrate the lab?"

"That is the general idea. It won't be as difficult as it might at first appear. It seems the lab was recently subjected to a purge. Several of the scientists and technicians were suspected of working for Mossad or being Israeli sympathizers, or drawing pictures of people or something. Several of them were rounded up and marched off, and presumably tortured and killed. This may have put the authorities' minds at rest, but it also left them shorthanded."

"Particularly in the warhead delivery department, I gather."

"Precisely. So Iran has been quietly fishing in Western waters, looking for rocket engineers with certain, very specific qualifications."

"Such as?"

"Rampant, unbridled anti-Semitism, for a start, sympathy with the Palestinian cause, a desire to acquire a very substantial amount of money, and above all, a degree of proven skills in the field of delivery systems for nuclear devices."

"I am struggling to see how I tick any of those boxes, sir."

"That's irrelevant. We will provide you with a credible résumé from MIT, and any phone calls directed to them about your background will be redirected to us."

"I am guessing I don't have to send them my résumé and apply for an interview."

He sighed. "No, Alex, we have arranged a meeting in London with an Iranian agent who is making discreet inquiries on the Ayatollah's behalf. You will go there and have an interview with him. On the face of it, it will all be very much above board and legitimate. The Iranian government is looking for talented scientists and technicians to work in Tehran and help train Iranian engineers."

"Who's the agent?"

"Sir Leo D'Arcy of Croftmore—"

"Is that the Isfahan D'Arcys of Croftmore or the Rafsanjani D'Arcys of Croftmore?"

"It's an old Scottish family with a long history of service in the British army, and support for the Palestinians. Sir Jeremiah D'Arcy was vocal in the '40s against the recognition of Israel as a Jewish state. He was also notoriously sympathetic to Mosley and his Black Shirts—the British Fascist party. They are a long line of reactionaries who favor a strong link with the Arab nations."

"So my first meeting will be with this interesting gentleman."

"Yes."

"Will we be liaising with the Mossad on this? I believe the IDF has a pretty uncompromising line on Iran and nuclear weapons. They are committed to a preemptive strike as far as I am aware."

"They are indeed. We may liaise with them at a later date. Right now we are keeping this very much in house."

Something in his face made me ask, "Is Captain Aila Gallin involved, sir?"

There was a slight coloring of his cheeks, something I had never seen before. He also hesitated, which in my experience was also a first.

"Captain Gallin has been abducted and..." He hesitated again, working his lips soundlessly. "And, I am sorry, Alex, she is in all probability dead."

The room seemed to rock violently. We were quiet for a moment while I tried to assimilate the news. I heard him vaguely in the background saying, "I know you were fond of her."

I seemed to watch myself as though from far above, saying, "How did it happen?" Oddly. It seemed like a cold, meaningless question, as if how might matter. His voice seemed to come from another room. "I am not at liberty, Alex. I believe it was a home invasion. I can't tell you any more. I'm sorry."

"Was there a body?"

He shook his huge head. I can't..."

Goddammit, sir!" He glared at me. I insisted. *"Was there a body?"*

"No!"

"Blood?"

"Yes!"

"Is she dead?"

"I don't know, Alex! Do not ask me any more questions! The subject is closed!" He sighed again and repeated, "I am sorry. I know you were fond of each other. I know this must be painful. Go home. You will receive your briefing papers and identity documents in the morning."

I nodded. "Thank you, sir." I remained seated for another fifteen or twenty seconds. Then I stood and made for the door. His voice stopped me.

"Alex." I turned back. "You are under no circumstances to attempt to investigate her murder. It will jeopardize your mission and your life."

I nodded. "Yes, sir. I understand."

I left the building and stood on the sidewalk for a little longer than was normal, wondering what to do. I considered and dismissed a visit to a number of DC's late-night bars and instead walked down Wilson Boulevard searching for a cab to take me home.

In the cab I considered sending Maria Garcia a message, but—illogically—felt it would be an insult to Gallin's memory. So in the end I paid off the cabby, climbed the steps to my door and sat in my living room working my way through half a bottle of ten-year-old Bushmills, while Manny Pacquiao lay on my lap and allowed me to scratch his belly.

At four in the morning I made my way up to my bedroom and collapsed on my bed.

Morning came with a hangover. Made instantly worse by the appalling recollection of the news I'd received the night before. And, as I sat up and my stomach lurched, the bell started to ring downstairs. I ran down the stairs, fighting hard not to leave undigested, ten-year-old Bushmills on the stairs, and opened the door to a FedEx delivery man. He handed me a very large envelope, made me sign for it and left. I closed the door and ran for the bathroom.

A little later, over strong black coffee, eggs and bacon, I opened the envelope. As promised it contained my brief, a passport, driver's permit and a couple of major credit cards. My name was Dr. Henry Bassett, born in New York, graduated from MIT with a degree in Rocket Propulsion and later got a PhD from Caltech in Autonomous Remote Robotic Delivery Systems Deployed from Rocket and Jet-Propelled Platforms. I wondered if the acronym would be any easier, but gave up at ARRDSD...

There was some reading material on robotic delivery systems, so I'd have some idea what I was talking about at the interview, some family background and a thumbnail sketch of my personality, so I'd know how friends and colleagues, if approached, would describe me.

This was not something that had been prepared overnight, and that made me wonder if ODIN had been collaborating with the Mossad, and this had been what Gallin was involved in when she was killed. It seemed likely, not least because my contact was in London, where Gallin was based. The Chief's refusal to discuss her death added weight to that possibility. The Mossad had told him they would take care of it.

It was as I was studying my brief over a second cup of coffee that the doorbell rang again. I peered through the spy hole in my door and saw it was a messenger from DHL. That made me suspicious, so I took the P226 from the drawer in the coat stand and slipped it into my waistband behind my back before I opened up.

"Yeah?"

"Are you Mr. Alex Mason?"

I slipped my hand behind my back like I had lumbar pain. "Yeah. You got something for me?"

"An urgent letter, sir. Can you sign here, please?"

I glanced at the envelope and saw it was from London. I signed, took the letter and carried it back to the kitchen. There I sat, opened the envelope and shook the contents out onto the table. There were two plastic bags. One contained a single slip of paper with a number on it. The other contained fifty pounds sterling, two twenties and one ten. I sat a long time staring at the items. I knew they were from Gallin. That much was obvious. There was no message, no indication of what the packages meant or why they were important.

That meant two things: she trusted that I would understand, and she was in a hurry. A real hurry. She was scared that she would be seen, or caught up with. She expected to be abducted or killed and she wanted me to—to what?

To have these items, clearly. Because they contained information. What information could these papers hold? A number—a telephone number? It did not look like any code I knew, and it was a digit short. I glanced at the other plastic envelope. Money. Money! It was a bribe. A payoff? And the information contained on these pieces of paper was fingerprints. Paper is one of the best surfaces for recovering prints, and she had wanted me to know who had offered her the payoff. Because that was the person who had killed her.

I called Lovelock. Her disturbingly attractive voice answered.

"Yes, Alex. What can I do for you?"

"I need a messenger yesterday to take some items to the lab. I need fingerprints run through our database before this afternoon."

She was silent for a while, then: "On his way. Don't leave the house. What makes this so urgent? The lab will want to know why they are prioritizing it."

"It might tell us who murdered Captain Aila Gallin."

"Is that a priority for us?"

"Yes! And tell Nero I said so." Nero was the Chief's nickname, because he was said to set fire to things when he got mad. I went on. "We want to be friends with the Institute right now, and if we can help them on this they will be grateful. Make it happen, Lovelock."

She said she would and hung up. And I went upstairs to book a flight to London Heathrow, have a shower and pack.

* * *

Three and a half thousand miles away to the north and the east, two men were also discussing Captain Aila Gallin. One of them was Ahmed, the owner of the fingerprints on the note and the fifty pounds sterling that were about to be analyzed in DC. He was sitting, with his legs stretched out and his fingers in his jeans pockets, on a white windowsill in Kensington. Behind him the tall, sash window was open, overlooking a leafy crossroads with a triangular garden at its center. At that moment the man went by the name Ahmed, though he had so many false identities that sometimes he could not remember the name his mother had given him.

It had certainly not been Ahmed.

He had olive skin, pockmarked from a bad case of acne when he was sixteen, and large brown eyes which, for some reason, misled women into believing he had compassion. Right then, however, he was looking at Aaron Goldman, the young man in the chair across the room from him, with eyes that did not speak much of compassion.

"You tell me that she dropped the car at Oxford Street at seven thirty." He hunched his shoulders, bunched his mouth and nodded. "That is consistent—for London at that time of night—with her leaving the pub at seven. She has to walk to the car, drive up Whitehall, Trafalgar Square. Sure, that can take half an hour. But now you tell me that she got home at nine PM? You are telling me it took her *one and a half hours* to get from Oxford Street to Holland Park?"

"I had to pull back at Trafalgar Square. She is very smart. She'd told me she did not want company, and she went round the roundabout five or six times. If I'd stayed with her she would have spotted me. All I could do was go ahead and wait for her at the parking garage."

"And?"

"She went in, parked, and I waited for her to come out. When she did she ducked into Portman Street, and by the time I'd turned and gone after her she was gone."

"Incompetence."

"I'm sorry."

"Your sorry does not help. What was she doing during that extra thirty to forty minutes? Was she abducted by aliens?"

Aaron Goldman had no answer, so he remained silent. Which made Ahmed scream at him, "*Answer me! Was she abducted by aliens?*"

"I don't know, Colonel. I imagine not."

"*But it is your job to know! That is why you were sent! So that you would know what she did!*"

"Yes, Colonel. I am sorry."

Ahmed's face flushed with repressed violence. "*So if it is your job to know and you don't know, then you are incompetent!*"

"I searched..."

"*Excuses!* One man in the car! One man on the street! It is basic technique!"

"Yes, sir, but I was alone."

Ahmed put his fingertips to his brow and closed his eyes. "Now, let me see if you are not too hopelessly mentally retarded for me to teach you something. If she disappeared for half an hour, forty minutes, where do you suppose she went?"

"I am not sure, Colonel. I thought probably she was just being careful."

The colonel nodded several times, with an insane light in his eyes. "Oh yes, oh yes, very good. So, let's see. Where do you suppose she assumed her prospective employer thought she was going?"

"...what?"

"In her mind! Put yourself in her mind! Where did she assume her employer thought she was going?"

"Home?"

"So, if she was being careful, why did she not just get a taxi *home?*"

"Uh…"

"*Because she wasn't going home, you jackass!*" He stared with bulging eyes at the younger man, who stared hard at the floor. The colonel shouted again. "*And she was not being careful! So where do you think she went?*"

"To…to…"

"To *co-mu-ni-cate!* She went to *co-mu-ni-cate to somebody!* And that means one thing, you stupid, moronic jerk! It means *she suspected the man she had spoken to! Me!*"

The moronic jerk babbled with bare, fragile coherence, "Yes, Colonel, I see that now. I am sorry. I will work very hard to learn these lessons and not fail you again."

Ahmed's voice was barely a whisper. "So whom did she contact?"

"Her father?"

"*No! Think!*" He thrust his face forward. "To communicate with her father she need only go and see him! He is a half-hour walk from her!" He sighed heavily. "Do you know why you are still alive, you wretched son of a bitch?"

The young man's cheeks flushed and tears welled in his eyes. He fought down the anger and the tears and said, "Through your compassion, Colonel."

The colonel shook his head. "No, because it would draw too much attention to kill you now. But keep looking over you scrawny shoulder, sad little man. Stay alert. Now get out of my sight."

The younger man nodded and stood, fighting back

tears of anger and hurt.

"I have been summoned back to Tel Aviv, sir. I fly this evening."

The colonel sneered. "Let's hope you're more use over there than you have been here."

"Yes, sir." He turned and left.

MASON'S LAW
CHAPTER TWO

I touched down at Heathrow just before breakfast, collected my Avis F-Type Jaguar and drove through the English drizzle to the Dorchester. The English drizzle is something that the Brits hate. Personally I love it. It is like a perfect frame that brings out the beauty of every aspect of the painting. The hedgerows, the thatched cottages, the chimney stacks and the red busses. Even the shiny wet blacktop which they call tarmac acquires a special beauty in the drizzle.

I checked into my room overlooking Park Lane and Hyde Park and called a number Gallin had given me in one of her more human moments, while we were discussing what we should do if the other "didn't make it" while on a job. A gravelly, slightly confused voice said, "Yes, who is this?"

"Good morning, my name is Alex Mason, I am a friend of Aila's."

There was a long silence. "I know who you are. How did you get this number?"

"Aila gave it to me."

"Where and when?"

She had told me he would ask that, and I knew the answer. "Where? In her cups. When? Just after the ice had settled in Greenland."

A soft grunt over the line, and then, as though he were speaking with difficulty. "Why?"

She told me he would ask that, too.

"Because she was my friend."

Another, heavy silence and finally, "All right, Mr. Mason. You do not want me to grieve alone and in peace. A car will come for you in about twenty minutes. Try to be inconspicuous."

I had a quick shower, dressed inconspicuously in jeans and a blazer and went down to wait in the lobby, reading the *Daily Telegraph* in a large chair. After five minutes a guy in a suit pushed through the door. He was with a woman in a pretty dress who wouldn't stop talking and laughing. They headed for the bar, but halfway across the floor she stopped dead in her tracks and stared at me.

"Oh my god," she said. "Is it? I don't believe it! It is you, isn't it?"

I smiled blandly back. "It is certainly me," I said.

"Steve! Don't you recognize me? Oh, I am so *wounded!*" She laughed and came toward me, reaching for my hands. "Steve! It is so good to see you!" She turned and gestured toward the guy. "You don't know my fiancé, George Gallin, do you?"

By now I was on my feet. The message was subtle but unmistakable. I shook George's hand and she kissed my cheek. "Say you'll have breakfast with us."

"I'd love to."

They bundled me out of the door and into a waiting cab, laughing and joking all the way. We pulled out onto Park Lane, circumscribed the whole of Hyde Park, went round the Marble Arch circus three times and then headed down past Notting Hill Gate toward the Shepherd's Bush circus. We went around that four times and finally turned into Holland Road, headed south toward Kensington High Street—all in total silence.

At High Street Kensington, they took a sharp right and a sharp right again and dropped me outside the Nox Hotel, on Russell Road.

"Go back seven doors. Ring the bell once. When they ask say it's Neil. Go. Fast!"

I got out, hunched my shoulders and looked at my feet as I walked down the wet sidewalk back the way we had come, toward High Street Kensington. As I went I counted seven front yards, then skipped up the steps to the door and pressed the bell. After a moment a deep voice asked, "Who is it?"

"It's Neil."

The door opened and there was a guy who looked like he'd been chipped out of concrete. He had a five-o'clock shadow and a cigarette that was too scared to give him lung cancer. He jerked his head like he thought words were for girls.

"Top floor."

"Thanks."

As I climbed I heard the volume of the TV increase and decrease again before the living-room door closed. At the top of the stairs I knocked on a white door and a voice told me to enter.

Inside, the room was large. There were two tall sash windows which overlooked Russell Road. Directly in front of the door there was a desk. It stood at right angles to the window so that whoever sat there had a direct view of anyone entering Russell Road from Kensington High Street. To my left there was a nest of chairs and a sofa arranged around a coal fire burning in the grate. Sitting staring at the fire was a large, heavyset man in a charcoal gray suit. His face was dark and saturnine, with dark pouches under his brown eyes. He looked up as I closed the door.

"Mr. Gallin?"

His thick eyebrows rose high on his forehead. "She told you my name." His English was exquisite.

"Yes."

"She must trust you."

He didn't invite me to sit so I stayed standing by the door. I said:

"Trust is a rare commodity in our business. But we learned to trust each other."

"Trustworthiness is even more rare than trust. You had better sit down."

I sat opposite him. I put him in his late fifties, but you could tell he had aged in the last few hours.

"Forgive me, Mr. Mason, if I am less than polite. I would like to grieve in private. What is it you want?"

"I want to know what happened."

"Nobody knows what happened."

I shook my head. "That's not true. Somebody knows. And I'll get to them in time. But right now I need to put together the little bit you know with the little bit he knows with the little bit she knows, until I have a picture that tells me something."

He frowned. "Is this you or ODIN?"

"Me."

"Does Nero know you are here?"

"Nero told me specifically not to look into this."

He looked away, back at the fire. "He was right. We asked him to stay out of it."

"I can't say I care."

"There is a greater fight. If we start putting our personal, emotional needs..."

I cut him dead. "What is the point of fighting to protect values, if we sacrifice those very values in order to defend them?"

He frowned. "What?"

"We risk losing sight of what we are fighting for, Mr. Gallin. Aila was my friend, maybe more than a friend. If I let her death go unavenged, unpunished, unanswered, then what the hell am I fighting for? To protect the military supremacy of a political entity, regardless, irrespective of its values?" I leaned forward and pointed at him. "I am not here to fight for my government, right or wrong. My government is charged with fighting for my values, come what may. And my values say that these bastards cannot come here and murder my friend, your daughter, and get away with it because it happens to be expedient for ODIN and the Mossad to let it slide. They will be punished, and I am going to punish them. So tell me, what happened?"

He surprised me by yawning and rubbing his face with his hands, and I was suddenly aware that this was that yawn that comes so often with extreme grief, where your mind just wants to shut down and retreat into the dark, silent safety inside.

He groaned softly. "She trusted you," he said at last, and wiped his mouth with the palm of his hand. "You're the same kind of pain in the ass she was. This is unofficial, this conversation never happened and my advice to you is to obey Nero's orders. He is a wise and a highly effective man."

"Understood."

"We received intelligence that Iran was in the final stages of developing a nuclear bomb. It was a big shock to us. We keep a very close watch on Iran's nuclear program and we did not believe they were anywhere close to completing a bomb.

"Now we learn suddenly that friends of Iran, their agents in Britain, are looking for a rocket engineer whose specialization is delivery systems for nuclear devices. We hear that they have a bomb which is near completion, and now they are seeking a system to target Israel."

He watched me a moment, studying my face. "You knew this," he said and gestured at me. "I can see you knew this already."

"Our position has always been that if Iran develops a nuclear bomb, we will make a preemptive strike. This is a fight for survival. We will not—we *cannot*—hesitate."

He spread his hands, shrugged and sank back in his chair. "So it became imperative to find out for sure, to confirm, where they were at in their development, and stop them before it was too late."

"So Aila posed as a rocket scientist."

"Yes."

"And they didn't buy it."

"Apparently not."

"Who did she meet with?"

I was half expecting him to say, Sir Leo D'Arcy of Croftmore, but he surprised me by saying, "An Iranian going by the name of Ahmed. That was all we knew about him. They had been in touch and had one meeting, the night before last, at the Westminster Arms, by St. James's Park. She left that meeting at seven PM, deposited her car at the Oxford Street Car Park at half-past seven, according to plan, and then went off the radar until her backup called to say he couldn't raise her to confirm she'd got home safe."

"What time was that?"

"A couple of minutes after nine."

"That's a long time to get from Oxford Street to Holland Park."

"I raised the same question with him. He made a valid point. Aila is...or was, a very effective maverick. She operated her own way and her way was often—usually—the best way. And she deeply resented interference. He gave her a half hour's leeway before calling her. She didn't answer."

"Who was her backup?"

"You know I can't tell you that."

"I need to talk to him."

"I'll see what I can arrange. He is not in London now."

"What did you find at the house?"

He pointed to his desk. "The folder."

I stood and retrieved a manila folder from his desk. I handed it to him as I sat down. He opened it and leafed through several photographs which he handed to me.

"She was not there. There was no body. There were signs, in the kitchen, as you can see, of a scuffle. There was a lot of blood. The greater part was not hers." A grim smile touched his lips with pride. "But there were traces of her blood too. Of course that means nothing, except that her body was not at the scene of her abduction."

I studied the large, glossy prints.

"They took her away alive." I glanced at him. "They wouldn't clean up most of her blood and leave their own. Even if they killed her bloodlessly, it would still make no sense to take her body away and leave some of her blood and all of her attacker's. The only sense in taking her away would have been to interrogate her."

He closed his eyes and his skin became pasty. "It is almost preferable that they had killed her."

"Steady, Mr. Gallin. Try to keep perspective. I know it's not easy, but you know as well as I do that these guys will interrogate you either to make an example of you or to get information from you. And it's completely different in each case. Even these bastards know by now that information obtained under torture is not reliable. If they want reliable information, it won't be a picnic, but they won't be making an example of her either."

"You overlook the most likely scenario: that they have taken her simply to execute her. Do not delude yourself, Mr. Mason. The chances are she is dead."

"Why would they take her away to execute her?"

He was barely audible when he answered. "To make an example of her..."

I thought about telling him about the fifty pounds and the note, but he seemed to be coping with enough as it was. I nodded and stood. "Would you like me to keep you posted on what I find?"

He thought for a long time, staring at the fire. I was about to leave when he said, "If you can bring me my daughter back from the dead, let me know. Otherwise, let me grieve in peace and lay her to rest."

There was nothing I could say, so I left the room

and went down the stairs into the mid-morning drizzle. My feet carried me back toward Kensington High Street. The cars and the red buses had their headlamps on in the dull, gray light, and there was a damp chill in the air that crawled up your ankles and down your neck. You could smell autumn creeping in, and on its tail was winter.

Around the corner I found a Costa Coffee, and as my cell started to ring I decided to push inside and have breakfast.

"Yeah, Mason."

"Hey, Alex, it's Caroline at forensics."

"Hello Caroline at forensics. Bear with me a minute, will you, I am just buying a coffee and some croissants." To the gap year student whom his employers insisted on calling a barista, I said, "I want four espressos in one cup, and I want two croissants. And I don't want them irradiated, please."

"You're like that with everyone, huh?"

"I'm even-handed."

"Are you going to sit down?"

The barista, or bartender, rung up the four coffees and the two croissants and I handed him ten English bucks.

"Yes," I said into the phone, which was now clenched on my shoulder. "Why?"

"Good. Tell me when you're sitting."

I took my meager change and my fare on a tray and weaved my way to a quiet corner where I sat. Then I took the phone in my hand and said, "So, tell me."

"You sent us the note and the English money."

"I knew that."

"So we isolated Captain Gallin's prints and looked

277

at the fresh prints that were clearly on top of the rest. That would be the person who handled the paper immediately before she did."

"Right."

"Then we ran comparisons with the prints we took from the money and matched them to the prints on the note. OK?"

"So the guy who gave her the money is the same guy who wrote the number on the paper."

"Correct. Then we ran those prints through the Five Eyes database."

"And, did you get a hit?"

"Kind of."

"What does that mean?"

"It means we got a very special kind of hit. It was flagged and the Chief was notified automatically. He called the lab and wanted to know what the hell was going on and I had to tell him. He went ballistic."

"Well, who the hell was it? Who do the prints belong to?"

"Wait. I'll tell you, but I also have to tell you somebody else was notified of the hit too."

"Who?"

"I don't know. Some department attached to Five Eyes in the United Kingdom. But the identity was suppressed. It's a bit like caller ID withheld. But somebody in the UK knows we ran those prints."

"So are you going to tell me who the prints belong to?"

She took a deep breath. "In a word, no."

"Why the hell not?"

"Because they are contained in a file which is

sealed. It is classified as top secret. From here I can't even see who *is* entitled to see it. Only people with top secret clearance."

"So the person who gave her that money and that note..."

"Probably works for either the Australians, the British, the Canadians, New Zealand or the USA."

I thanked her and hung up, and sat staring at my coffee and my croissants. Suddenly I had lost my appetite.

– END OF EXCERPT –

To see all purchasing options, please visit:
www.davidarcherbooks.com/masons-law
www.blakebanner.com/masons-law

ALSO BY DAVID ARCHER & BLAKE BANNER

To see what else we have to offer, please visit our respective websites.

www.davidarcherbooks.com
www.blakerbanner.com

Thank you once again for reading our work!

Made in the USA
Las Vegas, NV
22 December 2022

63848340R00157

To Chi Chi, our Boys, the leadership of New Life Covenant Church in Harare, Zimbabwe, and to the Leaders of Jabula in the many countries we have ministry functions. Your willingness to submit to the teachings of Apostolic Government, and to allow the process of the Kingdom of God to be manifest has been a blessing to all. And to my Dad, Mom, brothers and sisters who believe in me and have given our anointing space. God bless you all.

AUTHOR'S NOTE

As you read this book you will notice many references to types, symbols, and Biblical numerology. The Bible is written in metaphorical as well as literal language and in studying the types, symbols, and numbers one can gain a more thorough understanding of the message in each verse, chapter, book, and Bible as a whole. I encourage you to study the "hidden" truths throughout the Bible and would direct you to three books that have been instrumental in my own study: *Interpreting the Scriptures* and *Types and Symbols* by Kevin Conner, and *Dispensational Truths* by Larken.

CONTENTS

Introduction

The Spirit Keeps Moving – With Order

In the year 1900 the Spirit of the Lord was poured out in Topeka, Kansas, and at Azuza Street in Los Angeles. That great movement of God within the United States was placed into the custodianship of men who were called pastors. They should have been called apostles, but because of the evangelical thought of the day, it was commonly believed that apostles and prophets no longer existed, that they had passed from the scene with the advent of the early church.

Thus most of the mainline Pentecostal denominations were started by men who actually had an apostolic mandate, or mantle, upon their lives. When they died, and someone else began taking care of their ministries, these new individuals, in most cases, did not have an apostolic mantle on their lives; so they could not sustain what was started by the apostle of the house instead, they merely became managers of what an apostle had started. The work immediately began to decline and die; in the hands of caretakers without apostolic anointing, Pentecostal denominations struggled to survive.

But the Spirit, of course, could not be thwarted forever, and God began to restore the office and ministry of the apostle. Initially, the outpouring for the restoration of the five-fold ministry in its true sense – utilizing the Apostle, the Prophet, the Evangelist, the Pastor, and the Teacher – came in the very early 50s in what is commonly called today the Latter Rain Movement. This movement was an unprecedented outpouring of the Holy Spirit, particularly in Canada. It was there that our terminology regarding five-fold ministry, which you'll be exploring in the chapters to come, became accepted.

However, the mainline Pentecostal groups in the Western hemisphere eventually rejected the Latter Rain Movement as an authentic move of God, the so-called theologians saying the movement didn't have the aptitude and characteristics of an authentic working of God's Spirit. However, those who were birthed in the Latter Rain have maintained the integrity of that move of God. They, for forty years – from 1952 to 1992 – were in the wilderness as apostles and prophets holding on to what they believed God was doing in their midst. Then, in the late 80s, when the truths of spiritual warfare became incredibly real, and then later on in the early 90s we all saw the authenticity of the Apostolic ministry and function with intercessory prayer at its heart.

A Movement of Praying

The Intercessory Prayer Movement, which was being really pushed by the Holy Spirit, started initially in South Korea with Dr. Cho, and then moved to various parts of the Western hemisphere and also to Africa and to Argentina. We can relate it to Acts 12 where Peter was locked up in jail:

5 Peter therefore was kept in prison: but prayer was made without ceasing of the church unto God for him.

6 And when Herod would have brought him forth, the same night Peter was sleeping between two soldiers, bound with two chains: and the keepers before the door kept the prison.

7 And, behold, the angel of the Lord came upon him, and a light shined in the prison: and he smote Peter on the side, and raised him up, saying, Arise up quickly. And his chains fell off from his hands.

8 And the angel said unto him, Gird thyself, and bind on thy sandals. And so he did. And he saith unto him, Cast thy garment about thee, and follow me.

9 And he went out, and followed him; and wist not that it was true which was done by the angel; but thought he saw a vision.

10 When they were past the first and the second ward, they came unto the iron gate that leadeth unto the city; which opened to them of his own accord: and they went out, and passed on through one street; and forthwith the angel departed from him.

11 And when Peter was come to himself, he said, Now I know of a surety, that the Lord hath sent his angel, and hath delivered me out of the hand of Herod, and from all the expectation of the people of the Jews.

Peter was chained in prison with guards around him. But as the intercessors were praying, the angel of the Lord came and released Peter. We might say, then, that intercessory prayer was a precursor to the release of apostolic anointing.

Then in the 1990s, with the powerful working of the Holy Spirit, we saw the release of the apostolic movement in a significant way. This was characterized by reconciliation ministries; we had the reconciliation of races, reconciliation of denominations, reconciliation among genders, and so on. We also saw inner healing, which is part of the apostolic mantle. We've seen tremendous moves of God through deliverance, which is definitely an apostolic anointing, as seen in Luke 4:18, along with outpourings of the miraculous.

Communities and nations were becoming transformed as apostolic leaders came together. So now we have to acknowledge the fact that in Africa, for example, we find the fastest-growing independent church movement in the world. There, fifteen to twenty new churches start up every day, because daily in Africa there are almost 20,000 people opening their hearts to Christ as Savior. Part of the reason is that the African minister is becoming more innovative in his thinking and is moving forward with new vision. We're also seeing this in parts of Asia and, in particular, in South America. I recount this history simply to say: We are seeing a full restoration of the apostolic role.

I must add here that there have been counterfeits as well. False apostles do rise up and teach certain things merely to solicit financial support on what could be called a pseudo-spiritual multi-level marketing system. It's where a man is on top and junior ministers pay up, to be a part of the movement. Beware! But nevertheless, in a genuine sense, we've seen tremendous movements developing under apostolic houses.

An Exciting Entry

I want you to grasp that we're coming into the Kingdom like we've never done before. We're seeing the shaking; the birth pains of the Kingdom of God are being ushered in. The Kingdom of God is coming in demonstration and power. When the Kingdom of God comes there is: 1 Corinthians 2:1-4

♦ *Kingdom anointing;*

♦ *Kingdom power;*

♦ *Kingdom force.*

These three things operate throughout the Gospels. There are places where you see the anointing of the Kingdom, the power of the Kingdom, and the force of the Kingdom. There are also places where you see all three working together. There is a difference, by virtue of levels of anointing, between times when rank is being displayed and levels of acumen in terms of authority. The force of the Kingdom, for example, comes through when Jesus calmed the storm. When Jesus said, "Peace, be still" it was not anointing, but the force of the Kingdom. The power of the Kingdom occurs when the Spirit of the Lord is present to heal.

The anointing of the Kingdom is what we're beginning to experience globally. I want to encourage you to understand the Kingdom mentality and the working ability of Jesus Christ to manifest His presence. Christ Jesus will manifest Himself in the midst of the people. The Bible says in Matthew 18:20, *"For where two or three are gathered together in my name, there am I in the midst of them."*

Also, according to John 3:8, *"The wind bloweth where it listeth, and thou hearest the voice thereof, but knowest not whence it cometh, and whither it goeth: so is every one that is born of the Spirit."* So, there's a difference between Him being present and Him manifesting Himself while He's present. I have been in places where the Lord has manifested Himself and the anointing was so incredible. We are asking Him for His manifest presence. Amen. God's Manifest Presence

It is happening, we are beginning to experience the prelude to Kingdom entry, and we see this in five basic signs as shown in the Scripture:

1. Cutting away of flesh

We can live according to the flesh or we can live by the Spirit. If we choose the Spirit, then we'll experience pain as our flesh is cut away. *(See Joshua 6 and Romans 8.)* It's painful when a male is circumcised, and it is painful to give up our own wills to the will of God. It is hard to look to Him alone for our sustenance in life and our guidance for the future. It is hard to give up our favorite habits and addictions, the things that keep us attached to the world while Christ knocks at our hearts seeking daily fellowship with us. But let our hearts be circumcised that they may be moved and melted by the Lord's love!

2. Preparing of the soil.

God has to plow our lives. He will turn over soil so He can put in the good seed. It's not easy. The stones in your heart are inhibiting God from growing something marvelous in you: the likeness of His Son. The stones will be taken out of the field and used to build a wall, or a hedge, so that various animals cannot destroy what God is planting.

3. Harvesting and crushing of the fruit

The seed grows. Once the wheat or corn is harvested, it is threshed or tread upon. God is removing the chaff that has protected the seed. It is then ground and put in the oven and baked. It is preparation for Kingdom entry. If you can think of vineyard imagery, then realize that you must be pruned if you're going to produce fruit and be made into fine wine. You will be crushed like a grape. Threshing, grinding, baking and pruning are all necessary preparations for Kingdom entry.

In similar fashion, the olive is shaken from the tree, drops to the ground, is crushed and then the oil runs. The olive must be crushed four times; it is in the crushing process the oil flows forth. The Kingdom of God begins to manifest only after the crushing. The crushing process means that God is working on you – it is good and necessary, but you pray it will end quickly.

Surely every true believer has his "dark night of the soul" more than once in a lifetime. Yet, as Oswald Chambers once said: "Despair is always the gateway of faith."

4. Acceptance of the nighttime

Everyone goes into a night season. Nicodemus came to Jesus at night, because in the born-again process, in going higher in the Lord, the night season of your life moves you to seek salvation. It is in the night season that God does something special in your life for Kingdom entry. Thus Israel was in a time of night when Jesus came. He began to tell them that the Kingdom of God is coming. He sent John first to prepare the way. John plowed the ground, saying: "Repent, and prepare for the Kingdom."

5. Transforming of the mind

When the Kingdom of God begins to hit an individual, a people, a church, or a nation, the entire thought pattern begins to change. You begin to change in your concept of Christianity, because the Kingdom concept, in terms of what the Bible teaches, cannot fit into a denominational structure. It's too big for a denomination, and too big for a doctrinal ideology. It's too big for preconceived ideas or notions. The Kingdom of God is too big. When it begins to manifest, it has a diverse purpose in dimensions, it reaches in multitudinous ways in generations-you may start it and your great-grandchildren finish it.

That's when the Kingdom comes. But it will always come with order and government.

Ordered for Success

This book explains how the Kingdom of God functions according to rank in government and order. You see, certain demonic forces have been reigning in parts of the earth for centuries. Many of these spirits aren't going to move just because someone has come to preach the Gospel. Government, rank, and order must be established for the Kingdom of God to be effective against demonic forces.

That's why you'll read in the coming chapters that we're not going to be successful until the eldership in cities and nations come together. When the cities are together, each city with its eldership, a particular city becomes just a room, and the entire nation becomes a complete house, with cities providing individual rooms. On a city level, each church is just a room. On a local level, each church is a house. To accomplish this government and order, apostolic leaders are being raised up all over the world.

When God is building the house, and leaders get together, we plow the fields of harvest a lot easier. If you're plowing with an ox or with a horse, a horse can pull just so much tonnage. But if you put the two together, they can pull ten times more, not just twice as much. In biblical terms, we think of Kingdom warriors:

> 6 *And I will give peace in the land, and ye shall lie down, and none shall make you afraid: and I will rid evil beasts out of the land, neither shall the sword go through your land.*
> 7 *And ye shall chase your enemies, and they shall fall before you by the sword.*
> 8 *And five of you shall chase an hundred, and an hundred of you shall put ten thousand to flight: and your enemies shall fall before you by the sword.*
> —Leviticus 26:6-8

If you have one leader fighting this devil by himself, and each church every Sunday morning is fighting the same spirit but individually, rather than corporately-how effective can we be? But when we get together, with our accumulated power and strength, we're going to take nations.

In Argentina, for example, five notable apostles have virtually taken the entire nation. In thirty years, they've changed a communist nation into an evangelical powerhouse. The same thing is happening in Colombia. They're closing the drug cartel. The church is rising powerfully. Similarly, Guatemala is being saved, and also El Salvador and Venezuela. Our own ministry is opening churches in Venezuela. When we begin to put ourselves in a position for taking nations with the Gospel message, we're going to see the magnitude and blessing of God in a way we've never seen before. Let me show you how this works.

✳ Those Who Loved . . . Were Feared

When Jesus was crucified at Passover, the entire city had cried out: "Crucify him! Kill him! We have no king but Caesar." The entire city cried out against Him. The fear this struck into the disciples' hearts caused them to scatter and hide themselves. Later, when they gathered in the upper room, they were so afraid that when Jesus came through the wall, they shivered in their boots.

Jesus' followers were hiding, but the Bible says in Acts 1 that Jesus taught them many infallible truths concerning the Kingdom:

> 3 *He showed himself alive after his passion by many infallible proofs, being seen of them forty days,*

and speaking of the things pertaining to the kingdom of God:

4 *Being assembled together with them, commanded them that they should not depart from Jerusalem, but wait for the promise of the Father, which, saith he, ye have heard of me.*

5 *For John truly baptized with water; but ye shall be baptized with the Holy Ghost not many days hence.*
—Acts 1:3-5

For forty days He taught them their role and function, so that when He ascended from earth to heaven, he basically said to them: "Whatever you do, go to the upper room and wait until you receive power from on high. Don't leave there." This is the fortieth day from His resurrection. Ten days later at Pentecost, the same guys who were so scared, and so messed up-those same guys preached powerfully on the day of Pentecost. And on the day of Pentecost they gained more converts than Jesus had in three and a half years of ministry.

The people who had said, "Kill him!" were still in the city, because the Hellenic and traveling Jews would not leave Passover until Pentecost was over. So the same people who had hollered, "Kill him!" were still in the city . . . being converted!

What made the difference? My answer is this: A team of apostles had come together, joined together in mind, in strength, in agreement, to formulate the government of God in that place. What the enemy had done in killing Jesus, the enemy could not do in destroying the church. Because what happens when you have a group of elders in a city that rise up? The Bible says they filled the city with their doctrine. And in twenty-five years, more than one-tenth of the entire civilized world back then was evangelized. No telephones, no fax machines, no television, no satellite, no Tape of the Month, no written Bible. There was just travel by horses or by ship or by walking. One-tenth of the known world whose population was 250 million globally, was evangelized. These once-afraid disciples preached in the enemy's stronghold, and over 25 million bowed their knee to Christ within twenty years.

Because God built the church through government.

Think about how amazing this is in world history. Caesar: the most powerful man in his Rome; and his army: the most powerful military machine since Nebuchadnezzar — both feared the church! The Christians, men and women who never carried a sword, who never carried out any form of active aggression or political subversion, were feared by Caesar and his Rome.

But these were not people to fear by any normal way of thinking. After all, they had taken their Master's words to heart when he taught them: "Love your enemies."

Yet Caesar, the fighting machine of Rome, who feared no army, no political system, and no kingdom, feared a handful of Christians devoted to loving their neighbors, committed to praying for their persecutors. "We've got to kill them," Caesar said. When Nero came to power, he too said, "Throw them into the lion's dens. Cut them asunder. Pierce them with the sword. Burn them with fire. Torture them wherever you find them!"

How could the great leaders fear people who didn't have weapons? How could they fear these loving worshipers who had no church buildings, no money, no choirs, and met in the dark and damp catacombs under the streets?

It is imperative that we ask ourselves: Why were they feared? Because the government of God was in place, the demonic gods were being brought down, and the systems of man were being torn asunder. It was being accomplished by a handful of people who started out with God's government, with God building the house.

You see we can have millions of people all over the world claiming they are Christians. But without God's government, we Christians are just a bunch of individuals who are not empowered upon the earth. The demonic world will still rule.

Is He Lord of your life?

Writer David Rohr talks about this basic idea with reference to the motor home, so popular in America:

The motor home has allowed us to put all the conveniences of home on wheels. A camper no longer needs to contend with sleeping in a sleeping bag, cooking over a fire, or hauling water from a stream. Now he can park a fully equipped home on a cement slab in the midst of a few pine trees and hook up to a water line, a sewer line and electricity. Some motor homes have satellite dishes attached on top. No more bother with dirt, no more smoke from the fire, no more drudgery of walking to the stream. Now it is possible to go camping...and never have to go outside!

We buy a motor home with the hope of seeing new places, of getting out into the world. Yet we deck it out with the same furnishings as in our living room. Thus nothing really changes. We may drive to a new place, set ourselves in new surroundings, but the newness goes unnoticed, for we've simply carried along our old setting.[1]

The adventure of new life in Christ begins when the comfortable patterns of the old life are left behind. Two thousand years after Jesus died and rose from the dead, the church is only now starting to grab hold again of the heavenlies. We're taking dominion, we're possessing what rightfully belongs to us, and it's not coming only because of intercessory prayer; it's coming because of apostolic leaders taking their rightful place in rightful times and associations.

When Jesus introduces the Lord's Prayer, He says when we pray we should say: *"Thy kingdom come, Thy will be done."* That is, in heaven there is one will, one Kingdom. When we conclude our prayer, we are to say: *"For thine is the Kingdom, the power, and the glory."* So when we begin to pray the Kingdom of God, we're praying something that's beyond a culture, beyond a group of people. We're praying the Kingdom of God in a Davidic sense in which we have apostolic headship ruling the entire nations of the earth.

It is a lot easier said than done. That is why we intercessors must keep praying that God will release an anointing and fervor for unity among the headships within nations, a deep desire to come together. That is why things like racism, genderism, preferential treatment, and nepotism are enemies to the Kingdom of God. They all perpetuate division while God wants to bring us together in unity.

As you read this book, my prayer is that you will open your heart to this Kingdom that is moving, that is coming at every level. It may start on a very personal level as you seek to renew your love of the Lord and to deepen your fellowship with Him day by day. And I am confident it will progress as you work within your family and within your local church for the government and order that the Kingdom always brings. You will no doubt see this personal renewal flowing outward as you join with your brothers and sisters of a similar mind and heart, to bring cities and nations together until . . .

> . . . *at the name of Jesus every knee should bow, of things in heaven, and things in earth, and things under the earth. And that every tongue should confess that Jesus Christ is Lord, to the glory of God the Father.*
> —Philippians 2:10-11

CHAPTER 1

ENTERING A NEW ERA IN THE CHURCH

THE PRINCES OF THE GENTILES EXERCISE DOMINION OVER THEM, AND THEY THAT ARE GREAT EXERCISE AUTHORITY UPON THEM. BUT IT SHALL NOT BE SO AMONG YOU.

—Matthew 20:25-26

There was an old farmer who, in the prayer meetings of his church would describe his experience like this: "Well, I'm not making much progress, but I'm established." One spring when the farmer was setting out some fence posts, his wagon sank in the mud, and he couldn't get unstuck. As he sat on top of the logs, viewing the situation, a neighbor (who had never accepted the principle of the old farmer's religious experience) came along and greeted him, saying: "Well, Brother Jones, I see you aren't making much progress, but you certainly are established!" [2]

The principle is simple: In the Christian life, as in any form of vital endeavor, there must be growth and progress; a moving forward to what's new. We may be established for a while, and that's okay. But if we stay settled and satisfied for too long, it begins looking suspiciously like being stuck. I see this with my four sons. Each of them attends various grades in school. One is in the first grade, another is in fifth grade, another is in ninth grade, and the eldest is in twelfth grade. They have all migrated through a process of learning — through the transforming power of education — to where they are now. And I'm quite sure they will keep growing. But my point is that the son who's in grade 1 is not wrong; he just doesn't have as much knowledge and information as the one in grade 12, who also is not wrong.

Isn't it the same with the church? There is a moving ahead in knowledge and maturity. What was in the past wasn't necessarily wrong; it was unfinished. Therefore, we are moving ahead into a new era, something different and something new. That's why a century ago, the kind of church government that prevailed was not wrong for that time. It was simply incomplete.

You opened this book because you want to know what the Scriptures have to say about government and order in the church. Once we look at governmental systems in the Scripture, we can begin to see what Jesus meant when He said to the disciples: *"They that are great exercise authority upon them. But it shall not be so among you."* You see, the Kingdom of God has a different kind of government.

We could go to numerous scriptural sources to uncover this truth. But let's begin with Paul in 1 Corinthians. Through him we'll find two primary principles setting the stage for the text: (1) The spiritual gifts as illustrating the perfection of the governmental structure we're moving towards, and (2) extravagant love as the "more excellent way" to achieving this transformation.

Gifts: Clues to Government

As we look at the spiritual gifts, remember that Paul is showing us the protocol and governmental structure of the way things should function within an assembly. This is my main point, and we'll come back to it, again and again. Let's start by digging into some verses from 1 Corinthians 12 and 13.

¹ *Now concerning spiritual gifts, brethren, I would not have you ignorant.*

² *Ye know that ye were Gentiles, carried away unto these dumb idols, even as ye were led.*

³ *Wherefore I give you to understand, that no man speaking by the Spirit of God calleth Jesus accursed: and that no man can say that Jesus is the Lord, but by the Holy Ghost.*

⁴ *Now there are diversities of gifts, but the same Spirit.*

⁵ *And there are differences of administrations, but the same Lord.*

⁶ *And there are diversities of operations, but it is the same God which worketh all in all.*

⁷ *But the manifestation of the Spirit is given to every man to profit withal.*

> ⁸ *For to one is given by the Spirit the word of wisdom; to another the word of knowledge by the same Spirit.*
>
> ⁹ *To another faith by the same Spirit; to another the gifts of healing by the same Spirit;*
>
> ¹⁰ *To another the working of miracles; to another prophecy; to another discerning of spirits; to another divers kinds of tongues; to another the interpretation of tongues:*
>
> ¹¹ *But all these worketh that one and the selfsame Spirit, dividing to every man severally as he will.*
>
> —1 Corinthians 12:1-11

First, let me comment on two particular ideas that come through here-diversities of gifts, and differences of administrations. In verse 4, the word "gifts" is charis in the Bible's original Greek manuscripts. The word doesn't literally incorporate entirely the nine gifts of the Spirit; it goes beyond the gifts of the Spirit. You see, there are the gifts of the Spirit and then there are spiritual gifts. Spiritual gifts and the gifts of the Spirit are totally different things. The gifts of the Spirit are given to those who are anointed, who have been baptized in the Holy Spirit. Spiritual gifts refer to endowments from God, such as the gift of being able to engage effectively in intercessory prayer, or to give money freely, or to write and sing music. Those abilities aren't listed as part of the nine gifts of the Holy Spirit.

In verse 5, regarding the phrase differences of administrations, simply recognize that there are varying gifts but the same Spirit. This word "administrations" has to do with government. It has to do with the structuring of church protocol, religious or Christian protocol, or spiritual protocol.

Now in verses 12:8-11, we have the nine gifts of the Holy Spirit. I like to place them into three categories: the inspirational gifts, the power gifts, and the supreme gifts.

The Inspirational Gifts:

◆ *Prophecy*

◆ *Tongues*

◆ *Interpretation of tongues*

These three gifts form in the outer court of Moses' tabernacle. The greatest of the gifts in this group is prophecy, because every set of gifts forms a house, and each house has a head of that house. (Note: There are three dimensions within every dimension. Once we see these three dimensions within a dimension, we then can understand the greater dimensions of what God wants to do.)

The Power Gifts:

◆ *Faith*

◆ *Working of miracles*

◆ *Healing*

The gift of faith is different from the faith in God that comes by hearing. This gift of faith comes in power and is head of this house. In this second dimension, the gift of faith is the power gift and head of the house of power gifts.

The Supreme Gifts:

✳◆ *Word of wisdom*
  ◆ *Word of knowledge*
  ◆ *Discerning of Spirits*

These gifts are the greater gifts, the gifts of profound order, with word of wisdom as the head. These are signified by what was within Moses' tabernacle, inside the ark of the covenant: Aaron's rod that budded, a golden pot of manna, and the two tablets of the ten commandments. Aaron's rod represents the discernment the people of Israel needed in order to choose the tribe of Levi for the priesthood *(see Numbers 17:2-11)*; the pot of manna represents for the wisdom the people needed to follow God's instructions about how and when to eat in the desert *(see Exodus 16)*; the ten commandments stand for the knowledge the people needed about what was right and wrong behavior as they sought to live for God *(see Exodus 20:1-17)*.

Now notice two important points about the gifts that can help you understand them a bit better:

1. The gifts are works of milk, not meat.

What do I mean by that? The gifts of the Spirit are not meaty works; they are works of milk. They are juvenile gifts that will preoccupy immature believers.

Remember that the apostle Paul was addressing the Corinthian church members concerning their problems. They were, in many ways, a problem congregation. In THE MESSAGE version of 1 Corinthians 3:1-2, Paul had said to them: *"Friends, I am completely frustrated by your unspiritual dealings with each other and with God. You're acting like infants in relation to Christ, capable of nothing much more than nursing at the breast. Well, then, I'll nurse you since you don't seem to be capable of anything more."*

So Paul says, "I cannot deal with you as adults; I cannot deal with you as mature. You have to be on milk because meat belongs to those with strong theological teeth. You are unable to chew the meat issues." What about you? Are you mature enough in your Christian growth to consume the meat of the Word? It's an important question for any of us to contemplate. Here's how the great nineteenth-century preacher Charles Spurgeon "pictured" it:

"We have the likenesses of our boys taken on every birthday, so that we see them at a glance from their babyhood to their youth. Suppose such photographic memorials of our own spiritual life had been taken and preserved; would there be a regular advance, as in these boys, or would we still have been exhibited in the baby buggy? Have not some grown awhile, and then suddenly dwarfed? Have not others gone back to childhood? Here is a wide field for reflection."[3]

It is an important issue for individual believers, but in Corinth the entire church was still in the buggy! The whole of 1 Corinthians is the book of milk, food for infants, not grownups. Why? Because Paul had to patiently explain to them how to act — behaviors they should have learned long ago. He told them not to fight with each other, to learn how to be orderly, to learn the proper use of their gifts, to recognize that love is their highest calling.

What problem kids they were! They were hung up on comparing their gifts. They wanted to rank one another in importance in the Kingdom. They sought to compete in spirituality. Thus, they caused divisions in their fellowship and chaos in their worship services.

However, amidst all the milk of his instructions to these immature members, Paul threw a piece of meat-to show the church what was coming in the future. A new maturity is coming. That's where we need to pay particular attention.

2. The gifts lead to new levels of the Spirit's working.

The gifts, primarily, are for building up the body of Christ. We exercise them to edify one another in the church. But I also want to emphasize that they are leading us to something else in God, especially regarding church government and leadership. Now watch how Paul introduces this new level. He says in 12:13-18; 27-28:

13 For by one Spirit are we all baptized into one body, whether we be Jews or Gentiles, whether we be bond or free; and have been all made to drink into one Spirit.

14 For the body is not one member, but many.

15 If the foot shall say, Because I am not the hand, I am not of the body; is it therefore not of the body?

16 And if the ear shall say, Because I am not the eye, I am not of the body; is it therefore not of the body?

17 *If the whole body were an eye, where were the hearing? If the whole were hearing, where were the smelling?*

18 *But now hath God set the members every one of them in the body, as it hath pleased him. . . .*

27 *Now ye are the body of Christ, and members in particular.*

28 *And God hath set some in the church, first apostles, secondarily prophets, thirdly teachers, after that miracles, then gifts of healings, helps, governments, diversities of tongues.*

Paul used the human body of an adult to explain various levels of church government and leadership. In another chapter I'll explain what the foot is and what the hand is. But the foot here speaks of the gospel message; the hand speaks of a five-fold functional ministry. He continued to talk about the ear and the eye, which are headship gifts of authority and government. Then, in verses 27 and 28, Paul gave us the protocol and the governmental structure of the way things should function within an assembly.

Finally, over-arching these means of government and order within the church comes the primary motivation of it all (in verse 31): the more excellent way.

Love: The Means to Perfection

Love shines through so brightly in the Bible that we call 1 Corinthians 13 "The Love Chapter." Love is excellent because God is excellent, and because God is love. Also, since God is perfect, his church will be perfect. But notice two things about the movement toward that blessed state:

1. It comes in measured doses.

Paul says in 13:9: *"For we know in part and our prophecy is in part."* The words in part mean "given by measure." That is, given in pieces, in doses. For example, when a person is sick, the doctor prescribes a certain medication. Then the pharmacist puts the pills in a bottle and writes the daily dosage on the bottle. You can't ignore the dosage, and swallow an entire bottle of tablets! For the medicine to be effective you must take the number of pills indicated in the prescribed manner over a course of time.

Similarly, Paul says, "we are prophesying in part," a dose at a time, because the audience of this letter was unable to receive the fullness of what God had for them. Then he says: *"But when that which is perfect is come, that which is in part shall be done away."* The perfection he's talking about is a state of the church. He's not talking about an individual being perfect before God or even about the return of Jesus. He's talking about the state in which the church will be existing. It's called the state of perfection, arriving dose by dose.

You can see it previewed in the Old Testament. Once a year, on the Day of Atonement, Aaron the priest would sprinkle blood on the pure-gold covering over the ark of the covenant, known as the mercy seat.4 There God's glory would come, and it was there on that mercy seat, which represented God's government, that the state of perfection would be released. All the enemies of Israel-sickness, disease, poverty, demonic spirits, hostile kings and kingdoms-all would be subdued under the power of God. That Day of Atonement was called the state of perfection, when that which was perfect had come. That which was in part, which was in proxy, was done away.

The Scripture says that the Old Testament was the shadow of things to come. However, the actual body is Christ, the very entity Paul is teaching us about. But the body of Christ on the Day of Pentecost, and in the early church, was not in full perfection. It was still being formed . . . until Christ be formed in us. It was still being formed, transforming into a position of strength and structure. *"For now we see through a glass, darkly; but then face to face: now I know in part; but then shall I know even as also I am known"* (1 Corinthians 12:12).

2. It requires certain components.

A number of components are necessary for this metamorphosis to strength and structure. We'll touch upon them more fully later. But for now, consider:

♦ *Going through the stages.* In Revelation 2-3, the apostle John speaks of the church ages to come. He says there are seven church ages or seven completions, seven candlesticks, seven movements in the motion to bringing the state of perfection. In this state of perfection the church is going to come into the fullness of who Christ is.

♦ *Putting away the childish things.* Paul says here in 1 Corinthians 13:11: *"When I was a child, I spake as a child, I understood as a child, I thought as a child: but when I became a man, I put away childish things."* The body is childish at the moment, in a state of childish perfection. It's growing to adulthood. Paul says we need to come to the place where we put away childish things.

♦ *Knowing as we're known.* Then he says that, for now, where we're standing, we are looking through a smoky glass. THE MESSAGE version puts it this way: *"We do not yet see things clearly. We are squinting in a fog, piercing through mist, but we won't be in this mist for long because the weather will clear and the sun will shine bright. We'll see it all then. We'll see God clearly as He sees us. Knowing Him directly just as He knows us."* That wonderful day is still ahead.

But will we move ahead with the church to that state of perfection? It is not an easy question, because it's not an easy task. The church, after all, is under persecution. It is threatened on every side, held in the lowest esteem in secular societies around the world. In effect, it is taking a beating. I recall a kind of parable-of-the-church offered by writer Philip Anderson. He tells this story:

Not long ago I visited my sister, a director of patient services for the children's unit of a large southern California hospital. She was conducting me on a tour through that unit. All the time, echoing through the halls, we could hear the cry of a baby coming from one of the rooms. Finally we came to that room. It was a little child, about a year old, covered with terrible bruises, scratches, scars, from head to toe.

At first, I assumed the child must have been involved in a terrible accident. Then I looked closely at its legs. Written in ink all over them were obscenities. My sister told me that the child was the victim, not of an accident, but of its parents. Its internal injuries were so severe that it couldn't keep any food down. The scars on the bottom of its feet were burns caused by cigarettes.

If you have ever had trouble visualizing the consequences of human indifference, the perversion of life's basic relationships, what God himself is up against in this world of ours, then I wish you could have looked with me at that battered, crying baby.

But I want to tell you what happened then. My sister leaned over the crib and very carefully and tenderly lifted the child, and held it next to herself. At first the child screamed all the more, as if its innocent nature had come to be suspicious of every touch. But as she held it securely and warmly, the baby slowly began to quiet down. And finally, in spite of wounds and hurts and past experience, it felt the need to cry no more.

The baby remains in my memory as a living symbol of the choice we face in the mission of the church. Are we willing to let life's most precious values be battered and starved and crucified by default? Or will we reach out and pick them up and hold them close to our hearts? The time for commitment is not next year, next month, but now!" [5]

Be assured, the transformation to perfection is taking place right now. Commit to it; hold it close to your heart. Completeness is coming, and we are not planting posts like the poor farmer who sat established and stuck. However, right now, until that completeness, we have three things to lead us towards this consummation: trust in God, hope relentlessly, love extravagantly.

CHAPTER 2

NO MORE DIVISION

EVERY ONE OF YOU SAITH, I AM OF PAUL; AND I OF APOLLOS; AND I OF CEPHAS; AND I OF CHRIST. IS CHRIST DIVIDED? WAS PAUL CRUCIFIED FOR YOU? OR WERE YE BAPTIZED IN THE NAME OF PAUL?
—1 Corinthians 1:12-13

When it was built for an international exposition in the late 1800s, the structure was called monstrous. Many of the citizens demanded that it be torn down once the exposition ended. Yet its architect loyally defended his work. He knew it was destined for greatness. Today it is one of the architectural wonders of the modern world, the primary landmark of Paris, France. The architect, of course, was Alexandre Gustave Eiffel. His famous tower was built in 1889.

In the same way, we are struck by Jesus' loyalty to another structure-the church-which He entrusted to an unlikely band of disciples, whom He defended, prayed for, and prepared to spread the Gospel. To outsiders they (and we) must seem like inept blunderers. But Jesus, the architect of the church, knows this structure is destined for greatness.

If we go to the Book of Matthew we'll see some of the things Jesus dealt with in governmental structure. Scripture says that when Jesus was about to be released into full ministry, His cousin John began to preach in the wilderness of Judea (Matt. 3:2) saying, *"Repent, for the Kingdom of Heaven is at hand."* Similarly, when Jesus started preaching, the Scripture says He went where the prophet Isaiah had said a great light was coming. Many people that were in darkness saw a great light but didn't understand it. Then, in verse 4:17, *"from that time Jesus began to preach and to say, 'Repent, for the Kingdom of Heaven is at hand.'"*

So, we have two preachers (one of whom is God-in-the-flesh) heralding the future of God's reign on earth. It is a Kingdom not of meat and drink, but of righteousness, peace, and joy in the Holy Ghost *(see Matthew 5:6-12)*. That is, when we see righteousness, peace, and joy in the Holy Ghost we see Jesus initiating the Kingdom of God. What can we glean regarding Jesus' approach to what is at hand — to the coming church government? I'd like to suggest at least four ideas:

1. This Is a New Way for the Church

We must grasp, especially as we come into the twenty-first-century church, that God's governmental order is being released in a unique way today. For many years we've had a denominational structure that has provided its own system. That system is complete at a certain level, but it's not fully complete when it enters into the Kingdom.

For example, in the Greek Islands, you'll find the home of Hippocrates, the father of modern medicine. In the area, you can also find an olive tree, supposedly dating from his time. If this is so, then this tree would be well over two thousand years old. The trunk of the tree is very large but completely hollow! It is little more than thick bark. There are a few long, straggling branches, but they are supported by sturdy wooden poles placed every few feet around it. The branches produce an occasional leaf here and there and might produce a few olives each year. In the fields around, however, you can see olive groves unfolding across the landscape in many directions. The strong, healthy, young trees with narrow trunks are covered with a thick canopy of leaves, under which masses of olives flourish each year.

We can still call the tree of Hippocrates an olive by nature; it still displays the essential, unique characteristics. But it has long since ceased to fulfill an olive tree's function. Tourists file by to inspect this ancient relic that has some link to a dim history. However, the job of the olive tree passed long ago to many successions of replanted trees.

Do you know any churches (or even people) like the tree of Hippocrates? The form is there, but the function is not. They have stopped reproducing and are satisfied just being big, or having a noble history.

Perhaps that is the essence of our denominationalism today. It is hollow. It has caused us to lose sight of our true identity as Christ's one body. I think of the story told of John Wesley. He was concerned about the rise of denominations in the church, and he had a dream about it. In the dream, he was ushered to the gates of Hell. There he asked, "Are there any Presbyterians here?"

"Yes!" came the answer. Then he asked, "Are there any Baptists? Any Episcopalians? Any Methodists?" The answer was "Yes!" each time.

Much distressed, Wesley was then ushered to the gates of Heaven. There he asked the same questions, and the answer was always No! "No?" Wesley asked, "Who then is inside?" The answer came back, "There are only Christians here."

Isn't it true? Our foundational identity is Christian. And if this is so, then our church governmental structures should demonstrate it. Yet this will be a new way for the church, a new way that is on the way. To conclude this section, just listen to the apostle Paul on the matter:

> [10] *Now I beseech you, brethren, by the name of our Lord Jesus Christ, that ye all speak the same thing, and that there be no divisions among you; but that ye be perfectly joined together in the same mind and in the same judgment.*
>
> [11] *For it hath been declared unto me of you, my brethren, by them which are of the house of Chloe, that there are contentions among you.*
>
> [12] *Now this I say, that every one of you saith, I am of Paul; and I of Apollos; and I of Cephas; and I of Christ.*

13 *Is Christ divided? was Paul crucified for you? or were ye baptized in the name of Paul?*

14 *I thank God that I baptized none of you, but Crispus and Gaius;*

15 *Lest any should say that I had baptized in mine own name.*

16 *And I baptized also the household of Stephanas: besides, I know not whether I baptized any other.*

17 *For Christ sent me not to baptize, but to preach the gospel: not with wisdom of words, lest the cross of Christ should be made of none effect.*

—1 Corinthians 1:10-17

2. The Church Is a Kingdom of Three Levels

In Matthew 5:14, Jesus says: *"Ye are the light of the world."* He goes on to say, "A city that is set on a hill cannot be hid. Neither do men light a candle, and put it under a bushel." So here we see a candle in a house, a city on a hill, and the light of the world. Jesus implies government, and we see three distinct levels of existence of the church.

This is the basis of church government: The house, the city, the Kingdom throughout the earth. This comes through most clearly in Matthew 12. There, Jesus was casting out a devil from a man who was deaf and dumb. The Scripture says,

24 *But when the Pharisees heard it, they said, This fellow doth not cast out devils, but by Beelzebub the prince of the devils.*

> 25 *And Jesus knew their thoughts, and said unto them, Every kingdom divided against itself is brought to desolation; and every city or house divided against itself shall not stand.*
>
> —Matthew 12:24-25

Every city or house divided against itself cannot stand. So Jesus was bringing a revelation about this concept-the house, the city, the Kingdom. We have three different levels of government, three different levels of existence, and three different levels of function.

Look at Matthew 7. In this chapter, Jesus is coming to the close of his teaching on the Kingdom called the Sermon on the Mount. He ends his teaching basically saying that the wise man builds his house upon the rock-his house, not his city, not his kingdom. When the stormy test came against the house, the house stood.

Building the house is important. In the Kingdom of God, Jesus says in John 14:1-2, "Let not your heart be troubled: ye believe in God, believe also in me. In my Father's house are many mansions." That word mansions is also interpreted "rooms," or better translated as "houses." So Jesus is saying, in effect: "In my Father's house are many houses."

When Jesus says you have to build the house first, that house reveals the starting place upon which the Kingdom of God is to be built. That's why Jesus said to the disciples, "Don't go anywhere. You must first go to Jerusalem, until you be endowed with power from on high. Don't leave the city of Jerusalem, go to Jerusalem first." That's where the first house was to be built. It was an apostolic house. There was a governmental structure and order for that particular house.

3. The Leadership Is a Multiplicity

All of this leads us to a key truth: Every church that is significant is a house that God is building with a multiplicity of leaders. The governmental system of that house is different from the governmental system of a city and different from the governmental order in the kingdom. So, when we talk about the governmental system of a house, in my own words, you'll have a pastor who is "the set man." In New Life Covenant Church, for example, that would be me. I would be the set man, the man whom God has set in the position of authority.

The set man is the one to whom God will begin to relate and to release vision for the purpose of that house and its existence. I believe that such a church is structured in heaven. Now, by that I refer to when David gave Solomon the plans for the temple saying: "These are the plans of the House of God that I received by the Spirit." In other words, the house Solomon was going to build, with all of its furnishings and its personnel, was already structured and planned in the heavens. So if I am the set man of our church, it means that God has set me to fulfill a Kingdom purpose where I am. And it also means that there is a set structure.

In the New Testament, you do not find the word pastor referring to an individual who is leading a church. Rather, the Bible says in Ephesians 4:11-12, *"He gave some, apostles; and some, prophets; and some, evangelists; and some, pastors and teachers; for the perfecting of the saints, for the work of the ministry, for the edifying of the body of Christ.*" These functions are for building the church. The five-fold ministry is a governmental structure. But the word pastor was not meant to be an individual, singular person leading in the church.

I want to emphasize that even though we have migrated from the five-fold ministry concept to singular leadership, it is always God's preference to have a multiplicity of leaders. "To the church in Corinth, to the church in Philippi, and the leaders and the bishops," Paul was always saying. "To all those God has assembled in Ephesus" . . . you always find a corporate group of elders leading the church.

As the set man of New Life Covenant Church, I now have an administration and governmental system that will differ from another church in our city. They'll have a set man with a different governmental system to suit that house, because each house is run autonomously as the Spirit gives anointing, knowledge, and information. The purpose is to build a strong house so that a city like Harare, or a city like Dallas, Chicago, New York or London, can have many strong houses or churches.

And please be aware that in all of our talk about a "house," we are not dealing with bricks and mortar. In fact, there is no biblical norm as to where the church should meet. The early church wasn't connected with a church building. It was something else: a group of Christians united by the Holy Spirit wherever they lived and worked together in the Kingdom. I like how Howard Snyder put it in his book THE PROBLEM OF WINESKINS:

Theologically, the church does not need temples. Church buildings are not essential to the true nature of the church. For the meaning of the tabernacle is God's habitation, and God already dwells within the human community of Christian believers. The people are the temple and the tabernacle. . . . Thus, theologically church buildings are superfluous. They are not needed for priestly functions because all believers are priests and all have direct access, at whatever time and place, to the one great high priest. A church building cannot properly be "the Lord's house" because in the new covenant this title is reserved for the church as people (Ephesians 2; 1 Timothy 3:15; Hebrews 10:21). *A church building cannot be a "holy place" in any special sense, for holy places no longer exist. Christianity has no holy places, only holy people.*[6]

So we've seen that Jesus prepared the way for a new way for the church, a Kingdom of three levels, with a multiplicity leadership. Finally, we must recognize the unity at the heart of this structure. Without unity, we face severe difficulties in the Kingdom.

4. Divided, We Can't Stand

In Matthew 12:25, Jesus says *"Every kingdom divided against itself is brought to desolation; and every city or house divided against itself shall not stand."* With that word *every*, Jesus was literally saying that there are many, many kingdoms in the earth, more kingdoms than we can count on our hands.

Have you ever thought about all those kingdoms? Actually, there are seven basic kingdoms that we have to deal with on a daily basis:

1. The *mineral* kingdom

2. The *vegetable* kingdom

3. The *animal* kingdom

4. The *human* kingdom

5. The *galactic* kingdom (planets)

6. The *angelic* kingdom (demonic and angelic)

7. The *Spirit world* kingdom (the sovereign Kingdom of God)

All of these kingdoms function powerfully individually, but even more powerfully when they work together. So when Jesus says that every kingdom divided against itself cannot stand, recall the principle of kingdoms. For example, consider the animal kingdom for a moment. Within the animal kingdom, there are various animals from the water, from the land, and from the air. In the three basic levels of the animal kingdom, you'll find there are kings of the sea, kings of the land, and kings of the air. The kings, or rulers in these kingdoms, need to be fully understood if we're to have success in our dealings with that kingdom.

Yet again, Jesus reveals something else. He's saying in 12:26, *"If Satan cast out Satan, he is divided against himself; how then shall his kingdom stand?"* So Jesus is saying that in the demonic world, which is the sixth kingdom of spirits, Satan is the king of his kingdom and it's not divided against itself. This kingdom is divided into principalities, into kingships, into domains, into measures of rule, and the demonic kings and princes that rule over regents and cities. It's not a kingdom divided against itself. But Jesus then implies that the Kingdom of Heaven has come: *"If I cast out devils by the Spirit of God, then the kingdom of God is come unto you."* So Jesus interjects here that there is a unity in the Kingdom of God. That Kingdom must not be divided either!

Do you remember ever being at a carnival show and putting your face into a headless frame for a photograph? The frame may have been painted to represent a muscle man, a clown, or even a bathing beauty, and it had a hole cut out of it for your face. Many of us have had our pictures taken this way, and the photos are humorous. The photo looks funny because the head does not fit the body. If we could picture Christ as the head of our local body of believers, would the world laugh at the misfit? Or would they stand in awe of a human body so closely related to a divine head?

The church must not be divided; it must stay unified through Christ the head, and connected across the earth. During World War II, Hitler commanded all religious groups to "unite" so that he could control them. Among the Brethren church assemblies, half complied and half refused. Those who went along with the order had a much easier time. Those who did not, faced harsh persecution. In almost every family of those who resisted, someone died in a concentration camp. When the war was over, feelings of bitterness ran deep between the groups, and there was much tension.

Finally, they decided that the situation had to be healed. Leaders from each group met at a quiet retreat. For several days, each person spent time in prayer, examining his own heart in the light of Christ's commands, then they came together. Francis Schaeffer, who told of the incident, asked a friend who was there: "What did you do then?" "We were just one," he replied.

As they confessed their hostility and bitterness to God, and yielded to His control, the Holy Spirit created a spirit of unity among them. Love filled their hearts and dissolved their hatred. When love prevails among believers, especially in times of strong disagreement, it presents to the world an awesome mark of a true follower of Jesus Christ.[7]

CHAPTER 3

THE WAY OF THE ELDERS . . . AND DEACONS

VERILY, VERILY, I SAY UNTO YOU, THE SERVANT IS
NOT GREATER THAN HIS LORD; NEITHER HE THAT IS
SENT GREATER THAN HE THAT SENT HIM.

—John 13:16

In Matthew 13 Jesus speaks of the mustard seed, the least of all seeds, which grows to be the greatest among herbs. Indeed, the seed becomes a virtual tree, so big that birds lodge in its branches. The original Greek word for "tree" in this parable is *dendra*. Elsewhere, in Mark 4, that herb plant's branches are described as *mega-lous*. So, *dendra* being the word for tree, and *mega* meaning huge or abnormal size — this applies to the church. That is, within a city like London or Dallas or Harare, you will find God raising up some *mega-dendra* churches. They grow bigger than the normal.

The purpose for that mega house is to provide a kind of shelter for other houses. The governmental structure and order in that house is very important. You see, the apostolic headship of that house must have a corporate group of elders who serve there for the purpose of nurturing the corporate vision that God is releasing among them. Eventually, that house influences other houses . . . and then a whole city.

As God begins to release that vision, and it falls upon the set man (who is the apostolic headship of that house), that vision will also then be imparted to the elders of the house. We see this playing out in the experience of Moses:

> 14 *I am not able to bear all this people alone, because it is too heavy for me. . . .*
>
> 16 *And the LORD said unto Moses, Gather unto me seventy men of the elders of Israel, whom thou knowest to be the elders of the people, and officers over them; and bring them unto the tabernacle of the congregation, that they may stand there with thee.*
>
> 17 *And I will come down and talk with thee there: and I will take of the spirit which is upon thee, and will put it upon them; and they shall bear the burden of the people with thee, that thou bear it not thyself alone.*
>
> —Numbers 11:14, 16-17

The Hebrew people, traveling through the desert, had been complaining to their heroic leader about food. But Moses was the one getting fed up! He called upon the Lord for help, and He responded. How? Notice that the spirit of Moses was placed upon seventy other men.

In other words, God responded by providing elders to serve in leadership on behalf of Moses. When these seventy entered into the anointing to serve Israel as elders, they could not function with their own spirit; they received the spirit of Moses. Moses got his spirit and his mandate from God.

Do you see the progression? God gave His Spirit and His agenda to Moses. That Spirit was then translated and placed on seventy other men. So as the set man at our own church, God has given me His Spirit and His agenda for apostolic strategy; apostolic insight; revelation and wisdom into governmental structure; building a complete house; prosperity; healing; miracles; and prophesy. These things resident in me, which I receive from God, fall corporately on all the elders in our particular assembly. Can you see, then, how important it is to understand the role and function of elders? That is the theme I want to take up in this chapter, along with laying out the next level of house government as well: the role of deacons.

The Role of Elders

The biblical word for "elders" is *presbuteros*, or *presbytery*. It refers to leaders who have been appointed to serve in a governing capacity. So when you have a house that's being built, that house serves as a governmental institution over a local assembly. Thus, when any demonic attack occurs – whether it's poverty, disease, demonic overtones of tyranny, or any other spiritual opposition – the presbytery can actually stop the attack by intercessory prayer and asserting its authority from God. Also, the presbytery is given the power to open the heavens, to shut doors, and to release gifts in people:

> 6 *Wherefore I [Paul] put thee [Timothy] in remembrance that thou stir up the gift of God, which is in thee by the putting on of my hands.*
>
> 7 *For God hath not given us the spirit of fear; but of power, and of love, and of a sound mind.*
>
> 8 *Be not thou therefore ashamed of the testimony of our Lord, nor of me his prisoner: but be thou partaker of the afflictions of the gospel according to the power of God;*
>
> 9 *Who hath saved us, and called us with an holy calling, not according to our works, but according to his own purpose and grace, which was given us in Christ Jesus before the world began,*
>
> 10 *But is now made manifest by the appearing of our Savior Jesus Christ, who hath abolished death, and hath brought life and immortality to light through the gospel:*
>
> 11 *Whereunto I am appointed a preacher, and an apostle, and a teacher of the Gentiles.*
>
> —2 Timothy 1:6-11

In our local church, I, as the set man, have appointed men and women within whose lives we see the fruit of presbytery manifested. This is important: They were not voted in.

If you place individuals by voting, your church members will not see the kind of fruit that is necessary in Spirit-led leadership. That's why the Lord basically said to Moses, "You go amongst the people, and you select seventy men." The criterion is given for those men, and God said to Moses, "I will take your spirit and put it on them."

That is why we highly recommend that the headship, or the set man — the pastor, the bishop, the apostolic head of that house or church — appoints the men and women according to the fruit they clearly bear; according to the service they've been rendering. These folks are appointed to serve as elders. Throughout Scripture, in both the New Testament and the Old Testament, we see examples of this, with four classifications of elders coming through. Let's look more closely at each kind.

1. Governmental Elders

The Bible says, *"Let the elders that rule well be counted worthy of double honor, especially they who labor in the word and doctrine"* (1 Tim. 5:16). We must give double honor because these elders serve with the set man concerning governmental issues. By that, I mean they give spiritual guidance, nurturing and caretaking the vision. They make massive contributions concerning the vision of the house, serving the vision of the set man, who gets it from God. Such servant hood is always worthy of honor.

2. Yoke Elders

A yoke elder is one whom God yokes to the set man, yokes to the leadership. That yoke elder will plow anywhere the bishop is going to plow. If the bishop, or set man, says: "We are going to have church in a certain place because that's where we feel God is sending us," then that individual may not fully understand – or even fully agree with moving from one place to another. But because he's a yoke elder, and that anointing is on his/her life, they will go and plow with that bishop in the field. They will stand with that leader, no matter what happens.

3. Gate Elders

This elder sits in the gates to watch for both good and evil, to watch for spiritual trends, and what's coming into and going out of the city. Gate elders who are tuned into God can usually tell long before a demonic attack occurs that a destructive wave is coming. The Spirit will speak to them through visions, dreams, inspirations, songs, and feelings. They may get depressed, and through the years learn that this depression is a signal through which God is going to speak.

Gate elders can also identify wolves in sheep's clothing. They can be sitting in a service, and the Spirit of God will show them a man or a woman who is not in good standing with the church, or somebody who has come to hurt the church. For example, in Africa, gate elders can pick out witch doctors and witches who come to disrupt a service. Thank God, they can see these trouble-makers coming down the road!

Gate elders are very powerful individuals because the Spirit of God sits upon them heavily. They are the church's spiritual barometer. They can tell when the seasons are changing and they usually receive strong prophetic words that are more directional and positional rather than inspirational and encouraging. So, let me issue this warning: If a gate elder isn't placed correctly in the church, he may actually hurt the church or the set man. He may even end up splitting the church. Why? Because this elder may feel that the set man of the house is not in tune with God.

4. Domestic Elders

Given to the care of people, these elders have a deep heart of compassion. They love to care for the widows, orphans, and single mothers. They want to know if the pastor is taken care of. They care about all the cares of their particular assembly.

These four classifications of elders help bring balance and structure within a church and are of key importance to a church that's going to grow and become significant. You can place a tremendous amount of weight on these individuals and, because of their gifting and their anointing, they can hold that weight.

There is no numerical limit to the number of elders you may appoint. Jesus set the perfect example, though: He had twelve apostles and then he traveled with another seventy disciples. So, the twelve apostles were the four groups of elders. They are listed in Matthew 10 by their name, in their rank, and in the order of double-honor elders which are governmental elders, gate elders, yoke elders, and domestic elders. (Interestingly, that's why the apostle Peter refers to himself as an elder in various Scriptures, as does Paul; they are referring to their structural role in the house.)

The Role of Deacons

When we go to the next level of the house government, we deal with the deacons. This group of individuals, whose qualifications unfold in 2 Timothy and also in Titus, are not governmental. Deacons exercise the ministries of "helps." They carry out service ministries for the presbytery and the set man (or apostolic headship) within the local house.

Deacons do not serve in a city; they do not serve in the corporate kingdom. For example, you can't tell me who the corporate kingdom deacons are that serve over the nation of India, because there aren't any! Deacons serve in a house. They don't serve in the city of Harare or the city of London; they serve in a local church. For that reason, their ministry is not governmental but administrative and service oriented. Here is the beginning of their ministry:

1 *In those days, when the number of the disciples was multiplied, there arose a murmuring of the Grecians against the Hebrews, because their widows were neglected in the daily ministration.*

2 *Then the twelve called the multitude of the disciples unto them, and said, It is not reason that we should leave the word of God, and serve tables.*

3 *Wherefore, brethren, look ye out among you seven men of honest report, full of the Holy Ghost and wisdom, whom we may appoint over this business.*

4 *But we will give ourselves continually to prayer, and to the ministry of the word.*

5 *And the saying pleased the whole multitude: and they chose Stephen, a man full of faith and of the Holy*

Ghost, and Philip, and Prochorus, and Nicanor, and Timon, and Parmenas, and Nicolas a proselyte of Antioch:

6 Whom they set before the apostles: and when they had prayed, they laid their hands on them.

7 And the word of God increased; and the number of the disciples multiplied in Jerusalem greatly. . . .

—Acts 6:1-7

Clearly, deacons are critically important in the church. What would we do without these dedicated, servant-oriented people among us? But there is a clear restriction placed upon their function.

Deacons Do Not Dictate!

Many denominations in the past century have appointed individuals to a deacon board that tells the leadership what to do-what to preach, what's on the agenda, what they should pay the pastor, who should be employed. In our perspective, and from our understanding of the Scripture, that order is over.

It may have been acceptable at one time, because of the incomplete understanding of the Scriptures, or the level of maturity obtained. But from where we are in the 21st century, any deacon board that's functioning as a governmental structure is out of order. Let me be even clearer: Deacon-possessed churches have caused more problems and more hurts than any other entity within the contemporary church.

Deacons are given to the church strictly to serve with the helping gifts, as we saw in Acts 6 above. The Greek widows complained that they were being neglected and they claimed that their neglect was a racial issue. So the apostles, the higher level of leadership within the body — that is, the elders of the church who were given governmental anointing, said, "We are going to preach and pray, while deacons serve the practical needs of the people."

The deacon qualifications outlined in Acts tell us that deacons must be full of faith, know the word, and have the spirit of service. And these men were also Greeks so that they could more effectively serve their own culture, which was a wise move. Their ministry was not to tell Peter, James, and John what to do. Their ministry was to serve tables. Philip was one of the deacons, Stephen was another, and both were great men of God.

Deacons can be promoted. For example, though deacons aren't teachers and preachers, Philip ended up preaching in Samaria. Stephen preached and was stoned as the first official martyr. So a deacon can be promoted to other areas of service.

The Scripture also says women traveled with Jesus to serve. All of these ministries could be considered ministries of helps, ministries of service and mercy. Deacon ministry is always a ministry of service.

Finally, I'll briefly mention that below the deacons come departmental heads, men and women who serve in departments. They serve upward in their giving, in their loyalty, in their vision for the soundness of the local house. Strong churches are strong houses within a region that follow God's governmental structure can then go to the next level, which is the city.

Leading and Serving . . . Under the Master's Hand

From looking at a general synopsis of local church government, if you're serving a senior pastor or a set man, these are some of the things that have to be taught about levels of leadership. It is dangerous to ignore the scriptural teachings here, especially when it comes to appointing only mature believers for leadership in the church. Too many individuals are given responsibility prematurely. Too many people who don't produce fruit are placed in positions that require a certain type of fruit-and then they manifest a different fruit.

Isn't that why we often have splits and divisions and turmoil within some assemblies? I encourage you to adopt a better way: Those who are structuring churches need to spend time on these principles, and much time and energy in "building" individuals to support the structure. For everyone who is serving under a set man, you must find your place and serve with all of your heart, with all of your God-given gifts.

After all, in the final analysis it is not you who produce the Kingdom fruit but Christ in you. As the apostle Paul put it: *"I am crucified with Christ: nevertheless I live; yet not I, but Christ liveth in me: and the life which I now live in the flesh I live by the faith of the Son of God, who loved me, and gave himself for me"* (Galatians 2:20). I can't think of a better illustration of how we are to serve in the strength of God than this old legend of Poland's famous concert pianist, Ignace Paderewski:

A mother, wishing to encourage her young son's progress at the piano, bought tickets for a Paderewski performance.

When the night arrived, they found their seats near the front of the concert hall and eyed the majestic Steinway piano waiting on stage.

Soon the mother found a friend to talk to, and the boy slipped away. When eight o'clock arrived, the spotlights came on, the audience quieted, and only then did they notice the boy up on the bench, innocently picking out Twinkle, Twinkle, Little Star.

His mother gasped, but before she could retrieve her son, the master appeared on the stage and quickly moved to the keyboard. "Don't quit — keep playing," he whispered to the boy. Leaning over, Paderewski reached down with his left hand and began filling in a bass part. Soon his right arm reached around the other side, encircling the child, to add a running obbligato. Together, the old master and the young novice held the crowd mesmerized.[8]

In our church work, unpolished though we may be, it is the Master who surrounds us and whispers in our ear, time and again, "Don't quit — keep playing." And as we do, He augments and supplements until a work of amazing beauty is created. This is the vision for the church and all who lead and serve within it.

CHAPTER 4

KNOW YOUR MEASURE AND RANK

WE WILL NOT BOAST OF THINGS WITHOUT OUR MEASURE, BUT ACCORDING TO THE MEASURE OF THE RULE WHICH GOD HATH DISTRIBUTED TO US, A MEASURE TO REACH EVEN UNTO YOU.

—2 Corinthians 10:13

True authority is a marvelous thing, isn't it? In the magazine of the U.S. Naval Institute, *Proceedings*, Frank Koch illustrates the importance of knowing where authority resides and how it is to be exercised . . .

Two battleships assigned to the training squadron had been at sea on maneuvers in heavy weather for several days. I was serving on the lead battleship and was on watch on the bridge as night fell. The visibility was poor with patchy fog, so the captain remained on the bridge keeping an eye on all activities. Shortly after dark, the lookout on the wing reported, "Light, bearing on the starboard bow."

"Is it steady or moving astern?" the captain called out.

The lookout replied, "Steady, Captain," which meant we were on a dangerous collision course with that ship. The captain then called to the signalman, "Signal that ship: 'We are on a collision course; advise you change course twenty degrees.'"

Back came the signal, "Advisable for you to change course twenty degrees."

The captain said, "Send: "I'm a captain, change course twenty degrees.'"

"I'm a seaman second-class," came the reply. "You had better change course twenty degrees."

By that time the captain was furious. He spat out, "Send: 'I'm a battleship! Change course twenty degrees.'"

Back came the flashing light, "I'm a lighthouse."

We changed course.[9]

When you come up against an immovable authority, you cannot argue yourself out of its sphere of power or bluff away its demands. That was how the apostle Paul stood before the Christians in Corinth, those who seemingly wanted to ignore his voice, who refused the "light" he was shining into their hearts with God's truth. The apostle speaks about his own authority in terms of measure, the measure of rule that was given to him:

[13] *We will not boast of things without our measure, but according to the measure of the rule which God hath distributed to us, a measure to reach even unto you.*

¹⁴ *For we stretch not ourselves beyond our measure, as though we reached not unto you: for we are come as far as to you also in preaching the gospel of Christ:*

¹⁵ *Not boasting of things without our measure, that is, of other men's labours; but having hope, when your faith is increased, that we shall be enlarged by you according to our rule abundantly,*

¹⁶ *To preach the gospel in the regions beyond you, and not to boast in another man's line of things made ready to our hand.*

¹⁷ *But he that glorieth, let him glory in the Lord.*

¹⁸ *For not he that commendeth himself is approved, but whom the Lord commendeth.*

—2 Corinthians 10:13-18

Paul was saying that he was given a level of authority by which he could reach even a Corinthian church-a church in a place that should have had no chance for spiritual growth. Corinth was as pagan and as seemingly hopeless as any culture could ever be. Yet Paul became a powerful influence among them for the Kingdom. *"For we are come as far as to you also in preaching the gospel of Christ: Not boasting of things without our measure."* Now what Paul is saying is, "It was easy to reach you in Corinth, because you were in the confines of my measure."

What does this mean for us today? Here is what I suggest: Once you have a measure established, and you have rank understood, then you can begin to function competently in bringing Kingdom authority to pass.

I will address measure and rank, rule and authority in this chapter and the next. I'd like to do it by departing from a purely teaching mode and instead be mostly autobiographical, illustrating how God works with His called and anointed leaders. In telling my own story, I hope you'll be inspired and encouraged to know your measure and understand your rank. Then, in the chapter to follow, we'll explore what it means to exercise dominion in God's government.

Measure . . . and My Story

When a man or a woman is anointed with an apostolic mandate, God dispenses a measure that can sometimes be determined by geographical dominion. For example, when we first started in ministry in Zimbabwe, the Lord moved me from the city of Bulawayo to the city of Harare. When we came to Harare (which back then was called Salisbury), I had no idea what my ministry was going to be. So the Lord began to show me, through visions.

The First Vison

I was sitting alone in a boat, and I was supposed to be fishing. But I didn't have anything to fish with – no pole, no bait. The water was dark and thick like oil, carrying the boat along with its current, when that boat suddenly landed on a shore. God was showing me that this particular era of my life had come to an end; I was now entering something new.

Then I was walking, fully dressed in a suit, trudging down a railway line towards a city. But it was not the city where I was born or spent my teenage years. No, I recognized it as the city of Harare. As I continued walking along the railway line, I saw that on both sides of me the ground was growing wild and untilled. But as I walked further, I came into a plowed field. Then I came into a field where I could see people planting seeds.

As I kept on walking, the field then had small shoots of cornstalks growing out of the ground. As I kept on walking, the field kept on getting bigger, the stalks became shoulder-high, and finally began putting forth mature ears of corn. The closer I got to the city, the bigger the harvest seemingly became, until I was almost in the city, and the corn was twelve feet tall. And each stalk had three ears of corn, fully mature. When I came into the city, there were barrels and barrels of grain being poured out into the streets.

What was the Lord showing me in this vision in 1978? He was showing me that as my years progressed I would be seeing levels of growth and progress in measure and rank. I would be witnessing my measure increase.

In 1980, my wife, Chi Chi, and I traveled to the United States where I was offered a wonderful position of ministry that would mean living in the United States. But Chi Chi said to me, "I don't think this is God." We prayed, and that night I had another vision. . . .

The Second Vision

Again, I was sitting in a boat – it looked like the same one I had seen two years before. But this time there were two of us sitting in the boat. I knew it was Chi Chi. She was back to back with me, and we were fishing with poles in a huge pool. The water was dirty, and we caught nothing. In fact, when I took my line out of the water, there was no bait on my hook and we had no bait anywhere in the boat. But I threw the line back in the water because, after all, I was fishing – but with a baitless hook!

As we sat there, suddenly we were thrust into the future and sitting on the deck of a huge ocean vessel. One of the crewmen said to me, "Pastor, the first net is coming out." And on that net was written "New Life," a huge net with all kinds of fish flapping around within it. The Spirit of the Lord spoke to me and said, "This is the first harvest."

And then the men said the next net was coming out. This one was so filled with fish that the huge ship was almost tilting; they had to get a crane to draw that net out. It represented various countries with a huge harvest of souls.

So what the Lord was showing me in 1980 was that I had to come back to Zimbabwe, and I'd be fishing for a season without catching anything, and we'd be struggling. But as the years went by, our measure would increase.

Sitting on the Platform

I look back and see how God has increased my measure over the years. But a "hint," or a kind of foreshadowing, of my rank was there from my earliest years. From the earliest years, my life was, in a sense, prefigured.

We can actually live a metaphor of our lives. I'll explain what I mean by telling you that when I first started in ministry I never, ever sat in the pew. I was always invited to sit on the platform. From when I was in my late teens, I've never sat in the audience. See, in those years we used to put chairs in front of the pulpit where the pastors would sit, but I never sat in them. Anywhere I went to minister, I'd always be invited to sit on the platform.

It confused me, because some of the other guys, my same age in the ministry, would be angry. Why was I was invited to the platform, and they weren't invited? I wondered. But I eventually learned that I was living in metaphor; I was living my life. I was being told, subliminally and physically, that I was a man of rank.

Yet I hadn't understood my rank. I never knew there was such a thing as rank, and I didn't know that I had a measure of rule. The only thing I knew was that Joseph, who had a coat of many colors, also had a vision telling him that someday he'd be in charge. So I was living that.

When I began to understand my measure in a more significant way, I found I had great influence in certain aspects of ministry. In the early 80s, when I started preaching in the rural areas-Buhera, Gweru and in the bush-I would see a tremendous response to the Gospel message. I saw miracles, signs and wonders, blind eyes opened, powerful witchcraft defeated.

In fact, many witch doctors repented and began serving in our ministry. One such witch doctor was converted in my dad's church in Bulawayo, received the

Holy Spirit in our church here, and I went with him to Buhera. He was 76 years old, having been a witch doctor for almost forty years.

During the crusade we did in Buhera, the demons launched a heinous attack on him. One night while we were sleeping in a thatch hut with a mud floor, we awoke to the sounds of the ex-witch doctor screaming. We ran outside and found him standing in the cooking fire, his feet and ankles burning. The demons had taken over his body and marched him into the fire, saying: "You belong to us." He was in a trance-like state and unable to resist the demons or remove himself from the fire.

When we reached him, we grabbed him and rescued him from the fire, but his feet and ankles were badly burned. He lost several toes, but miraculously kept his feet and ankles. Though deliverance for him was an on-going process, that night the demonic strongholds were broken and he began his journey with Christ in true freedom. The Holy Spirit was powerful that night — very, very powerful.

While we were preaching in Buhera and surrounding areas, the Holy Spirit moved in awesome ways; we saw all kinds of people being delivered. Sickness and disease were overcome — it was miraculous! Even during this time, the Lord was teaching me and showing me my measure. Even though I ministered under the anointing, my authority and measure were not national.

Expanding the Ministry Boundaries

Then, in the city of Harare, God began to show me the geographical boundary of our influence. It wasn't very big, but every year I noticed our ministry was moving to another area, and another area, and so on. So by 1989, as we were starting New Life Ministries, our ministry began to take root throughout much of Harare. By 1993, the whole of Harare was being put in our hands, and God began to put the nation of Zimbabwe into our hands as well.

By 1993, the provinces of Mashonaland, Manicaland, and portions of Matabeleland were in our hands. But we didn't have anything happening in Masvingo, in Midlands, or throughout Matabeleland. But in 1996, when the Lord began to open Zambia, Congo, Tanzania, South Africa, Botswana, Namibia, Uganda, West Africa (we began churches in West Africa!) and God opened all of Zimbabwe to us, my measure of rule began to expand.

At the same time, in the early 90s, I was preaching in Europe, and God began to expand my measure in Europe, in the Caribbean, in the United States, and in Canada. How did it happen? I dreamed in January of 1998 that I was standing on a Canadian flag. I said to Chi Chi when I woke up, "God is going to open the door to Canada, I have to go to Canada." I didn't know anybody in Canada! But within four weeks, I received phone calls from five different groups there and ministered in Canada during the next few months. Incredible! Today we have churches in Canada. And we're opening them in Asia, Germany, Pakistan, and moving into India. I even received a call a few weeks ago from Vietnam, asking us to come and start churches there. Soon Chi Chi and I are going to New Zealand and Australia, because they've asked us to come there and start churches. The islands are now opening as well.

So God expands the measure.

When God expands your measure, you must understand that you are being given authority over demonic princes. You are able to cancel all the illegalities of the demonic spirits, and you are now able to release the Kingdom of God; not a church organization, not planting churches, but the Kingdom of God. And when we begin to release our measure, we notice that our rank is on display.

Measure and Rank: How Do They Work?

My subject is the exercise of authority, and I'll use a humorous story to show my point. In the mid 1950s, when a man named Christian Herter was governor of Massachusetts, he was fervently pursuing a second term in office. One day, after a busy morning chasing votes (and having no lunch) he arrived at a church barbecue. It was late afternoon, and Herter was famished. As he moved down the serving line, he held out his plate to the woman serving chicken. She put a piece on his plate and turned to the next person in line.

"Excuse me," Governor Herter said. "Do you mind if I have another piece of chicken?"

"Sorry," the woman told him. "I'm supposed to give one piece of chicken to each person."

"But I'm starved," the governor said.

"Sorry," the woman said again. "Only one to a customer."

Governor Herter was a modest and unassuming man, but he decided that this time he would throw a little weight around. "Do you know who I am?" he asked. "I am the governor of this state."

"Do you know who I am?" the woman replied. "I'm the lady in charge of the chicken. Move along, mister."[10]

Clearly, knowing our measure and rank establishes definite boundaries of authority! It is true in the spiritual realm, as I attest in my own experience. But you may be wondering exactly how you might expect it to benefit your own life and ministry. Consider:

♦ *It helps you know what God is saying.* If you don't know your measure, then you won't know what God is saying. For example, if I am speaking before a group, and the platform is my measure of rule, if anything is going to happen on that platform, God is going to show me. Because that is where my measure of rule is. Anything, whether it's good or bad, if God's going to do something special there, He shows you first-because you are a part of what God is doing in that region.

We see this coming through, for example, in Genesis 18. The Lord was leading an entourage to destroy Sodom and Gomorrah. The Lord said, *"I cannot hide this thing from Abraham."* He couldn't hide it from Abraham because Abraham was given an influence and measure throughout the entire land. So God, in a sense, couldn't do anything without His man, His apostolic type, His partner knowing what was going to happen.

The key is that if you know your measure of rule, if you understand your rank, if God is going to do anything in a place then He will show you what He's going to do and make you a part of it. You can say, "I don't want to be a part of it," of course. But if you say, "I am going to be a part of it," then God is going to anoint you to do that thing.

♦ *It helps you extend the boundaries of authority.* Consider how this took place in the ministry of the apostle Paul, when he said in 1 Corinthians 10:13-14 that he doesn't work outside of his measure. In other words, he knew where God had extended the boundaries for him to have influence and to take authority. Because whatever Paul could declare illegal in that area or within that boundary, the demonic forces could not overcome. They couldn't implement anything that they wanted to do, because God would counter it through the anointing of Paul.

How far will such boundaries extend? No doubt it depends upon how far your total submission to God extends. How far your heart and vision are yielded up to Him. After all, is there any limit to the ministry God can accomplish through one who is totally surrendered as a servant of the Kingdom? *Key to extension of authority.*

I think about the vast missionary expansion that occurred under fearless preacher John Wesley of 1700s England. He began by being kicked out of the established churches of his day, so his measure became the dirt roads and paths of the country side. He would preach on tree stumps while dodging the stones and bricks thrown at him. But he kept preaching Christ, and God eventually extended his boundaries throughout Europe-and even across the ocean to reap a great harvest in the New World. Wesley once said this about his fervor for influence: "I want the whole Christ for my Savior, the whole Bible for my book, the whole Church for my fellowship, and the whole world for my mission field." How is it with you?

♦ *It places you at God's disposal, to work His will.* Sometimes God will send you to a place for your rank to be utilized, even if you don't have a measure of rule in that area. It happened with Jonah, when the Lord sent him to Nineveh. Jonah's measure of rule did not extend to Nineveh, but God used Jonah's rank in Nineveh.

Remember that Jonah first went in the opposite direction, and because he was a man of rank going in the wrong direction, he disrupted the lives of an entire enterprise: his ship. That ship lost all its assets, throwing everything overboard in the storm. Why? Because a prophet out of order, or an apostle out of order, can cause any enterprise he's in to go under.

When they threw Jonah out of the boat, the Bible says God prepared a fish, because in the Creation there was no fish that had the rank Jonah had. So God had to prepare a fish, give that fish the same rank Jonah had, and allow that fish to swallow Jonah, because the Bible says, *"Touch not my anointed, and do my prophets no harm."* But when you have rank on rank, it's not doing the prophet harm.

So Jonah was swallowed, and he had to wait three days before his mind was changed. Then, when the fish spat him out, it spat him out close to Nineveh, where he had to do the ministry he was sent to do. His rank was so powerful that in Nineveh, an ungodly city, all the people repented in less than forty days. An entire city repented at the preaching of Jonah!

Jonah didn't have a pleasant message, either. Jonah's message was: "In forty days, God will destroy you!" That was his entire message. But his rank caused the demonic princes to move aside.

Sometimes measure may not extend to a certain place, but then rank will kick in. Where you have rank and measure, something will happen. Demonic spirits will move aside, the spirits of human beings submit, a nation or a city or a community will open. Once the spiritual climate begins to change the dynamics of the Kingdom will be released.

CHAPTER 5

TAKE DOMINION!

GOD BLESSED THEM, AND GOD SAID UNTO THEM,
BE FRUITFUL, AND MULTIPLY, AND REPLENISH THE
EARTH, AND SUBDUE IT: AND HAVE DOMINION . . .
—Genesis 1:28a

In Africa we are fighting the spiritual forces of darkness in a direct onslaught. The battle is overt and heinous. So the story at the beginning of this chapter may sound strange to Western ears, but please realize that the evil forces are just as powerful around the world, though they may use more subtle methods in other places.

While ministering in Zimbabwe I prayed for a lady — let's call her Auntie Mary — who used to be a fortune teller and a spirit medium in Harare. So I was surprised when she began coming to my morning Bible studies saying she wanted prayer. But when I began to pray for her, she would immediately manifest a demonic spirit. I had seen this type of thing before, but this particular case was unusual, because when I tried to cast the spirit out of her, it was as if I were standing above a bottomless pit, an unfathomable well.

A voice came from deep, deep within her, with a kind of echo, and I knew it was the voice of a very powerful demonic spirit. In fact, scores of demons inhabited her! When we began to challenge the spirits to come out, we smelled a vapor like sulfur. It was a demonic breath, followed by a foul yellow fluid that spilled out of her mouth. This happened on a Tuesday morning, and we had mid-week church meetings on Tuesday nights. That night she came to church, and we baptized her, and though the demons were fighting, we calmed her.

The following Sunday I took dominion and authority in the morning service. She came to the front, and I rebuked the demons. She waved her hands as if she were blocking her face and ducking. I prayed to the Holy Spirit, "You've got to show me what's happening."

The Spirit showed me a cluster of angels with swords flying over her, and as I rebuked the demons, the angels bashed them, although some went back into the woman. But the Word of God was so strong that they were moving and leaving the woman.

Now, observing the war going on in this woman I learned valuable lessons. For one thing, demons know how to help one another. While we were ministering to this woman, another woman on the other side of the church cried out with a demonic voice: "Hold on! He only preaches for forty minutes! If you can hold on for forty minutes, you'll still be in this woman by the time it's over!" The Lord was showing me how these things operate. I rebuked that woman to be silent and cast that spirit out with the power of the Word. I also observed that when people with demons came to church, the demons would not come in the building; they would wait at the door. I saw them waiting at the door, and as people were leaving, the demons were getting back inside their vessels and leaving with them.

But all through this time, the Lord was teaching me that I have dominion. So the next week I took oil and poured it all around the property. You see, the Lord had revealed to me that the ground where the church was built used to be a tribal killing area, a place where people were judged by the chiefs and sentenced to death. That's why we had trouble, why we fought powerful devils there. But I also learned that I could take authority. And when I did, we broke a powerful demonic stronghold. Our church never grew very much until God revealed the stronghold and showed me my ability to break it through Christ. *Then* the church then began to explode with new converts.

****

Do you know your dominion area? For two years before those demonic encounters, I walked the streets of Harare every day. When I walked in the town, I wasn't shopping! I was praying, taking dominion in the city. I knew Harare had to obey the apostle God had sent. I knew my dominion area, and I exercised authority and rank within it.

You are called to do the same. After all, we learned in the previous chapter that it's difficult to establish Kingdom rule with people who don't know their rank or their measure of rule. If that chapter was meant to explain such authority, then our focus on dominion in this chapter is to help you know how to exercise that authority. So let's look at two key points about dominion: what they must do and what you must do.

They Must Serve You

Now when you take dominion in your dominion area, everything that is submissive to the Kingdom of God must serve you. **Everything.** Whether it's gold, silver, businesses, money, bricks, banks, people, every-thing that exists is part of one of the seven kingdoms (mineral, vegetable, animal, humans, planets, angelic, spirit world) and all kingdoms are subject to The Kingdom — The Kingdom of God. **When you take dominion through Christ, every thing in every kingdom is subject to your authority.**

We have experienced this in many arenas in South Africa. There have been times that we've needed a place to have church services. We have taken dominion, commanded places to be available, and God has provided. We have needed money to advance the Kingdom of God and to buy church property. In this also, we took dominion and God provided. We have favor because God supplies all of our needs according to His riches, and His riches are inexhaustible. We have needed vehicles for transportation and God has literally brought them to our door.

Once you understand your rank and measure —
your dominion and authority through Christ Jesus —
and begin to exercise them things will happen.
Kingdoms will serve you; not just people in the
Kingdom of God, but those who are not because God
uses a Kingdom dynamic to position people and things
to serve you, thus serving His purpose.

You Must Choose: Exercise, or Not?

My point is this: You are faced with a choice every
day: Will I exercise my dominion and authority or not?
It is not a passive undertaking; it is an active step of
faith.

Let me show you what Jesus said in Matthew 8:

5 *When Jesus was entered into Capernaum, there
came unto him a centurion, beseeching him,*

6 *And saying, Lord, my servant lieth at home sick
of the palsy, grievously tormented.*

7 *And Jesus saith unto him, I will come and heal
him.*

8 *The centurion answered and said, Lord, I am not
worthy that thou shouldest come under my roof: but
speak the word only, and my servant shall be healed.*

9 *For I am a man under authority, having soldiers
under me: and I say to this man, Go, and he goeth; and
to another, Come, and he cometh; and to my servant,
Do this, and he doeth it.*

10 *When Jesus heard it, he marveled, and said to
them that followed, Verily I say unto you, I have not
found so great faith, no, not in Israel.*

11 *And I say unto you, That many shall come from the east and west, and shall sit down with Abraham, and Isaac, and Jacob, in the kingdom of heaven.*

12 *But the children of the kingdom shall be cast out into outer darkness: there shall be weeping and gnashing of teeth.*

13 *And Jesus said unto the centurion, Go thy way; and as thou hast believed, so be it done unto thee. And his servant was healed in the selfsame hour.*

The centurion said to Christ, "There's no need for you to come to my house. You have dominion in the entire area, so there's no need for you to move. Just speak the word and my servant will be healed because he is in your dominion area." Apply this Scripture to your life. When you have an area of dominion, you can send God's word forth and it will act. You can pray for someone to be healed without touching them and it will be done.

I have prayed for people with heartbreaking circumstances over the phone, and God has answered prayer. I believed and took dominion over circumstances within my area of dominion and it was done in Jesus' name.

When you're in your dominion area, you can take authority. Paul did that; he took authority in his dominion area. But you have to know your dominion area. Every person has a dominion area, whether it's your bedroom, your bed, or the chair you're sitting on. Wherever your dominion area, then take authority in that area.

13 *When Jesus came into the coasts of Caesarea Philippi, he asked his disciples, saying, Whom do men say that I the Son of man am?*

14 *And they said, Some say that thou art John the Baptist: some, Elias; and others, Jeremias, or one of the prophets.*

15 *He saith unto them, But whom say ye that I am?*

16 *And Simon Peter answered and said, Thou art the Christ, the Son of the living God.*

17 *And Jesus answered and said unto him, Blessed art thou, Simon Bar-jona: for flesh and blood hath not revealed it unto thee, but my Father which is in heaven.*

18 *And I say also unto thee, That thou art Peter, and upon this rock I will build my church; and the gates of hell shall not prevail against it.*

19 *And I will give unto thee the keys of the kingdom of heaven: and whatsoever thou shalt bind on earth shall be bound in heaven: and whatsoever thou shalt loose on earth shall be loosed in heaven.*

Jesus is the Christ, the son of the living God. And you are an adopted son or daughter of the same Father (Ephesians 1:5). Jesus is blessed, and so are you. The Bible says, in effect, that whatever you declare legal or illegal shall be declared legal or illegal by heaven. But you can't declare something illegal if it's not in your dominion area.

Dominion: Believe It!

In the mid-70s, Dr. Cho of Korea was in Japan and he tells the story of how he had a very difficult time loving the Japanese nation because of the atrocities committed against the Korean people by Japanese soldiers in the war years. But Dr. Cho, through the leading of the Holy Spirit, sent missionaries to Japan.

He sent two women, even though the Japanese are thought to be more of a male-oriented society, but the Lord told Dr. Cho to send two women to minister in Japan. For a long time the women saw very little progress in winning converts to Christ. So Dr. Cho decided to hold a conference and crusade.

The first night was very difficult and he felt nervous and lacking in freedom to proclaim the Word. The next night he wasn't feeling well as he sat on his bed before the service. His stomach was queasy and he had a fever. Suddenly, standing right in front of him, was the demonic prince over Japan. He said, "I'm going to kill you, it's taken me over four thousand years to build this, and you are not going to come and destroy what I have built."

The Holy Spirit began to say to Dr. Cho, "Quote the Scripture and believe that I have sent you here." He began to quote Scripture. The demonic spirit said, "Oh, you're quoting the Bible! That doesn't matter; I'm still going to kill you."

The Holy Spirit was telling Dr. Cho that the devil is a liar, that he's afraid of the Scripture, that he should keep on quoting, because the devil was just putting up a front. The devil was trying to destroy Dr. Cho with fear, so the devil said, "Oh, so you think you're strong now? I'm busy, but I'll come back later."

That next night in the meeting, though, there was a tremendous breakthrough in the Holy Spirit, because Dr. Cho took authority in his dominion area.

Can you believe when the evidence is clearly contrary? For centuries people believed that Aristotle was right when he said that the heavier an object is, the faster it would fall to earth. Aristotle was regarded as the greatest thinker of all time, and surely he would not be wrong! Anyone, of course, could have taken two objects, one heavy and one light, and dropped them from a great height to see whether or not the heavier object landed first.

But no one did until nearly two thousand years after Aristotle's death. In 1589, Galileo summoned learned professors to the base of the Leaning Tower of Pisa. Then he went to the top and pushed off a ten- pound and a one-pound weight. Both hit the ground at the same instant. The power of belief was so strong, however, that the professors denied their eyesight. They continued to say Aristotle was right.[11]

What about us? Why should we keep believing we are powerless in the face of all the evidence to the contrary? We have God's Word, we have the testimony of those who trust Him, and we have the powerful example of those who have moved ahead in faith to take dominion.

CHAPTER 6

FORMING KINGDOM RELATIONSHIPS

...THEY SUNG A NEW SONG, SAYING, THOU ART WORTHY TO TAKE THE BOOK, AND TO OPEN THE SEALS THEREOF: FOR THOU WAST SLAIN, AND HAST REDEEMED US TO GOD BY THY BLOOD OUT OF EVERY KINDRED, AND TONGUE, AND PEOPLE, AND NATION.

—Revelation 5:9

I've met with a number of men around the world during the last several years and found that we have many things in common. Some live in America, some in Canada, some in England, some in Asia, and many in Africa (West and East). We don't even come from the same religious background; we don't have the same denominational roots or the same styles of ministry and worship. But the minute we meet and share a program together or minister together, we know in our spirits that we are deeply related. We know that we are from the same tribe.

When you're from the same tribe, you relate in more than just doctrine, you relate in spirit, you also relate in your understanding of what needs to be done in the Kingdom of God. Being one in Christ, you are bound together in eternal fellowship and purpose.

Today God is bringing men and women together in just this kind of relationship; not just so we can preach for each other, but that we can have covenants together to fight in spiritual warfare and to depose the demonic spirits for the thrust of revival.

After all, the Scripture says in Isaiah 11:9 that the glory of the Lord will cover the earth as the waters cover the sea. This awesome vision will only come to pass as we form Kingdom relationships on various continents in various nations. What are some of the qualities of this type of joining together? Consider:

Joining Brings Greater than Individual Power

Think about the Kingdom of God at its very best: Jesus preaches for three and a half years. After those ministry years, He is crucified. All of Jerusalem is saying: *"Crucify him! His blood be upon us and upon our children!"* They literally said, "He is not our king. We have no king but Caesar." The bloodcurdling screams of a community led by the high priests and rulers of the house of Israel renounced and denounced the rulership of Jesus Christ.

Jesus' disciples had run away. John was the only disciple who stood with Jesus. The Bible says he stood at the foot of the cross. Mark says there was someone else who was hiding, following from afar, someone without clothes. Mark was talking about himself. Even he failed in courage. Only John stood by while Peter denied Christ and Judas betrayed Him. The others disappeared; they were afraid.

On the day of Pentecost, fifty days later, the same group that said "Kill him!" listened to Peter preach. The Bible says that on that day 3,000 were converted, the church began to grow spectacularly, and God added daily to the church *(see Acts 2)*.

Please realize something amazing and somewhat shocking: Jesus did not have the same results. Why? Because the disciples brought church government on a Kingdom level that Jesus did not bring. He was the Messiah, and served in ministry as such. In other words, there's greater power in Kingdom govern-ment than there is in individual anointing. God's people joining together brings greater power than individual ministry.

Charles Osgood, the radio and television commen-tator, told the story of two ladies who lived in a convalescent center. Each had suffered an incapacitating stroke; Margaret's stroke left her left side restricted, while Ruth's stroke damaged her right side. Both of these ladies were accomplished pianists but had given up hope of ever playing again. The director of the center sat them down at a piano and encouraged them to play solo pieces together, each using their good hand. They did, and a beautiful friendship developed. What a picture of the church's need to work together! What one member cannot do alone, two or more can do together-in harmony. It is true, not only on an individual basis — it must become true across the Kingdom, tribe-to-tribe, nation-to-nation.

It Restores Order to the Church

There is an apostolic council of governmental authority being called to a Round Table by God. This group of men and women are being anointed by the Holy Spirit to do some unique things:

♦ to restore order (this is the primary calling);

♦ to bring another level of strategy against the demonic world;

♦ to release the wealth of the Kingdom of God into its rightful hands;

♦ to loose a wave of miracle signs and wonders;

♦ to open the heavens to bring prosperity on another level;

♦ to bring emancipation, in terms of deliverance;

♦ to end demonic blocks of power in Third World countries and end the pain and suffering there;

♦ to bring another level of worship that will be signified throughout the globe, whether it be in Africa, India, South America, or America.

Worship is going to the next level: worship in the Spirit. Paul said in 1 Corinthians 14:15 (NIV), *"I will pray with the spirit, and I will pray with the understanding also: I will sing with the spirit, and I will sing with the understanding also."* So we're going to see worship on a different level-praying in the Spirit, singing in the Spirit, and blessing in the Spirit. That only comes with Kingdom government that has been placed in order.

The Apostolic Round Table is the apostolic leadership coming to a table and discussing various issues that have caused divisions in the past. Thus order is restored in the church. Now, when we look closer at order in the church, we want to observe the house of Noah, Nehemiah, and Gideon.

NOAH

Jesus said: *"Just as it was in the days of Noah, so also will it be in the days of the Son of Man"* (Luke 17:26, NIV). In those days, Noah began to build an ark in the midst of an extremely wicked generation. And it's frightening that God found just one man in the whole earth qualified to build a house for God-to build an apostolic kingdom house for God.

So Noah consulted his three sons. Each of them had three levels of anointing that would cover the entire globe. In this consultation, at what I call the apostolic round table, Noah — the presiding leader of the Kingdom of God and its events — began to dialogue with these three major strengths. They talked about what each of them was going to be responsible for in building the Kingdom of God.

The word *Noah* means *"consoler,"* or one who is to bring heaven to earth, one who is to bring judgment, bringing a standard by which God is going to rule. So Noah established this standard. Once the standard has been established, that God is going to do a certain work, then Noah began to preach for 120 years. But at the same time, he was building something.

You see, we cannot preach without building. And we don't build without preaching. Noah was preaching and declaring, but at the same time he was building.

Noah built a three-level entity, an ark of three levels. This speaks of the three dimensions in the Kingdom of God. The apostolic order is restoring these three dimensions influencing the way we experience God. This is the premise upon which we must gather apostolic training and teaching, and it can only come when we sit around the table. We cannot use the systems of Nebuchadnezzar, the Medes and the Persians, Alexander the Great, the Roman Empire; of authoritarian rule, of dictatorship, or monarchies. We cannot use democracy, the rule of the laity in the church. If we are going to have success, we must return to apostolic headship.

NEHEMIAH

This great man received a word from God, namely: *Rebuild Jerusalem.* Three men preceded Nehemiah: Ezra, who was already there preaching the word; Zerubbabel who had the anointing of the kingship; and Joshua who had the Aaronic priesthood system flowing through his veins. Still, it took an apostolic head like Nehemiah to come to the scene and bring the three together: The prophetic, kingship and the priesthood. By bringing these three together, Nehemiah did in fifty-two days what they had not been able to accomplish in seventy years. So the apostolic headship brought the entire city and the kingdom together.

GIDEON

The reluctant soldier was chosen for leadership. Unlike the other judges, the rule of Gideon created a level of leadership in which, the leaders together brought order to Israel. Gideon came as an apostolic headship and brought a level of order and headship.

Remember that the Bible says the church is built on the foundation of apostles and prophets, they that are wise master-builders given to us by God. When these apostolic governments begin to come together at the Round Table and dialogue to sort the mess out, we then can come to the point where these apostolic generals can pray together. They can then agree together, and then respect and endorse each other.

They can then open heaven together, and release gifts and blessings together. They can curse the power of the enemy together, and as they stand together in this way, the Bible says God commands the blessing in their unity.

On the other hand: *"Every kingdom divided against itself is brought to desolation; and every city or house divided against itself shall not stand"* (Matthew 12:25). That is, there's so much dearth, drought, and desolation in the Kingdom of God because the Kingdom is divided against itself. But when the Kingdom is united within

itself, the drought is over, the desolation ends, the
dearth is no more.

It Confronts Demonic Opposition

David's anointing as king was so important that he
was anointed even while Saul was still ruling *(see 1 Sam.
16)*. In addition, in Saul's household the heir apparent
for kingship certainly wasn't David. It was Saul's son,
Jonathan, who was to become the king when Saul died.

But that changed; Saul's apparently demonic-
inspired actions disqualified him and his son from
kingship. Jonathan died in the field with his father,
never becoming king because his allegiance was to his
father's house and not to the kingdom. Jonathan's legs
— his destiny as king — were broken and he could not
stand on his own, neither could he stand in the city.

So David was anointed king while Saul still reigned.
The Bible says that Jonathan was in covenant with
David. Their relationship was a kingdom relationship!
When Jonathan chose to serve his father (like we today
may choose to serve a denomination or organization)
over and above the kingdom, Jonathan signed the death
warrant on his life and ministry. When the house died,
so did his ministry and gift. If Jonathan had chosen to
run with David, he would have saved David much
pain. Moreover, together they would have been
indomitable in building the Kingdom.

When David became king after the death of Saul and
Jonathan, Johab became the main leader of David's
armies. Jonathan should have held that office. We know

this because of the anointing upon Jonathan when he went after the Philistines (1 Samuel 14):

> *⁴ On each side of the pass that Jonathan intended to cross to reach the Philistine outpost was a cliff; one was called Bozez, and the other Seneh. . . .*
>
> *⁶ Jonathan said to his young armor-bearer, "Come, let's go over to the outpost of those uncircumcised fellows. Perhaps the LORD will act in our behalf. Nothing can hinder the LORD from saving, whether by many or by few." . . .*
>
> *⁹ If they say to us, 'Wait there until we come to you,' we will stay where we are and not go up to them.*
>
> *¹⁰ But if they say, 'Come up to us,' we will climb up, because that will be our sign that the LORD has given them into our hands."*
>
> *¹¹ So both of them showed themselves to the Philistine outpost. "Look!" said the Philistines. "The Hebrews are crawling out of the holes they were hiding in."*
>
> *¹² The men of the outpost shouted to Jonathan and his armor-bearer, "Come up to us and we'll teach you a lesson." So Jonathan said to his armor-bearer, "Climb up after me; the LORD has given them into the hand of Israel."*
>
> *¹³ Jonathan climbed up, using his hands and feet, with his armor-bearer right behind him. The Philistines fell before Jonathan, and his armor-bearer followed and killed behind him.*
>
> *¹⁴ In that first attack Jonathan and his armor-bearer killed some twenty men in an area of about half an acre.*

15 *Then panic struck the whole army-those in the camp and field, and those in the outposts and raiding parties-and the ground shook. It was a panic sent by God.*

—1 Samuel 14:4, 6, 9-15

Clearly, heroic Jonathan was God's Kingdom man to serve as the ruling general in intercessory prayer. He was in covenant with David but didn't develop the relationship with David and stand with him in the Kingdom. If Jonathan had been the leader of the military, David would not have sinned with Bathsheba, and David would not have passed a death warrant on Uriah, because Jonathan could have, and would have, protected his covenant friend.

So, when we talk about the Kingdom of God and rulership, we see that there's a rare commodity of leaders confronting the demonic. In the New Testament, we see this in the Apostle Paul, who established the church in Ephesus. It was in Ephesus where Artemus or Diana-the god, or demonic prince-had ruled for many, many years. Paul said these forces faced him at Ephesus *(See Acts 19)*.

But when Paul was taken to be with the Lord, and John the apostle came out of his exile, he went into the temple of the goddess Artemus (Diana), and prayed a short prayer. When John prayed this prayer with the leaders and bishops of Ephesus, in corporate government, John had the apostolic headship. When that prayer concluded, there was a literal explosion on the altar of the false god, Artemus. And the temple collapsed under the prayer of John. That demonic prince and his government in the region was totally broken.[12]

You see, it took a group of Kingdom men led by apostolic headship to go to Ephesus and break the power of a demonic god. If we are going to have the same results — in India where the demonic gods like Kali rule, or Tibet, or Mongolia, where you have the most powerful demonic strongholds influencing the West even now — it's going to take a corporate Kingdom group of leaders who are sold out to the Kingdom. They will use their resources for the Kingdom and change the nations of the earth by their rulership.

Let me give an example of what is happening in Africa. The common problems in Africa are:

♦ Witchcraft. (It has caused God to be taken out of our societies and a curse brought upon us.)

♦ Poverty.

♦ Ignorance.

♦ Gross misappropriation and corruption in political, socioeconomic and religious sectors.

♦ Sexual perversion.

In Zimbabwe we deal with these problems by praying against the demonic strongholds. We might depose a demonic spirit in our country that will leave for a time and reside in another nation that is not prayerful. That spirit will wait in another nation until the prayers in Zimbabwe subside and then come back to our nation and re-establish its house.

The Scripture says very clearly, that when a demon is cast out of a person, or removed from a person's house, that demon goes to a dry place. It will wait there and then in another season will come back to his house. That's not only true of an individual, it's true of a community, even a nation. When he finds his house swept, that devil goes and gets seven worse than he is and establishes his house in that place, and the end thereof is worse than the beginning *(Matthew 12:44, 45)*.

Selah!!

Once the apostolic headship in a nation begins to rise to the top, the headship needs to move within the region and find out who God is lifting in that region. They must pursue relationships in order to work together so that, governmentally, they move the demonic spirits out of the region through their prayers.

We watch what's happening, for example, in Ethiopia and in Uganda. There's been an increase in the church there. Some folks say the demonic spirits of rage and anger and genocide were moved from Uganda to Sudan. That's why the Sudanese people are suffering the persecution and the struggle they are in. What would have happened if all the apostolic headships had come together and agreed to pray and unite their power together? Imagine where those spirits could be moved to! God wants to bring that kind of power through Kingdom government.

The Bible says the Kingdom of God suffers violence, and the violent take it by force *(Matthew 11:12)*. Yet God is raising up a regimented system and order of kingdoms. This interwovenness of kingdoms is bringing the strength and the anointing of the church on yet another level.

Therefore, our prayer is this: That God would bring the leaders in Zimbabwe together and the leaders in America together. We cannot build strong churches and ignore the city and the Kingdom. It's the house, the strong house, with leadership; the city, corporate leaders in the city of churches that are mega dendras. Then Kingdom houses and Kingdom cities are what change nations. Whole nations must be changed!

We thank God for what is coming. We must pray for Kingdom rule. We must live Kingdom rule.

CHAPTER 7

RESTORING THE
HEADSHIP GIFTS
(WE NEED EACH OTHER!)

THE EYE CANNOT SAY UNTO THE HAND, I HAVE NO NEED OF THEE: NOR AGAIN THE HEAD TO THE FEET, I HAVE NO NEED OF YOU.

—1 Corinthians 12:21

In March of 1981, President Reagan was shot by John Hinckley, Jr., and was hospitalized for several weeks. Although Reagan was the nation's chief executive, his hospitalization had little impact on the nation's activity, Government continued. On the other hand, suppose all the garbage collectors in this country went on strike, as they did recently in Philadelphia. That city was not only in a literal mess, the pile of decaying trash quickly became a health hazard. A three-week nationwide strike would paralyze the country. Who is more important;

the President or a garbage collector? In the body of Christ, seemingly insignificant ones are urgently needed. As Paul reminds us, the head cannot say to the feet, "I don't need you!" On the contrary, those parts of the body that seem to be weaker are indispensable.[13]

In fact, seeing, hearing, tasting, smelling, and touching must come together to successfully fight demonic forces. The Scripture says we have many tutors but very few fathers. God is restoring the headship gifts in this day so that fathers are walking into communities and cities and bringing order.

Though somewhat hidden, such a movement can be powerfully seen "in preview" throughout the Scripture. In this chapter, I'd like to unfold its manifestations in certain key Old Testament characters, particularly: Isaac; Jacob and Esau; Rebekah; Joseph; and Gideon. Let's see what principles we can glean from their experiences as we ask the question: What is the nature of the headship gifts today?

Let me begin with a simplified definition of the word *headship*. Headship is a governmental anointing on a person. It manifests as a father to sons, a leader to leaders, or a counselor to counselors. It is a "life source" releasing structure, systems, and strategies.

In 1 Corinthians 12:14-27, the apostle Paul uses the human body as a metaphor to convey the numerous functions in Christ's body. Here he also deals with the dynamics of headship gifts, and their role, in terms of authority in the church: *"The foot cannot say to the hand I have no need of thee (verse 15) . . . nor the eye to the ear"* (verse 17).

The Tabernacle of Moses illustrates three distinct dimensions: the courtyard, the holy place, and the holiest of holies. Within these dimensions are seven pieces of furniture, symbolizing the bleeding spots on the body of Christ crucified. The brazen altar of sacrifice, along with the brazen laver, were in the first dimension, and illustrate the nails driven thru the feet of Jesus.

In Revelation 1:15 we read that His feet were "like unto fine brass." So then the foot (the message of repentance) is the evangel. In the second dimension (the holy place), we have the candlesticks and the table of showbread. According to Revelation 1:20, in his right hand were the seven golden candlesticks, so then the hand represents the functional aspects and dynamics of ministry, the right hand of fellowship, the ability to build. The foot (the evangel) cannot say to the hand (the functional five-fold ministry): "I have no need of thee." The evangel needs the direction of the five-fold functional ministry.

In 1 Corinthians 12:21, the apostle discusses headship gifts. The eye is the headship gift of revelation, the ability to see into the heavenly realm. Throughout the Bible the eye always signifies an ability to visualize spiritual dimensions. The ear is the headship gift of hearing what the Spirit is saying. This is not natural hearing but attending to the voice of the Spirit. The ability to smell (previously mentioned in vs. 17), is the headship gift of discernment, in which one has an anointing to "sniff out" the presence of evil or demonic strongholds.

Notice there is a direct relationship here between functional ministry and headship ministry; they must work together. Headship gifts must give direction, correction, guidance, and order to the body. The lives and destinies of the Patriarchs — Abraham, Isaac, Jacob and his sons, and his sons' sons — clearly illustrate this.

No Place for Weakness

Headship is the role of strong leadership. Isaac is a poor example of headship; certain weaknesses hindered his ability to lead. Nevertheless, ironically, Isaac is a miracle, the result of a visitation from God. In Genesis 18, the Bible says God comes and speaks to Abraham:

9 *They said unto him, Where is Sarah thy wife? And he said, Behold, in the tent.*

10 *And he said, I will certainly return unto thee according to the time of life; and, lo, Sarah thy wife shall have a son. And Sarah heard it in the tent door, which was behind him.*

11 *Now Abraham and Sarah were old and well stricken in age; and it ceased to be with Sarah after the manner of women.*

12 *Therefore Sarah laughed within herself, saying, After I am waxed old shall I have pleasure, my lord being old also?*

13 *And the LORD said unto Abraham, Wherefore did Sarah laugh, saying, Shall I of a surety bear a child, which am old?*

14 *Is any thing too hard for the LORD? At the time appointed I will return unto thee, according to the time of life, and Sarah shall have a son.*

Abraham was sitting at the door of his tent, in the noonday sun, when three beings appear, and God was one of them. Abraham ran to get Sarah, who was then at ninety years of age, to make the meal for the guests. This is unusual, because Abraham had plenty of servants, and Sarah would never have cooked. Yet no servant was to touch God's food; therefore, Sarah herself had to prepare this meal, because God showed up in town.

While God was eating and enjoying the meal, He said, "Where is Sarah?" God was not inquiring about her physical location, but her spiritual status. That is, "Where is she positionally in her faith? In her metamorphic process, where is she? Does she still believe she can have a baby at ninety, for instance?"

The Lord said, "Tell Sarah that, at the set time, I will return. This is the sign: she will embrace a son." Now, he wasn't saying he was bringing a son. God wasn't operating like a stork to bring a son. No, he was giving Abraham a sign of his next visit, and the sign of his next visit was that Sarah would embrace a son. "When she's holding a son, watch it, because that's the time of my next visit."

We put so much emphasis on the birth of Isaac, when the emphasis is actually: when God is visiting. The sign was, "She'll hold a son, and that's the time I'm visiting."

Isaac was spoiled because his parents were old and had waited for him much of their lives. It's was very difficult for Isaac, living in the shadow of a strong leader like Abraham; therefore, Isaac developed a temperament that wasn't conducive to making sound decisions, as we'll soon see.

No Room for Disunity

If headship is about one's strength, then it is also about working together with others for more strength. So, the day came when Isaac needed a wife. He was forty years old, and he still didn't think he needed a wife, so his father had to step in to get a girl for him! Abraham sent a servant to find Isaac a wife.

This servant had the tremendous responsibility of finding just the right match for Isaac. When he arrived at Nahor in the evening time with his camels, Rebekah appeared, and the Bible says she was "fair to look upon." The implication is that not only was she fair-skinned, but she had a very powerful, obvious anointing emanating from her spirit. The Bible says when she saw the camels, she gave the servant water, and then "ran" to get water for the ten camels. Each of those huge animals are dry, each of them will drink a minimum of forty gallons apiece-four hundred gallons of water to draw from the well, running back and forth. Rebekah was something else!

When she finished giving the animals water, the servant took out two things: a headgear, which I think of as a crown, and two bracelets for her arms. She went to the well an ordinary woman, and returned from the well with an anointing of headship, prosperity on her right hand, and healing in her left hand. When you go to a well, don't just go to drink; go to serve.

She returned home with guests and had invited them for dinner, which was not the cultural thing to do. That night, after all the gifts were given, the servant said, "I'm leaving in the morning to go home." Rebekah said (to make a long story short), "I'm going with you." She'd never met Isaac and didn't know who those people were. She was a tough girl, a woman who knew how to make decisions. Her mother and brother said, "Why don't you stay ten more days and be with us?" She said, "No way; I'm leaving tomorrow morning." She knew how to make decisions.

62 *Now Isaac had come from Beer-lahai-roi, and was settled in the Negeb.*

63 *Isaac went out in the evening to walk in the field; and looking up, he saw camels coming.*

64 *And Rebekah looked up, and when she saw Isaac, she slipped quickly from the camel,*

65 *and said to the servant, "Who is the man over there, walking in the field to meet us?" The servant said, "It is my master." So she took her veil and covered herself.*

66 *And the servant told Isaac all the things that he had done.*

67 *Then Isaac brought her into his mother Sarah's tent. He took Rebekah, and she became his wife; and he loved her. So Isaac was comforted after his mother's death.*

–Genesis 24:62-67

When Rebecca saw Isaac, he was walking on his own, he didn't want to be messed with, he liked being on his own. It reveals his temperament.

The Bible says that Rebekah was barren, so Isaac entreated the Lord for his wife, and the Lord heard him. Rebekah became pregnant (with a little bit of help from Isaac).

God then spoke to Rebekah. He always spoke to Abraham about Isaac's birth, but in the next generation, He spoke to the matriarch. God didn't speak to Isaac concerning Esau and Jacob, instead, God spoke to Rebekah. He went to Rebekah and revealed, that there were two nations in her.

God spoke to Rebekah and not Isaac, because Isaac was a weak man; he had a weak temperament. God had to speak to Rebekah, because of the future of the nation; how she dealt with her sons, Jacob and Esau was of great importance.

Esau was born first. He was red, a man of the field. Jacob grabbed his heel at their birth, which revealed that Esau was the foot and Jacob the hand (the foot cannot say to the hand, "I have no need of thee). Esau became a man of the field. Jacob was a tent dweller, a strong man, who learned how money, books and administration worked (governmental anointing). Esau was the foot (functional ministry), he worked the fields and organized the soldiers.

There is a season when God will download His blessing and the season for the brothers to be blessed had come. Isaac said to Esau, "I'm going to give you the blessing," but that wasn't God's instruction! The instruction was: The blessing goes to Jacob.

Rebekah was listening and she said to Jacob, "Esau's gone to hunt game for Isaac's meal. Go and kill two goats, and I'll make a meal of goat meat for Isaac."

Jacob killed the goats, and Rebekah prepared the stew. Jacob entered, wearing Esau's clothes, and he had goat's hair on his arms and his neck. He walked in with the goat meat and, because Isaac's eyes were bad, Isaac asked: "Who is coming in?"

Jacob said, "It's me, Esau."

This is where headship gifts are needed to function and cooperate, especially when one headship gift fails. The eye says to the ear, because the eye is blind, "I have no need of thee." The ear must have said this is Jacob, but the eye said: "I have no need of thee." So Isaac's great mistake unfolds.

Isaac said, "Come closer." He could smell the goat stew and thought it was deer. He said, "Embrace me, my son." As he embraces Jacob, Smell says, "It is indeed Esau" but Hearing says, "No, not Esau!". The smell and the eye are saying to the ear: "We have no need of thee."

"Let me touch you now," said Isaac. He sought the headship gift of feeling. Is God in that place? He must have wondered. Yet Isaac couldn't even discern goat's hair from his son, Esau!

Then, the final test — taste. He ate the goat curry, thinking it was deer. The juice was running down his chin, yet he couldn't discern.

The headship gifts require that we come together in unity. Some things are better heard than seen; some things better seen than heard. Some things are better smelled than touched or better felt than tasted. All of the gifts are needed; all must work together in the body of Christ, with integrity.

No Need for Deception

It was the will of God for Jacob to get the blessing, of course, but deception and corruption were unnecessary. Dishonesty is not God's way. For example, imagine if Rebekah and Isaac had called the boys in and said, "Esau, you are the foot. You need to go out there and raise up an army. Jacob, you are the one God has called to govern. Now we're going to send you to Nahor because there are two girls that you have to marry there. The reason you have to marry those two girls is that there are twelve sons in you that are the foundation for the Kingdom of God." How wonderful!

However, Jacob received the blessing through conniving and corruption, incurring curses and hardships, because Isaac did not recognize God's will — the headship gifts were not in order.

Jacob received the blessing, which was God's will. When Jacob left to find his wife, he went without money. When Rebekah was brought, her solicitation came with ten camels, showing the force and the power of the Kingdom. But Jacob went in search of the destiny of his life . . . with no money. As a result, he wasted twenty-one years working as a slave when, in reality, he was a king. Twenty-one years of his life were wasted, because his headship gift was weak. God had to work on Jacob to make him the man he was to become.

The years went by, Jacob had a number of sons, yet he was still an incomplete man. But God was working on him, therefore Joseph was taken away from him. Jacob thought Joseph was dead, but the Scripture says in Psalms that God sent Joseph ahead to prepare the way. So Joseph saw his brothers coming to him in the midst of a famine, in the second year of the famine. His family was unable to prepare for adverse times because the headship gift was not in order.

When headship gift is in place, though, one can sow and reap bountifully, as did Isaac. He sowed in the famine and reaped a hundredfold. But Jacob could not follow because of the curses passed on to him.

No Mistake in This Blessing!

In Genesis 49, Jacob blessed all his twelve sons. But in chapter 48, Joseph brought his boys to Jacob (by that time called Israel). Jacob was old and had lost his eyesight. Joseph brought his sons to Jacob to be blessed. Joseph placed the oldest boy, Manasseh, by his left hand so he could face Jacob's right hand. Joseph puts Ephraim on his right side so that he could face Jacob's left hand. In this way, the right hand of fellowship and power and blessing could land upon the older boy.

> 13 *Joseph took them both, Ephraim in his right hand toward Israel's left, and Manasseh in his left hand toward Israel's right, and brought them near him.*
> 14 *But Israel stretched out his right hand and laid it on the head of Ephraim, who was the younger, and*

*his left hand on the head of Manasseh, crossing his
hands, for Manasseh was the firstborn.*

15 *He blessed Joseph, and said, The God before
whom my ancestors Abraham and Isaac walked, the
God who has been my shepherd all my life to this day,*

16 *the angel who has redeemed me from all harm,
bless the boys; and in them let my name be
perpetuated, and the name of my ancestors Abraham
and Isaac; and let them grow into a multitude on the
earth."*

17 *When Joseph saw that his father laid his right
hand on the head of Ephraim, it displeased him; so he
took his father's hand, to remove it from Ephraim's
head to Manasseh's head.*

18 *Joseph said to his father, "Not so, my father!
Since this one is the firstborn, put your right hand on
his head."*

19 *But his father refused, and said, "I know, my
son, I know; he also shall become a people, and he also
shall be great. Nevertheless his younger brother shall
be greater than he, and his offspring shall become a
multitude of nations."*

20 *So he blessed them that day, saying, By you
Israel will invoke blessings, saying, God make you like
Ephraim and like Manasseh.' " So he put Ephraim
ahead of Manasseh.*

Jacob was blind; he could not see. And Joseph
thought, Oh, no! Father was supposed to bless them the
other way! The ear says to the eye, "We have to work
together in this thing. If we fail, we are going to affect
generations unborn to the end of time." But when Jacob

switched his arms, Joseph became irritated. Joseph did not have the anointing Jacob had.

Joseph was a five-fold ministry that was a hand. He was the hand that built Egypt. He didn't have headship gifting. We know this because when Jacob came, the Bible says he prayed for Pharaoh and laid his hands on Pharaoh. Joseph never once prayed for Pharaoh. But Jacob put his hands on Pharaoh because Jacob was headship.

The eye was blind, but the eye said to the ear, "I need you in this moment. I need you." So when Jacob began to pray, Joseph said: "Not so, my father!"

Jacob's response was: "I know, my son, I know." He prayed for Ephraim and he pronounced upon him the greater blessing. Manasseh means "to forget those things which are behind." Ephraim means "to be fruitful." The reason he had to pray and pronounce the blessing on Ephraim was not because Ephraim needed the blessing, but because of what was coming in the future.

The day was coming when Egypt would release Israel and the people would travel to a Land of Promise. A leader would have to be selected to lead the children of Israel. They needed a fruitful leader that had the endorsement of the headship gift.

His name was Joshua.

He was from the tribe of Ephraim.

No Small Need: Restoring the Headship Gift

I want to show you the force of the headship gift and the way it works. In Judges 6, Israel is in pandemonium; total anarchy reigns, for the doors have been opened to the demonic. When those spirits came in, they put Israel in a continual state of slavery.

Gideon, who was a man of valor, lacked courage because of the system. He threshed wheat in a winepress. Bread, or wheat is used metaphorically throughout the Bible to represent the word. Word, or wheat without the Spirit, brings death. Wheat is the letter that kills; the Spirit gives life, but there was no wine flowing in Gideon's life. He had a form of godliness, but no power. But then God. God chose him. The Bible says it was the angel of the Lord who called him a "mighty man of valor." But Gideon didn't believe he was a man of valor. The Lord said to him, "I want you now to be the man I'm using to deliver Israel. Assemble the army."

Gideon obeyed. Thirty-two thousand men assembled. The Lord said, "Tell the ones who are afraid to go home." So, twenty-two thousand left, ten thousand remained. Gideon believed this to be right as ten thousand is the number of the Kingdom, and the violent take it by force.

God said, "No, I want to show you something here. There is a level that is deeper than the Kingdom. There is a kingdom within the Kingdom. Go down to the river and let them take the water taste-test." Because when you get done with the water, you'll end up with 300 (300 is a headship number). The 300 had an eye that the other 9,700 didn't have. They could see what others in the Kingdom couldn't see. They were listening for something the others didn't even know could be there. They were tasting and observing in a way the others weren't doing, because there was a headship gift that God was restoring.

Now see the significance of this headship gift; the Bible says that one night the Lord said to Gideon and his boys: "Go and spy out the Midianite camp." They did.

One of the Midianite sentries said, "I had a dream last night about a barley loaf that destroyed the entire camp." One of the men suddenly received discernment and interpreted the dream and said, "That barley loaf is none other than the armies of Gideon."

A barley loaf is created when individual barley kernels put aside their individual potency, so they can be sown in the ground and produce the next generation. They are ground to powder and die in order to subsume their unique individualism and combine with others to make one loaf. They are baked in God's army, where they die to self for significant performance. The three hundred men in Gideon's army were willing to put aside all of their gifts to be baked together in a community of unity.

How good, how pleasant it is for brethren to dwell together in unity! For there the Lord commanded the blessing. Gideon went to the Midianite camp and the three hundred surrounded the camp. They didn't lift a sword. All they had was a trumpet — the prophetic — and a fire — the covenant of the Holy Spirit descending.

When you are covenanted, married with Christ, He'll fight for you.

This level of headship gifting didn't have to stab a single enemy. All they said was *"The sword of the Lord and the sword of Gideon."* An entire slavery, an entire siege, an entire threat, was put out in one night. It happened when headship gifts said: "We need each other."

CHAPTER 8

MOVING TO THE CITY

YE ARE THE LIGHT OF THE WORLD. A CITY THAT IS SET ON AN HILL CANNOT BE HID.

—Matthew 5:14

Ready to move from the house into the city? As we come into a city setting, please understand this: God builds churches to strengthen cities, in order to establish His Kingdom throughout the earth.

In any large city there will be all kinds of churches, because the body of Christ in the city setting has a kind of "ecclesiastical ecosystem." Some churches are very large, others very small. And not all of the large churches became large because God blessed them. No, some churches are large because individuals know how to organize, structure, and administrate. On the other hand, some pastors are blessed but don't have a clue about how to structure and organize, so their ministry stays small. But within any city's ecosystem, all the churches play an important part in the development of the city church.

Why the need for a city-wide church? I've been to prayer meetings in various local churches, and I'll find church members praying to bind the demonic forces in their city. But it is very hard to bind a demonic force in a city if that local house isn't participating with other houses in the city. For this kind of power, churches must come together.

In Matthew 5:14, Jesus said, *"You are the light of the world."* Here's the whole world, the Kingdom. Then he said, *"A city that is set* (not built) *on a hill cannot be hid."* That word *set* refers to place of authority. That is, here we have a city church, in which houses in the body of Christ make up a corporate, governmental, city-wide place of authority.

It "cannot be hid." What is Jesus talking about here? He's talking about another level of ministry, moving to another level of government altogether. But how do we make that move? I'd like to suggest five steps in this chapter. The move to a new level of government happens as churches learn to work together, to discern major players, to transfer anointing, to form alliances, and to restore order.

1. Churches Working Together

One night I was flying from Houston, Texas, to Amsterdam and most of the East coast of the United States lay dark under thick cloud-cover. But even with the clouds, I could tell when we were flying over a major city, because the clouds themselves were aglow. The lights of those cities could not be hid.

Now, an individual light of a house would not have changed the clouds like that. It would have left the clouds as dark and black as ever. But because each individual house contributed its own light, each made a contribution to all the lights. It caused a huge glow of clouds up to maybe ten thousand feet above sea level. The same is applicable in the city church idea I'm offering here.

Let's talk about the city of Dallas for a moment. It has some major churches. For example, Covenant Church, a couple of huge Baptist churches, and Bishop T. D. Jakes' church. It has great learning institutes as well, such as Christ for the Nations and Dallas Theological Seminary. All of these churches and schools are examples of major players in God's plan.

However, if you look at the previous generation of mega churches in the Dallas metropolis, you'll notice a number of churches that could have been effective had they not fallen to the ground. Those churches didn't build a strong house. There was no strong government in the house, and so they couldn't continue standing. It's just as Jesus said: *"If a house be divided against itself, that house cannot stand"* (Mark 3:25). But if a house is united within itself, it will stand. So when you have a house that stands, it then can go to the next level, which is the city.

If the mega churches in a city like Dallas would commit to working together in their city, the light of their churches could not be hidden, unlike a candle under a bushel. Each candle, each church, has a light. The light of the house must be brought to the corporate, city level. All of the house lights placed together on the city level cannot be hid. If you take a house and you put it on a hill, that house can be hid because a bush can hide that light. But if you take the major apostolic houses in a city, each house being a strong light, and place all those lights on a hill, they form one awesome glow.

2. Discerning a City's Major Players

We've said that God builds houses in order to strengthen cities for establishment of His Kingdom. That's why the churches that God is raising up must become major players in a city. How does this work?

Consider what I call the Crèche Syndrome in schools. When the child comes to the crèche, or the preschool, that child is like an outsider — but not for very long. After a number of weeks, that child will fall into the routine and the system of the preschool. He becomes a normal part of the scene, just like all the other "figures" walking the halls.

There is another hidden law in that particular school. It's a particular pecking order. Those who have more authority and power can actually dictate the rules on the playground. You begin to know the tough ones, the strong ones, and the intelligent ones. The leader is automatically understood amongst the children. Throughout the year, while they are playing on the playground, swimming in the pool, or working in the art room, one child is always the one top guy in the pecking order.

Of course, this isn't just a childhood phenomenon. We adults, too, recognize differing personalities, powers, and roles-all of which could keep us apart in our denominations. I recall a study carried out by two psychologists about how members of the various sections of eleven major symphony orchestras perceived each other:

The percussionists were viewed as insensitive, unintelligent, and hard-of-hearing, yet fun-loving. String players were seen as arrogant, stuffy, and unauthentic. The orchestra members overwhelmingly chose "loud" as the primary adjective to describe the brass players. Woodwind players seemed to be held in the highest esteem, described as quiet and meticulous, though a bit egotistical. Interesting findings, to say the least! With such widely divergent personalities and perceptions, how could an orchestra ever come together to make such wonderful music? The answer is simple: regardless of how those musicians view each other, they subordinate their feelings and biases to the leadership of the conductor. Under his guidance, they play beautiful music.[14]

Can we all, churches and denominations alike, submit to our Great Heavenly Conductor, and play together?

When we come to a church like yours or mine, which needs to become a player in the city, we already know who the major players in that city are. Jesus made a statement in this regard that is truly incredible. *(See Mark 14:8-10.)* I'll just paraphrase it for you: When you go to somebody's house, don't take the high seats. Instead, take the lower seats, because if you are to be seated in a higher place of honor, they will come and tell you so. But if you take the high seats right away, and you don't have the rank for that seat, they're going to ask you to move down lower. How embarrassing!

In that teaching, we're seeing the unfolding of rank in the city and how we know who God has anointed as a superior to a not-so-powerful general. Until the body of Christ comes to the understanding of city government, we're never going to see the fulfillment of true Kingdom within a nation. We will see revival come to a nation, once we understand Kingdom government.

3. Transferring the Anointing

God is moving in the world today where unselfish cooperation prevails. In Uganda, for example, we're seeing major apostles in various parts of that nation begin to rise up and become influential. It's happening because God has anointed men there to first build strong churches or houses; then these strong leaders automatically transfer their anointing, not just on their people, but transfer their anointing to the city. They are willing to put together a combination of their light, heat, fervor, anointing, revelation, wisdom, and gifts. They are willing to join up with others in the city so that if there's a city-wide prayer meeting called, they all fall under that particular leadership. This is significant, because it eliminates disunity.

Disunity is disastrous! It's said that when the British and French were fighting in Canada in the 1750s,

Admiral Phipps, commander of the British fleet, was told to anchor outside Quebec. He had orders to wait for the British land forces to arrive, then support them when they attacked the city. Phipps's navy arrived early. As the admiral waited, he became annoyed by the statues of the saints that adorned the towers of a nearby cathedral, so he commanded his men to shoot at them with the ships' cannons. No one knows how many rounds were fired or how many statues were knocked out, but when the land forces arrived, and the attack was signaled, the admiral was of no help. He had used up all his ammunition shooting at the "saints."[15]

We can't afford to have that kind of rivalry in the church. Scripture is clear: *"A city divided against itself cannot stand."* We're seeing so many cities in the world, including in America, that are not standing because the demonic world is overrunning and overruling them. But when major churches in Chicago or Los Angeles come together, we're going to see a mega-dendra of awesome effectiveness. We'll see a number of incredible churches building a fruit tree with fruit that will affect an entire region.

Kingdom government on a city level is totally different from government in a local church. A denomination could be termed, in my words, a house. That house is led by the denominational leaders. Each denomination tends to perpetuate what it is doing to make itself grow, to become stronger, to have more money and more outreach programs. If that house denomination can move to a higher level and work with other house's denominations, then we'll have the light of that house join with the light of another house to form . . . a city on a hill.

4. Forming Strong Alliances

When we see governmental structure on this level, it's something that cannot be legislated, and cannot be voted into existence. Only through much fellowship and decisive action will the birth of relationships on three levels occur: allegiances, alliances, and covenants. That's when we see regional pockets of blessing in which God raises up the key men who, through the impact of their particular house, are changing the environment within their region. When these kinds of men — set men, apostolic men, bishops, overseers, if you like — come together in specific unity, then the city will be able to function and have strong leadership. It will have clear-cut decisive action because you won't have in-house discipline alone.

Why do we need broader discipline? Consider the case of having a minister in a city who falls into moral failure. No doubt, his denomination removes him, yet he will not repent or get his life right. So what does he do? He simply hooks up with another denomination! There he's accepted without being accountable for his actions. But once you have city elders coming together forming a city church, that kind of scenario cannot occur. I'm simply saying: We must have church alliances on a city level for the purpose of order. There has to be order.

In one of Charles Schultz's Peanuts cartoons, Lucy demanded that Linus change TV channels, threatening him with her fist if he didn't. "What makes you think you can walk right in here and take over?" asks Linus.

"These five fingers," says Lucy. "Individually they're nothing, but when I curl them together like this into a single unit, they form a weapon that is terrible to behold."

"Which channel do you want?" asks Linus. Turning away, he looks at his fingers and says, "Why can't you guys get organized like that?"

5. Restoring the Order

I want to mention the city of David as we close out this chapter. In 2 Samuel 4-7, David was being made king over not just Judah, the tribe from which he came, but also over the eleven tribes that came to him and offered their allegiance. David then became the king of Israel. The first thing he did was to clear the Jebusites out of Mt. Zion (or the fort of Zion). The Jebusites were there for almost seven hundred years after Joshua had taken the land, but David drove them out.

My point is simple: When you don't have city-level government as David did, you will still have pockets of demonic strength in a city that will inhibit the development of a church within that city. If elders in the church don't come together in the city, you'll have a Jebusite stronghold in the middle of what God is trying to do!

It took 700 years after Joshua had brought the people into a position of receiving their inheritance in the land. It took David, with a covenanted group of men and women who joined behind and underneath and together with David, to take the kingdom of God to another level. Again, the first thing David did, was call out Mt. Zion. Why? Two reasons: First, Zion became the resting place for the Ark of God. Second, it was the worship place for the children of Israel. The Ark of God, or the Tabernacle of David as it later became known, is not praise and worship, but government. When David went to fetch the Ark of God, which was resting at Obed-edom, that Ark had been away from Israel for almost a century.

David went to get this Ark. His first attempt failed when Uzzah touched the Ark, he died. He was trying to steady it but was killed. In touching the Ark, he was not touching the presence of God, but the government of God. Psalm 16:11 says, *"In* [God's] *presence, there is fullness of joy."* So when he touched the Ark, the touching was actually the man literally touching God's government. No one can touch God's government and get away with it. Ask Lucifer. He was expelled with lightning when he did it.

So when David went a second time to bring the Ark, he went with dancing. And something else occurs:

> *And it was so, that when they that bare the ark of the LORD had gone six paces, he sacrificed oxen and fatlings.*
>
> —2 Samuel 6 :13

They took six steps and then sacrificed. The taking of six steps meant something. The Bible says the steps of a good man are ordered of the Lord. David was a good man, and once his people took six steps while bringing the ark back, they had to stop and offer a sacrifice. It was the sacrifice of praise, the kind of restoration of praise and worship, which we are seeing today. Then, after the sixth step, they entered into a time of rest and celebration. What does all of this mean for us today? I suggest that after the six thousand years (or six years) in which mankind has lived, order is coming; after that, the restoration of order *(See Psalm 90:4; Conner; Larkin)*.

So David then took the Ark of God to Jerusalem and placed it on Mt. Zion. He became the governmental headship from which and in which God ruled and reigned. That is, David established a system of worship and a system of government, to rule in Jerusalem with him. He built a system of military might and he set up an economy. He actually established four things: *worship, economy, military might,* and *governmental rule and order*. All of these are directed in the New Testament church. It is citywide government.

David then set up garrisons in all of the other strongholds. He established garrisons to rule from a position of government into the regions throughout the land of Canaan or Palestine, now Israel.

This is so significant for our day and age. If we're going to see the power of God move beyond the local house, the set men are going to have to go from the house to the city. When the cities become strong, then we can become Kingdom players. The Kingdom of God is not a material world. It is righteousness, the Word of God, and peace, which means a war that was fought but is now over. In the Kingdom, peace and joy reign which is the very nature of God in the Holy Ghost.

It will take some swallowing of pride and some willingness to be broken and molded by the Spirit. The great preacher D.L. Moody once said: "There are two ways of being united — one is by being frozen together, and the other is by being melted together. What Christians need is to be united in brotherly love, and then they may expect to have power."

Do you agree? If so, are you willing to have your own heart touched and melted by the Lord? What is holding you back from loving your brother or sister in Christ? What is keeping your church from loving your brother church? What is hindering your entire city from being a light on a hill, a beacon of the Kingdom of God for all those lonely seekers who are walking aimlessly to and fro?

Chapter 9

From City to Kingdom

...In the days of these kings shall the God of heaven set up a kingdom, which shall never be destroyed: and the kingdom shall not be left to other people, but it shall break in pieces and consume all these kingdoms, and it shall stand for ever.

—Daniel 2:44

Been to a good football game lately? I like sports, but I've sometimes found it more interesting to observe the fans than to watch what might be happening on the field — especially at those tense moments when one of the teams will win or lose in the final thrilling seconds. At that point, long-suppressed emotions may suddenly leap out of their cages, transforming the gentlest personalities into raging fanatics.

Such transformations aren't limited to our sports arenas. Sadly, something similar can happen in the church, as well. I came out of a denominational structure that taught us we were a theocracy, ruled by God, we believed it. However, once a year, at the annual general conference, we nominated individuals to serve in various positions. Sometimes these leaders were nominated by the board, sometimes from the floor. In either case, all of the business procedures were governed by Robert's Rules of Order, and if an individual was to become head of the denomination, he would need a two-third's majority vote.

Here's my point: At some of those meetings, I'd see more fighting, more arguing, more disputes, and more enflamed spirits than I'd ever encountered at a football game! I can't truly say that our system of voting demonstrated a theocracy. It was much more like a democracy, with all its strengths and weaknesses.

In this chapter, I want to touch on leadership on a Kingdom level. But please realize that my concern is not so much the kind of structure (because that varies from place to place, culture to culture), but the result of the structure. That is, we want to look at what happens when we have Kingdom government. Kingdom government shouldn't be pursued only as an organizing and ruling structure. There must be relationships to go with structure.

As we explore this concept of Kingdom government — a system of rule in which God Himself is reigning in the earth — let's start with the book of Daniel. In Chapter 2 we find an unfolding of various governmental systems. In them we can see both the Gentile order of government and, in contrast, God's preference of government.

Daniel's Metals: They're about Governments

The Scripture says that King Nebuchadnezzar of Babylon had a dream *"wherewith his spirit was troubled, and his sleep brake from him"* (Daniel 2:1). He actually forgot his dream, but his spirit was troubled nevertheless, and he could not get back to sleep. So he called for all of his seers — the magicians, astrologers, and sorcerers — who should have been able to tell him his dream and what it meant. These so-called wise men were influenced by the demonic and could apparently see into the spirit world. Yet they didn't have the answer. So Daniel was finally summoned.

16 *Then Daniel went in, and desired of the king that he would give him time, and that he would show the king the interpretation.*

17 *Then Daniel went to his house, and made the thing known to Hananiah, Mishael, and Azariah, his companions:*

18 *That they would desire mercies of the God of heaven concerning this secret; that Daniel and his fellows should not perish with the rest of the wise men of Babylon.*

19 *Then was the secret revealed unto Daniel in a night vision. Then Daniel blessed the God of heaven...*

24 *Therefore Daniel went in unto Arioch, whom the king had ordained to destroy the wise men of Babylon: he went and said thus unto him; Destroy not the wise men of Babylon: bring me in before the king, and I will show unto the king the interpretation.*

25 *Then Arioch brought in Daniel before the king in haste, and said thus unto him, I have found a man*

of the captives of Judah, that will make known unto the king the interpretation.

26 The king answered and said to Daniel, whose name was Belteshazzar, Art thou able to make known unto me the dream which I have seen, and the interpretation thereof?

—Daniel 2:16-19, 24-26

Daniel went in to the king, and the king told him what he needed. "Give me a little time," Daniel said. So Daniel went to his house and joined in prayer with his associates, asking for God's help and mercy and God gave him the secret. [NOTE: Matthew 13:11 says that the mysteries of the Kingdom of God are given to a certain group of individuals. This is the group now participating in Kingdom government, the group that sees secrets. There are some in a local church who won't see what a true apostolic headship will see.]

Daniel saw a huge image:

31 Thou, O king, sawest, and behold a great image. This great image, whose brightness was excellent, stood before thee; and the form thereof was terrible.

32 This image's head was of fine gold, his breast and his arms of silver, his belly and his thighs of brass,

33 His legs of iron, his feet part of iron and part of clay.

34 Thou sawest till that a stone was cut out without hands, which smote the image upon his feet that were of iron and clay, and brake them to pieces.

35 Then was the iron, the clay, the brass, the silver, and the gold, broken to pieces together, and became like the chaff of the summer threshing floors; and the wind carried them away, that no place was found for them: and the stone that smote the image became a great mountain, and filled the whole earth.

—Daniel 2:31-35

The first thing he saw was a head of gold and a chest and arms of silver. The belly and thighs were of brass, legs or shins of iron, feet and toes of iron and clay mixed together. But what does it all mean? Daniel was ready to reveal it:

36 *This is the dream; and we will tell the interpretation thereof before the king.*

37 *Thou, O king, art a king of kings: for the God of heaven hath given thee a kingdom, power, strength, and glory.*

38 *And wheresoever the children of men dwell, the beasts of the field and the fowls of the heaven hath he given into thine hand, and hath made thee ruler over them all. Thou art this head of gold.*

39 *And after thee shall arise another kingdom inferior to thee, and another third kingdom of brass, which shall bear rule over all the earth.*

40 *And the fourth kingdom shall be strong as iron: forasmuch as iron breaketh in pieces and subdueth all things: and as iron that breaketh all these, shall it break in pieces and bruise.*

41 *And whereas thou sawest the feet and toes, part of potters' clay, and part of iron, the kingdom shall be divided; but there shall be in it of the strength of the iron, forasmuch as thou sawest the iron mixed with miry clay.*

42 *And as the toes of the feet were part of iron, and part of clay, so the kingdom shall be partly strong, and partly broken.*

⁴³ *And whereas thou sawest iron mixed with miry clay, they shall mingle themselves with the seed of men: but they shall not cleave one to another, even as iron is not mixed with clay.*

—Daniel 2:36-43

Daniel told Nebuchadnezzar that the king was the head of gold. The kingdom that was to come after Nebuchadnezzar's was silver, which was the Medo-Persian Empire. The next kingdom to follow was the kingdom of Greece, led by Alexander the Great, whose armies moved with lightning speed to destroy the kingdom of the Medes and the Persians. After the Greeks came the kingdom of the Romans.

But there is one more kingdom, after all of the human governments end. It is the kingdom of God, and it will last forever.

⁴⁴ *And in the days of these kings shall the God of heaven set up a kingdom, which shall never be destroyed: and the kingdom shall not be left to other people, but it shall break in pieces and consume all these kingdoms, and it shall stand for ever.*
⁴⁵ *Forasmuch as thou sawest that the stone was cut out of the mountain without hands, and that it brake in pieces the iron, the brass, the clay, the silver, and the gold; the great God hath made known to the king what shall come to pass hereafter: and the dream is certain, and the interpretation thereof sure.*

—Daniel 2: 44-45

So we see God used the kingdom of metals to reveal the governments coming in Daniel's future, one kingdom following another as history unfolded. And that is exactly how it happened. Let's look closer at the forms, or systems, of government these kingdoms employed:

1. Authoritarian/dictatorship government.

The head of gold is the Babylonian system of government. It was authoritarian and dictatorial.

You may be surprised to know that dictatorship is actually God's first order of preference. After all, imagine an all-powerful, all-loving ruler reigning over your nation; a truly benevolent dictatorship would be heaven on earth. Sadly, however, most dictatorships are hardly benevolent. They are often engineered by tyrants and merciless, power-hungry bullies.

In one sense, Jesus Christ is a dictator. When you become a Christian, you lose all your rights and become His bond-slave. Paul said, "I am a slave to Christ." So in service to Christ, you listen for what He tells you to do and where He tells you to go. It is the most joyful kind of life, because your Master always has your best interests in mind. The One who loves you unconditionally brings you into His work of reigning in the universe and makes you part of His cosmic plans. What could be better?

When we think of dictatorship, we normally think "Tyrant!" However, Jesus is different. He is a dictator with character. He cares more for you than He cares for His own policy.

That is why God's preference is firstly authoritarian: When the Word is spoken, it is settled. And every decision is always perfect and good.

2. Law-ordered government.

The silver, the second order of God's preference for government, is the system of the Medes and the Persians. Their system relied upon this foundation: If a word was written or spoken by the king in law, then that word could not be changed.

There are loopholes, though, with law because, as with a dictatorship, you can have a law-giver with bad character, or no character at all! Throughout history, we see such men. They weren't given to their people or to the needs of their people, and corruption very quickly crept in. Imperfections crept in, and imperfections began to rule. Nepotism began to rule as well.

Depending on one's understanding of the law, or even one's interpretation of the law, loopholes abound. That's what we're finding, especially in America today. There are so many interpretations of a single law, depending on what school you went to and what books you had available to you. That's why a certain president could say in a courtroom: "It depends on what the meaning of 'is' is"!

So those with the law — those who have a lot of money — can manipulate the law to serve their own purposes. On the other hand, some folks have died in the electric chair because they didn't have the money for the kind of help that would interpret the law in their favor.

That is why the system of law did not work very well when the children of Israel were on their journey to the land of Canaan. However, in spite of all these human flaws regarding law, this is still God's second order of preference for governing.

3. Rational (free-thinking) government.

God's third order of preference for government was the Greek system, which was called the "era of free thought." This form of government depended on thinking things through to logical conclusions. Within this framework, men like Socrates and Plato sought to create a city/state utopia where citizens would be educated, wise, and thoughtful. Thus they could govern themselves with rational purity in all matters of personal and social endeavor.

The problem? Not everyone is blessed with the same level of intellectual strength. Nor does intellectual ability ever guarantee moral rectitude.

In fact, there are three major disciplines in intelligence: Academia, Practical Engineering Knowledge, and Business Genius. You'll find that the key players in the Scripture who were the most effective, like Solomon, Paul, and Jesus, were quite developed in these three areas. They were very practical because they learned various trades. Paul was a tentmaker; Jesus was a carpenter. And when it came to business genius, they were all great businessmen.

The concept of government based on free thinking isn't God's preference. Furthermore, free thinking in a 21st-century setting is very dangerous because it can lead to moral relativism, a key characteristic of the postmodern philosophy so prevalent today. When all claims to truth are considered purely subjective (i.e., personal opinion), then that which is good might be considered evil; that which is evil isn't so bad . . . it's probably good.

4. Democratic government.

The fourth order of God's preference for government is exemplified by the Roman Empire, which was a democracy. Rome was ruled by an elected senate, which was to represent all the people. Again, as with any form of government, democracy can succumb to human failure, greed, or just plain evil intentions.

In addition, the best of democracies can only be as good as the quality of its citizenry. Democracy requires an educated and well-informed majority that can vote wisely for its representatives and laws. Of particular concern is the possibility of having a minority that begins voting only for entitlements to benefit itself. Once that minority becomes the majority, and constantly votes only to "spread the wealth," all revenue and property will soon be depleted — given away in massive tax breaks or entitlement programs — and the country can no longer exist. This is the worst-case scenario of a democracy; it can become little better than mob rule.

This is why the United States' government, for example, is not a strict democracy but a representative constitutional republic. Not even the president is chosen by "one man, one vote," as demonstrated in the Bush-Gore election of 2000. The founders feared a strict democracy in which an ignorant populace might become the majority.

Amidst these four types of government there are, of course, a multitude of variations. Throughout world history we find such systems as monarchies, parliaments, and communist politburos. All such forms of governing have strengths but they also have serious weaknesses.

5. Kingdom-of-God Government: A Complete Balance

Now we come to the key theme of this chapter. The four kingdoms shown to Daniel have long ago disappeared in the ash-heap of history. They are no more, though their modern counterparts might mirror a dim reflection of those once-great civilizations.

But at the end of both the vision of Daniel and that of Nebuchadnezzar, a stone was hewn out of the mountain, made without hands, and the Kingdom of God was then established. God's Kingdom is an amalgamation of all of these systems into a complete unit of balance. This conglomeration of government — this joining together of all these systems — won't work well in a house or a local church or even in the city setting. But it will work very well in the Kingdom of God at large — from nation to nation, where the apostolic headships and the governmental systems of the church within a nation can then begin to interact from nation to nation and continent to continent.

As an example, when we look at Paul serving as the apostle to the Gentiles, even though he made most of the decisions, and made most of the rulings concerning the Gentiles, the apostle Paul was directly responsible to Jerusalem. Not just to the city of Jerusalem, but to the elders in Jerusalem. That included Peter, John, and James, the bishop of Jerusalem.

Looking at the different roles of Peter and Paul in Jerusalem, we find that Peter was given to the circumcised — the Jews — while Paul was given to those who were formerly pagans — the Gentiles. Paul stated a number of rules and regulations for Gentiles that the Jews could not live by. For example, Paul said to the Gentile church: "It doesn't matter really what you eat, as long as it's received by thanksgiving" *(see Romans 14)*. The Gentile church could live with that, but the Jewish church couldn't because those members wouldn't even touch pork chops or a ham sandwich because of their former religious culture.

In addition, the apostle Paul said it was ludicrous to think the Gentile males needed to be physically circumcised to qualify for the Kingdom of God. However, the Jews said, "Our boys are going to be circumcised, no matter what." So they had to come to an agreement and a consensus, in which the Kingdom of God had to function outside of and within the confines of various rulings, cultures, customs, nationalities, ethnic groups, linguistic divisions, and tribes. This makes God's Kingdom supreme and transcendent in every way.

God's Kingdom has cosmic influence, but it is also very personal: *"The Kingdom of God is within you,"* Jesus said. So, as we close out this chapter, I must ask: Is the Kingdom in you? How can you tell? A rabbi told a story of a king and his son that applies perfectly here:

Once a king's son sinned against his father, so the king expelled him from his house. As long as he was near his home, people knew he was the king's son and befriended him and gave him food and drink. But as the days passed, and he got farther into his father's realm, no one knew him, and he had nothing to eat.

The young man began to sell his clothing to buy food. When he had nothing left to sell, he hired out as a shepherd. He would sit on the hills tending his flocks and singing like the other shepherds, and he forgot that he was a king's son and forgot all the pleasures he once knew.

Now it was the custom of the shepherds to make themselves small roofs of straw to keep out the rain. The king's son wanted to make such a roof, too, but he could not afford one, so he was deeply grieved.

Once the king happened to be passing through that province. It was common practice in the kingdom for those who had petitions to the king to write out their petitions and throw them into the king's chariot. The king's son came with the other petitioners and threw his note in; he asked for a small straw roof such as shepherds have. The king recognized the handwriting and was saddened to think how low his son had fallen, that he had forgotten that he was a king's son and felt only the lack of a straw roof.

It is the same way with our people. They have already forgotten that they are each of them King's sons and have forgotten what they really lack. One cries that he is in want of a living and another cries for children. But the truth — that we lack all the treasure of heaven — that is something they forget to pray for.[16]

Remember, you are a child of the King of the Universe. Are you living like it?

CHAPTER 10

PREPARE YOUR HEART FOR THIS KINGDOM!

FOR THE KINGDOM OF GOD IS NOT MEAT AND DRINK, BUT RIGHTEOUSNESS, PEACE, AND JOY IN THE HOLY GHOST.

—Romans 14:17

Nat Wyeth, engineer and inventor, once said this about his brother, artist Andrew Wyeth:

Andy did a picture of Lafayette's quarters near Chadds Ford, Pennsylvania, with a sycamore tree behind the building. When I first saw the painting, he wasn't finished with it. He showed me a lot of drawings of the trunk and the sycamore's gnarled roots, and I said, 'Where's all that in the picture?'

"It's not in the picture, Nat," he said. "For me to get what I want in the part of the tree that's showing, I've got to know thoroughly how it is anchored in back of the house." He could

draw the tree above the house with such authenticity because he knew exactly how the thing was in the ground.[17]

When it comes to the Kingdom, we must also have a thorough understanding of how it is anchored if we are to live and work within it according to God's will. Its roots must go down into the Rock, of course. And it must have a secure, biblical governmental structure. You see, we cannot have a full ruling of the Kingdom of God without government. That's why people who pursue praise and worship without governmental structure are foolish. They will rise and fall on their emotion and temperament.

Rather, what we need is structure that is sound, structure that can be built for three and four generations. The problem is that many evangelicals are willing to camp for one day in one place without building for the future. However, if we're not willing to build into the future, then what good is building at all?

In his Gospel, Matthew wrote to the Jewish community in order to reassure them during times of intense Roman persecution, that Jesus Christ is truly the King of kings. Yes, he wrote about the "lambness" of Jesus, too, because the two natures go hand in hand. Jesus is fully human and fully God.

As Matthew wrote, he related to a Jewish community that had placed Christ in a place of power in heaven. He wrote to bring that power of Christ down to earth. That is, through the discourses and actions of Jesus, we see the One who is king of heaven but who is also king of our hearts in a very personal way. Is this the Christ you know? Does He, indeed, reign within you?

Let's look together at some key portions of Matthew that can help us know what it means to answer "Yes." As if taking a flight over the text in an airplane, we'll survey the landscape of Matthew's writings and touch down upon some key teachings in answer to the question: How do I prepare myself for the Kingdom? The answers encompass the call to repentance, handling temptation, our character as leaders, and our desire for God's healing of body and soul.

The First Step: *Repent and Submit*

Jesus, the master teacher in word and in deed, ushered in His ministry through His forerunner John the Baptist. Even though John was a great Baptist, he had to move on to allow for what was coming after him: "I am the forerunner of what is yet to come."

> *In those days came John the Baptist, preaching in the wilderness of Judea, And saying, Repent ye: for the kingdom of heaven is at hand.*
> —Matthew 3:1-2

Matthew shows us that the way you usher in the Kingdom of God is through repentance. The word *repent* means "to turn away" from what you used to be and to go in the opposite direction. To repent is not merely to be remorseful; it means, in a sense, to return to the penthouse, the top. To be returned to the top. So Matthew said that Israel is about to be returned to the penthouse. It's time to return to the top floor of the building of the Kingdom of God. It will take some turning around.

How important is this repentance for all of us? Very! In his book *I Surrender*, Patrick Morley writes that the church's integrity problem is in the misconception "that we can add Christ to our lives, but not subtract sin. It is a change in belief without a change in behavior." He goes on to say, "It is revival without reformation, without repentance." Do you agree that this false kind of reformation is a very sad thing?

John the Baptist said we must repent because the Kingdom of heaven is at hand. He spoke of One who was to come: He is mighty, and John wasn't worthy to even carry His shoes. In a sense, this was true because John, the forerunner, was born of human beings, from Zacharias and Elizabeth. But the One to come was born through the Holy Spirit overshadowing a virgin girl who submitted and allowed God to use her. Mary said: *"Be it done to me according to thy word."* You see, when you say to God, Do whatever you want to do according to Your word, you might just be submitting to a time of confusion, hardship, and being misunderstood. But you will also be opening yourself to the rewards of heaven and of great glory — in God's own way and time.

Now in Matthew 3:15, Jesus came to John to be washed or baptized:

> *Suffer it to be so now: for thus it becometh us to fulfill all righteousness. Then he suffered him.*

The Kingdom of God is not meat and drink; it is righteousness. So Jesus said: "You've got to put me down in this water because you have to fulfill all righteousness." The first manifestation of the Kingdom is coming through the door now. The first words of

Jesus recorded in Matthew were, "I must be baptized because all righteousness must be fulfilled."

Then the heavens were opened unto Him. If there's no righteousness, heaven is never opened. God established a level of righteousness, so heaven would open and the devil would be defeated.

Where does this opening begin? It begins with repentance-now. As one anonymous quipster said: "If we put off repentance another day, we have a day more to repent of . . . and a day less to repent in."

The Second Step: *Expect Temptation*

To prepare your heart for the Kingdom requires not only repentance but the willingness to face **and overcome** the most powerful temptations. It happened to Jesus; it will happen to us.

1 *Then was Jesus led up of the Spirit into the wilderness to be tempted of the devil.*

2 *And when he had fasted forty days and forty nights, he was afterward an hungered.*

3 *And when the tempter came to him, he said, If thou be the Son of God, command that these stones be made bread.*

4 *But he answered and said, It is written, Man shall not live by bread alone, but by every word that proceedeth out of the mouth of God.*

5 *Then the devil taketh him up into the holy city, and setteth him on a pinnacle of the temple,*

6 *And saith unto him, If thou be the Son of God, cast thyself down: for it is written, He shall give his*

angels charge concerning thee: and in their hands they shall bear thee up, lest at any time thou dash thy foot against a stone.

7 Jesus said unto him, It is written again, Thou shalt not tempt the Lord thy God.

8 Again, the devil taketh him up into an exceeding high mountain, and showeth him all the kingdoms of the world, and the glory of them;

9 And saith unto him, All these things will I give thee, if thou wilt fall down and worship me.

10 Then saith Jesus unto him, Get thee hence, Satan: for it is written, Thou shalt worship the Lord thy God, and him only shalt thou serve.

11 Then the devil leaveth him, and, behold, angels came and ministered unto him.

—Matthew 4:1-11

The Spirit drove Jesus into the wilderness, where the devil came and tempted Him. Satan eventually showed Jesus all the kingdoms of the world and offered them as a reward for bowing His knee to all the evil in the cosmos. The word *kingdoms* used in this passage is from the Latin word *basilia*, meaning *the mechanism, the machinery,* or *the working parts of the devil's realm.* The devil said to Jesus that if He would bow down and worship, He would receive all this machinery for free. But Jesus told the devil to hit the road.

Why does the devil tempt God's people? He'll take a chance on us, he'll play on our instinctive greed and offer us the world so that heaven doesn't open over our heads. That's why, as it was with Jesus, the day of your blessing is the day of your greatest temptation. Let that sink in for a moment: The day you start being tempted in areas you never expected to be tempted in, before you mess up, think: Why is this temptation coming today . . . and not yesterday . . . or tomorrow?

Because heaven is about to open over your head!

But be prepared for that day of temptation! Know yourself, your special weaknesses and vulnerabilities. What are they? A survey of Discipleship Journal readers ranked areas of greatest spiritual challenge to them:

1. Materialism

2. Pride

3. Self-centeredness

4. Laziness

5. Sexual lust

6. Anger / bitterness

7. Envy

8. Gluttony

9. Lying

Do you see your particular place of vulnerability here? How are you guarding your heart, and when do you need to be most vigilant? On the old TV show "Hee Haw," Doc Campbell is confronted by a patient who says he broke his arm in two places. The doc replies, "Well then, stay out of them places!" We cannot regularly put ourselves in the face of temptation and not be affected.

The survey respondents said that their temptations were more potent when they had neglected their time with God *(81 percent)* and when they were physically tired *(57 percent)*. Can you relate? Also, resisting temptation was accomplished by prayer *(84 percent)*, avoiding compromising situations *(76 percent)*, Bible study *(66 percent)*, and being accountable to someone *(52 percent)*.[18]

We can supplement our accountability to others by reading slowly through literature designed to challenge our Christian maturity. Consider, as an example, these questions related to sexual purity in Kent Hughes' *LIBERATING MINISTRY FROM THE SUCCESS SYNDROME*:

♦ *Are we being desensitized by the present evil world? Do things that once shocked us now pass us by with little notice? Have our sexual ethics slackened?*

♦ *Where do our minds wander when we have no duties to perform?*

♦ *What are we reading? Are there books or magazines or files in our libraries that we want no one else to see?*

♦ *What are we renting at the local video stores? How many hours do we spend watching TV? How many adulteries did we watch last week? How many murders? How many did we watch with our children?*

♦ *How many chapters of the Bible did we read last week?*[19]

A scene from Bunyan's *PILGRIM'S PROGRESS* portrays Interpreter bringing Christian to a wall where fire is blazing from a grate. A man is trying to douse the fire with water. Then Interpreter shows Christian the other side of the wall, where another man is secretly pouring oil on the fire to keep it ablaze. Interpreter says, "You saw the man standing behind the wall to maintain the fire, teaching you that it is hard for the tempted to see how this work of grace is maintained in the soul." Satan tries to quench the flames of faith, but Christ keeps them alive.

Build upon Character

After the temptation, the devil left for a season and angels came to minister to Jesus. Then Jesus began preaching the same message that John had proclaimed from the beginning: *"From that time Jesus began to preach, and to say, Repent: for the kingdom of heaven is at hand"* (Matthew 4:17).

Jesus was beginning to work His selection program, selecting people He could build the Kingdom upon. He was about to structure the Kingdom of heaven, to build the foundation for it, so before He brought His message, He had to bring in the pillars. The Bible says a wise man builds his house upon the rock. So the first person Jesus encountered was Peter. Peter's name, *Petras*, meant "rock." Jesus had to build upon the rock of the apostles and the prophets in order to build what He said was coming.

Why is it important whom you choose to build upon? Because God always looks at the heart, not the talent. Jesus checks out our character not our résumé. Robert Murray McCheyne wrote to his friend Dan

Edwards after the latter's ordination as a missionary: *"In great measure, according to the purity and perfections of the instrument, will be the success. It is not great talents God blesses so much as great likeness to Jesus. A holy minister is an awful weapon in the hand of God."*[20]

Jesus then began traveling around all of Galilee teaching in their synagogues and preaching the Gospel of the Kingdom. Matthew 5, 6, and 7 are all part of His Kingdom discourse. He closes Matthew 6 by saying, "Seek ye first the Kingdom of God." You've got to make sure that when you're building your house, you're seeking the Kingdom. So as we build, we must ask: Who is God using in the city? Who is God using in the nation? Where is God blessing? Who are the men and women God has selected? Let's take a closer look at these people God selected:

1 *And seeing the multitudes, he went up into a mountain: and when he was set, his disciples came unto him:*

2 *And he opened his mouth, and taught them, saying,*

3 *Blessed are the poor in spirit: for theirs is the kingdom of heaven.*

4 *Blessed are they that mourn: for they shall be comforted.*

5 *Blessed are the meek: for they shall inherit the earth.*

6 *Blessed are they which do hunger and thirst after righteousness: for they shall be filled.*

7 *Blessed are the merciful: for they shall obtain mercy.*

8 *Blessed are the pure in heart: for they shall see God.*

9 *Blessed are the peacemakers: for they shall be called the children of God.*

10 *Blessed are they which are persecuted for righteousness' sake: for theirs is the kingdom of heaven.*

11 *Blessed are ye, when men shall revile you, and persecute you, and shall say all manner of evil against you falsely, for my sake.*

12 *Rejoice, and be exceeding glad: for great is your reward in heaven: for so persecuted they the prophets which were before you.*

13 *Ye are the salt of the earth: but if the salt have lost his savour, wherewith shall it be salted? it is thenceforth good for nothing, but to be cast out, and to be trodden under foot of men.*

14 *Ye are the light of the world. A city that is set on an hill cannot be hid.*

—Matthew 5:1-14

Do you recognize such people in your world? Do you recognize yourself in any ways? Three qualities stand out to me:

1. They are the pure in heart.

Verse 8, literally translated, means: "Blessed are those who have a pure heart, or the heart that King David had, which was the desire for the heart of God; these persons shall see as God."

In other words, you will look at something, and you won't see it the way you've always seen it. Instead, now that you have a Kingdom heart, you will see as God sees. That's why people who have a pure heart, who are seeking the Kingdom of God, are so effective in the Kingdom. We're coming into a generation of preachers who are not in it for the money, not interested in having their name in neon lights, and could care less about articles in the newspaper. In all purity of heart, they're in it for the building of the Kingdom of God.

2.   They are the salt of the earth.

Ushering in the Kingdom, Jesus continued in verse 13: "You are the salt of the earth." Not the salt of your kingdom or your town, but the salt of the earth. In other words, everything you touch — when you now have this Kingdom blessing of righteousness, peace, and joy — will come under your influence. You can be in a devil coven, but when you go there, you will bring them under your influence. You can be working with a bunch of God-haters, but the minute you walk into their building, you bring the influence of the Kingdom of God upon them. Sooner or later, that whole building's going to taste like salt!

3.   They are the light of the world.

Then Jesus said in verse 14, "Ye are the light of the world. A city that is set on a hill cannot be hid. Neither do men take a light and put it under the candlestick." Here we have the building of the Kingdom revealed. Later, in Matthew 12, when Jesus was accused of casting out devils by the prince of Beelezub, Jesus makes this profound statement: *"A Kingdom divided against itself is brought to desolation. Every city or house divided against itself cannot stand."* So there you see Jesus bringing a revelation of Kingdom, city, and house. You are the light of the world: that's the Kingdom. A city set on a hill: that's the city. You cannot take a light in your house and put it under a bushel: that's the house. House, city, Kingdom. My point: Today we have preachers who are trying to reach their city when they have yet to build their house!

What are the character qualities of a Kingdom pillar? They are obviously many, as Jesus' Beatitudes show us. The Beatitudes are a good place to start in evaluating our own readiness to accept the Kingdom. But consider, especially, the state of the heart — the softness, the openness, and the ability to let it melt when appropriately convicted.

If you are an older American, you may remember the popular cowboy humorist named Will Rogers (1879-1935). He was known for his laughter, but he also knew how to weep. One day he was entertaining at the Milton H. Berry Institute in Los Angeles, a hospital that specialized in rehabilitating polio victims and people with broken backs and other extreme physical handicaps. Of course, Rogers had everybody laughing, even patients in really bad condition. Suddenly he left the platform and went to the restroom. Milton Berry followed him to give him a towel. When he opened the door, he saw Will Rogers leaning against the wall, sobbing like a child. He closed the door, and in a few minutes, Rogers appeared back on the platform, as jovial as before. The point is, as Bible teacher Warren Wiersbe says:

If you want to learn what a person is really like, ask three questions: What makes him laugh? What makes him angry? What makes him weep? These are fairly good tests of

*character that are especially appropriate for Christian leaders.
I hear people saying, "We need angry leaders today!" or "The
time has come to practice militant Christianity!" Perhaps,
but "the wrath of man does not produce the righteousness of
God" (James 1:20).*

*What we need today is not anger but anguish, the kind of
anguish that Moses displayed when he broke the two tablets
of the law and then climbed the mountain to intercede for his
people, or that Jesus displayed when He cleansed the temple
and then wept over the city. The difference between anger and
anguish is a broken heart. It's easy to get angry, especially at
somebody else's sins; but it's not easy to look at sin, our own
included, and weep over it.*[21]

Watch for the Healing

I'd like you to consider that the entire book of
Matthew is written in a metaphoric language as well as
literal. That is, the things we see happening are
prototypes of the things to come in the future of the
Kingdom. In Matthew 8 and 9, we see Jesus healing,
healing, healing. He was approached by a man with
leprosy, for example. Jesus touched him and
immediately the leper was healed. Jesus healed a
centurion's servant, who was sick with palsy. He
expelled demons, healed Peter's mother-in-law, and
healed a woman with an issue of blood. He then
encountered the "asleep" daughter:

*18 While he spake these things unto them, behold,
there came a certain ruler, and worshipped him,
saying, My daughter is even now dead: but come and
lay thy hand upon her, and she shall live.*

19 And Jesus arose, and followed him, and so did his disciples. . . .

23 And when Jesus came into the ruler's house, and saw the minstrels and the people making a noise,

24 He said unto them, Give place: for the maid is not dead, but sleepeth. And they laughed him to scorn.

25 But when the people were put forth, he went in, and took her by the hand, and the maid arose.

26 And the fame hereof went abroad into all that land.

—Matthew 9:18-19, 23-26

Let's observe the metaphorical interpretation of this passage:

The number 12 speaks of foundation. The Bible tells us this girl was 12 years old, revealing that the foundational structure in Israel was dying. On Jesus' way to heal the daughter, a woman with an issue of blood for 12 years touched the hem of his garment; indicating that the system of foundation in Israel was hemorrhaging very badly — it was losing life and could not be productive. The hem of his garment represented part of his *Talmud*, which is a structure of word and robe (it also meant the outskirts of the fellowship of his ministry). By touching just the fellowship of His ministry, a restoration of a blood transfusion began. It was a sign that Jesus was building His house upon the rock.

When He healed the ruler's daughter, He kicked out all those who were religious only, who didn't understand the principle of why Jesus came. Jesus says, "This girl is not dead; she is asleep." And He brought her to life and told them, "Give her something to eat."

When Jesus commanded them to give her something to eat, he actually implied that they give her meat. Now, if someone's been sick for a long time and near death, you don't give them meat. You give them the broth of meat. Jesus was saying, When you begin to see me raise the foundation's structure again, it's there that meat can be ready to be received. My question is: Are you hungry for that kind of nourishment from the Lord?

I began this book by inviting you to prepare for the Kingdom's entrance as a new anointing, power, and force in the world. I said that preparing ourselves would involve a cutting away of the flesh so we could live, moment by moment, by the Spirit's guidance. We must let God plow our lives so that any hindering stones — sins, habits, attitudes — can be removed. And we need to accept the nighttimes of our lives as God enlightens our minds to His awesome vision for the world.

I hope you have kept these challenges in mind while soaking in the information and encouragement of these chapters. My prayer is that it will make a difference, not only in your personal life, but in the life of your family, neighborhood, city, and nation. For as God brings order and administration to a new level in our midst, no stone will be left unturned. All will be transformed. Behold, everything will be made new!

ॐ

BIBLIOGRAPHY

[1] David Rohr, quoted at
http://www.higherpraise.org/illustrations/transformation.htm

[2] Adapted from Spiros Zodhiates, ILLUSTRATIONS OF BIBLE TRUTHS (Chattanooga, TN: AMG Publishers, 1991), p. 115.

[3] Quoted at the Friends United Meeting website: http://www.fum.org/QL/issues/0101/valiant.htm.

[4] For references to the mercy seat, see such passages as: Exodus 25:17-22; 30:6; Leviticus 16:2, 13-14; Numbers 7:89.)

[5] Philip Anderson, quoted in James S. Hewett, ed., ILLUSTRATIONS UNLIMITED (Wheaton, IL: Tyndale House Publishers, 1988), p. 113.

[6] Howard A. Snyder, THE PROBLEM OF WINESKINS: CHURCH RENEWAL IN A TECHNOLOGICAL AGE (Wheaton, IL: InterVarsity Press, 1975), chapter 4.

[7] Closing story about the Brethren adapted from *Our Daily Bread*, October 4, 1992.

[8] Adapted from Craig Brian Larson, ed., ILLUSTRATIONS FOR PREACHING AND TEACHING (Grand Rapids, MI: Baker Book House, 1993), p. 221.

[9] Quoted from Max Lucado, IN THE EYE OF THE STORM (Nashville, TN: Word Publishing, 1991), p. 153.

10 *Bits & Pieces*, May 28, 1992, pp. 5-6.

11 *Bits & Pieces*, January 9, 1992, pp. 22-23.

12 *Christianizing the Roman Empire*, Ramsey MacMullen (Yale University Press, 1986), p. 25-26.

13 Source unknown, but remarks attributed to David Parsons at this website: http://www.bible.org/illus/b/b-70.htm

14 *Today in the Word*, June 22, 1992. Refers to a study presented to the American Psychological Association, by Jack Lipton and R. Scott Builione.

15 *Our Daily Bread*, October 6, 1997.

16 Rabbi Halverstan of Zans, quoted in E. Paul Hovey, ed., THE TREASURY OF INSPIRATIONAL ANECDOTES, QUOTATIONS, AND ILLUSTRATIONS (Grand Rapids, MI: Fleming H. Revell, 1994), p. 221.

17 Story by Kenneth A. Brown, INVENTORS AT WORK: INTERVIEWS WITH SIXTEEN NOTABLE INVENTORS (MicroSoft Press, 1988).

18 *Discipleship Journal*, November / December, 1992.

19 R. Kent Hughes, LIBERATING MINISTRY FROM THE SUCCESS SYNDROME (Wheaton, IL: Tyndale House Publishers, 1992).

20 Paul Borthwick, LEADING THE WAY (Carol Stream, IL: Navpress, 1989), p. 65.

21 Warren W. Wiersbe, THE INTEGRITY CRISIS (Nashville, TN: Thomas Nelson Publishers, 1991), pp. 75-76.

Covenant Partner Information

Dear Friend,

Thank you for taking the time to take a closer look at Jabula – New Life Ministries. While our ministry is taking us to the United States, Canada, the United Kingdom, and other nations around the world, we are endeavoring to answer the call of God in our homeland of Africa. God has given us a specific mandate to EMPOWER the people of Africa, by providing for them in a number of areas. Truly God is blessing in unprecedented ways, but at the same time, the needs of people are growing, the costs to bring this needed help are escalating, and our economy at home is in absolute demise. We must depend on the support of our friends in the United States and Europe to empower us to continue these efforts.

I want to personally ask you to prayerfully consider becoming a Covenant Partner with us on a financial level. As you covenant together with us for this Kingdom mandate, we believe that you become a part of God's blessing as well. Thank you in advance for your role in helping answer the call of God. May God richly bless you, and open the windows of heaven over you life!

Sincerely,

Bishop Tudor Bismark

Below is a basic outline of what God has called us to accomplish for His glory.

JABULA MEDICAL PROGRAM

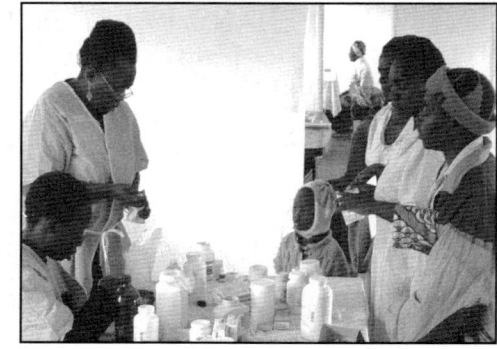

- Medical Mobile Clinic

- Ambulances for Emergency Transfers

- Seeing between 1,000 to 1,500 Weekly

- A wide range of diseases (HIV, Cholera, TB, Skin issues, etc.)

- Medical/Hygiene packets

ORPHAN RELIEF AND ASSISTANCE

- One in four Zimbabweans is an orphan

- Currently providing for over 100 children

- Provide housing (build orphanage facilities)

- Provide food, clothing, and medical care

- Provide educational assistance

EDUCATION PROGRAM (JABULA FOUNDATION)

- Currently providing education assistance to over 2,500 children
- Provide teachers' salaries
- Build schools and classrooms
- Provide books and supplies
- Commitment through college degree

WIDOWS/ELDERLY CARE

- Caring for over 3,000 widows and elderly
- Provide housing (build living facilities)
- Provide food, clothing, and medical care

MINISTRY/PASTORS SUPPORT

- Provide covering to over 1,000 pastors
- Operate Bible schools in several locations
- Provide monthly financial support for over 200 pastors
- Provide regional conference to train and empower

RESOURCES

The preeminence of the Kingdom at this time cannot be denied or ignored. God is indeed calling His church back to their rightful role and function in the earth. Contained in these messages are powerful principles and concepts as to the way the Kingdom of God is functioning in the earth today. As you engage the process of learning this material, we believe that you will be changed and transformed into the person that God intended you to be in the beginning of time. Welcome to the Kingdom!

The Kingdom Series   Volume I
"The Gospel of the Kingdom"

Tape One   *Kingdom I*
Tape Two   *Kingdom II*
Tape Three   *Kingdom III*
Tape Four   *Kingdom Aggression*
Tape Five   *The Might of God*

The Kingdom Series   Volume II
"Kingdom Dominion"

Tape One   *Kingdom Dominion I*
Tape Two   *Kingdom Dominion II*
Tape Three   *Kingdom Dominion III*
Tape Four   *Kingdom Dominion IV*

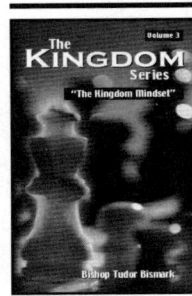

The Kingdom Series   Volume III
"The Kingdom Mindset"
Tape One   *Your Legal Rights I*
Tape Two   *Your Legal Rights II*
Tape Three   *Your Legal Rights III*
Tape Four   *Kingdom Authority - Healing*

The Kingdom Series   Volume IV
"Kingdom Resurrection"
Tape One   *Kingdom Resurrection I*
Tape Two   *Kingdom Resurrection II*
Tape Three   *Kingdom Resurrection III*
Tape Four   *Kingdom Resurrection IV*

Kingdom Series   Volume V
"Wisdom and Judgement"
Tape One   *Kingdom Wisdom*
Tape Two   *Commit Your Thoughts*
Tape Three   *Lawgiver I*
Tape Four   *Lawgiver II*

The Nature of the Beast

Tape One   *The Nature of the Beast*

Tape Two   *Breaking The Nature of the
             Beast*

*When mankind fell, we were thrust into the arena of the
nature and manifestation of the Antichrist, which in this
series we are calling "The Nature of the Beast. These
teachings are designed to help you to understand how Jesus
Christ and His Church, together, reverse this equation and
release us into the Kingdom restored to His image.*

The Spirit of the "Ites"

Tape One   *The Spirit of the "Ites"*

Tape Two   *The Spirit of the "Ites" II*

*When the Children of Israel took the land of Canaan, they
found and learned a number of things, one of which was what
we refer to as the "The Ites." This was an organized group of
nations designed as a system to oppose Israel. These same
systems exist in our world today, and are being used by Satan
to hinder development and progress of God's church. This
series deals with how to identify and how to be liberated from
"The Spirit of the Ites."*

Blessed, Beyond The Curse!

Tape One   *The Generational Blessing*

Tape Two   *Blessed Enough to Break The Curse*

Tape Three   *The Curse Can't Hold Me*

As sons of God, we have a destiny that requires us to be blessed. It is Satan's desire to interfere with this release, and impose curses on our lives and ministries. In this series, we deal with the process of coming out of curse oriented conditions and organized demonic schemes, into a sphere of blessing and freedom. I am blessed and NOT cursed!

Breakthrough Anointing

Tape One   *Children In The Marketplace*

Tape Two   *A Ridiculous Blessing*

Tape Three   *Kick That Door Open*

Immaturity is one of the greatest INHIBITING factors in the Body Of Christ today. Hebrews 6:1-2 reveals that we are to move on to perfection; a state where we can be trusted with "True" riches. In this series, we learn that God desires to systematically grow us, so that we are positioned to receive the fullness and the magnitude of God's release in our lives.

Manifestation of Destiny

Tape One   *The Manifestation of Destiny I*

Tape Two   *The Manifestation of Destiny II*

Tape Three   *Manifestation Destroys the Works of the Enemy*

Tape Four   *The Fourth Dimension of Revelation*

Everything that takes place in the earthly or physical realm, happens first in the heavenlies. Ecclesiates 3:14 & Acts 15:18 declare that all decisions were made in eternity before the world began. This series will elevate your faith and ability to step into the manifestation of what is already established in heaven as it relates to your life.

The Ministry of Intercessory Prayer

Tape One   *Intercessory Prayer*

Tape Two   *Intercessory Prayer — Taking Cities*

We are living in the day of the greatest prayer movement that has ever been seen in the history of mankind. The number of Christians praying today far exceeds the total number of believers that have prayed in preceding centuries and millenia.

Breaking Curses

Tape One   *Breaking Curses Part 1*

Tape Two   *Breaking Curses Part 2*

Tape Three *The Blessing*

Tape Four   *The Bastard Curse*

Are you continually encumbered with sickness, financial bondage, temptation, or poor relationships? Do you feel like you will never break through? Learn how to be free from issues you thought you had to live with!

Books

The Kingdom in Motion

In The Kingdom in Motion, *Bishop Tudor Bismark carefully unfolds key passages in the Gospel of Matthew, demonstrating how the ancient promises are coming to fruition in our day. The time has come when all Christians must become "Kingdom bearers," to rule and reign with Him!*

The Anointing of a Thousand Times More

This book will open your eyes to the power of God's anointing and will show you practical ways to prepare for this impartation. God is awakening the Church to be life changers, city changers, and world changers.

For more information or to send a donation, please visit one of our websites:

www.jabula.org
or
www.tudorbismark.org

or contact us:

United States
Jabula-New Life Ministries
445 E. FM 1382, Suite 3-371
Cedar Hill, Texas 75104

(800) 671-0844
(469) 272-7337

E-Mail :
info@jabula.org
or
info@tudorbismark.org